THE EX-DEBUTANTE

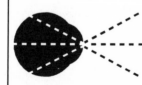

This Large Print Book carries the
Seal of Approval of N.A.V.H.

THE EX-DEBUTANTE

LINDA FRANCIS LEE

THORNDIKE PRESS

A part of Gale, Cengage Learning

GALE
CENGAGE Learning

Detroit • New York • San Francisco • New Haven, Conn • Waterville, Maine • London

GALE
CENGAGE Learning™

LIBRARY OF CONGRESS CATALOGING-IN-PUBLICATION DATA

Lee, Linda Francis.
   The ex-debutante / by Linda Francis Lee.
      p. cm. — (Thorndike Press large print laugh lines)
   ISBN-13: 978-1-4104-0947-8 (hardcover : alk. paper)
   ISBN-10: 1-4104-0947-3 (hardcover : alk. paper)
   1. Women lawyers—Fiction. 2. Women—Texas—Societies and clubs—Fiction. 3. Balls (Parties)—Texas—Fiction. 4. Rich people—Texas—Fiction. 5. Texas—Fiction. 6. Large type books.
I. Title.
PS3612.E225E93 2008b
813'.6—dc22   2008019495

Published in 2008 by arrangement with St. Martin's Press, LLC.

ACKNOWLEDGMENTS

The Ex-Debutante would not exist if not for the continuing support of the people in my life who talk, listen, advise, guide, and have even been known to hand-hold at just the right moments. At St. Martin's Press: Jennifer Weis, Sally Richardson, George Witte, Matthew Shear, John Murphy, Lisa Senz, John Karle, and Stefanie Lindskog. At Writers House: Amy Berkower, Genevieve Gagne-Hawes, Jodi Reamer, Lily Kim, and Maja Nikolic. On the family front: Tim, Carilyn, Grant, and Spencer for days of hot Texas sun and long walks along the river. And, of course — Michael.

CHAPTER ONE

Denial \de-ni-al\ n (1528): one small word crammed with three tiny syllables that quite frankly causes great big problems in a whole lot of lives; a word, like most, with multiple meanings. 1: refusal to recognize and/or critically test the truth, 2: repudiation of fact, and 3 (my personal favorite): the reason I got tangled up in what I now refer to as the Debutante Mess.

Granted, I had been around etiquette, manners, and the waltz since birth. And true, I had made my own bow to society eleven years earlier in one of Texas high society's premier social events. So on the surface there was no reason I shouldn't have gotten involved. But I had left Texas to get away from all of that.

Actually, I left Texas to get away from my mother's, let us say, larger-than-life personality and her renowned beauty she never let anyone forget; my sister Savannah's obsession with babies and her inability to have one; and all the complaining I had to endure over my sister-in-law Janice's lack of obsession with babies and her apparent inability to stop having them.

But as Michael Corleone in *Godfather III* said, "Just when I thought I was out, they pull me back in."

My name is Carlisle Wainwright Cushing, of the Texas Wainwright family. More specifically, I am a Wainwright of Willow Creek. My mother is Ridgely Wainwright . . . Cushing-Jameson-Lackley-Harper-Ogden. I kid you not.

Given my mother's predilection for divorce, not to mention her claim that growing up I had been the most disarmingly independent child she knew, is it any surprise that as an adult I had become a divorce lawyer?

It had seemed a natural choice given that as the only truly practical person in my family, I had been dealing with the dissolutions of my mother's marriages in one way or another since I was in ruffled ankle socks and patent leather Mary Janes — and not the Manolo kind.

To be specific, it was my mother's pending dissolution of her most recent marriage that initially dragged me back to my hometown from Boston where I had moved three years earlier. Then, once back in Texas, like Alice falling down the rabbit hole, I slid along the slippery slope from divorce court to the debutante court, all because I couldn't say no to responsibility. Or so I told myself.

See? Denial. Whitewashing the truth, a sleight of hand with reality until even I believed the convoluted excuse for why I had gone home.

But I'm getting ahead of myself.

"Carlisle is here," announced the woman who swore it was her face that had launched a thousand ships, "to deal with my pesky divorce situation."

My mother sat at the head of the formally set dining table, perfect in her cashmere and heirloom pearls.

"She is?" my sister asked.

"You are?" my brother demanded.

Even Lupe, our longtime family maid, who was serving her famous veal cordon bleu, froze for half a second in surprise.

"Have you lost your mind?" I stated in a way that was far more direct than any self-respecting Southern belle would ever be.

Ridgely Wainwright-Cushing-Jameson-Lackley-Harper-Ogden shot me, her youngest child, a glare. But I wasn't the same eager-to-please girl who'd left three years earlier. I returned my wine glass to the table and smiled tightly.

"Mother, could you join me in the kitchen? Please?"

"Not now, Carlisle. We are in the middle of dinner. Lupe, the veal looks divine."

"Mother."

She wore the cream cashmere sweater set with cream wool flannel pants, bone low-heeled shoes, her shoulder-length blond hair elegant and swept back with a cream velvet headband. She held her own wine glass in her perfectly manicured hand as she studied me over the length of fine linen, sterling silver, wafer-thin crystal, and tasteful fresh flower arrangements made of white roses, light pink peonies, and lavender hydrangeas. After a second, she nodded. My mother was more perceptive than her porcelain china-doll exterior would lead the average on-looker to believe. She understood without having to be told that Miss Never Make a Scene Carlisle Cushing was feeling a whole lot like making a scene. She probably followed me from the dining room more out of surprise than anything else.

As soon as we stepped into the service galley of stately Wainwright House, the dining room door swinging shut behind us, I stopped abruptly just outside the kitchen and turned back, bringing me face-to-face with my mother.

"Oh!" she squeaked.

"I really am not in a position to stay here and help you with your divorce. I have a job, remember? In Boston."

She only peered at me. "Dear, have you put on weight?"

I might have pressed my eyes closed and counted to ten. I definitely wondered how I had ever allowed her to trick me into coming back to Texas.

"And your skin, it looks dry. I don't like to brag, but you know I'm famous for my youthful appearance. But I look this good because I take care of myself, Carlisle. Don't the Pilgrims sell moisturizer?"

On principle, my mother is not fond of anyone who lives north of the Mason-Dixon line. In her personal dictionary, she refers to New Englanders \new en-gland-ers\ n (1620) as 1: The Pilgrim People (or assorted variations) 2: Yankeefied 3: Pantywaist Thurston Howell the Thirds.

I ignored her criticism and maintained focus, not easy to do when she was looking me over like a judge at a beauty pageant. "The only reason I am here is because you called me saying you were having an

11

emergency."

Tension settled around her eyes. "This divorce mess is an emergency. And if you don't clear it up then I swear to goodness it is going to be the end of me." She pressed her delicate hand to her chest. "Darling, really, I need you."

To be completely honest, to say that my mother was larger than life would be an understatement. She should have been a stage actress, probably would have if it had not been for the fact that as a direct descendant of Texas founding father Sam Houston himself, the great-granddaughter of the fifth Duke of Ridgely who arrived in Texas in the late 1880s, Debutante of the Year when she took her own bow more years ago than she was willing to admit, and with more money than even Ross Perot, she didn't do such base things as act on stage. Instead, she acted her way through life until I'm not sure anyone (including my mother) knew who she really was.

That said, I am a good daughter and love her, just as I love the rest of my family, though is it any surprise that I have found it easier to be a good daughter when I'm not living right in the middle of my mother's theatrics?

I was twenty-five when I came to this

realization, at which point I did the only sensible thing a sensible girl could do. I opened the big atlas in the Wainwright House study to the map of North America, closed my eyes, and took a stab at the page. My finger landed in the Atlantic Ocean, but it was reasonably close to Nova Scotia, Maine, and Boston. Not wanting to be referred to as a Canuck, and having no clue what anyone actually did in Maine other than wear plaid flannel and fish for lobster, I packed my bags and headed for the baked bean capital of the world, landing in a city with a great many people who had more onerous ancestries than I.

Even better, not one person in Boston knew my name. Which meant, I realized, on a not-so-sensible intake of breath, that I could be anyone I wanted, namely a New Me \new me\ adj n (2005) 1: not Sam Houston's descendant 2: not the duke's great-great-granddaughter 3: not even Ridgely Wainwright-Cushing-Jameson-Lackley-Harper-Ogden's youngest child.

Moving to Boston had been quite a feeling. Freeing. And given my Texas accent, when people stereotypically assumed I was white trash, probably inbred, ignorant, and undoubtedly poor, well, I didn't do anything to set the record straight. I let them assume the worst.

I know, it sounds terrible, and if I could do it all over again, believe me, I would. Not that I minded being considered that Texas girl from the wrong side of the tracks. But something that seemed like an adventure at twenty-five had a way of coming back to bite me three years later.

Though that was the least of my concerns just then.

"There are plenty of attorneys who can deal with this, Mother."

"Yes, just like that one I had for my last divorce who bungled everything so badly. Do you think for a second I am going to trust anyone else but you?"

My mother's last attorney had done such a horrible job with the divorce that one Mr. Lionel Harper (husband number four) had become a line item on the family accounting ledgers. Not to mention that the lawyer had been a publicity hound and our family had been in the news more in the ten months the negotiations raged on than in the previous ninety-nine years Wainwrights had been in Texas.

"We can't have our family name disparaged, dragged through the mud. Yet again. You are a Wainwright, even if you choose to live elsewhere."

"I can't stay in Texas. Whether you believe it or not, I really do have a job. A good job." And I did. I had a great position at Marcus, Flint, and Worthson, one of the largest and most prestigious law firms in Boston.

"Pshaw. You have a job using the law to make a bunch of those Kennedy types mind their *p*'s and *q*'s. I say tell them to start pronouncing their *r*'s and find a new attorney. Besides, you went to all that trouble to get your licenses so you could practice in both Massachusetts and Texas. Seems like this is as good a time as any to put that Texas certification to use, to make that sniveling Vincent Ogden rue the day he ever decided he didn't want to be married to me."

Tension settled around my eyes this time, not that there wasn't truth in what she was saying. If anyone could make anyone rue anything, it was me. I had gotten more than one of my clients out of sticky marital predicaments.

But, again, I lived in Boston.

I loved it there, loved the surprise of four true seasons, the lush green Boston Common in spring, picnics at the Hatch Shell listening to the Boston Pops in summer, the stunning orange, yellow, and red of autumn, and skating on the iced-over Frog Pond in winter.

Also, it just so happened that I was engaged. Not that my mother knew this, and not that I was about to tell her right there in the service galley amid the dessert china and coffee cups ready for the next course. But I was engaged to the extremely amazing Phillip Granger, a lawyer at my firm who had a warm smile, laughing blue eyes, and a kind soul that I wrapped around myself like a cashmere throw in winter.

There was just one problem. He wanted me to set a date for the wedding, and, well, even I couldn't set a date until I told my mother that I was getting married. But the minute I told her (after she recovered from the stupefying shock that I was marrying a Yankee; that is, if she did recover) she would dive headlong into the sort of traditional wedding plans she would expect. I had no interest in showers and teas and all the prewedding niceties my mother wouldn't see as negotiable. I planned to have a sensible, low-key civil affair, which would definitely kill my mother, bringing me full circle as to why I had yet to set a date for the wedding.

But there had to be a way to convince her that what I wanted to do was the best thing for everyone involved. Which was the only reason I didn't simply walk out of Wain-

16

wright House, get back on a plane, and return to Massachusetts. Instead if, say, I stayed, just for a little while, not dealing with the divorce so much as helping my mother find a decent lawyer, it would give me a little breathing room from a certain unset date, and time to figure out how to tell my mother I was getting married and not have to succumb to all that a large Texas wedding would entail.

"This is what I'll do," I said.

In copious detail I mapped out exactly how I would facilitate the process. I would help her find a lawyer. But there would be no other involvement.

"Well, that's fine, dear. Though before you do all that . . . organizing, Vincent has asked me to meet him at a lawyer's office. No surprise it's that disreputable Howard Grout's firm."

"I thought you liked Howard Grout."

"Of course I do. It's hard not to like the man. But that doesn't mean I approve of him."

Have I mentioned my mother has very distinct ideas on who it is appropriate to socialize with? Howard Grout, with his mountain of questionable money and lack of good breeding, did not make her list.

"Anyway," she continued, "the meeting is

17

tomorrow morning. Come with me, talk to your stepfather. Vincent always liked you. Maybe you can talk some sense into him. If not, turn on all that unladylike killer charm you are famous for and scare him a little."

I wasn't sure if I was flattered or insulted.

"If there has to be a divorce," she added, "then convince him it should be done quickly, quietly, and without a lot of fuss. Then depending on how the meeting goes, we'll think about getting another lawyer."

Sure enough, first thing the next morning, my mother's driver Ernesto drove us through the craggy live oaks, rolling green hills, and the perfectly kept streets of town, past the main square, alongside Willow Creek High, then the university, to the offices of Howard Grout, Attorneys at Law, LLP.

In court, I had heard he was supposed to be meaner than a junkyard dog and he only hired lawyers who were cut from the same cloth. Not that this worried me, but it was good to know these things going in.

The offices were nice in that *new* nice way meant to announce in bold letters that they had made it without the help of old money. After working out of his home the previous year, Howard had opened up shop in one of the best buildings in town. While the exterior was traditional limestone blocks, inside everything was made of glass, steel, and jutting granite sculpture. There wasn't an inch of dark walnut wood paneling, mahogany desks, or oil paintings to be found at Howard Grout, LLP.

Dressed in an Armani power suit that, thankfully, I had brought along, I had pulled my (unfortunately blond) shoulder-length hair back into a sleek ponytail. Never one to go far without my baby-soft black calfskin briefcase, I held it at my side, my low-heeled black Chanel pumps the only minor indulgence I allowed myself.

My mother followed in my wake (a rare occurrence in itself) looking stunning, her hair professionally done, her makeup perfectly applied, her nails a demure shade of barely pink that matched her lip color. She also wore her usual strand of Wainwright pearls around her neck.

We walked down the long wide hallways of marble flooring, the walls lined with modern art. At the end of the hall a Schnabel filled the space.

"Who is that?" I asked the receptionist.

"Who?"

"The woman in the portrait." I gestured toward the broken crockery forming a mosaic portrait, a signature Schnabel piece.

"Oh, that. It's Mrs. Grout."

"Nikki?"

"Yes. Mr. Grout had it done as a surprise." The girl shook her head. "He said it was like a mast on a ship; you know, their good-luck charm. I don't know about you, but I've never seen a picture painted on a bunch of broken teacups and saucers."

Howard Grout appeared out of an office. "Did I hear someone talking about my Nikki?" he said grandly.

"Mr. Grout. I'm Carlisle Cushing."

"Of course you are. And this is your mother. Prettiest lady in town, next to my Nikki, mind you."

My mother smiled like a coy schoolgirl. "Now, Mr. Grout. Aren't you just the sweetest man."

Mere lack of approval had never stopped my mother from flirting.

He chuckled and slapped his big round belly that lay beneath the three-thousand-dollar Italian suit. "We both know that's a bald-faced lie. I'm a lot of things, Miz Wainwright, but sweet ain't one of them."

He bid us goodbye, then barked out orders to some unfortunate soul in another office.

There wasn't anyone in Willow Creek my

mother didn't know, and as we continued on, she spoke to most everyone we passed.

"Isn't that a lovely blouse you're wearing, Lisabeth. Though you might consider blue next time. Pink really isn't your color."

Lisabeth stared, pretended the comment didn't bother her, then ran for the bathroom mirror just as soon as my mother was out of sight.

"My word, look at you, Burton Meyer. Looking younger and younger every time I see you. Is that hair dye you're using? Or have you given in and gotten Botox?" She kissed his cheek. "Whichever, you look just as handsome as any man your age can look, sugar."

Burton Meyer stammered.

"Morton Henderson, your sweet Mabel must be quite the cook for all the weight you've gained." She patted his round belly, which no other soul in all of Willow Creek dared do, given his reputation as blood-thirsty litigator. "Don't you worry though, I won't breathe a word of this to your mother. I know how she and Mabel don't get along."

Ridgely left her usual trail of destruction in her wake, like a hurricane racing through town. Anyone with half a brain got out of her way.

When I led my mother into the designated

conference room, my stepfather was waiting.

"Hello, Vincent."

Vincent Ogden was a fit man with reddish-brown hair tamed within an inch of its life, and a well-trimmed beard and mustache. He wore a tweed jacket and cuffed slacks, a white dress shirt but no tie. He looked as if he had just stepped out of the faculty lounge at Willow Creek University.

"Carlisle," he acknowledged, then with little more than a glare at my mother, he turned away and started to sit down at the conference table.

"Typical," Ridgely said. "Sits before a lady does."

"Lady? In your dreams! A lady knows how to treat a man!"

Technically, a *woman* knows how to treat a man, not necessarily a lady. But I kept that to myself.

My mother raised her chin. "When you turn into a real man, let me know. I was married to a milquetoast."

"I'm no milk toast! You're a shrew and it's just easier to lay low than have to deal with your theatrics on a regular basis."

"*My* theatrics," she shrilled. "If ever there was a drama queen in my house, it was you."

"Yeah, your house. Your money. Your everything!"

I had seen it before, dueling jabs.

"Mother, Vincent, please."

Not that it did any good. They went back and forth, each insult worse than the last, until the conference room door opened. Thankful that opposing counsel had finally arrived, I turned around with my best professional smile. But this time I stiffened and sucked in my breath like an overacting actor in a really bad play.

"Jack?"

"Carlisle Cushing. I heard you were back in town."

His voice was deep and smooth, with hints of fond amusement. Okay, "fond" might have been overly optimistic. In fact, "impatient disbelief" might be more accurate. Whatever, I was so stunned at the sight of him that my muscles refused to take signals from my brain.

He didn't look any different from the last time I'd seen him, unless even more dangerously handsome counted as different. He still had those same broad shoulders and narrow hips, still had the same dark brown hair and brown eyes, not to mention the full dark lashes that made him look like the angel he wasn't, and never had been. Not that Jack had ever tried to be an angel.

I knew he had gone to work for the district attorney straight out of law school. He had developed a reputation for being wild — as if anyone should have been surprised — and had become an aggressive prosecutor who was known to play it a little too close to the bone for the comfort of the DA.

When he left the DA's office no one was surprised. Going to work for Howard Grout hadn't so much as raised an eyebrow. Since then rumor had it that "ruthless" had been added to the adjectives used to describe him, i.e., not someone you wanted to meet in a dark courtroom . . . or, for that matter, even a lighted one with a judge sitting up front.

I had no reason to doubt the rumors since I knew Jack Blair well. It's probably worth mentioning here that he was the first guy I ever loved. He also played a starring role in a little thing I don't like to call my undoing three years earlier.

Not that I hold grudges.

The first time I met Jack I was a precocious freshman in high school. I had placed out of Algebra I and Geometry and entered Algebra II on my very first day at Willow Creek High School with the sort of arrogant pride that showed just how oblivious I was to how kids really work. I had dressed with care that day, wearing a starched white button-down shirt, a green plaid skirt, green knee-high socks, and penny loafers with a brilliant shine. Walking into class before the bell rang, I was quite pleased with myself until I realized the room was filled with juniors who stopped what they were doing when I entered.

"Hey, babe, kindergarten is a block away at Willow Creek Elementary."

"Call the Geek Squad. One of their members has gone missing."

I ignored them and found a seat, which, unfortunately, was at the back of the room.

The desk was like nothing I had seen before in my days of learning, a black-topped table for two with high wooden legs. You can probably guess who walked into the class and into my life and sat down next to me. Jack Blair.

The teacher hadn't arrived yet, and it didn't take a math whiz to see that the girls adored Jack, some of the cooler boys wanted to be like him, and every squeaky nerd in the class was afraid of him. I fell solidly into the Adore Him at First Sight category.

"Hey," he said, ambling up to the table in a T-shirt, jeans, and work boots that could have used a good tying.

He was disheveled, as if he had gone

straight from bed to class, but his smile gave my heart its first taste of internal gymnastics.

"Mind if I sit here?" he asked.

Did I mind?

Would you please?

Could I bronze the chair afterward?

"Sure," I said with remarkable cool, considering the calisthenics going on in my chest.

He collapsed into the chair with a groan, then proceeded to fall asleep. He didn't so much as move a muscle when the bell rang and Mr. Hawkins walked into the room.

The short math teacher with his Napolean-era hair went on about something, though I could barely focus given the, well, god sitting mere inches from me. Until that moment, I can safely say that I hadn't given boys a thought. My only interest was in school and making excellent grades on my way to becoming an even more excellent lawyer. In the scenario in my head, there was no room for romantic entanglements. I'd leave that up to my mother, sister, and brother — all of whom seemed to be obsessed with the opposite sex, their lives altered as a result of it.

No doubt it was because I was working so hard to ignore the amazingly muscled and tanned arm lying on the desktop next to me that I didn't realize Mr. Hawkins's monotone voice was getting closer by the syllable. When the teacher slammed his yardstick against our table I nearly had a heart attack, though Jack barely moved. He sat up and yawned. "How ya doin'?" he asked the man.

The teacher seemed at a frustrated loss, words working themselves slowly to the surface, until he bit out, "Not so good."

"Sorry to hear it. Life's rough, no question."

I thought Mr. Hawkins would explode.

"I've heard about you, know all about how you slide through class, getting A's because you're Hunter Blair's little brother."

Even I had heard of Hunter Blair. Let us just say that he surpassed even Howard Grout in both the money and unacceptable categories.

All Jack Blair's easy charm evaporated, though I could tell he was trying not to show it. Clearly there was more beneath the surface of My Heart's Desire than easy charm.

"For a change, you're going to have to do the work." The teacher sneered. "Now sit up and pay attention."

Everyone watched as Jack sat up with a

shrug as if not embarrassed in the least, while I felt heat burn in my cheeks from all the stares.

Mr. Hawkins returned to the front, passed out books, and gave us our first assignment just as the bell rang.

I did my best to forget Jack Blair until the next day when he returned to class and sat down at my table again as if that were his assigned seat.

"Hey," he said with a grunt, and promptly put his head on his arms and fell asleep.

Mr. Hawkins started class, going a hundred miles an hour. The barrage of words came fast enough to make me only partially aware of my neighbor as I worked to solve for x and y in case I was called on.

It was after I finished a particularly difficult equation that Mr. Hawkins whipped the yardstick down on his own desk, jarring the entire class, with the exception of Jack.

"Mr. Blair," he bellowed. "The answer, please."

I still don't know why I did it. But I kicked him under the table, bringing him upright. I'll never forget the look in his eyes when he glanced at me. By day two, my adoration had turned to dumbstruck love. Who would have guessed.

"Mr. Blair," the teacher repeated. "The

28

answer?"

It wasn't hard to realize that Jack walked a fine line. One slip over to the other side and there would be hell to pay. Mr. Hawkins was looking for an excuse to get rid of him. And hello, I was madly in love, and not thinking about consequences. So I did the only thing a lovestruck math whiz could do. I wrote the answer on the corner of my paper so he could see.

Jack looked at it, then me. He debated for a lifetime, then shrugged.

"X equals 3,458."

You'd have thought the teacher would have been pleased and let it go. No such luck. He was furious. And his fury was directed at me.

Mr. Hawkins bore down on us like a tornado headed for Kansas. I realized right then that I was going to be kicked out. For cheating. Me, Miss Never Get in Trouble. Me, Miss Obnoxious Do-gooder, was going to get kicked out of class.

The heart attack that had been threatening was banging at the door. And Jack Blair knew it. With what I swear was a curse, he locked eyes with the approaching storm, cursed again, then smiled. Yes, smiled.

Slowly and with great relish, he tore off the edge of paper revealing the answer, then put it in his mouth and ate it.

You really can't make something like that up.

Mr. Hawkins went crazy, screaming, threatening to kick us both out for crimes ranging from disrespect to cheating.

"Go ahead, send us to the office," Jack said, the tone a taunt.

I whipped my head around to gape at him, my mouth slack with an expression of: *Are you crazy!* I had never been sent to the office in my life.

He just chuckled, burped, then added, "What are you gonna tell them, Hawkins? That you kicked us out because I ate a piece of paper and she watched?"

The math teacher glared, fumed, but knew when he was beaten. Muttering, he retreated to the front.

The next day Jack showed up for class and didn't fall immediately asleep when he sat down.

"Thanks for yesterday," he said.

I fumbled around in my normally large vocabulary and came up with, "Oh, well . . ." and that was it.

He reached into the pocket of his leather jacket and pulled out a plastic egg, the kind from a bubble gum machine. "Here."

"What is it?" I breathed.

"I'm not sure. But it came out of the machine and, hell, I figured it was the least I could do." Then he promptly went to sleep.

I knew on sight that whatever was inside was nothing more than a silly gesture, but still, my heart beat wildly. When I cracked it open, a plastic ring with a strange blue plastic "stone" fell out. Jack didn't so much as move when I whispered "thank you," and he certainly didn't notice when I slipped it on my finger.

CHAPTER TWO

In the granite-lined law office conference room, with a view looking out over all of Willow Creek, my mother was tight-faced and grim at the realization that my current stepfather had retained Jack Blair to deal with the divorce.

My mother was not a big fan of the Blair family, though as far as I knew, her dislike centered on Jack's older brother, Hunter. As mentioned, Hunter had made massive amounts of money, but he had done it as a redneck oil fighter, and was supposedly meaner than a Siamese cat tossed into a tub of cold water.

I had never met the man, but I had heard more than a few stories about how the Blair patriarch had died, leaving two sons and a daughter. Hunter had been only eighteen, Jack only five, the sister a newborn, when Hunter was forced to care for his mother and siblings. But he had done it, and pulled out of poverty into extreme wealth, all by the time he was thirty.

My guess had always been that it was Jack's past that pushed him toward the wildness — like pushing hard and fast to outdistance demons. But what did I know. I had hated psychology in college.

Most Texans were impressed by what Hunter had accomplished. My mother, well, not so much, saying, "He's brash and a braggart, and never lets a soul forget he was a poor boy who made good. You'd think he'd try to hide his unfortunate past like any respectable man of importance would."

Remember, this is my mother we're talking about, the one who calls New Englanders the Pilgrim People, and thinks the Kennedys should take elocution lessons.

Jack and my mother exchanged barely pleasant pleasantries before he returned his attention to me. His brown-eyed gaze ran the length of my severely clad form in true alpha male, Neanderthal fashion, his arms crossed over a file he held against his chest. I felt ticking indignation and I opened my mouth to give him a searing set-down with my impressive vocabulary.

"You look good, Carlisle," he said.

My heart leaped. He thought I looked good.

Which was a completely unacceptable form of girly behavior to which I did not subscribe. I was long since over my star-struck status with Jack Blair.

"Thank you," I said, my voice crisp and efficient. "You look the same."

Of course, that was a good thing, but the way it came out it didn't sound like it.

He raised one dark brow, then walked past me, all six feet of him, broad shoulders, narrow waist, and chiseled jaw included. I could feel the raw energy of him, primal, I swear, despite the civilized surroundings. He gestured for us to take our seats.

"I suggest we get started," he said abruptly, as if not interested in wasting time. I wasn't sure if this was a billable-hour issue, or a me issue.

I sat next to my mother, across the modernly fashionable cement table from Jack and Vincent. Forcefully, I put Jack and his narrow hips out of my mind.

"I am only here to help until I find my mother an attorney."

Jack leaned back in the thousand-dollar, ergonomically correct captain's chair, those dark eyes assessing, before I saw the first hint of a smile crook up his mouth. "Good idea," he said. "I'd hate to think I had an unfair advantage over one of you Northerners with your fondness for oversized silver buckles, square-toed shoes, and horns of plenty. Even if you are just a convert. But sometimes those are the worst kind."

A shift occurred in me like a key turning in a lock. I leaned back as well, finding my center, and said, "Clearly you haven't done your homework, counselor. The Pilgrims never wore silver buckles or those big black hats, for that matter." I held my number 2 pencil at both ends. "Moreover, I have a win-loss record that should make you shake in your boots."

"A Yankee win-loss record."

"Mr. Blair." I tsked at him. "If I'm not mistaken, the Yankees won the last time the South tangled with them."

Vincent looked confused, my mother groaned, but I could tell Jack swallowed back a laugh. "Looks like we've got a full-blown traitor on our hands," he said.

True. You weren't born and raised in Texas, then started siding with the North. Ever. You could become a Democrat, fight for gun control (okay, maybe not gun control), even wear black. But you could never, ever choose a Northern point of view over your own state's. Just look what happened to the Dixie Chicks if you want proof, despite their slew of Grammys.

"Traitor? No," I equivocated. "I prefer to think of it as broadening my point of view. But enough about me. Let's talk about our clients. Based on what I've seen today between my mother and her husband, I'd say it's a safe guess that there will be no reconciliation."

Ridgely and Vincent harrumphed.

"I agree," Jack said. "And I think it's also safe to say we all would like this to go away as quietly as possible."

"Agreed."

"Good." Jack extended a stack of papers. "Here are the terms to make this easy as pie for everyone."

Easy as pie, as if he were an easygoing Southern gentleman on the veranda with a cigar and a splash of bourbon. But I wasn't that naïve. Jack Blair never made anything easy as pie, and beneath the gentleman act I sensed the ruthlessness that simmered just below the surface.

With the cool, calm, and collected manner I had perfected over the last three years, I glanced through the pages. At the end of the last page I forced myself not to drop my jaw. "You seem to have mistaken the divorce case we are here to deal with today with someone else's."

"No, we've got *Ogden* versus *Ogden.*"

"What is going on?" my mother wanted to know.

Without looking at her, I said to Jack, "They want spousal support in the amount of twenty thousand a month."

My mother stiffened at my side.

If Jack noticed, he didn't let on. "My client has grown accustomed to the lifestyle he and your mother shared. No judge in town would expect him to do without."

I ignored him. "He wants both the BMW and the Escalade —"

"He needs the sedan for city driving and the SUV for rugged terrain, of which Texas has a lot."

I rolled my eyes, then read the next line. "He wants the house in Aspen?"

"Yes."

"He doesn't even ski."

"He proposed to your mother there."

"Are you kidding me? He's the one who wants the divorce, why would he want to remember where he proposed?"

"It reminds him of better days."

This time my mother rolled her eyes.

"Plus he wants the house on Lake Travis," Jack added.

"What? Did he write her a poem there?"

Jack eyed me in a way that I knew didn't

bode well. "They had sex there for the first time."

My mother gasped. As much as I hate to admit it, I felt a blush try to creep up my face because I just might have been thinking about sex between two people in the room . . . two people other than my mother and her husband. Sue me, but Jack really did look good.

I shook the thought away. "More Kodak moments for the man who doesn't like what's in the pictures. That makes sense. This is a waste of our time."

"We're not asking for Wainwright House."

"Because no judge in their right mind would give Vincent property that is the Wainwright family's, not my mother's."

He tapped his pen on the table and considered me. "Hard to say. Your mother is a Wainwright, ergo she owns a percentage of the property."

"We are done here." I pushed up from the table and stood. "Come along, Mother."

"Is that a no?" he asked.

"Is that a no?" I cocked my head and studied him as if he were a troublesome child. "That isn't just no, but —"

He held up his hand. "Don't say something you'll regret, Cushing."

"There are a lot of things in life I regret,

but that wouldn't be one of them. Something else I don't regret is my mother's prenup."

"Ah, that. It won't stand up in court."

I might have blinked. "You came to that conclusion . . . how?"

"Vincent was a good husband to your mother, not to mention a supportive helpmeet."

My very proper mother scoffed, and why not. Helpmeet?

Jack tossed the pen on top of the file, all flashes of humor gone. "Vincent was a man who added more to her life than is represented by the one-sided prenup your mother forced on him."

"Forced?"

"He has also been a loving companion."

"Oh, please." More from my mother.

"And we feel our terms are more than fair, fair enough to keep us out of court where we would be forced to contest the prenuptial agreement. What do you say?"

"Just rewind and replay the 'no' comment of earlier."

"Have it your way," he said, retrieving the pen and flipping his folder shut. "But don't say I didn't warn you."

"We will see you in court, counselor."

"Then you're taking the case?"

I ground my teeth.

"*My mother* will see you in court after I find her a lawyer who will happily make you rue the day you ever walked into my life."

Which pretty much made us all freeze. Just for a bit of clarification, this wasn't about me. I knew that.

"I mean, the day Vincent walked into my mother's life."

With an impressive display of dignity in spite of my heart doing flip-flops, I gathered my things then directed my mother from the room as my thoughts slid back to Willow Creek High and Mr. Hawkins's math class. I remembered going home that day, all but floating on air. I couldn't wait to get back to school, back to math class, back to the table that forced me to sit so close to Jack that his knee brushed against mine. For the first time in my life I had understood attraction.

When I got home that day, my mother wasn't there, my sister out of town, my brother already living in California with his wife and the first of their children. Before I could think better of it, I went to Savannah's room to borrow some clothes; just a simple sundress, but a far cry from my usual plaid skirt and button-down shirt.

The next morning I dressed with care,

prayed my mother would still be in bed, then winced when I entered the kitchen and found her dressed in a flowing peignoir, her hair pulled up in a loose twist of blond curls, tendrils framing her face, as she sipped a cup of coffee out of her favorite breakfast china.

"Carlisle," she enthused.

I knew right away she had met a man.

It was always the same after she had met someone new, the pendulum of her euphoria swinging wildly, like a child getting a new toy. When she was in this phase she was exhausting, but only because I had learned it wouldn't last, the pendulum swinging back with the inevitability of white and pink tearoses at a debutante ball.

"Good morning," she sang. "Isn't it a glorious day?"

"Who is he?"

She tossed her head back and laughed. "You naughty girl. Who says I met someone?"

I raised a brow.

"Fine. Have it your way. I did meet a man. And he's fabulous! Simply fabulous! He's coming to dinner tonight."

"So soon? In this day and age, aren't you supposed to go someplace and meet him, get the lay of the land first, figure out if he's a serial murderer or something, then decide if you should bring him home?"

"Nonsense, I am nothing if not an expert judge of men."

Which made me laugh. Sorry. If my mother had a talent, it was for falling for men who inevitably hurt her.

Her smile went coy. "If he asks, you're ten."

"Excuse me? Ten?"

"Would it kill you to try?"

"It might. And what's the difference between me being ten and thirteen?"

"It's one thing to have a child in junior high, but a teenager in high school? I think not."

"Mother, in case you've forgotten, you have two married, adult children. And last I heard, you're a grandmother."

"Bite your tongue."

As promised, Mr. Rhys McDougal arrived at our doorstep, tall, dark, and handsome — as was my mother's preference. No surprise that he bore gifts. Flowers for my mother, a baby doll for me. He clearly hadn't a clue what a "ten-year-old" played with, though he was smarter than that misstep would make him seem. After one look at me, he said, "You look a mite big for ten."

I sliced a smile at my mother. Ridgely only

laughed and guided him into the receiving room. "She's always been big for her age," she cooed, her drawl going extra soft. "And you know how sensitive girls can be if someone says they are b-i-g."

Pink colored his ears. "Well, I'm sorry —"

"No need," she said, then turned to me. "Carlisle, sugar, tell Lupe we are ready for drinks in the parlor."

My mother seated herself on the French settee, fanning the chiffon skirt of her gossamer dress over the brocade, crossing her legs like a model in a hosiery commercial.

Lupe entered with a silver tray lined with crystal and ice, which she set down on the highboy server that housed the liquor. I was there to chaperone and was served lemonade.

Mr. McDougal drank bourbon with a splash of water.

My mother said, "Oh, my, maybe I'll have just a tiny bit of sherry. Though Lord have mercy, I rarely imbibe."

She shot me a withering glare when I laughed.

It was all very Old South, as if we lived in Atlanta or even New Orleans at the turn of the last century, and my mother was eighteen getting ready to make her debut.

That first night I ate dinner with them.

Roast duckling, fingerling potatoes, asparagus, and more than a bit of wine. The second night, I was dismissed after my lemonade on the pretext that I had "scads" of homework to do and had already eaten dinner. The third night, Lupe's night off, I was conveniently spending the night with a girlfriend (of which I had none) and had to cover my head with a pillow to block out the sound of my mother's girlish laughter and Mr. McDougal's deep baritone voice coming from her bedroom.

The night after that he didn't call.

Wearing her sensible housecoat and slippers, my mother paced and stared at the phone, willing it to ring. I might have said something about a watched pot never boils, which she didn't appreciate, but she took to pacing in the other room, flying to the phone every time it rang. But it was never Mr. McDougal.

When she determined he wasn't going to call, she left him messages, which he didn't return. A week after the first dinner, she dragged me out of bed in the middle of the night and into the truck she had bought Ernesto, taking that instead of the Mercedes so that no one would know it was her. Both of us still wore nightgowns as we drove through the darkened streets to see just what Rhys McDougal was up to. A car she didn't recognize sat out front of his ramshackle house, so she threw the pickup into park and we waited.

"Mother, this isn't a good idea, not to mention totally creepy, and probably isn't the kind of example you should be setting for an impressionable thirteen-year-old, as in: me."

"Hush. I need to concentrate."

Unfortunately I knew the drill. I had been through it with disheartening regularity.

I was just dozing off when she stiffened and cursed. "That bastard."

Blinking awake, I saw Mr. McDougal coming out of his house with a woman.

"Rhys McDougal, shame on you for your cheatin' heart!" Her shrill whisper echoed through the truck as she sank low in her seat, careful as always not to be seen. "I hate him!"

Her anger filled the space until it shifted into despair as she ranted against the injustice of men. When she started to cry, I knew what I had to do. I leaped out of the truck, my legs tangling in my nightgown, then raced around to the driver's side. Opening the door, I cringed at the creak of hinges, then stepped up on the running board in order to get inside. Scooting

45

Mother over to the passenger seat, I had to sit on the phone book she kept under the seat in order to drive us home just as I had learned to do.

"They're all the same," she cried, her head flung back, tears she would have never shown in the daylight streaming down her cheeks. "They always break your heart. Remember that, Carlisle."

When we got to the house I went to my room and put Jack's plastic ring in my drawer. And after sitting in the back of the classroom beside him that entire week, I got to school early the next day and found a seat in the front row. When Jack walked in, he looked at me in surprise. Mr. Hawkins didn't give him a chance to question me, and once the bell rang I was gone, then managed to avoid him like the plague until he graduated from Willow Creek High. I had learned my mother's lesson. If only she had taken her own advice.

After we left the law offices of Howard Grout, Ernesto drove my mother and me home. Willow Creek looked much the same as it always had, the curving tree-lined streets, manicured lawns, mixed with sprawling mansions and the university. We arrived at Wainwright House on Hildebrand

Square, close to the heart of the city, Ernesto swinging up the long drive, bypassing the front door, heading around back to the garage.

The house was nothing if not stately, a sprawling three-story structure built to resemble a medieval castle made from limestone and granite, replete with turrets and crenellated rooftop. I was surprised my great-great-grandfather hadn't gone all-out in his dream of regal grandeur and installed a moat and drawbridge.

My ancestors had lived in this same spot since the early 1900s after Gerald Wainwright, the Duke of Ridgely, hit a million-dollar-a-week oil field. And let me just say, a million dollars a week back then made my great-great-grandfather better off than the king of England.

Since then, the family had hit more oil and invested wisely so that the crash of 1987 didn't so much as cause a blip in the Wainwright assets. My ancestors had been a conservative bunch, at least until my mother took her first breath.

When Ernesto put the car in park, I started to get out. My mother stopped me. Her lips pursed, then she consciously smoothed her features. "You're going to make Vincent pay for putting me through this, right?"

"The lawyer will make him pay," I clarified.

My mother frowned at me, as if I were some sort of traitor, a theme I was getting extremely tired of. Regardless, I still had every intention of finding my mother another lawyer. I didn't need this, I didn't want this. I had nothing to prove to this town. I had nothing to prove to Jack Blair.

I thought of Phillip and instantly felt my mind ease. I'd return to Boston soon. We'd go to La Fenice for lasagna and a nice bottle of red wine. We would set a date for the wedding. Then life would get back to normal. Just as I had planned.

Nodding, I promised myself I would start doing research into lawyers as soon as I got inside. But inside, everything had gone crazy.

CHAPTER THREE

When we entered Wainwright House through the wide sweep of the back veranda, noise came from every direction. My older brother, Henry, and his wife, Janice (of fertile fame), had arrived in Texas from California only a few weeks before me.

As far as my mother was concerned, there were three kinds of women. The ones who were born fabulous. (Think Jacqueline Bouvier Kennedy Onassis.) The ones who learned to be fabulous. (Think Princess Diana.) And the ones who would never, no matter what, be fabulous. (Think Jessica Simpson.)

There were others who said there was a fourth variety. The ones who swore they could be fabulous if they wanted to, but it was beneath them to try. (Think the no-makeup, Birkenstock sort who believes a razor is nothing more than a form of female subjugation.)

My mother does not subscribe to this fourth distinction, her argument being, "Who doesn't want to be fabulous?"

My mother swore that if I, with my own blond hair, blue eyes, and Wainwright alabaster skin, just tried I would fall solidly under the second category (as in Could Learn to Be Fabulous, i.e., Princess Di — I was her daughter, after all), but I had never put any effort into it, and now I was wasting said dormant fabulousness living north of the Mason-Dixon line. I couldn't imagine what she would think (and no doubt say) if she learned I was living as "that penniless girl from Texas" in Boston. But I didn't argue. Not that I was interested in arguing any point in regard to fabulousness (who wants to compare themselves to a potentially crazy, though more recently, totally dead princess), nor did I want to argue the case in defense of my sister-in-law.

Janice Josephine Reager was a Pulitzer Prize–winning journalist for the *San Francisco Chronicle*. Despite the fact that she had been born and raised in Willow Creek, she had found her like-minded brethren among the granola and Birkenstock crowd who believed they were saving the world . . . and anyone who didn't agree with them was not. You'd think she had never heard of

Texas if it weren't for the fact that with a little digging it was easy to find her Lone Star roots.

Despite her Southern origins, she was a rabid, card-carrying women's rights activist who once compared all things social to ethnic cleansing in third world countries. If I recall correctly, she made this statement during what my mother now refers to as the Thanksgiving from Hell. Given that Ridgely Wainwright-Cushing-Jameson-Lackley-Harper-Ogden was all about everything social, it was not hard to see why their relationship was strained.

Their affiliation had been less than perfect from the beginning. The first thing Janice did wrong was be born into the Buford Reager family, as in the Buford Reager of Nuts, Bolts, and Scrap Metal, Inc., fame.

The second thing Janice did wrong was, well, be herself when she met my mother back when she and my brother started dating in high school.

Number three on the list was that Janice got pregnant during her and my brother's senior year at Willow Creek High.

There were times when I swore my outwardly laid-back brother married Janice just to make my mother insane.

"Why are Henry and Janice here?" I asked.

"Because of Morgan," my mother explained, referring to my eighteen-year-old niece. "Lord have mercy, did you see her last night at dinner? The child sulks and carries on as if she has been dragged against her will to the land of hillbillies and hayseeds. While no one has bothered to tell me why they showed up here unexpectedly, I just happened to overhear them talking. It turns out that Morgan has been kicked out of yet another school in the greater San Francisco Bay area. From what I heard no one else would take her, especially this late in her senior year. So Texas, here they came, apparently." She smoothed her St. John suit, then raised a perfectly plucked brow. "Though you didn't hear that from me."

"Why in the world are they staying with you?"

Janice wasn't an idiot (proof surely found in the Pulitzer), and she didn't like my mother any more than my mother liked her. I couldn't imagine her moving anywhere near Wainwright House, much less into it. Beyond that, after Janice and Henry's unexpected pregnancy in high school, they hadn't slowed down since and Janice had managed to produce three additional offspring along with her Pulitzer.

"I offered, of course," my mother said,

"couldn't do anything less. But I never expected them to accept."

My mother had a habit of saying what she should say without meaning it, then bemoaning the fact that people didn't know better than to simply give her credit for being nice and decline her generous offers.

Inside the house, it sounded as if my brother's children had gone berserk. Lupe was in the kitchen cleaning, her iPod turned up so loud that even we could hear Rick Martin singing "La Vida Loca." Ernesto couldn't be coaxed through the door, complaining that his hearing aids couldn't take the noise.

Neither Henry's nor Janice's car was in the drive when we pulled up. Though my sister, Savannah, appeared as soon as we walked in.

"Finally!" she said. "Mother, you have to do something about those children."

My sister, Savannah Wainwright Cushing Carter, was a younger version of my mother. Beautiful, ethereal, and used to getting her way. Standing in the kitchen, she looked like yet another china doll pulled out of a glass cabinet, her blond hair brushed back, her skin so perfect it looked like porcelain, her eyes as blue as . . . well, something really blue.

My mother stiffened. I knew she was rattled after the meeting with Jack and Vincent. In fact, I expected her to head for the bedroom at any second to lie down. Instead she walked into the living room where her only grandchildren were sprawled and carrying on among her antique furniture and family heirlooms.

"What is going on here?"

Morgan slouched in the Louis XIV settee, one leg slung over the delicate arm, fiddling with a long strand of her orange-dyed hair. Henry Herbert Cushing the fifth, aka Cinco, a ten-year-old bundle of energy, slid down the stairs on a piece of cardboard. Priscilla, the eight-year-old princess, looked as if she should be Savannah's child with her blond hair, blue eyes, and a fondness for pink. A screech interrupted everything as two-year-old Robbie woke up from a nap with a wail of displeasure.

"Where is your mother?" my mother asked Morgan.

"Mom says that raising kids is a shared responsibility. Today's my dad's day to deal with us."

Ridgely's jaw tightened. "Forget my feelings on where a woman belongs, just tell me where your father is."

54

"He went out. Said there was too much noise."

My mother did some screeching of her own. She pressed her eyes closed, shook herself, then tried to get the children to behave. But no such luck.

"Call 911 if you see blood. I'm going to Brightlee." She turned to Savannah and me. "Girls, come along. We're going to the tearoom for lunch."

Savannah glanced from my mother to me, then back. "We're taking her?"

"What's wrong with me?" I demanded.

My mother and sister looked at me.

"Nothing," my mother said.

My sister rolled her eyes.

"The fact is," Ridgely added, "I have to be seen. Everyone has to know that I'm doing great, better than great. Besides" — she glanced at her grandchildren — "seems like a good day to get out of the house."

We arrived at Brightlee and as soon as my mother, sister, and I entered the tearoom everyone turned to stare. Brightlee is the Junior League of Willow Creek's headquarters. It was just off the center of town, an old sprawling mansion made of limestone with a wraparound porch, and a cedar shingle roof. Inside, they have a tearoom

55

with high ceilings and antique furniture. It was the place for ladies of a certain distinction to go to be seen.

The tearoom waitresses were Junior League volunteers, so there was no guarantee of an efficient use of anyone's time. Fortunately, the cooks and bakers were professionals, so while it might take forever to get a waitress's attention, whatever she brought would be divine. The orange rolls were something not to miss.

We walked into the dining room, our heels sounding overly loud against the hardwood floor. Even I sensed the knowing whispers that floated through the room at the sight of us.

Not one to be intimidated, my mother smiled and strode forward, her Hermès crocodile Kelly bag swinging on her forearm. My sister, more a Birkin bag girl, followed, with me bringing up the rear with my plain black briefcase. As the three of us walked through the tables, women said hello, but even I could tell that Ridgely was not getting the usual homage that women generally afforded her.

"Carlisle?" more than one Junior Leaguer said in surprise. "I hardly recognized you. What with all the flat hair and black clothes . . . Well, never you mind about that, sugar. How are you?"

A barb wrapped in smiles and "sugars" and "aren't you sweets." A Southern specialty that ranked right up there with sweet tea and barbecue.

We were seated at an antique oak table set with silver flatware and fine bone china, though it took even longer than normal before a waitress appeared. It was Carol Simmons, a shy member who blushed as she took our order. I had the distinct impression that she had been forced to take our table, and I was certain of it when I noticed that the rest of her tables were clear on the other side of the room.

"What is going on?" I asked.

Savannah snapped her compact closed. "Some of the women are saying that the debutante ball is a mess. And there's a nasty rumor going around that this year's group of debs are going to back out and go to San Antonio or Dallas to make their debuts," she explained, glancing around the room, preening in all her blond hair, perfect cashmere, and heirloom pearls. The strand had been a gift from our grandmother.

I had a strand, but couldn't bring myself to wear it. One, because somehow I felt it turned me into someone I didn't want to be. But there was a two in the equation: I

57

missed my grandmother dearly since she had passed away the year before. She had always supported me, told me to go after what I wanted. Which I had, in Boston.

The times I had put the pearls on they never ceased to remind me of her, and quite frankly it was hard to be a cutthroat, ball-busting divorce lawyer when you were choked up over your deceased grandmother. So when I moved away from Texas, I left the pearls in a small velvet-lined jewelry box in my childhood bedroom dresser.

"To make matters worse," Savannah added, "after last year's debacle, the symphony is having money problems."

The annual Willow Creek Symphony Association Debutante Ball was one of the oldest and most prestigious debutante balls in the country and *the* most prestigious in the state of Texas. More important, the Willow Creek Symphony, along with its debutante ball, was founded by a Wainwright one hundred years ago. Everything deb-related had been a priority to my grandmother until the day she died.

"How bad are the problems?" I asked.

"Very bad."

I swung my head to look at my mother in disbelief. "Is the symphony going bankrupt?"

My mother glowered at my sister.

Savannah just smiled. "Yes, they are."

After my grandmother died, my mother had stepped into Grand-mère's shoes and taken over last year's event. Unfortunately the ball had been an unmitigated disaster when the famous (now infamous) conductor Alberto Guiseppe Rinaldi was caught in the young debutantes' dressing room the night of the big event. Not with one of the girls (which would have been a disaster), but secretly slipping into one of the girls' ten-thousand-dollar ball gowns (in Texas, a bigger disaster). The reporter who found him snapped his picture, and the next day the photo ran on the front page of just about every newspaper across the state of Texas with the caption:

**Willow Creek's
Debutante of the Year**
They don't make them like they used to.

Worse yet, the picture was taken from behind, Signor Rinaldi glancing over his shoulder like an innocent coquette, unfortunate amounts of hairy back revealed where the zipper wouldn't zip.

As you might imagine, my mother was mortified. But I thought she had moved

59

beyond it, pulling together another set of the traditional eight girls with money and old-family connections who would make their debut in a little more than three months. The names were supposed to be announced in just over a week. Soon, last year's debacle would be nothing more than a bad memory.

"According to the rumor the current crop of debutante mothers are going to boycott the ball unless the reins are handed over to someone else," Savannah explained, seeming amused. "They blame Mother for last year's debacle and don't want to risk another repeat."

"Is this true, Mother?"

"Yes. And we can't let it happen. We can't let those women destroy a hundred years of our family history. A Wainwright has always been in charge of the debutante ball."

My eyes narrowed. While I hated that my grandmother's beloved event had taken a hit, I really hated the sudden use of the "we" word.

Several women whispered to one another as they glanced our way.

"Keep smiling, girls," my mother hissed, her own smile plastered on her face.

I got a headache from the tension of my minor supporting role. All I had to do was sit, smile, and make mindless small talk, offering up the requisite laugh now and again to "show" what a fabulous time we were having, and how nothing, certainly not any gossip, was bothering me any more than it bothered my mother. I might have lived in the Northeast's cutthroat world of divorce law for the last three years, but I still remembered how to act in Texas polite society.

My mother started looking a tad stressed around the mouth, a huge no-no for her since she prided herself on her younger-than-her-years good looks. Everyone marveled that without a lick of surgery, she could pass for our sister. "I'm so fortunate to have such good genes," she was fond of saying.

"Here," Mother said, pulling a letter from her purse. "You need to read this. Grand-mère wrote it before she passed."

"A letter?" I frowned. "What letter? Why haven't I heard about a letter before now?"

Savannah scoffed. "Because Mother didn't want you to see it." She laughed. "Now she's desperate."

I gaped.

My mother smoothed her hair. "It's not like you cared one whit for your heritage, proof being that no sooner was your grand-

61

mother's funeral over than you hightailed it back to Boston."

Confused, I took the envelope.

I held it for a long second before I lifted the flap. Instantly I could smell my grandmother's subtle perfume. L'Air du Temps.

I took a deep breath, swallowing back a traitorous swell of tears, then started to read. My mother eyed me in speculation. Savannah waved to someone across the room.

Dear Carlisle,

I'm sure you'll be surprised by this letter, but in time I believe you will come to understand. As a concession to the Wainwright family for starting the Willow Creek Symphony, the founding charter states that a Wainwright is to be in charge of the annual debutante ball. For one hundred years it has been part of who we are.

But now, the truth is Savannah has other things on her mind than debutante balls. And your mother, bless her heart, while she loves the ball, she has no interest in the many details that go into making such a function truly work. If she were in charge, I'm afraid the ball would, let us say, incur problems.

As had been exhibited the first year my
mother took over.

We need someone at the helm who
understands the importance of details.
You, my lovely girl, are all about details.
Step up to your legacy, Carlisle. Please.
If you can't, I understand. But know,
the position is yours unless you say otherwise.

All my Love,
Grand-mère

Me?
Take over?
"I can't do that!"
My mother took another sip of tea.
"That's exactly why I didn't give you the
letter in the first place."
Savannah smirked with her special version
of disdain and condescension, combined
with perverse glee. "It was a crazy idea
anyway, given your own experience with deb
balls."
My mother shuddered. "True. After your
own debut disaster, we certainly didn't need
you anywhere near the ball. I couldn't
imagine what Grand-mère was thinking."
Sorry, I might have left out a small (read:
gigantic) detail. While I had been around

etiquette, manners, and the waltz since I was born, no one had ever accused me of being Debutante of the Year. As it turned out, my debut had been something short of successful. But they didn't have to get ugly about it.

"However, that was years ago," my mother added. "No one remembers Carlisle's debut."

My sister snorted. "See? She's desperate."

"Savannah, enough. The fact is," my mother continued, "our family's legacy is at stake. And Grand-mère asked Carlisle to do this."

My heart pounded, and not in a good way. "What about you, Savannah? Why don't you do it?"

"As Grand-mère pointed out, I have other things to deal with now."

"Like what?" I asked.

"Excuse me. Like get pregnant."

My sister had spent the last seventeen years trying to have a child. She was on her second husband (had announced with not a little superiority that this one was her perfect match) though still had no baby with forty and its corresponding plunge in fertility rates just around the corner.

Savannah launched into her latest theory on why she was sans children. She went on

64

about acupuncture, soy-rich diets, and even something called imaginary wombs. I hadn't a clue what she was talking about, didn't ask, didn't want to know.

I needed a break. Without a word, I pushed up from the table, then headed for the front door. But I knew Ernesto was out there waiting. Not interested in running into him, I hurried down a long hall that took me the back way to the ladies' room.

Two League members were fixing their lipstick when I entered. Not wanting conversation, I went into the very last stall, closed the lid, and slid the lock securely in place. I needed a few minutes alone to gather my wits and clear my head.

I heard the women snap their handbags shut and leave the ladies' room. I started to get up, but the door swung open again and two other women entered.

"Can you believe it!" a woman said. "Can you believe Ridgely sits there and pretends everything is still the same. Ha! Is she ever going to be in for a surprise when she has to address the ultimatum of stepping down or losing the debs. Everyone is going to look at her and her crazy family differently, now." The woman laughed. "And Carlisle! Can you believe she's back? Remember her debut?"

Insult melted into a cringe as the two women laughed.

"How could I forget? I swear her nose is crooked from the fall."

I had to swallow back a groan by covering my face as I remembered my big night. I had worn the requisite long white gown with white gloves, my hair pulled up in an elegant twist. I felt on top of the world, beautiful, as I came down the formal staircase, a barely remembered stepfather at my side, my escort waiting for me at the bottom. When I reached the end of the stairs I stood for one perfect moment between my escort and the stepfather, then began the famous Texas Dip, a deep, full curtsy where a girl sinks so low that she touches her forehead to her skirt. Tricky for most girls, a disaster for me when I lost my balance and did a face-plant into the hardwood floor.

Hiding in the bathroom stall, I felt the humiliation of eleven years earlier as if it were yesterday.

The two Junior Leaguers stood side by side in front of the sinks and mirrors. Through the crack between the door and jamb, I could make out each of them fluffing their hair as they laughed with wicked glee as if they were girls in the bathroom at Willow Creek Junior High.

Normally, I would have barged out and demanded an apology. But somehow I couldn't force myself to do it. Instead, I carefully (in an embarrassingly juvenile *Witness* [the movie] moment) pulled my feet up off the floor.

"I hear she's a lawyer now. A divorce lawyer."

More laughter, not coming from the stall.

"Have you ever heard of a plain-as-vanilla-cream-pie divorce lawyer? No doubt she'd get eaten alive in a Texas court."

My mouth fell open. These women could insult my clothes, ridicule my hair, but how dare they question my abilities as an attorney?

Suddenly my cell phone vibrated in my purse. The supposedly silent sound made a faint buzz.

"What was that?"

"What was what?"

"That noise?"

"I didn't hear anything."

I hugged my purse close to my chest, though fortunately the phone didn't buzz again.

One of the women leaned down and I could see her long strawberry-blond curls swing low as she looked under the first stall.

Great, my mind shrieked. Bad enough not

to confront them, but then to get caught hiding?

Then the hair swung down again as she looked under the next stall.

My heart jammed in my throat as my mind raced. What to do? What to say?

I was just about to burst out of the stall when the outer door slammed open and the head waitress burst in. "What are you two doing in here? We have customers! And they want their tea!"

"Fine, fine, we're coming."

My breath gasped out of me as all three women departed.

I sank back against the commode in relief, though I only gave myself a second before I unlocked the door and went to the sink. Splashing water on my face, I glanced at my reflection in the mirror. "I am Carlisle Cushing. Strong. Tough. In control," I whispered. I was no longer the fatherless girl, the one whose mother was drawn to drama like the queen bee to honey, the girl who did the face-plant into the floor.

My reflection stared back and, quite frankly, it didn't look convinced, which made me angry.

Feeling strangely determined for reasons that in that second I couldn't have named, I went back to my mother's table. As soon as

I sat down two women swept over and stopped. Loud enough for everyone to hear, a petite strawberry-blonde said, "Ridgely, I was just sick when I heard the news."

I knew this couldn't be good, especially since I realized right away that this was one of the women from the bathroom.

"Maylee Pearson," my mother said, "I'm not sure who you think you're speaking to with that tone of voice?"

Maylee glanced around the room and saw that everyone was watching.

"Why, Ridgely, sugar, I'm speaking to you of course. And after the embarrassment of last year's ball, this year's event is irrevocably tarnished. Everyone says so. I thought it only fair that someone told you to your face that the debutantes are reconsidering the wisdom of being a part of the Symphony Association ball if you stay in charge."

A collective gasp shuddered through Brightlee. Not that everyone didn't already know this; there were no secrets in Willow Creek. But no one could have expected such a blatant challenge thrown down in the middle of teatime at the Junior League tearoom.

I saw the embarrassment on my mother's face. As much as I wanted to ignore it, I couldn't. Emotion surged up, of the sort I really don't do.

As a child, I used to pull a red beach towel from the linen closet and tie it around my shoulders like a magic cape. It was the first time I felt I had power, different from my mother's, different from Savannah's, but still a certain strength that I wrapped myself in.

It was with the thought of that silly cape that I stood. "Why, girls, haven't you heard?" I asked with the sweetest Texas accent you can imagine.

Their brows furrowed as they glanced nervously from table to table, then back.

"My mother is so busy, what with all her tremendous responsibilities managing the Wainwright assets and charitable contributions, that I am taking over this year's debutante ball."

After a moment of surprise, the girls looked more relieved than worried. "You, in charge of a debutante ball?"

I heard the snickers, which made me even more determined.

"It is going to be pure heaven," I cooed dramatically. "And after living in Boston with all those Mayflower descendants and their seriously prestigious old-money debutante balls, I can't tell you all the fabulous things I have learned and plan to implement." Of course I knew absolutely nothing about deb balls in Boston, imagined they were austere sorts of events, given their Puritan roots, but these women didn't need to know that. "We'll be written up in all the major Texas media. It's going to be fabulous!"

Crazy, I know. Foolhardy, no doubt. And who knows why I said it. The mounting stress of the fake me in Boston? The sudden unsettling thought that I had to be fake to succeed? Or maybe it was simply my closing in on thirty and the chest-squeezing tick-tick-tick I woke up with in the mornings? It was hard to say. All I knew was that I couldn't stand by and watch my mother be humiliated.

"This year's debutante ball is going to be a true affair to remember." I smiled serenely. "Mother. Savannah. I believe we are done here."

Ridgely and my sister sat at the table, surrounded by the better women of Willow Creek, looking as if they had been shot. Without too much effort, I bustled them out to the parking lot, gossip surging up behind us like a wave in our wake.

Ernesto leaped out of the car and raced around to open my mother's door. With just one look at her, he yelped, "Wha happen to you mama?"

I didn't respond. I herded my mother and sister into the Mercedes. It only took five minutes to arrive at Wainwright House, but long enough for my mother to recover her wits. When we pulled into the drive, she turned to me. I expected her to take my hand and thank me profusely.

She shook her head. "Let's just hope Grand-mère wasn't losing her marbles when she wrote that letter and didn't have a clue what she was talking about."

"I can do this," I found myself saying. "And I'll do a great job."

"Now, dear, let's not get carried away. You have never been *great* at anything social. I'm just hoping for something higher on the scale than disaster to give us time to regroup before next year."

"Mother!"

"Well, that's no lie. And quite frankly, I'm surprised you care. You've never cared about being good at anything except intellectual matters like the law."

"Which is why I am taking the case."

Both of us were surprised by that, but as soon as the words were out of my mouth I knew it was true. I might have built a life in Boston, but I wasn't going to let Jack Blair or anyone else look at me as someone who couldn't hack it in Texas.

"I'm going to take the case *and* whip the deb ball into shape. It's going to be fine."

Mother might have snorted, but I was too busy planning to notice.

I was going to do whatever it took to fix the Hundredth Annual Willow Creek Symphony Association Debutante Ball *and* my mother's divorce. And good manners or not, I had the exceedingly inappropriate thought that by the end of it I would make those women regret the day they insulted my family, my mother, and, well, me.

CHAPTER FOUR

Panic is an odd thing.

As a rule, I don't do panic. But after my belief that I could make magic happen wore off, panic was exactly what I felt.

Standing in the big old sprawling house where I had grown up, listening to the familiar creaks and groans of my past, I tried the breathing exercises they taught us at the firm-sponsored (and requisite) stress management course. I had thought it ridiculous at the time (one of my major assets in the courtroom being my ability to thrive on, even relish, any stress opposing counsel threw my way), but standing there with my heart crammed in my throat, I wished I had paid better attention. Making grand declarations about debutante balls in front of a group of society women wasn't like me any more than overblown displays of affection were. And I was nothing if not proud of the fact that I could always count on me being

Just Like Me.

By noon the next day, I had explained to the managing partner of Marcus, Flint, and Worthson back in Boston that I had to take a leave of absence. When he said that was unacceptable, I said, fine, tell Stanley Marcus I'd have to quit. He backed down, though not without a lot of unflattering grumbles, then gave me the leave, calling it a sabbatical. The fact was, after I had put together a prenuptial agreement for the firm's managing partner that had proved ironclad when the man's wife filed for a divorce, Marcus, Flint, and Worthson had bent over backward to make sure I was happy. On top of which, given the firm's predilection for new hires from Harvard, Princeton, and Yale, I suspected they had hired me as some sort of quota requirement. Excellent grades, star moot court team member, and a woman, more specifically, a "financially challenged" woman from Texas.

Next I pressed 3 on my cell phone, speed-dialing my fiancé.

To say Phillip wasn't happy would be an understatement.

"What do you mean, you'll be staying for a while? What is a while? A week?"

"No."

"A month?"

"Not exactly."

"More than a month? Did you quit your job, Carlisle?"

There was a trace of hysteria in his voice, and I realized that I didn't know if it was caused by my potentially deserting him or by my losing my standing at the firm.

Phillip Granger was on the fast track at Marcus, Flint, and Worthson. He was considered a catch despite the fact that he was a Boston Southie, aka a Boston boy born (another quota satisfied?) on the wrong side of the tracks, at least in the eyes of the venerable Boston Brahmin law firm. It wasn't a surprise that Phillip loved that I had come from "poor" origins "as well." He also loved the way I put myself together with careful sensibility, even if I did have the same blond hair and violet-blue eyes that marked me as my mother's child as clearly as any DNA chart ever could. The difference, however, was that there were no off-the-wall theatrics from me.

No question, I should have told him the truth, but again, in my defense, it's not as if I *told* him I was money challenged. Somehow the rumor got out there, and well, I just never corrected it. But we've been over that.

"I've taken a leave of absence." I hesitated.

"Technically, I'm on sabbatical."

There was a very long pause of disbelief crackling over the airwaves before the burst of: "That's crazy. You're going places, Carlisle. Ducking out now is career suicide." He hesitated. "Hold on."

I heard him get up, go over to his door, and close it. When he came back on the line his voice was low but excited.

"You can't tell anyone," he said, his rough voice low in a whisper, "but now that Skaggs was caught sleeping with Worthson's wife, I'm next in line to make partner!"

I might have gaped. Bernie Skaggs and Martha Worthson? Think hideously ugly and exceedingly old. In that order. Clearly Bernie had something else going besides billable hours to get a leg up.

"Can you believe it?" Phillip went on. "This is great. I should be a partner by the end of the month. Come back, Carlisle. I want you to be here for this. We'll start planning our wedding as soon as you get here."

As has been established, he was a great catch. More than that, I really did love him. I loved the life we led together in Boston, the way he swung by my apartment on the way to work, how we would hold hands as we walked across the Public Garden and Boston Common to the high-rise offices of

77

the firm regardless of the weather. The way he would stick his head around the door to my office at lunchtime, asking me where I wanted to go that day.

On weekends we drove somewhere. Up the coast to Maine, out to Cape Cod, down to New York City. Just before I left, we had decided to get a dog. As soon as I got back, we were heading straight for the pound.

Phillip far exceeded every requirement I had on my list for the Perfect Husband. And is it really a surprise that the daughter of a woman who had been married five times might be trying to figure out what made someone a keeper?

Keeper \kee-per\ n (and not the 14c kind) a man who 1: was honest 2: loved me 3: shared my goals 4: could never, in any way, make me act like my mother.

Phillip had all these attributes.

"Oh, Phillip, I'm so happy for you. Truly. But I can't come back now. I'm staying to work on a divorce case."

"A divorce case? Whose?"

I stepped right into that one. "My mother's."

"Your mother's?" As in, *You have a mother?* "You are handling your own mother's divorce case?"

For the record, had he shown even a tad

of concern over the fact that my newly acquired mother was getting a divorce, I might have felt guilty, or might even have reconsidered. He showed no such consideration.

"Phillip." There was that whole tight-edge-in-my-voice thing again. "I can't leave my mother to deal with this herself."

He grumbled and muttered all the first-year-law stuff that I already knew about representing relatives in a matter of law, then he added, "Though why it would take more than a few weeks, I can't imagine. With no money in the family, how complicated a case can it be?" He seemed to consider. "No custody issues given your age. And I suspect Texas is a no-fault state like most others these days. Seems like she could file the proper forms, sit tight for the waiting period, then sign the papers. I don't see why you have to stay there at all?"

I could hear him sit back in his chair, and I imagined him in his starched white shirt, conservative blue tie, and gray pin-striped suit looking out his office window.

"I still can't believe you're doing this. Even though you're dealing with a case rather than just taking time off, it's a risk." His chair squeaked. "Plus, I miss you."

It should have been too little too late, but

I felt myself soften at the words. I found myself placating him with the promise that as soon as my mother was settled I would ask him down for a visit.

"As soon as you meet my mother, Phillip, we'll set a date. It will be perfect."

"All right." He hesitated. "How can I help? You definitely should be visible while you're there. You should get some press for the work you're doing."

"No press!" I blurted.

"Why not? The press loves stories about poor people making good. This could be a bonanza for you. I can see the story now: 'Poor girl makes good and helps her poor mother out.' "

Way too many "poors" in the sentence.

"Phillip, really. No attention. And as soon as I have things in order you can come down."

It was a workable plan. He'd have to learn about my unfortunate money situation sooner or later, and this would be the perfect way to do it. We would set a date. I'd pick him up at the airport, then explain the situation to him in a way that he would understand it wasn't my fault my mother had money. But I would cross that bridge when I came to it. In the interim, there were more immediate concerns, specifically my upcoming meeting at Symphony Hall.

Attendees: the debutantes and their mothers.

Purpose: convince them to stay on board.

How to achieve: discuss the unique qualities I bring to the table . . . but will beg if necessary.

Symphony Hall stood on the corner of Hildebrand Boulevard and Willow Creek Avenue, just off Hildebrand Square. My grandmother had loved the building, and had been taking me to hear the symphony perform since I was old enough to walk. Whenever I entered the hall, it brought me a sense of bone-deep peace, like walking into a cathedral.

I was the first to arrive for the meeting, though coffee, sweet tea, and finger sandwiches were already laid out on a sideboard.

Giselda Montserat walked in. She blinked at the sight of me. "Who are you?"

Giselda was a short plug of a woman, with hair dyed so red she looked like a cardinal. She had worked for the symphony since I was a girl. Which meant that she had been around during my unfortunate days as a deb.

"I'm Carlisle Cushing."

At first there was confusion. Then it hit

her, and confusion was replaced by horror.

I've learned in life that there are times when it's best to put your cards on the table, acknowledge the issue, and be done with it. But there are other times when it's best to ignore the issue, pretend that the elephant in the room doesn't exist. Which basically makes life a crap shoot, and the people who are best at it are the ones who are best at gauging when to ignore the beast and when to acknowledge it.

That day it seemed best to take something of a dual approach. Let her know that I knew what she was thinking, then dare her to do something as stupid as mention it.

I raised my chin, gave her a look, and said, "I'm Carlisle Cushing. I'm sure you remember me."

I had honed my instincts over the last three years in the courtroom and they worked quite well with Miss Montserat. She sniffed, then turned to fuss with the perfectly arranged sandwiches.

The first of the girls arrived with their mothers. They weren't nearly as confused or surprised to see me, which could only mean that word of my display at Brightlee had gotten around. The good news was that all the girls arrived.

The cluster of well-dressed mothers and

their daughters sipped tea, held sandwiches but didn't eat them, gossiped, and glanced my way repeatedly like uneasy pedestrians being forced to cross paths with a bellowing homeless man.

"Hello," I began, from the front of the room.

"Carlisle? I can't believe it's you!"

This from Genny Jenkins (married to Edward Jenkins of Jenkins Technology), who had grown up with Savannah.

"Lord have mercy, I didn't believe it when I heard you'd be here."

By then, several other mothers had circled around and a wave of general dissatisfaction rose in the ranks.

"I thought it was a joke."

I forced a smile. "No joke."

I barely recognized Anda Wilkinson. Time had not been kind to her, though when she was young she had been a blond bombshell. Now her tanned skin looked so much like leather that even her Chanel suit and perfectly highlighted blond hair couldn't detract.

"It's bad enough that your grandmother isn't here," Anda said. "But really, how can you possibly think you can do this? We felt we needed someone else besides your mother after last year's debacle, true, but you, Carlisle?"

The teenagers had been utterly uninterested in the proceedings until then. Suddenly the eight mothers had eight daughters peering on with keen interest. Not about to let them see me weak, I introduced myself.

"I'm Carlisle Cushing and, as you have probably heard, I'm taking over this year's ball. The event is just over three months away, with names to be announced in a week in Sunday's newspaper. So we don't have a second to lose."

One of the girls looked me up and down. "Weren't you voted something like the worst deb known to man, like a hundred years ago?"

"Oh, my God! You're the one?"

"Yes, well." I swear I wasn't blushing, it was just hot in the room. "But as you pointed out yourself, that was eons ago. It has nothing to do with my ability to carry out a fabulous ball now."

"This could actually prove true," said a short plump girl with thick glasses. "When I heard the rumors that she was taking over, I Googled her. She's won all her cases and is considered a top lawyer in Boston. Surely she can put on a deb ball."

The rest of the girls turned to her, looking

her over with disdain, stopping at her loafers.

"Didn't you get the memo?" one of them asked.

"Memo?" The girl's confidence wavered.

"Pennies are out. Dimes are in."

The rest of the girls burst out laughing. The chubby girl went bright red. Her mother went bright red. One of the mothers admonished her daughter, though without a great deal of conviction.

I hated this year's gaggle of debs at that second. Not a good sign since I would have to work with them for the next three months.

"Ladies, as has already been noted," I added in my best lawyerly voice, "I've been living in Boston for the last few years." I gave them my spiel on the land of long lineage and long-held traditions, and what a great ball it was going to be.

I nearly convinced myself.

"How'd it go?" Savannah asked with her signature smirk when I got home.

"It went great."

"Really?"

I should have been forewarned by her superior look. But I had been away from Savannah for so long that I was out of practice. When Mother walked into the kitchen, she looked ill.

"What is it?" I asked.

Savannah just smiled.

"The debutantes have canceled."

"What?" My gasp was indignant. "That can't be. We had a great meeting and no one said anything about canceling."

"Then 'great' has taken on new meaning since every single girl's mother has called, regretting that they can no longer in good conscience be involved in the Willow Creek Symphony Association's Debutante Ball."

To my credit, I suppressed every unfortunate emotion I felt knocking at my staggering psyche. I smiled and shrugged with a great deal of bravado. "Not to worry, Mother. I'll fix this."

Though how, exactly, I couldn't say.

CHAPTER FIVE

The solution to my problem hit me in the middle of the night. All I needed to do was get eight new debutantes, thereby raising the money necessary to save the symphony through the amazing ball I would put on with said new debutantes.

How hard could it be?

I took to my mission like a general plotting a war. My mother was no help since she had about fainted dead away when I told her the news.

"You're getting new debutantes?"

"Exactly. The girls haven't been officially announced yet. Plus the fact is, they weren't good enough."

"Those girls were from the finest families in town. That alone makes them good enough."

I heard a snort and we turned to find Janice standing in the hallway from the kitchen, eating a container of live yeast yogurt with one of my mother's favorite French Provincial silver spoons.

We ignored her.

Never faint of heart, I got to work on my plan of action.

Fortunately, even I knew there were five components to any Debutante Season \deb-u-tante sea-son\ n (1748) 1: selecting eight eligible graduating senior girls, and hoping they looked as if they had at least a fleeting acquaintance with innocence 2: announcing the names of the young ladies who would be launched into Society, and praying that no reporter had a slow enough day to dig around on the Internet for revealing photos of any of our supposedly chaste chosen 3: playing referee as each debutante's mother tried to outdo the other mothers with the extravagance of their individual (and required) coming-out parties 4: acting as overall den mother to the girls who were secretly vying to be named Debutante of the Year by the Texas press corps (perhaps they should contact Signor Rinaldi for pointers) 5: all the while planning and carrying out the grand finale of every season, the actual Debutante Ball.

The plans were generally executed over an entire calendar year. Given the last-minute desertion of this year's girls, all of the above would have to be accomplished over the following three months.

With my confidence firmly back in place (and feeling quite pleased with my ability to regroup so quickly), I started making a list of potential candidates in a black composition book.

There are four strata within Willow Creek society who potentially could afford a debutante season. In order of importance they are:

1. moneyed families with fine old names: my target debutante pool
2. passably moneyed families with fine old names: perfectly acceptable possibilities
3. moneyed families with new names, aka the haute bourgeoisie: only if I were desperate
4. moneyed families with cringeworthy names: no way, no how, my mother would kill me

I managed to drum up ten names of families who, if not exactly level one, were at least kissing cousins. I called them, made appointments to "visit," then got to work.

I wasn't sure how the mothers would feel about getting the belated invitation, but sometimes a woman is just happy for her daughter to get the chance, however it comes to pass.

I started my quest with Kitty Hayes. No question, she was old Willow Creek and had plenty of money, which made me wonder why her daughter had been overlooked in the first place.

Borrowing clothes from my sister (I told myself I wasn't compromising my standards, simply smart enough to know I needed more than black Armani), I dressed in a cream cashmere sweater set, matching wool flannel pants, and a pair of brown suede Ferragamo low heels, then headed for the Hayes home. I took the Volvo Lupe used to shop for groceries and made my way through town. I managed to hit Hildebrand Square just when classes were changing at the university, cars and students everywhere. It took forever to get through the intersection of Hildebrand Avenue and Moss Street because the gaggle of students kept streaming across the road despite the DON'T WALK sign that flashed.

Finally impatient, I forgot the cardinal rule of no honking in Texas, and gave the horn a good hard blast. Everyone within a hundred yards, with the exception of the students, turned to look at me. Too late, I noticed the way-too-handsome Jack Blair coming out of Starbucks at the corner.

The sun hit his dark hair, highlighting those infamously chiseled cheeks and strong jaw. More than that, he didn't have on his new uniform of blue blazer and gray slacks. He wore 501 jeans that cupped him in places that a sensible girl like me shouldn't notice, his black T-shirt molding to his broad shoulders. This was the Jack Blair I remembered.

"God, you look great," I accused him through the windshield.

I wasn't the only one who noticed him. Every female within a fifty-foot radius craned her neck to look at him, not that he noticed, or if he did, he didn't appear to care.

When he saw me I felt the shift. In me, sure, but in him as well. He stopped and looked at me with his brow furrowed, as if trying to understand something. Why I had come back? What did he feel? Why was I sitting at the intersection not moving?

Without thinking, I raised my hand in acknowledgment. He stood there and just looked at me . . . until a woman I had never seen before walked up beside him and hooked her arm through his. As if the whole world were moving in ridiculously slow motion, he came out of the staring stance, and when he looked at the woman he smiled at her. A real smile. Not a teasing smile. The kind that says louder than words that he was happy to see her.

Jerking my gaze away, I saw that the crosswalk had cleared, the light blazing green. With enough embarrassment surging through me to make me curse, I drove through the intersection (perhaps depositing a tiny bit of rubber on the pavement), leaving Jack and the woman far behind.

Of course I didn't really leave him behind. He lurked in my brain, both as a sexy god, and also as a reminder that I needed to get up to speed on my mother's divorce. Yep, a little thing like that.

I made it to the Hayes home five minutes later. Kitty had been a cheerleader at Willow Creek High School and a Kappa at UT. When she graduated, she married Russell Hayes, the university's star running back. With her money and his godlike status as a Texas football player (enhanced later by his success as a real estate tycoon), they were considered one of Willow Creek's golden couples.

The Hayes family lived in a sprawling mansion made of limestone, lots of windows, with a cobbled drive leading up to the front doors. It was an impressive place in a new development called Live Oak Estates, one of Russell's real estate projects.

The house was part home, part advertisement, and actually seemed more ad than family quarters once you got inside. It appeared as if someone had gone to the local furniture store for One Stop Shopping. Everything screamed "Matching Suite," or more specifically, "Expensive Matching Suite." My mother wouldn't have approved.

The long and short was that there was no sign of antiques handed down from generation to generation or evidence that anyone had traveled farther than Ferdinand's Fine Furniture to fill the space with "treasures." They hadn't even bothered to "coordinate" fabrics rather than "match" them.

But let them decorate as they may, as long as Kitty said yes to my request.

"Thank you for seeing me on such short notice," I said.

"Absolutely," she enthused, remnants of her cheerleading days still present. "I was thrilled when you called!"

A maid served us tea in the garden room, complete with matching wicker set. We chatted about Boston and the weather, then made it through the obligatory this and that, before I got to the point. "I am heading up this year's deb committee —"

"Oh, Lord, what a mess."

My teacup froze halfway to my mouth, but only for a second before I forced myself to take a sip. "It's all straightened out now, I assure you. You might have heard that I've taken over and I have everything under control." Hardly. "And the hundredth annual ball is going to be the best ever."

She leaned forward, tsked, and actually patted my leg. "Sweetie, I know you'll try your little ol' heart out."

Just so you know, I have always had a problem with the sweet-as-pie routine, even if I have been known to use it to effect. But whatever.

"Regardless," she went on, "I can't believe everyone is causing such a ruckus. You know I just adore your mama. And for anyone to work to destroy all those years of history, it's a cryin' shame. The fact is, it's Willow Creek history, not just your family's. I can't imagine what people are thinking."

I ignored the "ruckus," "mama," and "cryin' shame," and said, "Then you'll help me out?"

"Oh, gawd, no."

"Why not?"

"For one, I can't afford to get on the wrong side of most of Willow Creek, what with Russell's investment here in Live Oak Estates. He has a lot of property to sell and it just wouldn't do for me to get tangled up in any messes right now. And for another, well, I just don't have the time. I have gone back to work."

This was a surprise. Though when I finally focused on something besides my debutante problem (or her decorating sense), I noticed that she did look more businesswoman than do-gooder with her durable navy blue suit and silk shell underneath instead of cashmere and elegant wool.

Her spine went stiff when she realized I had noticed. "It's not that I have to work," she explained. "But I need something to do with myself now that Cecelia is going off to college. Empty-nest syndrome, and all."

During one of my mother's weekly phone calls while I was still in Boston, she had shared the rumors that Russell Hayes was having cash flow problems. I had dismissed them as absurd. Though maybe not. It certainly would explain why Cecelia hadn't been a member of the original group of eight. She no doubt had been asked, but her mother had said no.

And empty-nest syndrome? Certainly the oldest daughter would be leaving at the end of the summer. But the Hayes family had two other children of the younger variety who hadn't even flown the grade school coop, much less forced Kitty to face a midlife crisis.

I was ushered out much faster than I had been ushered in. But since I wasn't the type to be discouraged easily, I headed for my next quarry with unabated optimism.

For the rest of the day and the day after that, I went through the list of every mother of every graduating senior in Willow Creek who was of a proper family, supposedly had money, and reportedly had two X chromosomes. I visited with Lalee Dubois, Georgina Weatherman, Pamela Prescott. And the list went on. When I got to the end with no takers, for half a second I wondered about debuting boys.

Talk about a scandal.

I swear I wasn't feeling desperate when I went to visit Merrily Bennett.

Fortunately, Merrily had married into a fine old family. On the unfortunate side of the fence, she was madder than a hatter, and larger than, well . . . never mind. She laughed loudly and wasn't afraid to speak her mind. She hadn't been asked to join the Junior League when she was younger, and no question she wasn't the perfect deb mom by a long shot. But she had money, and lots of it since the price of oil was at an all-time high.

She had married into the Bennett Oil family, had been the light of Old Man Bennett's eye before he died. He had pampered her beyond any of the other daughters-in-law in the family, or even the daughters. It had been an eyebrow-raising situation, all very *Cat on a Hot Tin Roof,* Big Daddy and Maggie the Cat, sans Elizabeth Taylor's beauty. Moreover, up until the moment Frank junior married Merrily, everyone was sure he played for the other team. Not to imply that anything untoward had gone on between father-in-law and daughter-in-law. I'm just saying.

The Bennett juniors lived across the street from my mother, in a massive Victorian house that was covered in gingerbread molding and multicolored accents. The yard was dotted with gnomes, pink flamingos, and large plastic daisies that spun in the wind. My mother called the Bennett home the carnival quarters. No question it was lively.

Merrily welcomed me inside like we were long-lost friends. She wore a flowing muumuu that matched the theme of the house, her face lined from the sun, her gray hair done up in a twist of braids like a milkmaid on the front of a hot cocoa box. Not a good look on anyone who was over the age of six and lived beyond the Swiss border, but one of which Merrily Bennett was tremendously fond.

She led me into the kitchen where we were greeted by a tiny woman (not so unlike a real-life gnome) with sparkling eyes.

"Carlisle, you know my mother-in-law, don't you? Mama Bennett, this is the youngest Wainwright girl."

"Oh, my," she twittered, her voice squeaky. "Not that awful Ridgely's girl?"

"Now, Mama Bennett, never you mind about that."

The older woman giggled at some joke I was not privy to, crammed her house frock pockets with cookies, and disappeared.

"Sorry about that," Merrily said. "Your mama and Mama Bennett never did get along."

Merrily served me a tall glass of ice-cold sweet tea. The room was massive and welcoming with cakes under glass and fresh flowers in porcelain vases.

"I couldn't have been more surprised when you called than if an armadillo had jumped out of my double broiler." She gave a big belly laugh. "So, tell me. What can I do for you?"

I set my handbag down on the counter, my hands still clutching the handle, and said, "I'm here to invite your daughter to make her debut at the Hundredth Annual Willow Creek Symphony Association Debutante Ball."

Sorry, but I was fresh out of pleasantries. I got right to the point.

Merrily's eyes went round as saucers. She didn't say a word, then startled me when she marched to the kitchen door and banged it open. I jumped a little.

"Betty!" she hollered. "Come down here. Someone's here to ask you something."

This wasn't how things were done. First an invitation was extended to the parents, generally via the mother. Then a formal, handwritten invitation was issued to the daughter. Not that I thought for a second that the parents didn't tell their offspring the news before the official invite arrived, but they certainly didn't call them into the room during the visit.

"Merrily, I really don't think —"

But it was too late.

The daughter pushed into the kitchen.

Betty Bennett entered. She looked just like her mother, only a fraction of the size, both in height and weight. Beyond that, she had golden brown eyes that you could hardly notice for the wild bush of golden brown medusa hair that would have made a perfect "before" photo for a late-night television infomercial.

"What, Mama?"

"Miss Cushing is here to invite you to be a debutante. Isn't that wonderful?"

The girl caught her breath, then went beet red, and I'm sure it wasn't from lack of oxygen.

"Oh, no," she gasped. "I couldn't. I'd die of embarrassment."

Which made me feel horrible and relieved all at the same time.

"I couldn't possibly do the Texas Dip," the girl added, then turned on her heel and fled.

The Dip could do that to a girl, and I don't think I need to remind you why.

Her mother sighed. "She's a shy one, my Betty. Can't imagine where she gets it either. But it's nice of you to ask."

Yet again, I found myself on another front porch, the door closed firmly at my back.

I returned home, and over dinner with the family, I talked up a storm about anything and everything but my progress, or lack thereof. I monopolized the conversation, not allowing anyone else the chance to speak. I went through all my mother's favorite topics (sans any mention of the debutante ball), starting with her prize-winning roses, muddled through upcoming spring hats, then went into a rather impressive exposé on the difference between Francis I and Burgundy silverware.

"Carlisle," my mother interrupted.

Even bad manners wouldn't keep her from her goal.

"How many girls have you gotten so far?"

Everyone at the table stopped eating to look at me. The pressure was on and the words "none, zero, zip" didn't seem like the perfect answer, so I went with: "I'm still working on it."

Which everyone knew meant "none, zero, zip."

When I finished my update, Ridgely blotted her lips and set her linen napkin beside her plate with quiet precision. FYI, this was not a good sign, one I had lived with my whole life.

"Carlisle, you have to fix this. You promised you would fix this."

My mother locked eyes with mine, not in hope, not in a plea, but in a demand. I wanted to toss in my promise to help like tossing in the towel. But I realized sitting there that suddenly it wasn't about saving my mother from embarrassment anymore. Somehow I had to do it for me.

The next morning, I sat at the granite-topped island in the kitchen. I had my notebook in front of me, Lupe buzzing around, talking up a storm in Spanish. I listened as best I could, but I was distracted. I was almost glad when Janice entered wearing her uniform of willowy skirt and canvas sandals.

"Good morning," she said with an efficient use of syllables, her long dark hair pulled back in a loose, earth-mother twist. "I see you're writing in your little black book again."

She poured her own cup of coffee before Lupe could get it for her, then sat down on a high stool across from me. Tilting her head, Janice took in the heading I had written out.

" 'Possible Debs,' " she read out loud. "I can't believe you're really going to stay here, deal with your mother's divorce and this idiotic ball."

"Well, when family is in need —"

"In need." She looked at me like I was demented. "I can't believe anyone still does anything as antiquated and debasing as make a debut. We live in the twenty-first century, for chrissake."

Though it was early and I hadn't had more than half a cup of coffee, I plastered on my fake smile.

"Come on, Carlisle," she continued, planting her elbows on the granite. "How can you feel good about yourself if you get a bunch of girls together and show them off like livestock?"

My fake smile got even faker.

"Take me, for example," she continued. "There was no way I was going to be a deb back in my day. Even then I stood for women's progress."

I didn't point out that no one would have asked Nita Reager, wife of Buford, to have her daughter make her debut. I just smiled.

"I have always refused to be a cookie cutter girl. In fact, I've taught Morgan the same thing."

Perhaps she should have taught her how not to get kicked out of school. I know, bad me.

"I've drilled into my daughter's head the importance of being whoever she wants to be, without embarrassment, no matter what anyone says. I've told her to go for what she wants. Don't let anyone else's opinions or desires stand in her way if something is important to her."

Given that, no surprise in what happened next.

Morgan walked in (her orange hair uncombed, her robe clownish, her multi-pierced ear glittering with rings), refused a glass of fresh-squeezed orange juice from Lupe as she looked at her mother with a smile that even I, the unmarried childless one, knew was not good, then said, "I've made a decision."

Janice glanced at her daughter, nodding her head importantly. "About what, Morgan?" she asked in the "See, I'm the perfect caring mother who asks questions" sort of way, then took a sip of coffee.

"I've decided to be a debutante at the Hundredth Annual Willow Creek Symphony Association Debutante Ball."

CHAPTER SIX

Janice blew coffee clear across the room.

Silence reigned, everyone staring at Janice or the spew of fine French roast that trickled down my mother's handcrafted cherry cabinets. Only Morgan wasn't fazed. She took the coffeepot from Lupe's hand with a dramatic flourish that would have done my mother proud, poured herself a cup, added generous portions of cream and sugar, then stirred with a clink of silver on china that felt like the ominous tick of a time bomb.

"What do you think, Mom?" she finally said, a smile lurking on her orange-lipsticked mouth.

From the expression on her mother's face, it wasn't hard to guess what Janice thought. And no doubt she would have spewed more than coffee if my mother hadn't walked in.

"Morning, good morning," she sang, her mood clearly back into the rose-colored shades. That was one of the hardest things to anticipate with my mother. Her mood. Given the impending divorce, I'd expect that pendulum swinging off the charts. But she had been surprisingly happy this time — as if she were in the stage of finding a man rather than losing one.

"*Bonjour,* my little kittens."

She accepted a cup of coffee from Lupe and took a sip. "Dee-vine," she added, giving a little shiver of delight, then stopped and looked around. "What? What is going on?"

Morgan smiled at her grandmother. "I've decided to be a debutante and I just told Mom."

A little technicality here: she hadn't actually been invited. But hey, as they say, the devil is in the details.

My mother froze much like everyone else, then she set her cup down and opened her arms to her grandchild. "Oh, my stars, you are going to be the most fabulous debutante ever born!"

In light of Morgan's fashion sense and attitude, this was a stretch. What's more, I doubted she had been practicing the Texas Dip since birth and felt she had the very real potential of following in her aunt's infamous footsteps. But what was more important, I applauded my mother for this surprising burst of altruism.

Ridgely turned to Janice, grabbed her by the shoulders, and hugged her close. "You must be so proud."

You can imagine.

I could tell Janice was composing herself, her sense of women's rights doing battle with her teachings of being true to oneself. Talk about being caught on the dual prongs of the proverbial pitchfork. If she stated the emotion that was on her face (No way in hell any daughter of mine is going to be a deb.), she'd prove that everything she had taught Morgan about being whoever she wanted to be was a lie. But if she agreed, well, even I could see that would be a hard pill for her to swallow. I might not be overly enamored of debutante balls, but my sister-in-law was rabidly against them.

Sue me, but I was amused.

"What do you think, Mom?" Morgan persisted, barely holding back a grin.

"Well, I —"

"I think it is simply grand," Ridgely said. "In fact," — she glanced at Janice — "I have a brilliant idea! You and Carlisle will work on the ball together."

This, I didn't find so amusing.

"Think of it. The Wainwright family sticking together, and all that." Mother gave a general wave of her hand. "It will send a message loud and clear that no one messes with us. It's a master stroke of genius. I should have thought of it sooner."

"Now, Mother," I began. "I think it's great that Morgan wants to be a deb. But really, Janice doesn't want anything to do with any stuffy social committee. I can handle it myself."

"Ridgely, really," Janice began through clenched teeth. But she got no further.

"Pshaw! It's a marvelous plan!"

My mother really must have been desperate if she was willing to let me and my sister-in-law get involved with the ball.

Janice didn't look any happier about this turn of events than I was, and her jaw muscles ticked as if she were trying extremely hard to hold herself together.

My brother, Henry, pushed through the swinging door to the kitchen. At the sight of us, his ever-ready smile went still, his eyes narrowing as he stopped and took a look around. He was smarter than his dashing good looks might lead one to believe and he knew something was up. So he did what any sane male would do in similar circumstances. He turned on his heel and attempted to make a hasty retreat.

"Henry Herbert Cushing, stop right

there." This from my mother.

He did as he was told, hanging his head. I heard him grunt before he straightened and turned around. "What's wrong?"

Ridgely went from stern to excited in the blink of an eye. "Morgan is going to make her debut! And Janice is going to serve on the steering committee with Carlisle. Isn't this wonderful news!"

Henry stared in disbelief, glancing from his daughter to his wife. "You've agreed to this?"

"Of course not."

Morgan preened in triumph as if to say, *See, you're all talk, Mom.*

Janice telegraphed silent (frantic) messages my brother's way. *Back me on this! Tell her no!*

Henry turned to me, those eyes boring deep, followed by a hard glance at our mother. Then he burst out laughing.

"Hell. This will be better than fireworks at a Fourth of July picnic." He walked over to the coffeepot where Lupe handed him a cup. "The lovely Lupe," he teased and accepted.

When he turned back, his wife was right there, and he nearly washed her with coffee when he jerked in surprise. But Janice Josephine Reager wasn't going to take this lying down. "Honey," Janice said to her husband, her smile more a baring of teeth. "Are you saying you approve of not only our daughter being herded out on stage trussed up like cattle at auction —"

"Mom!"

"— but me helping her do it?"

"Good Lord, Janice," my mother snapped. "There is no auction. The debutante ball is an age-old tradition that makes a girl feel special. Nothing more, nothing less."

"Forget it, Gigi," Morgan said, referring to my mother. "Mom isn't going to say yes. I knew she was a hypocrite. Yeah, right, I should be anyone I want to be. Only if it's what she wants me to be."

Morgan banged down her cup like a two-year-old, coffee sloshing over on the granite countertop.

I swear I could hear the gears working in Janice's feminist brain as she desperately foraged for a Pulitzer Prize–worthy speech to convince her wayward daughter of the error of her ways.

But then she surprised us all. "You're right, Morgan."

She was?

Though on closer inspection I could see that Janice had something up her sleeve.

"That was hypocritical of me," she conceded. "If this is what you want, you can be a debutante. In fact, I'll be on the committee just as Gigi wants." She hesitated, her brow furrowing with exaggerated seriousness. "I'll even go with you to have your hair redyed its natural color and the rings taken out of your ears and that one from your lip. You'll look fantastic," she gushed with enough fake enthusiasm to impress even me. "And, of course, you'll have to get rid of the orange nail polish and the brightly colored clothes. But it's going to be great!"

"What?"

"You don't think that in the lily-white world of debutantes they let you look like a Rorschach ink blot test recast in color, do you, sweetheart?"

Morgan's face screwed up with fury. This, apparently, had not occurred to my niece.

And the point goes to Janice.

Morgan swung her head around to look at my mother.

"Yes, dear, you'll have to fix yourself up a bit."

Now it was Janice's turn to look smug.

Mother and daughter faced off in the Wainwright family kitchen, and I could see that Janice was certain she had found the perfect means to get her way. Morgan saw it too. And Morgan was no dummy.

The teenager who was supposedly on the verge of true womanhood (not to mention swore she wanted to be launched into the world as a true lady) drew a deep breath, then said with Grace Kelly aplomb, "I was getting tired of orange anyway. I am going to be a debutante." Then her eyes narrowed. "And I'm going to be the best freaking debutante this godforsaken, sheep-happy hillbilly town has ever seen."

Chapter Seven

We had our first debutante and an actual committee of two.

Progress, of a sort.

The only problem was that the Pultizer Prize–winning Janice Reager had very different ideas on how we should proceed from there. It's not as though this should be a surprise, I realized, but that didn't make it any less irritating.

First, it was clear that at any moment she expected her daughter to back down. Second, in the interest of steering the "unfortunate event" in what she termed an appropriate direction, she dove into committee participation like a kamikaze pilot going full throttle in his tiny metal World War II airplane. She was either going to succeed at getting her way or die trying.

"All right," Janice said, her journalist's pencil poised over a pad of paper. "If I have to be involved in this travesty, then I say we make it about something other than a cattle call. I say we go for smart girls," she added with dogged determination. "We go to the high school and find out which senior girls have the highest GPAs."

Not that I was looking for airheads, but she was missing the point (or didn't understand the point) of a debutante ball. So I tried to explain about raising money the symphony needed to continue to provide music and culture to Central Texas, not to mention keep it solvent. To do this we needed to choose girls whose families had spent years donating time and money to the symphony, showing their commitment, and would continue to do so, yada yada. It had a very Do the Right Thing sound to it, and I felt certain it was just the sort of speech she'd go crazy for.

"Yeah, right."

So I was wrong.

"People just tack on the goody-two-shoes business to whitewash the fact that it's a meat market."

Her with the meat market. I felt the beginnings of a headache pressing at the backs of my eyes.

"Fine, think what you will," I said. "But the point is, the Willow Creek Symphony has money problems, and if we don't raise enough money to get them out of the red they will go bankrupt."

"How did that happen?"

"From what I could tell, they spent every penny they made at last year's ball for damage control. Hired a publicist, ran ads touting the fabulous music of the symphony. That sort of thing."

"So what are you trying to say?"

"Grade point averages alone do not a good deb make. We need girls from the kind of old families who are willing to donate generously to the cause and pay for the tables and extravagant parties, not to mention the clothes, with the resulting funds going directly to the symphony. Girls with high GPAs don't necessarily have the kind of money to do anything for the symphony's bottom line."

Janice in all her socialist prowess hated the reality of this. Especially since her family had tons of money, but lacked the fine old and illustrious name.

"Fine, we'll get girls with money," she conceded. "But forget the fine old family stuff."

Normally I wouldn't have agreed so quickly, but really, I'd already been through the fine-old-name category and had come up empty-handed. I was more than ready to move on to moneyed families with new names. "Fine, we'll do it your way," I told her, regardless of the fact that I could hear my mother now. *"You've gotten second-rate girls?"*

But that was another bridge I would cross when I came to it.

"Okay, let's make a list of potential candidates," Janice said.

We sat at the kitchen table ready to write, and couldn't come up with the name of a single girl. Of course that's to be expected from two women who hadn't lived in Willow Creek in recent years.

"I haven't a clue," she said.

"Neither do I."

We sat for a second longer.

"We're going to have to go to your mother."

"No!"

"Carlisle, I know what you're thinking. But the fact is, she's going to find out who we get eventually."

" 'Eventually' being the operative word. I'd prefer she find out later rather than sooner . . . after the deed is done and she can't do anything about it."

Janice made a face. "I see your point. Fine. We're two intelligent women and I'm an investigative journalist. We should be able to find out who in town has money on our own."

We were deciding exactly how to do just that when Savannah marched into the kitchen. She and husband, Ben, had been living at Wainwright House since they got married, swearing they were moving out just as soon as Savannah found the perfect house. Truthfully, I couldn't imagine my sister living anywhere other than our old family home.

Savannah clipped into the kitchen wearing pink feathered kitten mules and a feathered lounging set of the diaphanous variety. Her hair was done up in an elegant twist, her excessive-even-by-Texas-standards diamond wedding ring glittering on her finger. She would have looked ready to pose for a Victoria's Secret catalogue except for the black satin sleeping mask perched on her forehead.

Janice glanced at me. "Is that really how she sleeps?"

I shrugged.

"What?" Savannah demanded, as petulant as two-year-old Robbie.

It was at the thought of Robbie that the noise finally registered. A crash in the upper regions of the house made me wince, followed by screaming.

Janice tilted her head to listen and only then seemed to hear. After a second, she announced, "No emergency. You can always tell when blood or broken bones are involved. It's a different sort of scream."

For all Janice's intellect, clearly she wasn't too smart regarding her sister-in-law.

"Janice," my sister cried, clearly not caring why the children were screaming, "you have to do something about those . . . those . . . derelicts of yours. How am I supposed to get a decent night's sleep with all that caterwauling?"

"Derelicts? Caterwauling?" Janice asked, somewhat dangerously.

"What do you call it?"

"Normal playing by normal children."

"Normal?" Savannah threw her hands up. "How would you know the first thing about normal children? From what I've heard you aren't around yours enough to know good from bad!"

I think I cringed.

Janice did not.

"I'm not sure I need to take child-rearing advice from a woman who can't have any."

Which made everyone in the room suck in their breaths.

Disastrous behavior \dis-as-trous\ adj (c1600) \be-ha-vior\ n (15c) 1: criticizing

118

someone else's children or parenting skills 2: calling said children caterwauling derelicts, and/or 3: throwing childless state at woman who is desperately seeking children.

"I'm sorry, Savannah," Janice said, with a sigh.

She cradled her coffee cup between her palms and appeared contrite. "You just pushed a button. Not that that's an excuse for being unkind. It's just that I try hard as a mother, but can't just be a mom all the time. I have to do other things too."

Surprisingly, my sister looked uncomfortable, then couldn't have surprised me more when she said, "No, no. I'm the one who's sorry. I had no right to say that about your kids."

Then, in an even bigger shocker, my sister's lips trembled. "It's just so hard," she said, fighting off the tears that have never been acceptable among the Wainwright clan, at least in broad daylight. "I want a baby so bad. And when I see yours I just . . . start acting crazy."

The two women faced each other awkwardly.

"I could loan you Robbie," Janice said, trying to joke.

Savannah started to cry.

Oh, man.

"I'll never have a baby! Ben and I hardly ever have sex anymore. First I thought it was because all the timed-sex was making him crazy. But now he's just so busy! How will I ever have a baby when Ben is too busy to have sex with me?"

Janice made another of her disbelieving faces. "Look. If you want to have sex, then seduce your husband."

Not exactly a speech you would expect from a card-carrying NOW member.

"Seduce?" Savannah asked, without the blush I expected. "What do you mean?"

"Haven't you ever seduced Ben?"

"Well, no," Savannah said.

"Savannah. This isn't the fifties."

I could tell my sister would have been insulted, but she was too interested in what Janice had to teach her. "You mean like wrap myself in Saran wrap and answer the door when he comes home?"

I laughed. Sorry.

Janice and Savannah scowled at me.

"What?" I shot back. "She lives in a house with her mother, her brother, sister-in-law, four kids, and now me. I doubt naked, Saran wrap, and the front door really go together in that scenario."

"True," Janice conceded. "But the sentiment is right. You'll have to find a different

120

way to do it. And with so many people around, I bet it's hard to feel all that sexy." She considered. "Okay, you've got to go out. Get drunk. Get Ben drunk, then follow him when he gets up from the table."

"When he gets up?" My sister was confused.

"Yes. When he goes out for a cigarette."

"He doesn't smoke."

"Then when he goes to the bar for another drink."

"But waiters take care of that."

Janice sighed her impatience. "Then follow him to the men's room, for God's sake."

"I can't do that!"

Janice shrugged. "Sure you can. The minute another man sees you in there, I guarantee they'll bolt once they realize you aren't there for them."

"Sounds like you have experience with this," I said.

My sister-in-law got a very devilish look on her face. "Let's just say that your brother will never forget the men's room at Bubba's BBQ on Sixth Street in Austin."

I winced. I really didn't want to think about my brother and sex in the same sentence. But I also couldn't help but laugh.

"No way will Savannah follow Ben into a men's room," I predicted. "If for no other

121

reason than she wouldn't like the mess."

"A nice men's room then. Or something like that. Just make it kind of kinky. Who knows why, but guys like kinky."

"My Ben does not like kinky," Savannah stated.

Janice rolled her eyes. "Just try it. I'd put money on it that he backs you into a stall and makes you forget where you are."

Now Savannah did blush, but I could see in her violet-blue eyes that she was already planning her method of seduction.

I am a firm believer in boundaries. Establishing them. Keeping them. Making sure no one crosses over them to muddy my perfectly constructed world.

In Boston, that was easy to do. Up at six, the gym at six forty-five, the office at nine, in court by ten, working until the sun had long been down, dinner in my tiny kitchen with Phillip, discussing our respective cases over candles and a good red wine. I loved my life there, a quiet simple life of curling up in a blanket and reading books when the snow fell fast and deep, or picnic dinners along the Charles River in the sort of summer that was like spring in Texas.

I had built a life in Boston that both challenged me careerwise and filled me with a quiet peace when I wasn't in the office. In Willow Creek, keeping my boundaries secure was, well, not so easy. No one else from my old world seemed to subscribe to the idea that maintaining an ordered world with planning and boundaries was a good thing.

But I was nothing if not a determined soldier, and kept drawing lines in the sand with the persistence of General Patton at the Battle of the Bulge. Though with my sister wanting to discuss kinky seductions and my niece using my precariously positioned debutante ball as a sharp stick to poke in her mother's fervent feministic eye, I had to hope I wasn't really General Custer at Little Big Horn.

It was with my warrior's heart, and a ticking clock leading up to the traditional announcement day of the first Sunday in March, that I went to see Isabel Foley, wife of Werner, at the offices of Foley Construction. The Foley Building was just south of town, a jutting high-rise of pink marble that stood out like an overlarge male appendage surrounded by the low rolling hills of Texas covered by the thatch of live oak trees. Around town, the building was not-so-fondly referred to as the *Folly* Building, one, because it was so out of place among the tasteful low-rise buildings of Willow Creek, and two, because no matter how hard Werner tried to coax tenants into occupancy, no one bit. Really, who wanted to work in a big pink penis on the wrong side of town?

Unlike everyone else who steered clear of said building, I went there in need. Namely, in need of teenage girls with money, and the Foleys had one. While their folly hadn't been a hit with business professionals in need of office space, every other property they built went for record dollars per square foot. Which meant the Foleys had plenty of cash.

I arrived at the Foleys' offices at ten to ten for a ten o'clock appointment with Isabel, vice president of Foley Construction. While the women at the country club speculated that Isabel's position was purely for show, quite frankly I thought Isabel was a whole lot smarter than her husband. Whatever the case, having a woman VP of a big company was good for Willow Creek. Janice had been all for me contacting the family.

"Good morning, Miss Cushing," the receptionist said. "Mrs. Foley is just finishing up with her nine o'clock. If you'll have a seat in the waiting room, I'll come get you

124

when she's ready."

"Thank you."

The offices were decorated in lots more of the pink marble (no doubt they got some sort of a deal), the furniture sleek and modern, floor-to-ceiling windows looking out over Central Texas as far as the eye could see. In the waiting room, coffee and doughnuts were laid out on a sideboard. Not one to pass up a good doughnut or hot coffee, I went in search, then about jumped out of my skin when none other than Jack Blair came up and stood next to me.

"You're jumpy today," he noted, pouring himself a cup. "Are you sure coffee is a good idea?"

Turning to face me, he took a sip and waited for an answer.

I focused on the fare, but barely registered the platter of breakfast sweets, the urn of coffee, the silver bowl filled with sugar cubes, or even the tiny silver tongs perched next to the bowl. He stood no more than a few inches away, the heat of him doing strange things to my brain. In the interest of full disclosure, the last time I had been this close to Jack Blair and alone, I had been naked. In his bed. At his little house just north of the center of town. His black Harley parked out front at an odd angle due to our haste to get inside and get . . . well, naked.

I reminded myself that it had been three years ago, and I cursed the way my lips itched to part on a deep shuddering breath just remembering.

I reached for a china cup just as he reached for something and our hands touched — or banged together. Whatever, the sensation was electric. Which was ridiculous.

With a calm I didn't feel, I persevered and took the cup, filled it with coffee, then picked up a glazed doughnut. "A little caffeine never hurt anyone. Besides," I added, going for humor, albeit forced, "I like living on the edge."

I took a bite of the doughnut, turning to face him since I couldn't very well stare at the table all day. However, facing him was a mistake given the uncanny ability he had to make my breath stick in my lungs. His dark hair was raked back, his chiseled jaw, well, chiseled, his shoulders way too broad and strong beneath his blue blazer. All I can say is thank God he didn't have on the 501s.

"Caffeine and trans fats." He raised a brow. "Not quite my idea of life on the edge."

He shook his head, a hint of amusement

dancing in those brown eyes as he reached out, brushing the corner of my mouth, so easy, so normal, as if he touched me every day. Though no sooner had his finger come away with glazed icing than both of us froze.

His brow furrowed when he realized what he had done, then I swear he cursed, dropping his hand. I, on the other hand, froze because a traitorous shiver ran through me, pooling in places shivers have no business pooling, at least not in regard to Jack Blair. He was no longer part of my life.

When I graduated from Willow Creek High, I went to college at Willow Creek University. Jack was there, gorgeous, brooding, wild, with a reputation for fighting. Despite that (or perhaps because of it), he was the fantasy of every girl on the WCU campus.

My resolve to stay away from guys had remained throughout the rest of high school and was firmly in place when I arrived as an undergraduate. I focused on my studies, determined to become a top attorney, though even I couldn't spend every second with my nose in a book. With the need for exercise all over the news, I took up running, frequently on the treadmill at the gym.

The day I saw Jack again I was distracted. It was hard not to be around my roommate,

Betsy, who had opted for sex with her boyfriend as a physical activity instead of running. Eddie spent hours at our house. Along with Eddie came his assortment of friends. Who knew Jack was one of his friends.

I had just gotten back from the gym, my running shoes shoved into the oversized purse I used as a gym bag, and was trying to avoid the gaggle of Eddie and his friends by tiptoeing through the front door and heading straight for my room.

"If it isn't little Carlisle Cushing."

I cringed, one, because of the realization that if I somehow didn't get into law school, spy school clearly couldn't provide a fallback position, and two, the voice belonged to Roger Dubac, a senior who fell into the not-very-nice category. He was a giant of a guy who drank beer as a sport.

"Hello, Roger." Head down. Keep going.

"You been out runnin' in that nasty-wear of yours?"

Running shorts and a short-sleeved cotton T-shirt hardly seemed like something anyone would buy at Sluts' Us, but whatever. I had to count to ten to keep myself from saying something that would only make things worse.

"I've seen your mother and sister around

town," he went on with a lewd chuckle. "They might not wear the nasty stuff, but boy howdy, I wouldn't mind getting me some of that."

So counting didn't work. I whirled around to give him a piece of my mind, or maybe a whack with my purse. But I wasn't given the chance.

"What the fuck is your problem, Roger?"

Jack stood there like some knight in black leather armor, his dark hair raked back and brushing his shoulders, his leather jacket showing just a hint of black T-shirt.

In high school he'd had trouble written all over him. In college, everything about him warned "Danger" in big yellow flashing lights.

"What's it to you?" Roger shot back.

Jack was taller than Roger, but Roger had to outweigh him by a good hundred pounds of sheer fat. But one glimpse at Jack's expression would make a pit bull terrier trade in its metal stud collar for pink lace and rhinestones. Roger looked leery, but he didn't back down.

"More than you'd think," Jack said. "And if I were you, I'd get the hell out of here before I decide to let her take after you with that purse. It looks like it could do some damage."

Roger muttered and started to return to the kitchen. Jack turned to me. "Sorry —"

Roger spun around, leaping on Jack, catching him off guard. Jack staggered, but only for a second. They grappled for a minute or two, everyone from the kitchen racing out.

"Shit!" Eddie yelled. "What are you two doing?"

"Damn," another offered, clearly impressed with the fight.

"Hey, hey, hey," I yelped. They were banging up the walls and I was the one who had paid the deposit on the house. "Stop right now!"

Not that anyone was listening. Jack and Roger crashed between the wall and the thankfully sturdy oak table like two drunken dancers, before I saw something in Jack shift. He groaned deep in his throat, jerking Roger hard, then quickly pinning the oversized beer guzzler to the wall.

Jack's breath came in short bursts, those brown eyes violent.

"Whoa," the other guys said, taking a step back.

"Hell," Eddie added in a loud voice. "You've been friends too long for this kind of shit."

I swear it looked like Jack would kill Roger.

"Jack?" I said softly.

I saw the shudder that raced through him, then he drew a deep breath, letting Roger go with a shove. He sort of shook himself, then that smile came up. After a second, he gave a quick brush at Roger's shoulders, as if straightening up a little brother.

"Don't mess with her, Rog. That's all I ask."

I saw the tension in Roger ease. "Yeah, sorry, man."

Jack nodded, then the guys actually shook hands.

I hadn't a clue what to make of it all. Not having much experience with guys, even in my own household, I had never seen anything like it. Clutching said handbag to my chest, and with the little house out of immediate danger of more damage, I didn't wait around to see what happened next. But Jack wasn't done with me yet.

"Sorry about that," he said, coming into my bedroom as if it hadn't been four years since I'd seen him last, or that he hadn't just been in a fight. "How are you?"

Heart fluttering and all that, though mainly because he started walking about my room, taking in the bulletin board filled with calendar, class schedule, current diet. He stopped when he came to my desk. My heart went from fluttering to a dead stop when he looked confused and he reached out and touched the plastic bubble gum ring he had given me in high school. I had attached it to a chain and hung it from the decorative knob on the mirror frame. Yes, it was pathetic. But in my defense, I was only eighteen.

I could see the wheels working in his head, but meaning hadn't come clear to him.

"Jack!" I blurted.

He turned around, still confused.

"You were saying?" I enthused, interrupting his train of thought.

"What?"

"You were asking me how I was?" I clarified.

Sure it was lame, but I really didn't want him to remember where that ring came from. Talk about embarrassing.

I hurried on. "I'm good, by the way. How are you? Aside from being none the worse for wear after your little tiff."

He chuckled then. "Roger and I have 'tiffed' more than once over the years. I suspect this won't be the last either."

Geez.

"Well." How do you respond to that? "Well, fine, and I bet you really need to go."

"Yeah. I do." He shrugged then looked at

me. "I just wanted to make sure you were okay."

How was it possible that such a rugged bad boy whom I had zero in common with constantly made me feel . . . I don't know, safe? "Me? I'm fine. Completely fine."

"Roger isn't all that bad. He just knows you don't like him."

First, he was on the verge of killing the guy, now he was defending him?

"I don't dislike anyone."

He just laughed. "We're not all like him."

"Trust me. I'm not worried about Roger. It's the ones like you that worry me."

"Me?"

Like a scene break in a bad play, a girl's voice called out. *"Jack, where are you?"*

I nodded. "Yep, it's the ones like you a girl has to be careful of."

"Why is that?"

"They have heartbreak written all over them."

"I don't want to break your heart."

This time I laughed. "I assure you, Jack Blair, you won't have the chance."

"Jack!"

"You better hurry," I said, pushing him toward the door.

As soon as he crossed the threshold, I banged the door shut. Protection shield up, radar on. I was never going to be like my mother, whose life always revolved around a man.

And I felt the same way years later standing in the Foley Building. I closed my eyes in that pink marble building and thought of Boston, the ordered grid of streets in the Back Bay, the perfectly manicured lawns in the Public Gardens, Phillip and the comforting ease of his sandy blond hair and pale green eyes.

"Boundaries," I half whispered.

When I opened my eyes Jack was studying me, and he didn't look any happier than I felt.

"Stop doing that," I managed.

"Doing what?"

I waved my finger (trans fats and all) in a wild gesture toward his face. "That."

"I didn't do anything."

"Whatever. Now, if you'll excuse me."

"Sure."

I started to turn away.

"But first, help me understand," he repeated, stopping me. He set his coffee aside.

I groaned. "Understand what?"

Quite frankly, he didn't look like he had any idea what he meant, and might not actually want to know the answer.

"Look, no fraternizing, okay?" I said,

though even to me it sounded ridiculous.

He actually tipped his head back and laughed out loud.

"But fraternizing can be so much fun," he said, moving even closer, the old Jack I was used to surfacing, the one who was bad, yes, and wild, true, but not ruthless.

Thoughts of me, him, and "fun" swirled through my head like cotton candy at a local fair.

"There will be no fun." I choked on the words. But really, the last thing I needed was another complication in what was already proving to be a complicated trip home.

"Come on." His lips twitched. "Not even a little? For old time's sake?"

"No. No fun." I ran my toe back and forth across the floor in emphasis. "You and me. Boundaries," I repeated.

That dark place reappeared. "You and your boundaries." Then he cursed again and pulled me to him, my arms out on either side of me, one hand holding my coffee, the other the doughnut, before he kissed me. And I'm not talking about some peck on the cheek. It was a shake-me-to-the-core, possession-of-my-mouth kind of kiss that knocked the sense right out of me. My body shuddered. My boundaries crossed.

For half a second I remained stiff. But I felt it the instant my traitorous body melted, the kiss going deep and hot, and I might have moaned.

When he set me back, thank God he didn't let go because I swear I would have fallen in a puddle on the floor. He leaned close and whispered, "When are you finally going to learn that the only way life's any fun is when it's messy?"

I barely heard the footsteps approaching. Thankfully Jack must have because he stood back, though he did have to reach out to steady me.

"Mr. Blair, Mr. Foley will see you now."

"Thank you, Adele," he said, though he was looking at me. "Remember," he said, the darkness gone, his infuriating grin back in place. "Messy is good."

He left before I could respond, not that I could have said anything since my brain was filled with the fireworks that had taken over my body. I felt the distinct need to race after him and slap him . . . okay, so I really wanted to launch myself at him and demand he have his way with me right there in the big pink marble penis. Instead, I am proud to say, I got ahold of my wayward thoughts, pointed my toe, and drew the line over and over again, this time with more determination. The receptionist looked at me as if debating a call to security.

CHAPTER EIGHT

For the next three days I racked my brain for potential debs. I hardly remember my meeting with Isabel Foley, but I do know I was still muttering about boundaries when I was shown out of her office (Jack nowhere to be seen), with Isabel regretting that they had already committed to debuting their daughter in New York. In fact, I soon learned that the nouveau riche crowd (having been snubbed by haut Willow Creek Society for a century) had started taking their daughters to New York and Paris to make their debuts with the offspring of Hollywood movie people and faded rock stars.

Fortunately, Janice and I found fifteen names of people who had plenty of money sans old family names once we went through past issues of the *Willow Creek Times* and *Texas Monthly* at the Willow Creek Public Library. Armed with phone numbers, I set up appointments.

Phillip called at least once a day if not more, each call a little more strained than the last when I wouldn't commit to a date for him to travel to Texas. Moreover, despite the sabbatical I was technically on, my office called me nearly as often.

"Allison," I said to the managing partner's assistant, "Deirdre in Bill Patterson's office can help Walter with his new prenup."

"But Walter doesn't want Deirdre or anyone else doing it. He wants you."

If it wasn't Walter with a new prenup, it was someone who had gotten my name from a friend whom I had represented. For reasons that I never quite got, no one seemed to understand the word "sabbatical" and what exactly that meant. I had gotten so I cringed every time my cell phone buzzed. Diving into the new round of deb appointments in search of the elusive debs was actually a relief.

Out of the first ten names Janice and I had found in our search, we only got three families to commit to the deb ball, which gave us four girls, including Morgan. Not a great average of success, especially since we only had four more days before the traditional announcement was supposed to be made in the newspaper.

At one point, questioning my abilities, Janice went with me on one of the appointments.

"So tell me about your daughter," she asked the wealthy and well-dressed Elizabeth Peters, leaning forward like a reporter trying to get to the bottom of who really had opened the neighborhood crack house.

"What is her grade point average?" Janice wanted to know.

Elizabeth stared.

"Would you consider your daughter smart? Or is she just your average boy-crazy girl?"

Elizabeth stiffened.

"Mrs. Peters," I interjected politely, shooting Janice a glare, "we are here because we would like to invite your daughter Emily to be a debutante at this year's debutante ball."

Janice leaned forward again. "We know this is an abomination, so don't be insulted that we're inviting her. As hard as it is, try to think of it as doing good for the community, not as a meat market."

We were out on the front porch, door slammed at our backs, in record time. I swear I didn't gloat.

Though who was I to feel smug? With only forty-eight hours left before we had to submit the names to the newspaper and my mother breathing down my neck demanding to know who we had gotten, we still only had four debutantes when tradition required eight. By the time we got home, desperation rode me like a barrel rider at the rodeo.

The doorbell rang as Janice and I sat in the kitchen debating a new plan of attack. Lupe went out to answer, followed by unpleasant voices slicing through the walls, before the maid pushed through the kitchen door with a bang.

"Lupe? What in the world is going on?"

"Dat girl. India. She no nice."

"India? India who?"

"India Blair," she sniffed indignantly. "I see her around town when I go chopping." (Translation: shopping.)

"Blair, as in *the* Blair family?" Janice asked.

"*Sí.*" Lupe harrumphed. "She say she hear about you debutante ball."

"Hunter Blair's daughter? She wants to be a deb?" Janice persisted.

"I tink so, and she out there waiting for you."

I grimaced. Hunter Blair \Hunt-er Blair\ pn (1963) a man who 1: fell very solidly under the (very) big money category with a (hugely) cringeworthy name 2: was the older brother of my mother's opposing

141

counsel (aka Jack Blair) . . . all of which led to 3: definitely not Ridgely Wainwright-Cushing-Jameson-Lackley-Harper-Ogden Approved.

"Tell her I'm not here," I said.

Janice didn't say anything at first, then she sort of *hmmmed*. And it didn't sound like a "send her on her way" *hmmm*.

"Say what you will about Hunter Blair," Janice said, "but he has become as rich as they grow them here in Texas. More importantly, it sounds as though he has an eighteen-year-old daughter. And she's standing in the foyer. Haven't you heard the saying 'Beggars can't be choosers'?"

She had a point.

With more than a little trepidation, I followed Janice out of the kitchen. I shuddered to think what sort of child Hunter Blair could produce. I had seen pictures of him in the newspaper. Where Jack was dark and chiseled, Hunter Blair was wiry, and had nothing in common with beauty. While this could be used to a certain effect for a man, let me just say it could never, ever, work for a woman. At least not in Texas.

Though when I actually saw India Blair, it was worse than I had imagined. The girl was pretty . . . that is, if you go for the slutty, Britney Spears pre-shaved head, Oops, I've

Done It Again look.

India was short, made taller by four-inch stilettos, had dark blond hair streaked with chunky highlights, and wore spandex paint-on pants, with some sort of diaphanous baby doll minidress fluttering over her hips, and a Day-Glo bra underneath.

"Oh, my God," Janice whispered, "who let that child out of the house looking like that?"

"That would be Hunter Blair, whom you were just waxing eloquent about."

She groaned.

But India wasn't alone. She had two equally chastity-challenged girls standing a pace behind her.

A rich trollop with an entourage.

India glanced at Janice, then me. "You must be Carlisle Wainwright Cushing." She looked back at Janice. "Who are you?"

Janice stiffened. "Janice Reager," she said with not a little importance.

"Never heard of you."

"Then you must not read the newspaper."

India snorted. "As if."

A pissing match between a thirty-seven-year-old journalist and a teenager. I should have known right then and there to turn tail and run all the way back to Boston and the Pilgrim People.

143

"So. Carlisle," India said coolly. "You obviously know who I am."

I don't think I have to tell you that an eighteen-year-old (even an exceedingly advanced one) was not about to intimidate me. "I'm told you are India Blair and you want to be a debutante."

"Exactly. So do my friends. Abby Bateman and Tiki Beeker. Don't worry. They've got money. And our parents will spend it on your ball."

The entourage preened.

"You've probably heard of their fathers. Grady Bateman and Armand Beeker. They're totally rich. Not as rich as my dad, but close enough."

Abby was dressed in a lace blouse, the proper effect ruined by the orange bra underneath, her short, tight blue-jean skirt, and the red crocodile clutch under her arm. Tiki wore a spandex cropped T-shirt, low-cut rolled-up jeans, with four-inch-high chunky heels and ankle socks with a lace ruffle around the edge.

I couldn't imagine any of these girls dressed in the required virginal white debutante gowns.

"Well, India," I managed, "you are sweet to come by, but —"

"But what? I know all about debutante

144

balls," she stated. "You've got to have like a bazillion of your friends and your parents' friends sitting at massively expensive tables. Just so you know, my dad has tons of friends and tons of money and I know he'd buy at least four tables."

My head swam with numbers. Four at twenty thousand a pop — just for one girl's tables.

India smirked. "Plus, Abby's and Tiki's dads will do the same. They always do what my dad does."

Girls with money, and lots of it. I felt light-headed.

Then I reminded myself of what kind of money it was. Cringe-worthy money. We'd be a laughingstock.

Janice leaned close. "After Signor Rinaldi, the ball is already a laughingstock. I say we go for it. What do you think?"

Actually, what I thought was that I had to stop wearing my thoughts on my face.

"And for my party," India continued, "I am going to fly everyone in my dad's plane (a G4, thank you very much) to New York for a party at the top of the Blair Building."

Talk about blatant displays of wealth. A very un–Willow Creek Society thing to do.

"Abby and Tiki will each do something cool too."

"Can Abby and Tiki talk?" I asked.

India rolled her eyes, and Abby and Tiki giggled, suddenly seeming more like the teenagers they were.

"Well, this is very nice of you," I said. The words just came out, primarily because money or no, I knew my mother would kill me if I let a Blair anywhere near the debutante ball. "Let us present your . . . generous offer to the committee."

Janice stared at me in disbelief.

"Look, you need debs," India said. "I want to be a deb. Make your decision now."

She must have learned negotiating technique at the knee of her father, who was renowned for his ability to get what he wanted.

"How do you know all this?" I asked.

She considered for a second. "Betty Bennett. She's, like, practically in love with me. Always trying to impress me." She shrugged, bored. "She was slobbering all over me as usual. Hanging out at my locker. And told me that you asked her to be a debutante."

"She said no."

"Thank God," India replied with a singsong snort. "Who'd want to be a deb with a loser like her?"

For the record, it did not make me feel better that I'd had much the same thought

146

about the girl a few days earlier.

"What do you say? Are we in?"

I didn't know how to say yes. Though I couldn't seem to say no either. We were sinking to new lows. My mother would kill me. But I couldn't escape the fact that we were desperate. Which meant one thing . . .

"Fine, you're in."

"All three of us?"

"Yes. All three of you."

The Entourage nodded with cool superiority. India looked at me with the gloating smile of a victor.

"Have your father call me, and we'll get everything arranged."

Miss Victory's hardened gaze wavered. "Oh, that." She laughed, but I could tell it was strained. "Oops. My bad. He doesn't exactly know that I'm here."

"What?" Janice demanded.

"It's no big deal," she scoffed. "All you have to do is convince him to let me be a debutante."

"What?" This time it came from me.

"My father isn't all that crazy about social stuff," India explained. "He says he won't lower himself. But if anyone could convince him to let me do it, it is Carlisle Wainwright Cushing."

"I am not going to convince anyone" —

147

most especially Hunter Blair — "to 'lower' themselves to be part of a time-honored Willow Creek tradition. It is a privilege to be invited."

India made a face. "A tradition that is going up in smoke if you don't get your eight debutantes. Hello."

It all came back to that.

Which is how it came to pass that I, me, Carlisle Wainwright Cushing, had the unenviable task of going head-to-head with Jack Blair's older brother to convince the man to let his not-so-darling daughter make her debut at the Hundredth Annual Willow Creek Symphony Association Debutante Ball.

Chapter Nine

The next night, with no time to waste and without a word to my mother, I made my way to Blair House. India said I should come over that evening at seven. Her father would be there. Guaranteed.

I (along with everyone else in Willow Creek) knew that Hunter Blair was divorced. His young wife, clearly aspiring to the cliché, had run off to Hollywood as soon as she had given birth to India. What was not so cliché was that she had given up all rights to India in order to gain her freedom, then hadn't tried to regain any of said rights when she tired of not making it in the movie business and remarried and started a new family not five minutes away in South Willow Creek.

Hunter had never remarried and lived with his daughter in the Willows of Willow Creek, a prestigious gated community that admitted no one but the very wealthy, their servants, and expected guests.

I arrived at the entrance gate where I was grilled like a common criminal by a short man in a uniform. He returned to his guardhouse, called what I assumed was the Blair home, then returned. "They espetting you."

He then wrote down my license plate number, filled out a form, placed it inside my windshield, told me where to go (ha-ha), then sent me on my way.

The winding streets and lanes of the Willows were carved into the rolling hills of Central Texas, covered with willow, cedar, pecan, and live oak trees draped in Spanish moss. Willow Creek is as sophisticated as Dallas, but has maintained the lovely charm that Austin had before the state capital filled with the sort of new politicians who treated politics as a sport.

I drove up the cobbled length of Blue Willow Lane, made a right as instructed onto Weeping Willow Drive, and thought I would indeed weep when I came to the Blairs' home and found a great many cars and half a dozen valets. Clearly there was some sort of event going on inside.

"Welcome," the uniformed young valet said. "You're a little late, but if you hurry no one will notice."

No wonder India was certain her father would be home. Yet again, she had manipulated me. The girl was good.

Frankly, I would have turned around and departed had it not been for the fact that I had already been announced and would not want it to look as if I would flee from anything. So I exited the Volvo, and hoped the St. John knit top and skirt I had appropriated from Savannah's closet was suitable attire.

I rang the bell and the door was immediately opened by a butler.

"I am Miss Cushing, here to see Mr. Blair."

India swept into the foyer. She was still in high bitch mode, and her cornflower-blue eyes sparkled with triumph.

"Ingenious way to get you here, don't you think?" she said.

I might have scowled.

"Whatever. This was the only way to get you in front of him. He is like always busy."

"India," I said as kindly as I could. "I really don't think this is a good idea, or that it will work." The latter being the more important issue. "I'll call him in the morning."

"Yeah, right. Like you have the time. Hello. Clock ticking, and all that."

Irritating as she was, she wasn't wrong.

She made a disparaging noise in her throat. "I mean, really, just meet him now."

Not waiting for an answer, she pulled me through a magnificent foyer, my sensible heels clicking on the marble floor, into a grand room. Let me just say that the house was spectacular. I entered what I realized was a rotunda, the ceiling two to three stories high, with a dome made of glazed glass, a contemporary chandelier hanging from the center. A mezzanine of sorts ran around the perimeter, overlooking the grand space. Whoever built the house was a master.

However, the furnishings were not so grand. Not that they weren't expensive. Clearly the man had spent a small fortune on antiques. But not one of them went with the stunningly modern palatial home of marble, glass, steel, and granite.

The pieces were a mishmash of boxy Early American, delicately curved Louis XV, Chippendale, and Shaker. Hooked rugs and Aubussons ran together with the congruity of frozen waffles and fine bars of French chocolate. Mass-produced reproductions hung next to what I was sure was an original Rembrandt.

Fortunately, given the gold accent buttons

on the St. John, I didn't look too out of place among the glittery set attending the event. After a quick scan, I knew there wasn't a respectable old name in the crowd, but they all looked to have plenty of money. The men were in their forties and fifties, their wives in their twenties and thirties. Early thirties. Even given the tender years of the women, I also could tell there was enough Botox in the room to poison a small country, tanned faces frozen in their perfection, only the eyes and smiles registering any emotion.

The only woman in the room who appeared normal was Nikki Grout, wife of Howard Grout. We had gone to school together forever, though given my predilection for advanced mathematics and studying we had never hung out together. She was more Frede Ware's type, and well, look at the trouble she got herself into.

The good news was that Nikki, even decked out in feathers and paint-on clothes, was sweet as sweet could be.

"Carlisle?" she practically hollered across the rotunda. "Is that you?"

She clipped across the marble floor, her heels echoing like machine-gun fire.

"Good Lord, how are you?" she cried, pulling me into a full bear hug. When she set me at arm's length, she added, "Don't you look just as pretty as pretty can be."

Nikki was from the old school that believed, If you can't say anything nice, then don't say anything at all.

"Thank you, Nikki. How are you?"

"Just grand. Better than grand. My Howard is just wonderful, though I am adjusting to him working in an office now rather than at home." She giggled guiltily. "Though it is kinda fun to surprise him, ya know, when he comes home."

I thought of Janice and her advice to Savannah. I fought back a cringe, gave her another hug, then went in search of India's father.

I scanned the room (not looking for Jack), found India, then saw an older woman who gained my attention. She was sixty-five if she was a day, with far too much makeup on (even by Texas standards) and bustled around the room acting as hostess. Could this be Hunter Blair's official or unofficial hostess? Somehow she looked familiar.

While Hunter was Jack's older brother, there was a big age difference, though Hunter wasn't close to sixty-five. The woman couldn't be a second wife.

The woman bustled up to India and me.

"India," she twittered. "Who is this?"

"Gramma, this is Miss Wainwright Cushing," India said with importance.

The woman peered at me, then said, "Carlisle? Is that you?"

I looked closer and realized it was Jack's mother. I remembered then my mother's scoffing explanation over the phone about a year ago regarding how Gertrude Blair had restyled and colored her hair, been to a plastic surgeon, dabbled in Botox and who knows what else. My mother made it clear she didn't approve of unnatural forms of beauty enhancement. I didn't point out she had been coloring her hair since I had been in third grade.

"You know her?" India said.

"Well, yes, sweetie. I know Carlisle. She's a friend of your uncle Jack's."

India glanced back and forth between us. "You are?"

"Friend" hardly seemed the right word.

"Oh, my," the woman twittered even more, pressing her hand to her ample chest. "I'm not sure you should be here, dear."

And she wasn't talking to India.

I'm not sure what else she would have said or done, but I was saved (relatively speaking) when Hunter Blair headed our way.

I suspected it was him the second I saw

him. He was shorter than I expected (isn't everyone?), but it was hard to mistake the wiry man. His face was craggy from years in the punishing oil fields where he had made his fortune, and he looked meaner than a sleeping bear poked in winter.

Until recently, Hunter hadn't spent that much time in Willow Creek, given his job as a wildcat oil fighter. He had made millions with his oil-fighting company, and traveled the world putting out fires in places that had always been dangerous but were deadly now.

As I understood it, the Hunter lore had it that he had gone to the oil fields as soon as he graduated from high school, and excelled. Perhaps it's because I have a bit of poet underneath the lawyer in me, but I'd say Hunter felt that fighting raging oil fires in death traps was easier than fighting the demons of being dirt poor and from the wrong side of the tracks in a town like Willow Creek.

Who knows. Hunter was good at what he did, made a fortune, and made his little brother stay in school, go to college, and eventually get his law degree. I knew for a fact that Jack felt equal parts frustration and admiration for his brother.

I received confirmation that the man was

Hunter himself when he saw me standing there, no doubt looking guilty, and approached. Now, you'd think that a host of a party would be, maybe, gracious. Not this guy. He walked over, stopped, looked me up and down, and said, "Who the hell are you?"

My horror movie–worthy deb ball party duties were getting more horrifying by the second. I wanted out of there bad.

"Nobody," I said, turning on my heel, determined to leave the house, leave Willow Creek, return to Boston, and say, *Yes, yes, yes, I'll marry you, Phillip, whether my mother approves or not.*

But India caught my arm. "Daddy, this is Miss Carlisle Wainwright Cushing." India seemed to change, smiling at her father like a dreamy-eyed grade-schooler. "I invited her to have dinner with us."

He looked suspicious, then even more so when I said, "Dinner? Really, I can't intrude."

"Then why are you here if not to eat?"

Direct. To the point. No messing around.

Fine. I'd play it his way.

I pulled up General Patton. "Actually, I'm here because your daughter would like to make her debut at the Hundredth Annual Willow Creek Symphony Association Debutante Ball. I am here to extend an invitation to you and your family to participate."

India groaned since she had specifically said I should "sort of ease into it." I had been in the courtroom long enough to take this man's measure. "Easing into" wasn't a part of his vocabulary much less was it anything he would respect.

The man's first response was confusion. "The debutante ball?" Then shock, before his craggy face broke out in a glower.

His mother looked at me with speculation, then at her granddaughter who literally held her breath. After a second, Gertie Blair tutted. "Now, Hunter, don't get that look about you," his mother said. "It's an honor to be asked."

"It's an honor for me to fork over a pantload of money?"

"Daddy," India pleaded.

"Don't daddy me. I didn't raise you to be a citified snob."

I must have raised my brow because Hunter gave me a look of the not-nice variety. And might I add that up close, he was pure grit and spit and a "look" could turn cream to butter in an instant.

"Debutante balls are for sissies," he said.

"Fine," India huffed. "Then call me a sissy. I am going to be a debutante. If I have to, I'll use my trust fund money to pay for it."

"You don't have access to your trust fund." Check.

"I will in three months." And mate.

More glowering, an impasse of sorts, until Hunter Blair raised what I could tell was a triumphant brow. "Even I know debutantes have to be escorted by their father. Seems a mite embarrassing having to make your debut all alone." Again, check.

But he had raised his daughter in his image. One of India's perfect brows arched, the adoring daughter gone. "Just so you know, Daddy, a girl only has to be escorted by a male relative."

Daddy's brows slammed together.

"I bet Uncle Jacky will escort me if you won't."

Daddy's heart wasn't the only one to stop in the room at the mention of Uncle Jacky. Mine did a cartwheel, especially when I heard his voice.

"What kind of trouble are you stirring up this time, Indie?"

We all turned to find Jack entering the foyer, slapping the butler on the back. "Good to see you, old man."

"Mr. Jack," the man said with fatherly pride.

He wore a black, three-button suit with a not-quite-royal-blue shirt with barely black buttons marching up the center, the top button undone, and no tie in sight. His dark hair was racked back and I don't think I need to spell out just how amazing he looked.

He walked up to us, gave his mother a big hug, all but lifting her off the black and white marble tiles, for which the woman squealed with delight. "Oh, Jacky, you bad boy." Though it was clear she adored her youngest son.

Jack followed up by giving India a sternly teasing scowl. "I can tell by the look in those beautiful blue eyes of yours that you are causing trouble." Then he hugged her too. "Good girl."

He shook his brother's hand. "Not sure what you two are arguing about, big brother, but I'd think you would have learned just to give in early and avoid all the hassle. You know your little girl is going to get her way eventually." At which point he laughed, though Hunter decidedly did not.

Then Jack turned. As had become the norm, his smile flatlined when he looked at me. His expression was a mix of ice and heat, and I felt blood rush up from my toes to my cheeks. What I wanted to do was run, more specifically, run like my hair was on fire, as fast and as far away as possible. But given my status as cool, calm, and collected woman, I stood my ground.

"I am here at India's request," I blurted without being asked.

So much for cool, calm, and collected.

One dark brow rose, the corner of his mouth crooking. "This should be good."

"India wants to be a debutante," their mother explained.

In short order, his niece and mother filled Jack in on the details, with Hunter Blair adding his not so flattering commentary along the way.

This back-and-forth went on for a bit more, gaining everyone's attention. Not that the Blair clan appeared to care since they only got louder and louder until even Hunter couldn't ignore the growing quiet as people turned to stare.

"Time to eat," the man barked angrily.

The crowd scurried to the dining room in an ostentatious wave of jewelry, elaborately coiffed hair, and designer clothes, led by the host himself, India marching away toward the stairway with a mutinous scowl. I started to leave, but Jack stopped me.

"You've made this mess, I suspect it's only fair you stay to see it through to the end.

Don't you want to know if Hunter will give in and let his daughter be a . . . what did he call it? A pantywaist sissy girl?"

His amusement made my teeth grind. "He already said no."

He tsked. "Now, now, Miss Cushing. I thought you were made of sterner stuff than that. Besides, clearly you don't know anything about how India works."

Actually, I did. I was there, wasn't I?

"Come on," he said. "Dinner's getting cold."

Which is how I ended up at Hunter Blair's dinner party of twenty-two, now twenty-three, seated next to none other than the host's little brother.

As has already been established, the house was filled with expensive, if ill-matched, antiques. The dining room table was no exception. At a mere glance, I would say the table was a delicately beautiful antique Queen Anne piece, extended to its max and laden with the gaudiest display of silver, gold, crystal, and china I had ever seen.

With Jack sitting so close, my skin tingled like an idiotic schoolgirl's, so much so that I hardly noticed that the other guests had to scoot down to accommodate me. Jack sat back, his legs crossed casually at the knee as he spoke to the woman on his left. I pretty

162

much forgot all about India and debutantes and found myself staring at his hands; I might have been remembering how they had touched me in the Foley Building. The probability that my breath caught was high. I was so engrossed that I didn't notice when Jack turned to me until it was too late.

"Relax," he said.

My head shot up. "What?"

"I said relax."

"I am relaxed."

He tilted his head. "You're a lot of things, but relaxed isn't one of them." He turned just a hair. "Listen, if you want Hunter to say yes to this deb thing, you have to work it. He's a businessman, sell him on the idea."

I had been staring at the tablecloth. At this, I glanced up. "How does anyone sell Hunter Blair on anything?"

He studied me, his fingers idly turning the stem of his wine glass. He'd always had the ability to alternately make me love him then hate him. I had loved him the instant he sat down next to me in that math class. But he had undone me as well, changing the course of my life forever when I finally gave in to everything I had felt for Jack Blair. Dramatic, I know, but that didn't make it any less true.

Fortunately, I was long over him, over any

foolish infatuations that made me act Not Like Me.

He shrugged. "I have no doubt that that brain of yours can figure out a way to convince my brother to do what you want." He ran his gaze over me. "Though maybe not when you're wearing your mother's clothes. Those two never did get along."

I sat up straight. "These are not my mother's clothes."

"Okay, Savannah's."

He had me there, but I saw no reason to confirm his suspicions. "What, he's like you and prefers stiletto heels and spandex pants?"

Jack chuckled. "It's a start. Hell, you show up looking like that and I'll convince him for you."

Which made me laugh. God, how I hated the way he could charm me even when I was fast telling myself to stay clear.

Thankfully, a man across the table asked Jack a question, forcing him to look away.

Course after course of the meal was served, Hunter's mother chatting up a storm, telling the group the origins of this piece of furniture and that piece of silver and all but stating the price of each. My mother would have been appalled.

I was a little queasy when they served the

main course. I am all for beef; I'm a Texan after all. But the steak that stared up at me was so rare I was afraid it might bite back when I stuck my knife in it.

The entire meal was like that, an odd mix of gastronomic delights and trailer-park delicacies. During the first course, they served pâté along with sausage rolls that I suspected were made from a tube of Pillsbury crescent rolls and Jimmy Dean sausage.

I ignored the discussion among the guests (and Jack) and forced myself to "sell" Hunter Blair on the deb ball. With no help for it, I turned to my host who sat on my right at the head of the table, and said, "I really think a girl of India's caliber would be a great asset to the debutante ball. And she would reap a lifetime of benefit from it as well."

He grunted. "My India has everything she needs. And she has my mother to show her the ropes of being a lady."

I glanced down the length of the table, peeking through the tall silver candelabras and multiple centerpieces, along with the bloody steaks. "Your mother is a lovely woman, and clearly she is interested in the finer graces of life." Interested in and excelling at being two completely separate kettle

165

of fish. "Becoming a debutante would simply be icing on the cake."

"My daughter doesn't need any more cake."

Over the length of the eight-course meal, I came at the problem from every direction. And none of them worked. For a second Hunter gave me such an irritated scowl that I thought he would tell me to leave.

It was during dessert, an actually delicious concoction of chocolate and cream soufflé, when India's grandmother leaped up, the tablecloth caught in her ornate belt of turquoise and jewels, tipping the stemware and candelabras over like dominos. Everyone watched in shock, unable to move, until the last candelabra fell and the tablecloth burst into flames. You've never seen twenty-three adults scramble backward so quickly in your life.

"Oh, my," India's grandmother said.

Oh, my, was right.

After a few obligatory offers to help, the group practically trampled over one another to escape to the relative safety outside . . . or get to the phone lines to report in on Hunter Blair's disastrous dinner.

Hunter Blair looked as if he wanted to murder someone. Jack was busy putting out the fire.

"Oh, Hunter," his mother said with a quaver. "I'm so sorry."

Then she ran from the room. India and the servants had raced in.

India looked her father in the eye, and said, "Yeah, right, you know how to deal with society."

She flipped her hair and walked out.

Servants hopped to, helping Jack with the fire. Hunter Blair still hadn't moved.

"Well, then, I'll just be going," I said, thinking I could tiptoe away. Maybe a year off for the symphony event wasn't such a bad idea after all.

"Miss Cushing."

Hunter Blair's voice shuddered through the room.

I didn't really want to stop; in fact, I told myself not just to run, but run like hell. I didn't need any more trouble, and this family spelled nothing but.

I turned back. "Yes, Mr. Blair?"

"I accept the invitation."

"Invitation?"

Yes, I was being dense, intentionally. But my mind raced with how to get out of what was promising to be an even bigger mess than the former conductor caught in a dress. Standing there with Hunter glaring at me, India poised at the bottom of the stairs, not to mention Jack looking on with streaks of ash on his face like some kind of warrior, I felt far too tangled up with Blairs. On the other hand, in reality I was far too tangled up with the debutante ball. I had a family history to save and a grandmother whom I hoped I could make proud.

"India will be a debutante at your fancy party," Hunter clarified.

India leaped up and down, then got control of herself. "Thank you, Daddy," she said, racing across the foyer and throwing her arms around the bear of a man.

What was odd was that the man didn't hug her back. He pulled away with a curse and strode from the hall. At first India looked hurt. But then the India I had come to know and not love returned.

"Then it's settled," she stated coldly, and headed up the stairs like a queen.

I had gotten what I came for and had no interest in getting involved in any further Blair family drama. I had enough family drama of my own.

"Very good. I'll get back to you with the details," I said, then fled.

For the record, I could feel Jack staring at my back as I disappeared into the cool Central Texas night.

CHAPTER TEN

The general mood at Wainwright House was a cross between bedlam and despair. The children were still not on intimate terms with discipline, my sister's mood swung wildly between overly dramatic and depressed, and my mother had taken to calling me on my cell phone rather than talking to me directly. I was sitting at a long worktable in Miss Montserat's symphony headquarters office waiting for her return when my mother launched her latest bombshell.

"I just want you to know," she said without any sort of expected niceties to ease into conversation, "that I'm upset and haven't gotten out of bed all day."

At first blush, this news didn't worry me. My mother was frequently upset and took to her bed. She pulled the sheets over her head for a week when Matt Lauer cut his hair.

"Are you sick?" I asked.

She didn't sound sick and the day before she had looked perfectly fine after coming home from a late lunch date. She didn't tell us where she had gone, but she returned happier than she had been since I arrived in Willow Creek.

"Of course I'm sick. Why else would I be in bed?"

"Ah . . . maybe because you're afraid Gwyneth Paltrow will get pregnant again and name this one Pear?"

"I'm hanging up now."

"Fine. Sorry. What's wrong?"

Miss Montserat returned with her own black notebook. Every year she compiled one that included all plans for the upcoming ball. She raised a brow when she saw me on the phone. I gave her what I hoped was a winning smile and turned away.

My mother sniffed. "Rumor has it that Vincent is going to the country club for dinner."

"And?"

"And it's my membership. My world. My friends."

"Then who's he going with?"

"That Jack Blair is taking him."

My spine tingled like a knee jerking when hit with a rubber hammer. Unintended, but it happens unless you are dead or dying of

170

some strange neurological disorder.

"It's obviously a PR move," I surmised.

"My thoughts exactly. So I must counter."

"How?"

"By going to the club for dinner as well. I'll expect you and the rest of the family to be ready by seven."

She hung up before I could say "no, thanks."

At seven on the nose my mother descended the stairs ready for dinner at the country club. I had barely made it through the front door, and no one else was in sight.

"What is going on here?" she demanded.

The gold buttons on her St. John's suit winked all their perfectly proper Southern lady power. In contrast, I had on a pair of old Converse sneakers, white T-shirt, khakis, and notepads bundled against my chest.

"Good Lord, Carlisle, you can't go to the club looking like that. And where is your sister?"

Savannah strode in from the kitchen. "What is it, Mother?"

"Heaven have mercy," she said, her tone exasperated. "I thought I could at least count on you to be ready . . . and not look like some sort of third world refugee."

In my sister's defense she didn't look that bad, just not particularly familiar with a brush and comb.

Like animals sensing blood, the rest of the family entered and weren't intuitive enough to realize the blood was about to be their own. My mother took one look at them and closed her eyes. No one else was dressed much better.

She clapped her hands. "Chop-chop, everyone. Our reservations are in thirty minutes. Get dressed."

There was plenty of grumbling, but even Janice's kids seemed to realize that you didn't argue with Ridgely.

In record time the family was ready and bundling out the door. We took multiple cars.

"Where's Ben?" I asked.

Savannah's expression made a strange swing between anger and despair. "I called him at work and he said he didn't know if he could make it."

"I'm sure he's just busy."

"He's always busy."

I searched my brain for a suitable response. "Well." I was stumped, so I resorted to a standard. "Savannah, don't worry. Ben loves you."

Of course as a divorce attorney I figured it was probably highly likely that my brother-in-law was out doing who knows what with who knows who. But I'm also a sister and know that sister-talk is extremely different from lawyer talk. And sister-talk proved to be just the thing when we arrived at the WCCC and found Ben waiting for us at the entry.

Savannah fell into his arms and he kissed her in such a tender way that he either deserved an Academy Award for acting in love or he really was.

The Willow Creek Country Club was north of Willow Square, built a hundred years ago, and was harder to get into than the Junior League, mainly because the initiation fee alone was more than the average person made in an entire year.

The entrance to the property was announced by limestone pillars and tall wrought-iron gates, the grounds surrounded by a high green hedge. The main clubhouse sat back from the main gate like an antebellum mansion underneath a sprawl of willow and live oak trees. The tennis courts and golf course were to the west, the swimming pool to the east.

The club was busy on Friday nights. But no matter how busy, Hector the maître d' always saved my mother's table.

She acted like the queen entering the high-ceilinged dining room, tall French doors lining the far wall, floor-to-ceiling draperies pulled back with swags to let in the moonlit night. She waved discreetly to some, stopping to chat briefly with others, a light touch of fingers to someone's sleeve.

I scanned the room and didn't see Vincent or Jack. Good, I told myself.

The Friday night country club crowd was generally an older lot. The younger group came on Saturdays. We didn't get nearly as many whispers behind hands as we had at Brightlee given that most people over a certain age no longer cared about who was doing what to whom, with whom, or the like. Life, they had finally learned, is too short for that.

Drinks were ordered and served, menus distributed, small talk made, smiles a must. Finally, dinner arrived, though no sooner did we take our first bites than Ben pushed up from the table, and set his napkin on his chair. "If you'll excuse me."

Given that good breeding prohibited leaving the table while people were eating, my mother was looking unhappier by the second. Savannah didn't look much better, her delicate fingers holding a shrimp fork, the shrimp dangling uneaten. But suddenly, her eyes went wide. She sat frozen for a second, then dropped the fork to her plate with a clatter, took her glass of wine and threw it back like a soldier just returned from war. Slamming the stemware back on the table, she leaped up. "Excuse me," she shot over her shoulder as she hurried away.

Janice and I exchanged a panicked glance.

No way, she mouthed to me.

Surely not, I mouthed back.

Even I knew the Willow Creek Country Club wouldn't fall under the heading of Kinky to anyone. But then again, my sister had never been just anyone.

Hoping to head off an even bigger potential disaster, I hurried after my sister. I hurtled through the tables, then down the long dimly lit hallway toward the restrooms, stopping short outside the big oak door marked GENTLEMEN. Unfortunately, there was no sign of my sister or her husband.

Scowling, I glanced up and down the hall, then inched open the door. "Savannah," I hissed.

The door lurched open and I would have fallen inside if I hadn't landed in someone's arms.

"Carlisle, this is a surprise. Are you lost? The ladies' room is next door."

I pushed away and came face-to-face with Jack Blair. "I am not lost." Said as if he were the demented one.

"When I told you boundaries were ill-advised, I didn't realize you'd take me so literally."

"Ever the comedian."

"I try."

I backed up. He followed and my stomach gave a lurch as the door swung shut behind him.

"How are you?" he asked, when my back hit the opposite wall.

"I told you, no fraternizing." Admittedly, I was sort of breathless, but really, my heart was going a hundred miles an hour and my skin tingled with a mix of panic and completely inappropriate excitement.

"We *fraternized* at Hunter's dinner party. Oh, but you needed something then. So the rule is no fraternizing unless I can help you?"

"You make it sound so wrong."

A smile threatened, but he held it back, then just more of him looking at me as if still trying to figure something out.

I tried to duck past him, but he put his arm out, bracing it against the wall, blocking me. I stared at the tan skin, the corded muscles. Forget the fact that a man should never wear any sort of short-sleeved anything on a Friday night at the club; my heart beat (wildly) and my whole body itched to give in and throw myself at him as he always made me want to do.

No, no, no, I told myself firmly.

But when I dragged my gaze up from his arm to his shoulders, then finally to that ruggedly chiseled face, he hadn't looked away. In the dim light he was more the Jack I had always known, completely dangerous, sure, but caring. And yes, he was beautiful. I mean, really. What was I supposed to do?

"Damn," I muttered, then did the very thing I swore I wouldn't do after I saw him at the Foley Building. I launched myself at him in the dimly lit hallway of the Willow Creek Country Club. Yes, me, the totally together, in-control person. Yes, me, the engaged-to-the-perfect-man person. Yes, me, the woman who had sworn off Jack Blair three years ago like Britney Spears swearing off hair shears.

The kiss was instant, intense, as if we had simply picked up where we left off. His breath came fast, his hands caressing places that shouldn't have been caressed — at least by him. There was plenty of panting and all sorts of noises a girl like me just didn't make.

He framed my face with his hands, those strong, capable hands, tilting my head back. "This isn't a good idea," he said.

"Like I don't know that?"

I curled my arms around his shoulders, and he groaned, seeming to give in, lifting me up. As much as I hate to admit it, when he wrapped my legs around his waist I let him. Not that you want to know this, but I had on a skirt.

He buried his face in my neck, his hands cupping my, well, lower parts. And no telling where the craziness would have led if the men's room door hadn't opened again.

I disentangled as quickly as I could, leaping away to find my sister standing in the doorway.

"Carlisle? Jack?"

"Savannah! I was just looking for you."

She didn't appear convinced. "What were you two doing?"

"Nothing, absolutely nothing."

She smiled wickedly. "Nothing?"

"I had an eyelash in my eye."

"Good Lord, Carlisle," my sister said, "surely you can come up with something better than that. You know, like, I've become a clinging vine and I was practicing on the enemy's hot lawyer?"

Jack's brow furrowed. I gasped. Savannah giggled. Then all of us froze when the rear door from the back parking lot pushed open.

A woman entered the building pulling a

silk scarf from around her neck, her handbag swinging on her forearm, and after a second I realized it was the same woman I had seen with Jack outside of Starbucks.

She stopped in all her long-legged, willowy dark-haired beauty and looked Savannah and me up and down. Not seeming to find anything threatening (Savannah was incensed), she turned to Jack, smiled a smile that said as plain as day that she could be very, very bad, then hooked her arm through his.

"Sorry I took so long, darling."

Darling?

"I hope I'm not too late for dinner."

Jack had a date? And I had just thrown myself at him? (Had I been inclined toward exclamation marks I would have used them here.)

I grabbed my sister's arm and dragged her away. "Thanks for the help, Jack," I tossed over my shoulder.

When I got to the end of the hall I couldn't help myself. I looked back. Big mistake given the fact that Jack was watching me — and the woman was watching me too.

Just between you and me, neither of them looked happy (good) . . . more to the point, he looked as if he as wondering what kind of crazy, stupid-ass thing he had just done, with me, aka Satan's spawn (not so good).

"So really, what was that?" Savannah asked, thankfully breaking into my unfortunate thoughts.

"As I said, nothing." Nothing, that is, if you call knees trembling and my head swimming nothing. I felt a pressure at the back of my eyes, like unshed tears. Though what exactly I wanted to cry about I couldn't say.

My sister, completely oblivious to the turmoil in my head, just smiled. "I bet that's her."

"Her? Who?"

"His fiancée. Racine Bertolli."

"What?"

She smiled that wicked smile of hers. "Jack's taken, sister mine. Engaged. About to be married. No longer single. Which in Willow Creek, Texas, means hands off."

She left me standing at the entrance to the dining room with my mouth on the parquet floor. Jack, engaged?

Had I been fifty, I would have sworn I'd had my first hot flash. Given I was a good two decades away from running dry in the hormone department, I can only explain the prickling heat that rushed through me as an unpleasant variety of shock. How could he not tell me he was engaged? How could he *be* engaged?

I snapped my mouth shut given my own pesky little issue that I was engaged, too, and had failed to mention said engagement. But still . . .

I headed (marched) back to the table, following Savannah. As has been established, no question she was beautiful. But as she walked along, saying hello to this person, waving at that person, her bee-stung lips smiling in a very guilty way, her cheeks flushed and her blond hair no longer so perfectly styled, even I could tell men would think she was gorgeous.

My mother looked confused, then, I swear, a little jealous. At first I didn't believe it. But then I conceded that my mother always had to be the most beautiful woman in the room. She had never subscribed to the idea that a parent's goal was to help their children do better than they had in life.

But confusion and jealousy took a turn for the worse on my mother's perfect face when Ben reappeared shortly after his wife. The very proper man was flushed, too, and I swear, a piece of his shirttail hung exposed from beneath his blue blazer, his blue-and-gold striped tie hanging askew against the white broadcloth.

Ridgely's spine went stiff, her eyes narrowed. After a furtive glance around the room, she pulled up a ragged smile.

"Ben, dear, I suggest you make yourself presentable before you grace us with your presence."

He noticed his untucked shirt and blushed. Ben. Blushing. More than that, Savannah laughed.

I shook my head, though why I couldn't say since, like my mother, when it came to men, my sister had always been willing to do crazy things to get what she wanted. Though who was I to cast stones? I had just fraternized (or whatever) with the enemy (the engaged enemy) without bothering to mention I had taken my mother's case. I wasn't sure which would be considered worse: the legs around his waist or the missing detail about my new position as my mother's counsel of choice. Or, for that matter, that I had engaged in said activities with one man while I was promised to another.

My cell phone buzzed. When I saw the readout showed Phillip's number I cringed, then let it go to voice mail.

CHAPTER ELEVEN

For a girl who wasn't particularly fond of multitasking, I certainly had my plate \plate\ n (15c) full \full\ adj (before 12c) given that I was 1: avoiding my (unequivocally great) fiancé 2: juggling phone calls from my (exceedingly persistent) office assistant back in Boston 3: planning a (potentially disastrous) ball 4: being manipulated by a (totally spoiled) teenager 5: gathering ammunition for my mother's (extremely troublesome) divorce 6: lusting after (the unfortunately sexy — not to mention completely engaged) Jack Blair.

On the bright side, I had my requisite eight girls. Eight, not seven, because as it turned out, India provided not only her entourage, but when she learned that the clock had struck the hour and we still needed one more girl, she rolled her eyes, said something about having to do everything, then reappeared with Betty Bennett.

Betty might die of embarrassment in the process of making her debut, but the girl would do anything for her idol.

India sighed in exasperation at the fawning, but she had come too far to have everything fall apart because we lacked one girl.

We were set. Eight girls, the announcement made, the *Willow Creek Times* running the article on the front page of the Society Section. Janice might not have been a lot of help getting the girls, but she had whipped up eight short bios that made our debutantes sound like true diamonds who simply hadn't been discovered yet.

My mother read the announcement in the newspaper (from bed where she had been since hearing the news of just who would be making their debut) and said, "No wonder she won the Pulitzer."

The next day, I had a receiving room full of eighteen-year-old girls of not perfect lineage, and their mothers. Or in India's case, her grandmother.

"Thank you for coming," I said, walking to the front of the formal room.

Unlike Gertie Blair, my mother had undeniable style, having decorated the hundred-year-old house with a combination of subdued color and unquestionable quality.

Treasured family antiques mixed with stylish fabrics to create a room that was both dignified and inviting.

Lupe had laid out cucumber sandwiches with the crusts cut off, and a large crystal bowl of sweet tea. Small linen luncheon napkins fanned out on the sideboard, and everyone there but India had something to eat or drink.

The mothers sat nervously. The only girls talking were the Entourage, and they were giggling quietly about who knew what, though from the beet-red expression on Betty's face, I'd say it was about her.

I was saved from having to figure out what to do about it when Janice walked into the room with someone behind her. I did a double take.

"Morgan?" I said.

The other girls stiffened and India scowled. After Morgan's trip to the hair salon, her relic Cyndi Lauper rainbow-of-color hair had been neutralized, ending up a deep dark brown that matched her mother's. Combine that with her big dark violet eyes and creamy skin, and she was by far the prettiest girl in the room. Who would have guessed that beneath the oranges and reds a beauty lurked?

"You're beautiful," I said.

She didn't look happy as she marched over to the sofa, her straight dark hair swinging as she dropped down and sat with her arms crossed on her chest. "Whatever."

"If you don't like the new look," Janice said, "you can always back out now and avoid participating in this travesty."

"Give it up, Mom. I'm doing this."

The rest of the group glanced at one another.

"Travesty?"

"Back out?"

"Janice," I stated tightly, "I believe you are giving our ladies the wrong impression."

Janice, much like her daughter, marched up to stand next to me and flashed the group a massively fake smile. "Yeah, yeah, it's going to be great."

I felt the beginnings of a headache coming on, and I hadn't even said hello. But at least now we had all eight debutantes in attendance.

"Let's get started," I said.

I stood at the mantel, Janice next to me.

"In just under three months, each and every girl here is going to have an experience she will treasure for a lifetime."

The Janice I knew and didn't love snorted, though quietly. And who could blame her? Certainly not me, since my own debutante experience, while it would be remembered for a lifetime, certainly would never be treasured.

"Let's start by going around the room and each of you introducing yourselves and your mother . . . or grandmother."

India started, standing up proudly, the majority of her skirt appearing to have stayed home sick. Her chunky blond hair was clipped back helter-skelter in an assortment of butterfly clips.

"I'm India Blair. Though you all know that. And this is my grandmother, Gertrude Blair. My mother isn't here today, but she will be at the ball because she totally loves me."

Gertrude appeared concerned while everyone else looked nonplussed, probably because rumor had it that India's mother had made it abundantly clear that she wanted nothing to do with her oldest child. Or so the gossip mill would have you think.

The awkward moment was broken when the Entourage stood, both dressed as scantily as they had been that first day they arrived with India to secure a spot in the deb ball.

"My name is Tiki Beeker, and this is my mom, Persy."

Persy Beeker had the perfectly put-together look of a woman who spent great amounts of time and money putting herself together. Her hair was perfectly highlighted. Her nails done to perfection. Her clothes expensive but not flashy. Given that each girl had to host a party, I had high hopes that Persy Beeker would make sure theirs was a tasteful affair. Then again, she did let her daughter dress like a trollop.

Abby Bateman went next, announced her name, said only, "I'm best friends with India and Tiki, and this is my mom," before she sat down.

Wilma Bateman smiled, said her name, but didn't stand. For all of Persy Beeker's taste, Wilma wore serviceable clothes, and her thick legs were covered with the murky sheen of support hose.

Next up were Merrily Bennett and Betty. After that we met Ruth Smith, Janice's dream girl given the girl's status as president of the debate team, reporter for the *Willow Creek High Gazette,* and all-around intellectual. Her short brown hair had a slight curl to it, and her sand-colored eyes were about as nondescript as her clothes. The only thing that stood out about Ruth was the lace-up oxfords she wore. I wasn't sure if it was a vintage statement of individuality or if she just hadn't seen the need to grow out of elementary school shoes.

Her mother was Olive. She stood briefly to tell us of her husband, Thomas, who owned a chain of drive-thru liquor stores across the state of Texas, and promised each of us a discount if we ever shopped there. It was odd, but not so bad since the Smiths were new to town and we didn't know that much about them. I had gotten their name from Miss Montserat at Symphony Hall when she told me that the Smiths were making donations all over town. At that point, as far as I was concerned, they were just the sort of family we needed. Had money. Were willing to spend. Case closed.

Nellie Kraft was there along with her mother, June, both of them natural redheads with the pale white skin that had to be awkward in the unforgiving Texas sun. The Krafts were even newer to town than the Smiths, but in the short time they had been there June had made a name for herself with her hard work at the Junior League.

After the newly stunning Morgan introduced herself with a grunt, the group was rounded out by Sasha Winthorpe and her mother, Waverly. Sasha was the one girl there who actually acted like a lady, wearing a cream turtleneck and cream wool skirt and cream flats, her light brown hair pulled back with a headband.

When we were done with introductions, I began with the basic instructions.

"We have a lot of work to do," I explained, then passed out a handout I had gotten from Giselda Montserat at Symphony Hall.

"What's this?"

" '*A Girl's Guide to Etiquette*,' " Ruth read.

"I want each of you to read this from cover to cover before our next meeting."

"Homework?"

"It isn't that long."

The girls grumbled.

I persevered. "Today I wanted to explain the basics. Each girl will need a white ball gown, white gloves, white shoes, and a single strand of pearls for the night of the debut."

"I already have my dress," India announced. "My father paid like a fortune for it. But that's my dad. Always buying me great stuff, cars, and trips and jewelry, because he totally loves me more than like anything." She flipped her hair. "And he's going to fly in a hair guy from New York to do my hair for the ball. And I'm going to have one of those fabulous Sylvia Weinstock cakes at my party! You know *InStyle* magazine called her 'the Leonardo da Vinci' of cakes! I'm going to be Deb of the Year."

"Modest, are we?" Ruth snipped.

"Jealous, debate nerd?" India shot back.

Pretty much every mouth in the room dropped, followed by all the girls talking at once, arguing, accusing, muttering. The mothers looked as if someone had hosed them down with a fire extinguisher, startled into a painful, back-arching grimace. They looked to me for help.

"Girls," I said.

Nothing.

"Girls, please."

Which did no good.

"Quiet," Janice barked.

Which did a lot of good.

I drew a deep breath. "Thank you," I said politely.

Janice rolled her eyes.

"Where were we?"

"Gloves, pearls, white dresses," Sasha interjected helpfully.

"There we go. Miss Know It All is at it again," Abby giggled.

"In addition," I plowed on, praying my mother was nowhere near the front receiving room, "each girl is required to host an individual party, to which all other debutantes are invited, plus any other guests the host family wishes to include. The theme of each party is up to the families, though it should be appropriate to your ages and the integrity of the debutante season."

Before the girls could start in on this one, I lurched on through the rest of the list. I went over escorts, and their need for one in addition to their fathers to present them. Everyone but India looked panicked at the news.

"Are there any questions?"

A slew of hands went up, not that anyone waited to be called on. Questions came at me all at once.

"When you say theme parties, what exactly do you mean?"

"White gloves. Like how long?"

"Escort?"

"Do you mean a guy?"

"No one said anything about having to ask a guy."

"Of course we ask guys to escort us," India stated with a scoff. "That's part of the fun."

To which a chorus of groans rang out, including from the Entourage.

"Girls," I said, "I know it seems over-whelming now, but it's going to be fine. Isn't it, Janice?"

She heaved a sigh. "Yep. Sure."

So much for help from the committee ranks.

"Everything is listed in the handout, along

with certain 'rules' of good behavior. We'll go over those when we meet again tomorrow after school. Until then, I think the mothers can go ahead and leave so the girls can start going over one of the most fundamental pieces of a Texas debutante ball."

"The Dip!" several cheered, though several others looked terrified. And why not. Just the thought of explaining the deep (potentially dangerous) bow gave me a chill. But there was no avoiding it, and the longer the girls had to practice, the better off they would be.

"Does anyone here know how to do the Dip?" I asked as soon as the mothers had departed, trying not to sound too hopeful.

Sasha Winthorpe sat up even straighter than she already was. "If you'd like, Miss Cushing, I can demonstrate."

"God, Sasha. If you suck up any more you'll explode," India scoffed and looked at me. "She's always doing this crap. Kissing everyone's ass. Pretending like she's so innocent."

"At least when a guy asks me out I know it's *not* because he assumes I'm easy."

India's eyes narrowed, then she shrugged. "At least guys ask me out. Tell me, Sasha, when was the last time you had a date?"

Red flooded Sasha's cheeks. "For your

information, I went to the movies with Tommy Brown two weekends in a row."

"Ooo, the movies."

I ignored the exchange and said, "Sasha, I would be happy to have you demonstrate for us."

Sasha shot India a withering glare, then stood. Given my own precarious past with the Dip, I assumed she would show a little bit of nerves. But no, she walked to the front of the room, pivoted back to her audience on a space of hardwood floor, then extended her arms.

"It goes something like this," she said, then put her left leg behind her and started to bow. At the beginning, it looked like any normal curtsy. But when she came to that point where normal stopped, she kept going. Inch by inch, lower and lower.

One by one (with the exception of India) the girls sucked in their breaths, a wave of gasps washing across my mother's tastefully decorated receiving room. You could feel the tension, the fear (and a little hope on one or two of the girls' faces) that Sasha's precarious balance would fail.

She didn't stop until her back knee nearly touched the floor, her head bowed low, then she stayed that way for what seemed like an eternity, before she started to rise like a phoenix. I could tell even Janice was impressed. What they didn't know, but I did, was that while Sasha had been impressive, she hadn't gotten low enough to touch her forehead to what eventually would be the flowing skirts of her debutante gown. But as far as I was concerned it was good enough.

When Sasha stood, proudly (smugly), it was as if the group suddenly got religion.

"Oh, my gosh!" Betty cried out, impulsively standing and starting to clap.

Everyone else followed suit, bursting into applause and circling around Sasha . . . everyone, that is, except India who hung back. I couldn't tell if she was jealous, terrified, or some combination of both.

"Girls," I called out.

They whipped around to me and said, "We have to do that too?"

"So low?"

"I couldn't!"

"Just couldn't!"

"I'll fall and make an idiot of myself."

"I'll be the laughingstock of the century!"

Which made me grimace.

Dragging up a nonchalant shrug, I said, "I guess you don't have to do the Dip. Though most girls do."

It was Ruth Smith, our intellectual, who said, "All it will take is balance, steady nerves, and practice."

Immediately, the girls started doing varying forms of the Dip, Sasha demonstrating again and again. But not one girl made it closer to the floor than about three feet. And they didn't even have on high heels yet.

Daredevil Morgan showed her true colors when she kept going, and kept going, with every other girl in the room holding her breath. With about a foot left, she tipped, squealed, and rolled over onto her side with a bellowing laugh.

Once we had one fall, the other girls weren't as worried. They started going lower and lower, each managing some variation of the Fall instead of the Dip, until soon just about every girl there was on the floor of my mother's very proper receiving room, rolling with laughter.

Morgan's shoes had fallen off, and while all outward color had been eradicated, one glance at her toenails showed my niece's true stripes. Namely, hot pink and orange striped nail polish.

"Cool," Tiki said. "I've never seen stripes before."

Morgan looked guilty but pleased at the same time.

"Can you lend me both colors?" Abby asked.

"Sure. They're upstairs. Come on."

The girls leaped up, and flew out of the room. India watched her best friends leave with Morgan. Her teenage face, quite frankly, looked scary.

I turned to stop the girls from leaving, but found none other than my mother standing in the doorway. If India's expression was scary, my mother's expression made India look tame. Though I doubted the two of them were concerned about the same thing.

"Hello, Mother," I said.

She didn't respond. Instead, she turned around without a word, and headed back upstairs, to bed no doubt.

Following her, I hurried out into the foyer. "Mother, it isn't that bad."

She turned back on the stairs. "No?"

"No. It's going to be fine. You're getting worked up for no reason."

"We are descendants of Texas's first family, not to mention English royalty, and now we are turning into embarrassments. I'll have to pack up and leave town."

My mother's dramatics had always seemed at the very least nothing more than tiring. But standing in the foyer, I'd had it. "Fine. Then we'll cancel."

Her manicured nails curled around the banister. "We can't cancel. Certainly not the Hundredth Annual Ball."

"Then find someone else. I give up. I'll leave it to you to pull this event together and move forward without me."

"And leave me with this disaster? I think not."

Lupe walked in. "Meese Carlisle. The phone is for you. Señor Jack. I tell him you busy, but he say eets important."

I glanced from my mother to the room full of undebutanteish debutantes. For a change, Jack Blair seemed the least of all my problems.

"Thank you, Lupe. I'll take the call in the library."

CHAPTER TWELVE

"Carlisle Cushing here."

"Ah, Miss Professional," Jack said on the other end of the phone. "I like it. Not quite as nice as talking dirty in a hallway outside the men's room, but it certainly conjures up all sorts of images."

"Where did you go to law school again? Law 'R Us: Become a lawyer in ten easy online lessons?"

He laughed. "Same law school as you, sweetheart. Don't you remember?"

Yes. Very well, thank you. "Oh, that's right. I seem to remember you there, barely."

Just more of his one-note laughter came over the phone line.

"What can I do for you?" I asked, in a voice that even I could tell sounded curt.

"Rumor has it you're taking your mother's case."

"If by rumor you mean the official documents I filed with the court clerk, then yes, the rumor is true."

"Funny you didn't bother to mention it any one of the last three times I saw you."

"Just like you didn't bother to mention you were engaged any one of the last three times I saw *you.*" I swallowed back any guilt I might have felt over my own engagement omissions.

"So you heard," he said.

"Yes, Savannah shared the news after she found us in the country club hallway engaging in . . . inappropriate behavior."

He actually laughed out loud at that. "Listen, cupcake, as I recall, you started it —"

No one would accuse Jack Blair of being a gentleman.

"— but you're right, it shouldn't have happened and it won't happen again."

"Good." I hesitated, then because my mind seemed to have, well, a mind of its own, I said, "Where'd you meet her?"

"For someone who swore there'd be no fraternizing between us, you're doing an awful lot of it."

"I am only being polite." And nosy, but I left that part out.

"I met her in Dallas. She's a lawyer for —"

"She's a lawyer?"

"Don't sound so surprised, Cushing. Not all lawyers are uptight and . . . oh, sorry, I forgot about you throwing yourself at me in the hallway."

The capillaries in my brain dilated, my chest constricted, making me gasp.

But Jack just laughed some more. "So, I'll see you at the hearing tomorrow," he said.

"Hearing! What hearing?"

"You're probably not so good at poker, are you?"

"What hearing, Jack?"

"I love it when you say my name. Maybe you could sorta drag it out, moan a little."

"Excuse me. Inappropriate."

"Sorry. There's just something about you, Cushing, that brings out the worst in me."

"Don't blame this on me. You were plenty bad before I ever came into the picture."

"You got me there."

"Now, seriously, what hearing?" I persisted.

"The hearing's at eight. With Judge Howard."

Even I had heard of Judge Howard, and not for any reason that had to do with law, lawyers, or courtrooms. My mother had dated him once, though thankfully she never got as far as marrying him.

I was lucky that Jack hung up before I

could emit the screech that was brewing and embarrass myself. I set down the phone, intent on calling the courthouse to find out if this could possibly be true. But then I realized it was Sunday.

My mother walked in, and I suspected she had been lurking outside the door.

"Did you know we have a hearing tomorrow?" I demanded.

"Yes."

"Why didn't you bother mentioning it to me?"

"Didn't I?"

"No."

"Oh, well then, we have a hearing tomorrow. At . . ." She fished around on her desk. "Here it is. Hearing. Eight a.m. Tomorrow. With that lovely Judge Howard. Did I ever tell you he adored me?"

"Yes, you did tell me. Many times. They all adore you."

At eight the next morning, we found ourselves in the Willow Creek Municipal Building just off Hildebrand Square.

The courtroom was packed, the judge's docket full. The benches were lined with an assortment of people. Given the small size of Willow Creek, judges heard a variety of cases, causing my perfectly clad mother to sit amid the masses of humanity.

"Reason enough not to get a divorce," she had snipped when she was forced to sit next to a man who leered at her while we waited for our case to be called.

Jack and Vincent walked in.

"Miss Cushing," Jack said with a nod.

Vincent and my mother ignored each other.

Given the way Jack and I had been interacting since my return to Willow Creek, I felt it only wise to get things on a better footing. "I apologize for not mentioning that I had taken the case." I started to add that I really hadn't been thinking about lawsuits when I had thrown myself at him. But I felt that would only add to the unprofessional thing we had going, so I held that back. "I would like to think that we can . . . well, clear the air. Start over. As friends."

He raised one of those dark brows. "Friends?"

"Yes, friends."

I'm not sure what he would have said, probably something of the not-nice variety, based on his expression, but he was cut off by the court clerk.

"*Ogden* versus *Ogden!*"

"Showtime," Jack said.

We strode to the counsel tables, Jack holding the swinging gate for us like a perfect gentleman.

With the formalities adhered to, I was finally able to address the court.

"What do you mean you want a continuance?" Judge Howard barked.

I had barely said a word and he was being testy already. I glanced between him and my mother. My guess was that he hadn't loved her as much as she let on.

Note to self: ask for new judge.

"I'm a busy man, Miss Cushing, my time valuable. Not that you or anyone else in your family has ever seemed to realize that."

Suspicion confirmed. Revised note to self: demand new judge.

"Yes, sir. I realize that. But I've only recently returned to town and I'm in the process of familiarizing myself with the situation."

Jack stood, a slow unwinding of muscle, the power palpable, every trace of the man who called me "cupcake" gone. "Your honor," he began, smoothing his tie against his shirt as he stood. "My client would prefer to resolve the matter of the divorce. The emotional stress is very difficult for him."

My mother snorted.

Vincent glared at her.

"Opposing counsel was notified of the hearing, your honor," Jack added. "And in fact, she attended an earlier meeting regarding the case . . . a meeting held a full week ago," he said as if apologizing.

I counted to ten.

Judge Howard turned to me. "Is this true, Miss Cushing?" he asked, his gravelly voice sharp.

"Your honor, you see —"

"Is it true or not, young lady?"

As if I were ten years old.

"Yes, it is true, sir. But —"

"No buts. Proceed." He banged his gavel.

Fuming, I stood there. Jack shrugged with an insincere apology. When I glanced back at the judge, he looked just as smug. Whether they liked it or not, I needed time. And I planned to get it.

"Your honor —"

"Miss Cushing, I am not going to change my mind."

"May I approach the bench?"

He started to bark something else.

"It's important. To both of us."

The man eyed me from beneath full, bushy eyebrows that had gone gray some time ago. "This better be good, Miss Cushing."

I approached the bench, Jack leaping up

to follow me.

"Your honor," I said with quiet dignity. "Given the fact that you once dated my mother —"

He sat back in his chair, his bushy gray eyebrows flapping up and down like I had shot him.

"— I request that you recuse yourself from the case."

"You are out of line, young lady. There was never anything improper or even serious between your mother and me."

I gave him a look of resigned innocence, as if I hated to be the bearer of bad news. "I didn't say anything about improper, your honor. But" — I shrugged — "my mother swears you loved her. If we move forward with this case in your courtroom, I will feel obliged to find out the extent of your past relationship with my mother, which might lead to comparisons with other women you've had relationships with . . ." I let the words trail off, the implication clear.

"I barely went out with her once!"

"But you did go out with her."

He glowered, then banged the gavel. "Court is in recess," he snapped. Then he leaned forward and added quietly, "I will consider your request."

Mr. Smooth evaporated and the killer Jack

I knew so well showed his true colors. I mouthed, *Not so good at poker, huh?* And this time as we left, I held the gate for him.

That afternoon at three forty-five I was ready, or as ready as I was going to be, when the girls arrived. They walked into the house, went straight to the receiving room, and plopped down on sofas and overstuffed chairs. India filed her nails, the Entourage chattered nonstop, the others chomped on gum. Only Sasha sat up straight in a stiff-backed settee and smoothed her skirt.

When Morgan entered, the Entourage sat up straight and waved. "Morgan, look!"

They displayed striped toenails.

India seemed to consider. "Scoot down, Abby. Morgan, come sit here by me."

Morgan appeared suspicious, or maybe she was just leery. Either way, it meant she was smarter than being kicked out of every private school in the Bay Area would lead one to believe. Though I was forced to re-assess when she walked over and sat down next to India.

"What did you all learn from the handout I gave you?" I asked without preamble, Janice standing next to me.

India studied her hands. "That Tommy Brown kisses better than anyone in the entire school." She displayed her fingernails to the group. "I went with French tips in honor of the event." She looked at Sasha. "Oops. Is that the guy you said you went to the movies with?"

Sasha's mouth dropped open.

"Well, be that as it may," I said smoothly, if tightly, "what did you read in your homework assignment that applies to your kiss with Mr. Brown?"

India looked at me like I was crazy. As did Janice.

I glanced at the other girls. "Does anyone know the answer?"

Miss Intellectual's hand shot up, straining in the air.

"Ruth?"

"A lady never tells anyone anything that's private," she announced proudly. "And a kiss should remain private."

"Oh, yeah!" Abby said, her hand up, waving in the air. "Like: don't kiss and tell."

"Exactly," I said. "Even slang can come from manners."

"Who cares about manners?" India stated.

"Clearly not you," Sasha retorted.

I thought India might launch herself off the sofa, but then she laughed. "Jealous?"

"A debutante cares about manners," I leaped in. "And last I heard, India, you wanted to be a debutante. Though if you've changed your mind . . ."

"Whatever," she huffed, then breathed out sharply until a sly smile appeared. "When Tommy and I go out again and get massively serious in his father's hunting cabin, I'll be sure not to mention it."

The Entourage twittered. Janice hung her head. Sasha looked like she was going to cry. I hurried on, whipping out a dry erase board from behind a wing chair and setting it on an easel.

"We have five areas to work on." I wrote on the board with each item. "They are:

1. walking
2. talking
3. dancing
4. table manners
5. attire."

"Attire?"

"How you dress."

India looked me up and down, then Janice. "And the two of you are going to tell us how to dress?"

"Funny." Which it wasn't, and wasn't intended to be. "For today, let's begin with walking."

I had been up late the night before practicing what I would say and how I would demonstrate. It had been late because I had to wait until everyone had gone to bed and I was sure they were all asleep. I didn't want anyone to know I needed the practice. By the time I made it to bed that night, I was rather pleased with myself. But standing in front of eight teenage girls and a sister-in-law who thought the whole thing was lower than low, I felt that stomach-churn of nerves like I was back in high school myself.

Determined, I placed an encyclopedia volume on the top of my head and started off toward the other side of the room. "I'm sure you've heard of learning how to walk properly by placing a book on your head," I said, concentrating on keeping said book from falling to the floor.

"You want us to walk like that?" Nellie asked. "Sorry, but you look pretty stupid."

I stopped, the book fell, thankfully I caught it, and I turned back.

Janice covered a laugh. When I gave her a questioning look, she nodded. "Yeah, a little . . . strange."

I shoved the book at her. "Then you do it."

She backed up. "Oh, no, not me."

Sasha stood, smiled perfectly, and said, "I'll do it."

India was not about to let that happen. She snatched the book away from me before I could hand it to Sasha. With a smirk, India walked over to the end of the room. "Let me show you how it's done."

She planted the pages on top of her head and started off. Given her four-inch heels and scantily clad form, she did a surprisingly good job — for a hooker prowling the Mexican border.

"Maybe a little less hip," I suggested.

She snorted, though she did tone it down. When she finished a second lap, her audience applauded. She dropped the tome from her head, smiled, and curtsied. I noticed she didn't do the Dip, however.

Each girl wanted a try and I had to supply more books. We had moved into the marble foyer, and no question there was a lot of racket going on from the whack of books hitting the floor. So is anyone surprised that my mother appeared at the top of the stairs?

I smiled with the confident smile of *See how well things are going?*

Next, Morgan took the stage, and I sent up a little prayer.

We watched her place a book on her head and start off across the foyer, but she couldn't get the hang of it.

"Errr," she ground out. "This is so lame."

Janice smiled serenely. "You don't have to do it."

"What are you, a broken record?"

"Just trying to help."

"Yeah, right," she snapped.

"I am. In fact, in the interest of helping, I might suggest that if you stopped wearing those boots, you'd be able to walk better."

I thought that my young niece was going to explode. India, never the peacemaker, nodded with cool superiority and threw flames on the fire. "Combat boots really are so over."

"What do you say, Morgan?" Janice persisted.

If I hadn't been standing at the front of the room, I would have waved my sister-in-law off like an emergency crew heading off accidents with bright orange flags. Even I knew she was headed into dangerous territory.

My niece glared at India, then wrenched back around to her mother, her newly dark hair flying about her shoulders, her blue eyes narrowed. "Say about what, Mom? You'd rather I wear old lady shoes like Sasha? Or four-inch heels like India? What kind of shoes do you want me to wear?" She made a condescending noise in her throat. "Oh, I know. You want me to wear those retarded hippie sandals you think are so cool. News flash. They're 'so over' too. Looks like we're both freaks."

She whirled away, and raced out of the room, flying past my mother who stood way too still.

I started to say something, what I don't know, only to hear another gasping cry. I turned around just in time to see India grab Sasha's book off her head and throw it down on the floor.

"You think you're so great," India said. "Well, you're not. You're a stuck-up bitch who no one likes."

"Better a stuck-up bitch than a slut!"

I leaped forward and separated the girls just before they tumbled into a brawl, shooing them back into the receiving room.

I pressed my eyes closed, and when I opened them my mother shook her head.

"It's not just the Symphony Association and our family name that's going to be ruined with this debacle," she said. "Those girls are going to be the laughingstock of Willow Creek and will never live it down the way this is headed. I'd think after your own deb ball, you'd remember that."

She looked at me hard, then turned on her heels and returned to her room.

Chapter Thirteen

I went to the kitchen, heading straight for the pot of coffee I knew Lupe always had going. It was that or a stiff swig of something eighty proof.

Lupe sat at the center counter polishing silver. My mother had at least four sets of silverware, which she actually took pride in polishing herself. Though her bed schedule of late had left the silver flatware to its own devices.

The timer rang on the oven and Lupe set the rag and silver down, pulled off the rubber gloves, before she went and pulled out a baking sheet of cookies. While I'm not a silver freak like the rest of my clan, I had grown up around it my whole life and could polish the stuff in my sleep. Right then it sounded like the perfect thing to do. Like meditation. Giving me time to clear my brain and figure out how to proceed.

The truth was that all the money in Willow Creek couldn't make a person truly acceptable in society. It had to be accompanied by grace, wit, style, and a sense of noblesse oblige. While I could count noblesse oblige among the girls, given the money their families would be contributing to the symphony, I was hard-pressed in the remaining three categories.

My cell phone rang and I saw that it was my office. "Yes?" I said.

"Carlisle, it's Pam."

Actually, it sounded like "Car . . . it . . . mmmm" given the bad connection.

"Pam, I can't hear you."

She added something about big news.

"Let me call you back on the land line," I told my assistant.

I flipped my cell shut and went over to the phone on the kitchen wall. I dialed my office number.

"Miss Cushing's office."

"Pam, it's me."

"What is Wainwright House?"

"What?"

"On the caller ID, it says 'Wainwright House.' "

"Oh, it's . . . ah, where I'm staying. What were you saying before?"

"You won't believe it! Mel Townsend, the richest guy in Boston, he called and wants to talk to you about handling his divorce! I swear, Carlisle, we are going places! I mean, you are going places. You have to come back."

I admit, my heart did a little jig, or maybe a big jig. But what was I going to do? "Pam, I can't come back now. I'm in the middle of my mother's divorce."

"But this is Mel Townsend we are talking about! How can you say no?"

"Give me his number and I'll call him."

After taking his contact information, I hung up. Talk about feeling conflicted. Mel Townsend really could solidify my career, but how could I walk away from what I had promised to do here?

With Lupe bustling around the kitchen, I picked up the gloves and soft rag, and got to work, needing time to think more than ever. Piece by piece, my hands fell into a rhythm until my brain finally stopped spinning. I was halfway through a set of antique silver handed down from generation to generation when the phone rang.

Lupe answered, but I barely noticed. I was only vaguely aware that she was her less-than-pleasant self to whoever had been unlucky enough to disturb her work.

"She no available, I tell you," she said with an impatient sigh. "You bother me. I tell you. She working. Polish sealver. Who these?" She listened. "Feel up?"

This got my attention. Feel up? I started to smile before my eyes went wide and I lunged for the phone, silver clattering to the floor.

"Phillip!"

Lupe huffed and I pressed the receiver to my chest. "I've got it!"

She muttered something I didn't understand.

"And let's keep this call between ourselves, okay, Lupe?"

"Bah," she muttered and marched away.

I waited until she was out of earshot before I took a deep breath. "Phillip," I said again, this time into the receiver.

"What is going on there?" he asked.

"Nothing, nothing. Just polishing silver. Lupe didn't want the job interrupted."

"Is Lupe your mother's boss?"

"Ah —"

"Have you gone home only to be put to work at menial tasks?"

"Ah —"

"I thought you were working on a divorce case."

Short on answers, I went with diversion \di-ver-sion\ n (17c) 1: "How did you get this number?"

"Pam. She just told me about the Townsend deal."

"She shouldn't have done that."

"What, give me the number? Or tell me that you are thinking about passing up a jewel of a case?"

Both?

"Phillip, I haven't passed on anything. But I have to finish here first."

He sighed. "Listen, I'm getting ready to start a big case, and before I do I thought I could come down this weekend. We can talk, figure this out."

"No!"

I could almost feel Phillip's stiffening shoulders.

"I mean, this weekend isn't good. Things are crazy here." I launched into a detailed summary of the divorce case to distract him.

"The judge dated your mother?" he asked.

"Exactly! So I'm swamped. But I promise, as soon as things are a little more settled I want you to come down."

The doorbell rang in the distance.

"But if I came down now we could talk strategy," he persisted.

"Phillip, that's great of you but right now I need to get my thoughts together."

"Well . . ."

I heard Lupe answer the door, then voices

approaching. When the door pushed open, Jack appeared.

The minute he entered he saw me, stopping to look at me, his brow furrowed.

"I miss you, Carlisle."

"What?" I focused on the phone with effort.

"I said, I miss you, Carlisle."

With Jack studying me, I might have blushed. Even Lupe stopped and watched me too.

What could I say in front of an audience? "I appreciate that, Phillip."

Yet again I hadn't provided the answer that would win any prizes. And what did that mean? That I didn't want the prize?

I shook the thought away, pulling up the reassuring image of Phillip and his kind green eyes, his sandy blond hair, the way he could make me breathe easily regardless of how stressful my day had been in court. The day he proposed, he took me out on a Swan Boat in the Public Gardens. The grass had been so green, the willow trees lining the water's edge, the centuries-old buildings surrounding the public space standing like sentinels at the perimeter of the park. When he asked me to marry him, he turned me to face him on the narrow plank seat and told me how proud he would be if I would agree to be his wife. I had said yes so fast that I knew right then and there it was meant to be. I loved him. With this man, I could be filled with love and not feel as if I were drowning.

"I've got to go," I said over the phone. "Someone's here about the case. I'll call you later."

Hanging up, I pretended I didn't hear Phillip saying something as I put the phone in the cradle.

"You up to somting," Lupe noted.

"You are an astute woman, Lupe," Jack added. "Who's Phillip?"

"Hello. None of your business."

Lupe raised a brow. Jack just laughed.

There was silver polish all over the receiver, and rather than have to look at Jack and potentially do the weak-kneed thing, I peeled off the rubber gloves and got a paper towel.

Janice pushed through the door. She stopped when she saw all three of us standing there. "What's going on?"

"Nothing," I said.

"Mees Carlisle talking to feel up."

"Feel up?"

"Lupe, I asked you to keep that to yourself."

She just shrugged.

I turned to my sister-in-law. "Let's not mention this, okay?"

"Sure." She headed for the refrigerator.

The door pushed open again. "What's going on?" Savannah asked, clipping into the room on dainty kitten heels. Though at the sight of Jack she cocked her head in surprise, then made another of her "enemy's lawyer" cracks, adding "engaged" and "unavailable" this time.

Janice stopped and looked back. "Carlisle is doing something with a feel up on the phone, whatever that means."

"Janice!" I said.

"Sorry," Janice explained, "it just came out. Besides, you know how hard it is to keep anything from Savannah. She's like Chinese water torture and the Spanish Inquisition rolled into one. Might as well give in right away and get it over with."

"True. But you, Janice? Giving in to her? I always thought you were stronger than that."

Frankly, she looked disappointed in herself.

I had the sudden thought that Janice's entire existence was being challenged. Moving back to her hometown, her husband constantly working, her daughter wanting to be a debutante, and Janice herself work-

221

ing hard to make the event, well, successful if not overly debutant-ish. She had to be questioning whether all the strides she had made after leaving Willow Creek had been real.

Savannah's smile was wicked. "So, getting a little feel up, I take it?" she asked.

"Lord have mercy," my mother demanded, pushing into the kitchen, "what kind of talk do I hear going on in my very own home?" Then she saw Jack. "What is this? Fraternizing with the enemy?"

Savannah smiled her most wicked smile. "She likes doing that lately."

Mother glared.

"Mrs. Ogden." Jack greeted her with a smile that rivaled Savannah's.

"Carlisle appears to be engaging in phone sex," Savannah went on.

My mother, Savannah, Janice, and Lupe studied me, then glanced at Jack, looking him up and down.

He raised his hands. "Don't look at me. I have nothing to do with this."

"Stop! All of you. Jack, why are you here?" I asked, my jaw tight and starting to ache.

"I just got word that Judge Howard has removed himself from the case."

My mother sighed. "He really was such a nice man."

"He's being replaced by Judge Theodore Weston."

"Oh, my, Theo is lovely. I dated him too, you know."

We all looked at my mother.

"Who haven't you dated?"

She just laughed and flitted away. Lupe, Janice, and my sister followed suit. Jack didn't budge.

"So, tell me, who's this Phillip guy?"

Like I was going to tell him. I might have snorted. I didn't believe for a second that Jack would keep any information I told him a secret. He'd probably use it against me in court. And for the record, my not telling him I was engaged was completely different from his not telling me because mine was actually a secret. Could anyone expect me to tell Jack I was engaged before I had told my own mother?

"None of your business," I said.

"Come on, Cushing," he teased. "We're friends, remember? You can tell me."

Another thing I didn't believe, despite what I had said before, was that we could ever be friends. We had already tried it.

In college, as has been established, my roommate's boyfriend spent an inordinate amount of time at our house, as did his friends. It was the same every time I walked into the kitchen. A shift in the room when Jack looked at me. The completely crazy awareness.

Beyond that, there was something else between us that had always been there. I had kept people, especially guys, locked out. I was not and would never be my mother — I think I've been more than clear on that point. But that first day in high school, then again that day he saved me from Roger Dubac, he had gotten in, even if it was only for a second. No matter how hard I tried to close him out, somehow I couldn't, at least not entirely.

Things changed the day I was alone in the little house just off campus, making a grilled cheese sandwich. Jack showed up at my front door, his motorcycle parked out front. "I left my economics book here yesterday."

That was the thing about him. Massive bad boy who was massively smart. Though most people couldn't see beyond the wildness to what lay beneath it.

He grimaced. "Damn, is something burning?"

No one had ever accused me of being Wolfgang Puck.

I yelped, then wheeled away, but Jack beat me to the kitchen. The cheese from my sandwich had dripped onto the heating element of the toaster oven, a flame starting to spark. Before I could say "Oh, dear," he yanked out the plug, picked up the appliance, and dumped the sandwich into the sink with a sizzle.

Side by side, we stared at my ruined lunch. Then he turned and leaned his hip against the counter. "You want to go to a movie?"

"So much for the expected trajectory of conversation. Are you asking me out?"

"I suppose I am."

A thrill raced through me, which I promptly squelched. "Sorry, no can do. I don't date."

He raked his hand back through his hair. "What does that mean?"

"What's so confusing?"

"I mean, who doesn't date?"

His tone suggested freaks, losers, morons, et al.

"Not everyone is hormone crazy."

I didn't add that I didn't have time. Couldn't afford to get sucked in. Refused to be like all the other girls. The list was long.

I studied him for a second, then couldn't help myself when I blurted, "I suppose I could do friends."

He chuckled grimly and those dark eyes

ran the length of me. My mind started screaming *Danger, Will Robinson!*, but all I could do was smile back.

"Friends, you say?" he said.

"Heck, why not."

"Living on the wild side?"

Based on the hitch in his smile, I was pretty sure his idea of the wild side differed vastly from mine.

Over the next few days we went to the movies, bookstores, the library, all as Friends. Jack seemed fine with the arrangement, if you discounted how every once in a while he would distractedly curl a strand of my hair around his finger or simply stop doing something to study me.

"What?" I'd say.

But he'd just smile, then turn back to his reading.

At least that's how it went until late one night when he walked down the hall to my bedroom and woke me.

"Hey, Jack," I said, my voice rough with sleep. "Is something wrong?"

He sat down on the edge of the mattress. "I don't want to be your friend, Carlisle."

What was I supposed to say? My brain doesn't work all that well in the middle of REM cycles, and it really didn't work well with Jack sitting on my bed with me wanting to forget everything I had witnessed my mother experience with men.

My eyes started adjusting to the dark room and I pushed myself up on the pillows.

I blinked. "Oh, my gosh! You're hurt!"

"It's nothing."

"Nothing!"

I scrambled out the other side of the bed, forgetting that I only wore a T-shirt to sleep in, and turned on the lamp.

"Oh, my gosh!"

"You already said that."

"What happened to you?"

His left eye was red and swollen, and I knew given the rate at which blood coagulated, it would be black and blue by morning. His knuckles looked like ground beef.

He fell back against the mattress and I raced to my bathroom and collected the closest thing I had to medical supplies. I doused a washcloth with water and grabbed a bottle of alcohol. When I got to work, I cleaned him up, then put the alcohol on his knuckles.

He barely flinched, but he closed his eyes. "My brother asked me to go to law school."

I couldn't imagine Jack anywhere near a law school, unless it happened to be next door to a county jail.

"And?"

"And fuck, I owe him."

It was the first time I wondered what it would be like to live in the shadow of someone as legendary as Hunter Blair. Nobody had to tell me how a family member's life could affect you.

"So you were mad you owed him so you got in a fight with him to . . . what?"

He looked at me as if I were crazy. "I didn't fight my brother." He eased back. "I went out afterwards, and some guy started mouthing off . . ." He shrugged, then grimaced in pain. "Shit happens."

He didn't say anything else, just lay there until I thought he was asleep. Not sure what to do, and somehow not able to kick him out, I pulled my comforter over him. When I backed away, he caught my hand and pulled me close.

Oh, dear.

He tugged me down to him. As much as I would like to say that I pulled away, I have always had an out-and-out aversion to lying. He felt hot and cold, and quite frankly, I felt pretty much the same. I told myself we were both coming down with the flu. Probably an epidemic. Good news, I wasn't so delirious that I believed it.

"Jack, this isn't a good idea."

"It's the best idea I've had all night."

"Maybe it doesn't make sense to you, but I have dreams. Goals. But somehow girls get distracted when they fall for a guy." This, however, I believed with all my pounding heart.

Not that this fazed Jack. He ran his fingertips down my arm, and my body started doing crazy things.

"This can't happen," I managed.

"Why?"

I tilted my head back and looked at him. "Ah, because, I've never been kissed before."

That surprised him. "You're kidding. You're in college."

"I've been busy." I sort of smiled. "You know. Those goals."

He hung his head, then chuckled grimly. But when he started to roll away, my fingers curled into his shirtfront.

"Fuck," he whispered, then kissed me.

Given that I had never been kissed before, this wasn't as easy as it sounds.

"Open your mouth, Carlisle," he instructed softly.

And we know I am nothing if not good at taking instruction, at least of the educational sort.

When his tongue touched mine, my body

went crazy. The kiss was slow and deep, hot. I reciprocated, and felt certain, based on his slow deep moan, that I was earning an A, and not just for effort.

His hands explored while I did some investigating of my own. I felt on fire as he pushed up my T-shirt. Yep, I went from never been kissed to getting felt up in one easy step. Clearly I had more of my mother in me than I had bargained for.

He rolled over, his thigh crossing over mine, and when the phone started to ring I barely heard it. He came over me, his shirt long gone, his mouth moving over my skin. But just when I ran my hands up his back, amazed at the feel of hard muscle, my mother's voice came through the answering machine that was beside my bed.

"Where are you, Carlisle?" my mother cried. "Bernard is seeing another woman. You have to help me prove it!" She sniffed back her tears. "We'll take Ernesto's truck over to his house to see who he's with."

I pushed up with a jerk, leaped for the machine, and hit the hang-up button. My mother had always taken great pains to make sure that no one in Willow Creek knew of her completely unacceptable night-time driving and spying habits. Jack and I stared at each other and I could see he was trying to figure out who had called.

"You better go," I told him, pulling my shirt down.

"Carlisle —"

"Really."

I could tell he wanted to ask questions, but really, what was there to say about my mother and her never-ending dramas revolving around men?

Before he could say anything else I pushed him out of the room. "Go, Jack. Just go."

I slammed the door behind him, then fell back at the thought of my mother. But what was I going to do? She was my mother.

In the kitchen I found my keys and I went to Wainwright House. In the dark, we drove to Bernard's apartment building, parked out front, and waited. The only thing that had changed over the years was that I no longer had to sit on a phone book when the time came to drive my mother home.

CHAPTER FOURTEEN

"Orphans?"

Janice and I sat at the kitchen table discussing our progress with the ball when my sister-in-law announced her latest brainchild.

"Yes, orphans," she said. "They are exactly what we need at the Hundredth Annual Willow Creek Symphony Association Debutante Ball."

I stared at Janice in all her relic hippie earth-mother organic wear and could hardly believe my ears, me, the woman who was not all that crazy about deb balls, me, the person who was all about proving I wasn't a piece of fluff like my mother and sister.

"Are you out of your mind?" I bleated.

Yes, me, cool, calm, collected attorney who never ever bleats.

I took a deep breath. In my defense, I would like to say that we had already been at this planning session for the better part of the morning. I'd been through more coffee than was good for a three-hundred-and-fifty-pound man, much less me. I had a buzz that made my nerve endings scream and I had a craving to do violence. "What do orphans have to do with debutante balls?"

"Nothing. Which is the point I have been trying to make for the last hour. Deb balls are worthless."

"Soooo, by bringing orphans to the event it makes them . . . somehow . . . worthy? What are you going to do, bring them along so they can watch? Dress them up in white too? Have them serve as pages? Rub in their faces what they don't have?"

Janice considered, a pencil tapping on her jaw. "Okay, so orphans aren't such a great idea. Even I can't figure out a good way to tie them into the event."

She tilted her head, her eyes narrowing, then said, "I got it!"

Great.

"We'll have each deb wear a sash —"

"Like a Miss America sash?"

"Yeah" — said with a snicker and a sneer — "but instead of listing each state, our sashes will list topics of human rights."

I went back to staring.

Clearly taking my mute state as encouragement, she got into her plan. "One girl will wear 'Slaves.' Another, 'Suffrage.' We can have 'Poverty,' 'Homelessness.' You get the point."

"At the risk of being repetitive, Are you out of your mind?"

Janice considered some more. "Too much?"

A "yes" bubbled up and burst out along with a scoff.

"Okay, how about this," she said. "Each girl stands for a pillar of good. 'Work,' 'Children' —"

"Janice, you are . . . not making sense. This is a debutante ball we're putting on. Remember? Not an activist rally. We are trying to raise money to support the symphony. Not run off the support."

"Err. This whole notion of parading girls to raise money is archaic. I dream about it. I have nightmares about Susan Sontag and Betty Friedan condemning me."

I didn't mention that both women were dead, and even if they weren't, a debutante ball in Willow Creek, Texas, probably wouldn't rate high on their scale of Things in Desperate Need of Their Attention.

"Listen," I said. "No one is going to condemn you . . . unless this turns into a bigger disaster than last year's event. Then your nightmares will be justified." For all of us, but I held that back. "So let's put our brains together and make this work. To do that, even I know we have to adhere to a strict set of rules established by one hundred years of tradition."

Janice looked irritated. "Yeah, rules that caused me no end of grief while I was growing up here."

It was the first time ever I had a hint that Janice wasn't all that thrilled that her father made it big selling nuts, bolts, and metal stuff and she wasn't of the "society" crowd.

"Don't give me that pity look," she snipped. "I was perfectly fine growing up as I did. My past is what got me where I am today. It made me tough and a fighter. I didn't want to be a part of that snobby crowd, but if I diss them, it reeks of sour grapes. If you or anyone else in the crowd disses them, it sounds like you're above it all. I know the difference."

What could I possibly say to that? True? No wonder you won the Pulitzer?

Thankfully, the back door banged open, then footsteps hurried through the mudroom until Savannah burst into the kitchen wearing a raincoat and Jackie O sunglasses despite the muggy and overcast day.

She looked around. "Is anyone else here?" she whispered.

"Just us," I said.

Her eyes went wide. "I'm pregnant!" she announced, tossing her keys and purse on the counter.

Never a dull moment at Wainwright House.

"Pregnant?" I asked.

Janice looked equal parts smug and doubtful.

In case you're keeping track of the timeline, it was barely over a week since the big inappropriate scene at the Willow Creek Country Club. Not that I know a lot about being pregnant (as in nothing) but I couldn't imagine anyone would know so quickly.

"You don't believe me," she said, smiling like a Cheshire cat. "Look at this!"

She whipped off her sunglasses and raincoat to reveal pink flannel pajamas and pink Keds. She tossed the coat aside and rummaged in her oversized purse, producing a plastic Walgreens bag. After an excited look at us, she whipped out a pregnancy kit. "Voilà!"

"But it's still in plastic. Not to be dense, but I'm not getting how this proves you're pregnant."

Savannah headed out of the kitchen. "It won't be in the plastic for long. I'm about to prove I'm with child."

Janice looked at me, then at Savannah's retreating back, before she jumped up. "This I've got to see."

Well, what was I supposed to do? Sit there? I leaped up and followed them.

We hurried upstairs like ducks in a row, racing into my sister and her husband's bedroom suite of tastefully neutral colors, fine fabrics, and magazine-perfect flowers. But when Janice and I got to the bathroom, Savannah slammed the door in our faces.

We looked at each other and shrugged, then started to pace.

"Hurry up in there," Janice called out.

"I'm peeing as fast as I can!"

Finally, we heard the flush, then seconds more passed before the door opened. Savannah's face was white.

"What is it?" Janice asked, her brow furrowed.

Savannah pointed and we saw the stick sitting on the marble counter. "I can't look."

Janice marched in, I followed, and she and I circled around the stick like scientists observing a lab experiment. My sister hung back.

"What does it say?" she asked.

"Nothing yet. It takes two minutes," Janice explained.

Then Savannah surprised me when she rushed forward and took both of our hands. "Wish me luck," she whispered.

My sister, vulnerable? No way. Regardless, my heart suddenly started racing as we watched that stick.

Like magic, two pink lines appeared on the early pregnancy test.

"I knew it!" she shrieked. "Janice, you're a miracle worker! All it took was seducing my husband and the next thing I know I'm pregnant!"

"What's all the noise about?"

My mother stood in the doorway, wearing another lingerie set.

"Mother, I'm pregnant! Isn't it marvelous?"

Our mother appeared perplexed.

Seconds later, Ben walked into the room behind my mother, dressed in what even I knew was his usual attire of blue blazer, white shirt, striped tie, and khaki slacks. He even wore horn-rimmed glasses, and if he hadn't had a distinct Texas drawl he could have passed for a preppy Northeasterner.

"What's going on?" he asked, his sandy hair falling forward.

Before my sister could tell her husband the news, my mother said, "Your wife is pregnant."

Silence.

"Mother!" Savannah whined. "That's my job."

Ben stood stock-still, then sighed and raked his hair back. "But, Savannah, sweetheart, the doctor said —"

"Pooh on the doctors." She sniffed. "I'm pregnant and this time I know it will work."

"This time?" Janice asked. "Have there been problems before?"

Savannah stamped her foot. "Everyone stop this instant! Stop being sticks in the mud." Her bottom lip trembled, then suddenly she smiled wide and clasped her hands. "Did you see that? Mood swings. I'm having mood swings. This is wonderful. Every baby book I've read said that mood swings are a sign of great surging hormones. See, it's going to be fine. My moods are all over the place! And morning sickness. I was sick all morning long!"

Ben didn't look so convinced. "But we talked about adoption."

Back went the mood, and if indeed swings were a sign that all was well, Savannah was on the way to having the healthiest baby ever born in the state of Texas.

I was having a mood swing of my own, from coffee buzz to concern, elation, then back to a concern I couldn't quite get my head around.

"Just stop it, Ben," Savannah said.

Tears started to well up and he relented. The man my sister swore was perfect for her stepped forward and took his wife in his arms. "Don't cry," he said.

My mother shook her head and left the room.

"You're right, it's going to be great." Ben said the words with a firm nod, then suddenly he smiled. "You're right," he repeated, ease coming into his voice. "It is going to be great."

She stayed in his arms for a second, and you could see a visible easing. Then she sprang away. "Oh, my gosh! I have so much to do. The nursery to decorate, names to choose . . ."

My cell phone rang, and thankful for any diversion, I flipped it open. "Carlisle Cushing," I said without bothering to look at the number.

"Carlisle, listen." I knew right away it was Phillip. "Morton Bagwell thinks his wife is cheating on him. But he hasn't been able to prove it."

This was Divorce Law 101. "He needs a PI to tail her."

"He did. But they came up empty-handed."

"Who'd he use?"

"Trotter."

"No wonder. Trotter is worthless."

"He's the best in town."

"Yeah, if you want Internet searches, credit reports, county re-cords, the easy stuff. But when he tails people, they know it."

"No way."

"Yes, way. He's a six-foot-four-inch Russian. He stands out, Phillip."

My fiancé grumbled. "Fine. Then who should I tell Morton to use?"

"Becky Mumps."

"That airhead?"

"She is not an airhead."

He scoffed.

"Fine. Keep using Trotter. But I'm telling you, Becky is the best. She blends in, and even if people notice her they forget her the next second. She doesn't look like someone who'd be tailing you."

I heard Phillip tapping his pencil on his desk. "Okay. What's her number."

I reeled off the number by heart. "Tell her I told you to call."

Another pause.

"I miss you," he said.

Instantly I felt the ease. "I miss you too," I said. "Has your big case started?"

241

"Not yet. Let me come down. Meet your mother. Charm her." I could tell he smiled.

"Right now isn't a good time." Which wasn't a lie.

He hesitated. "Are you embarrassed of me, Carlisle?"

"Oh, my gosh, no!" Guilt kicked at me. "I know you are going to dazzle my mother. But right now, I just hate for you to come down here when she's distracted. That's not how I want things to start off with you two. But soon, Phillip. I promise."

"If you're sure."

"Positive. I love you, Phillip. Really, I do."

CHAPTER FIFTEEN

It had taken an entire week for the Willow Creek court system to come up with a judge who hadn't dated my mother. I walked into Judge Edward Melton's courtroom just as order was called.

"All rise."

The judge entered looking distinguished in his black robes, gray hair, and the kind of sun-kissed skin that looks good on an older man. Not so good, my mother would say, on a woman of any age.

Clearly noticing how handsome the man of law looked, Ridgely stood up straighter than she had in days. Judge Melton caught her eye for a second. Even I could see the spark that flared before he grumbled and glanced away with a jerk. He might not have dated her, but clearly he had heard about her.

"Mother," I hissed.

"What, a woman can't show her appreciation for the male of the species?"

"No, not in court." Though why I bothered I couldn't say. Some of my earliest memories were of my mother flirting in an assortment of inappropriate places — St. James Episcopal Church, the Brightlee tearoom, at old Miss Peter's funeral — like an addict needing her latest fix.

"Be seated," the clerk instructed.

The judge flipped open the file.

"Your Honor," I said, standing.

"Miss Cushing, sit down," he barked. "I am in no mood to hear from you yet."

"Well." My mother sniffed. "I never."

The judge actually blushed before he caught himself, then he grumbled again.

He returned his attention to the file, read, then read some more. You'd think he'd come to class prepared.

Looking up, he slapped the file shut. "Now, Miss Cushing, what did you want?"

"This hearing is a waste of the court's time."

One gray eyebrow rose. "Really? I thought that was my job to determine."

The gallery chuckled.

Jack smiled and ducked his head.

"Now what, pray tell, has brought you to this conclusion, Miss Cushing?"

"Your Honor, there is a prenuptial agreement in place. I see no reason for the court to be involved in this matter. The agreement states very specifically what the terms of divorce are."

Jack stood. "Your Honor, I beg to differ with Miss Cushing. This hearing is scheduled to discuss the veracity of said prenuptial agreement in light of the change in Mr. Ogden's circumstances since his marriage to Mrs. Ogden."

My mother snorted. "As in, for the better."

Jack kept his eye on the judge. "As in, for the worse, Your Honor. Since my client signed the prenuptial agreement, Mrs. Ogden encouraged my client to quit working at the university with the promise, a verbal contract, that she would take care of him."

"Your client was fired, Mr. Blair," I stated calmly, "he did not quit. Any promise my client made was only that of a loving and devoted wife who promised to be there for her fired husband. But Mr. Ogden changed that. He walked out on her, Mr. Blair. Not the other way around. Though this hardly matters given the *prenup* that is in place."

"He did not walk out, Miss Cushing. He was forced to leave for his own mental health."

Forget the judge. I leaned toward Jack. "You can't be serious," I said with the sweetest and most insincere smile I could muster.

"You bet I'm serious."

"You are making a mess of this," I snapped.

"Like I said, messy is good."

"Messy my a—"

"Counselors." The judge broke in with the gavel, cutting me off. "Do . . . whatever it is you are doing on your own time. In my courtroom, you will stick to the relevant issue. Whatever is going on between you two is not relevant."

"You're correct, Your Honor," Jack said evenly. "The only relevant discussion today is in regard to the terms."

"Terms?" my mother asked me, loud enough for everyone to hear. "We've already been over the terms." She glanced at the judge. "They are ridiculous, mind you. Good Lord, he wants to divide the assets. But he doesn't *have* any assets. He wants my assets. Look at him. I paid for everything on his back. And believe you me, he has expensive tastes. Why, look at those shoes. Have you ever heard of spending four hundred and ninety-five dollars on a pair of loafers?"

Even I glanced over at Vincent's feet, the fancy monograms giving the "loafers" away as designer. Men in designer shoes didn't go over that well in this part of Texas, as well my mother knew.

The gallery tutted about the choice of footwear.

Vincent sneered. "Believe me, I paid for everything on my back, if not in cash, then in aggravation by living with you!"

This got an outright laugh. There wasn't a person in the courtroom who didn't know or hadn't heard that Ridgely Wainwright could be a handful.

"You are no bed of roses, sir," Ridgely added.

The judge cleared his throat. "Miss Cushing, please control your client."

Mother glared at him.

"Mother, please."

"Your Honor," Jack interjected, "given the preliminary state of this hearing, I request permission to submit an amendment to our original petition of divorce."

"You can't do that," I stated.

The judge looked as though he agreed. But Jack didn't hesitate.

"Your Honor, it has come to my attention that Mrs. Ogden has not fully disclosed the extent of her estate — most specifically as it applies to Lucky Stars."

My mother turned indignant. "You can't have Lucky Stars! Lucky Stars is mine." She turned to the judge. "It is insane to think this man deserves so much as a blade of grass from my beloved farm."

"Miss Cushing," the judge said ominously, "you will advise your client that when she is addressing this courtroom she is to refer to me as 'Your Honor,' or at the very least, 'Judge.' " He turned to Jack. "And Mr. Blair, let me see your petition."

He read quickly, considered some more, then turned his gaze on my mother. "Mrs. Ogden, your husband is asking for fifty percent of Lucky Stars, Inc., the horse farm establishment at 524 Old Trail Road."

"He can't have it!"

"Miss Cushing," the judge warned me again.

"Mother, please." But my own brain was reeling.

"But he can't," she whispered. "It's covered in the prenuptial agreement."

Which was true, and I had no doubt Jack knew that as well. I glanced over at him. He didn't come in asking for something if he didn't think he had a chance of getting it . . . or getting something else he wanted.

"Your Honor, according to the prenuptial

agreement," I said carefully, giving the date it was signed, "Lucky Stars is precluded, established firmly as property owned before the parties involved were married. Moreover, as noted, the farm was clearly my client's prior to marriage, which according to Texas law is not subject to reversal of decision."

"Your Honor," Jack interjected, "Miss Cushing has failed to consider economic contribution in this case."

My eyes narrowed. "Economic contribution? To what? Contribution to my mother's debts? Contributions to BMW's bottom line?" Sorry, it just came out.

"Miss Cushing," the judge stated. "If Mr. Blair can prove economic contribution to the entity known as Lucky Stars, then all bets are off."

"That is what I intend to prove, Your Honor," Jack supplied. "In fact, it will be made clear that Vincent Ogden has significantly increased the value of Lucky Stars since he started working there —"

"Working there?" my mother blurted. "Last I heard, hanging out and betting on horses wasn't considered a job."

"I worked hard there," Vincent shot back. "And I gave up any chance of getting another teaching position in order to spend my time helping with the farm, making it portable."

Confusion reigned in the courtroom. "Portable?" more than one person asked.

Vincent glanced from person to person. Jack grimaced.

"Portable?" the judge inquired.

Vincent looked at Jack, but Jack was no fool and didn't dare venture anything that might be perceived as coaching.

"Oh! Profitable," Vincent finally interjected.

"Your Honor," I said. "Clearly the man has no idea of what he has or has not done."

"That's right," my mother stated. "On top of that, he never even tried to find another job. He never so much as sent out a single resume or made a single phone call to find alternate employment! I'm convinced you married me so you could spend time with the horses!"

"Better than having to spend time with you!"

"Miss Cushing," the judge blurted out. "Mr. Blair. This is the last time I am going to warn you. Control your clients."

"Mother," I hissed.

"Vincent," Jack added, before readdressing the court. "Your Honor, regardless of what Mrs. Ogden has said, I can prove that

Vincent Ogden's contribution to Lucky Stars added to the farm's value, and as a result, he is entitled to benefit from his efforts."

"Fine, you do that. In the interim, I'm granting a temporary injunction preventing either party from transferring or selling any property until the matter of *Ogden* versus *Ogden* is settled. And based on the financials that have been filed, I order Mrs. Ogden to pay spousal support in the amount requested until an agreement is reached or until the evidentiary hearing. Whichever comes first."

My mother was incensed. I was furious.

"Unless you reach an agreement before then," the judge added, "this court will reconvene in the matter of *Ogden* versus *Ogden* on May first. Court dismissed."

My mother went on and on during the ride home from the courthouse. Ernesto tsked and glared at me, as if it were my fault my mother was upset. I only had a month and a half to work discovery and pull my case together. But I had worked more difficult cases than this in less time. I wasn't worried. It was the debutante ball that gave me pause.

My mother was still carrying on when we

arrived home, the front drive filled with a variety of vehicles that I knew belonged to my tribe of young debs.

They didn't hear me enter for all the laughing. At first I was glad someone was in a good mood. But then I noticed that Betty Bennett was on the verge of tears, her lips quivering.

"What's going on?" I asked in my best lawyer voice.

The laughing cut off as abruptly as Marie Antoinette's head under the guillotine, eyes wide with guilt. I might not have intimidated Jack Blair, but I did a great job with the girls . . . at least all of them but India. No surprise there.

"Betty? What's wrong?"

"I don't know," she stammered, her medusa hair puffed and wild around her head. "Everyone's laughing at me."

I glared at the other girls, then she turned around and I saw piece of notebook paper taped to her back.

Big Bush Betty

I might have taken a step back involuntarily. The meanness of these girls staggered me. Had I been born a male of the species, I might have punched someone. But while I might work hard to not be my mother, I did have two X chromosomes and right then I was just plain mad that girls weren't more supportive of one another.

The front door banged open and Janice marched into the room.

"Sorry I'm late," she stated. "But I found the perfect deb dress."

Janice whipped out a froth of white lace and muslin, high collar and about a thousand tiny lace-covered buttons. "What do you think?"

We all sort of gasped.

"What is that?" India wanted to know.

"India," I admonished. Not that I didn't agree with her question of disbelief.

Morgan scoffed. "Yeah, Mom. What *is* that?"

"Oh, my gosh!" Ruth beamed. "It's beautiful!"

Which goes to show the kind of taste Ruth Smith had.

Janice looked confused, as if she couldn't imagine how anyone could think the froth in her arms wasn't the most beautiful dress ever made.

I had to wonder if Janice was at some level reliving her own past, rewritten as "Janice Reager: Activist Princess." The long dress looked remarkably like something a suffragette would have worn on a picket line — in the 1900s.

My sister-in-law glanced from Morgan to the gown, then back. "It's your debutante dress," she explained, her militant form of enthusiasm waning.

India laughed out loud. "I guess we don't have to worry about Morgan being voted Deb of the Year." She leaned back on the sofa and crossed her legs. "Did I tell you all that my mom and are I going shopping together to find her a dress to wear to the ball? She is totally amazing. She used to be famous in Hollywood."

Not that anyone was listening. By then Janice had noticed the tears on Betty's face.

"What's wrong?" she asked.

Betty turned just a bit, just enough. My sister-in-law's arms fell, crunching the gown when she saw the sign. "Who did this?"

She tossed aside the dress, which barely landed on a beige silk settee, marched over to Betty, and yanked off the piece of paper.

Sue me, but I had planned to discreetly take it off Betty then send her to the bathroom to clean up while I gave the girls a piece of my mind.

"I can't believe you girls would do this!" Janice stated.

Betty started to cry even more when she

saw the whole BIG BUSH BETTY thing. Her face turned bright red, then she ran to the bathroom.

Janice turned wild eyes on Morgan. "I never would have believed a daughter of mine could be part of such a thing."

Morgan looked far from contrite. "Yeah, well, you know me. Always full of surprises." She rose. "And FYI. I'm not wearing that hideous piece of crap you call a dress." Then my niece bolted from the room.

"Morgan," I called after her. "We have a lot to go over."

Janice snatched up the dress and followed.

"Janice!" I called after the mother.

But both were gone, storming up the stairs, each yelling until a door in the distance slammed shut, cutting them off.

Like we had time for this.

I closed my eyes and tried to remember what I was supposed to be imaging to calm myself. An ocean? A meadow? A ballroom filled with five hundred of Willow Creek's finest all turning out to witness these girls make their entrance into society? Obviously that was not on the serenity-approved list since my blood pressure made my ears ring.

I turned back to the girls, determined to do the adult thing — at least with regard to Betty. "How would you feel if someone put a sign like that on you all?"

India smirked. "As if. Though is anyone surprised that Betty is a loser given her mother? Hello? Did you see those totally insane braids she wrapped around her head at the introduction meeting? Where is she from? Planet Alps?"

Tiki and Abby laughed until I glared.

"Oh, sorry," India said, without an ounce of contrition. "If you really want to 'talk' about this, then you should ask your question of someone who would know." She turned to Sasha. "Tell us, how do you feel when people call you 'stuck up' or 'prude'?"

Sasha's face went white, then red. "Get real, India. If I was such a prude, Tommy Brown wouldn't have come over to my house last night begging me to take him back."

And the red face goes to India.

But I underestimated the girl. "Like I care about two losers ending up together. He is totally idiotic and I told him so."

My head started to throb and I had never been so thankful as when Betty returned.

"Everyone, just shut . . . stop talking," I ground out with a frustrated sigh. I still held my briefcase in front of me. "I guess we should go ahead and get started."

India interrupted. "So, Miss Cushing,"

she said, giving me a sly look. "I heard you fell or something when you were a deb? What's up with that?"

My briefcase dropped to the floor. What was I going to say? With the unfortunate exception of the fake me in Boston, I really did feel that honesty was the best policy. Besides, it wasn't a big secret. Unfortunately.

I raised my chin. "When I made my bow, I fell."

The girls gasped.

"Oh, man!"

"You're kidding!"

"Totally no fun!"

India looked me over with not a little disdain. "Maybe we should have put a loser sign on you."

I forced back the burn of embarrassment with sheer willpower.

"How did you fall, Miss Cushing?" Ruth asked.

"When I was doing the Dip."

India laughed out loud.

"Enough about me, girls. We really need to practice How to Carry Yourself."

Which made India laugh even harder. "Are you sure you're qualified?"

No. But I didn't tell her that.

To my credit, I had gone to the library

and filled my little black book with copious details on comportment, and launched into credible explanations of how to enter the room, how to speak eloquently, and the tone in which a lady spoke. Though why I bothered to discuss the topic was anyone's guess.

"Why in the world would I want to *not* be noticed?" India wanted to know.

"That's not what I said. The point is that you don't want to demand attention by being loud or dressing loudly. It is through quiet confidence and inner beauty that you can truly be noticed."

Okay, so it sounded sappy even to me.

"Give me a break," India said.

Ruth shrugged. "I tend to agree with India, Miss Cushing. While I don't advocate making a spectacle of oneself, even I know that sitting around like a wallflower isn't a plus in this day and age. Maybe in your day . . ." She considered. "Nah. You might be old, but not old enough to be around when Betty Crocker was a big hit. No, even you should know that we have to scream our accomplishments."

My brain churned for a decent response.

"Then you're saying *loud* is good?" Nellie asked, confused as she smoothed her already smooth skirt.

"Loud, quiet, I don't care," Ruth continued, taking control. "But you better be out there letting people know all the good things you're doing. And if you aren't doing good things, then you better start . . . or spin stuff so it sounds good."

Spin? In high school they were already thinking about spin?

Sasha blinked like a mad person. "We should lie?"

Ruth shrugged. "What's a lie?"

"A lie is a nontruth," I said, cutting off the conversation. "It's not my job to teach you morals or ethics. I just have to get you through one night acting like something approximating a lady of good breeding."

"Old-fashioned breeding."

"Fine. Old-fashioned breeding. Call it what you want. I don't care. Please just follow the rules for this one night. That's all I ask. Then you can go back to hiking up your skirts, screaming out your accomplishments, and slathering on makeup like plaster on a wall."

Nellie's eyes went wide.

I cringed.

"Sorry," I said. "I've had a long day. Let's pick up with introductions tomorrow."

Chapter Sixteen

While Janice maintained a strange determination that her daughter wear the godawful suffragette gown, as if this would somehow prove Morgan wasn't an insipid conformist, Savannah had started obsessively preparing for the arrival of her child.

Benjamin Wainwright Carter if it was a boy.

Benita Wainwright Carter if it was a girl.

I wasn't crazy about either name, but was smart enough to keep my opinions to myself.

I worked in the small study next to the nursery, pulling together my case. Working in such close proximity to the next room, I found it impossible to ignore the complete redo that even I knew had been completely redone a year earlier the last time Savannah had been pregnant. I'm not certain, but I don't think Savannah had entered the room since the day she miscarried. How Janice didn't know all this was beyond me, though Henry had rarely brought his family back to Texas until their unexpected return.

When Savannah wasn't decorating, she was listening to Mozart, reading inspiring stories aloud, all directed at her belly and the baby growing inside her. She shopped for baby clothes, put Benjamin/Benita on waiting lists for all the right schools, debated disposable diapers against washable diapers and diaper services. If ever there was a prepared mother, Savannah was going to be it.

It was late morning when I realized that all had gone quiet in the house. Standing up from the desk, I walked the few steps down the hall into the baby's room. Savannah had fallen asleep in the rocker, a copy of *Peter the Rabbit* resting on the tiny bulge in her stomach. I was reminded of just how pretty my sister was, and that when I was growing up how kind I had always thought she was whenever she was asleep, and how surprised I'd always been when she woke up and wasn't.

Tiptoeing across the carpet, I gently took the book away and set it on the white dresser. A tiny book with a latch key caught my eye. It was the sort of diary girls keep when they are young.

I heard Savannah move.

"What are you doing?" she snapped with a sleep-roughened voice.

"Just putting the book away before it fell."

Then I couldn't help it. "You still keep a diary?"

She reached up and snatched it away from me. "Yes. Do you have a problem with that?"

"Well, no. I'm just surprised."

Though why I should be was anyone's guess. Savannah had been writing in a diary for as long as I could remember.

The next day, UPS arrived with a load of boxes. Savannah dove in, pulling out the fanciest baby bedding you have ever seen. Stunningly beautiful white silk shams with borders and coverlets.

"You know," I said (my brain actually screaming for me to stop while I was ahead), "seems like baby bedding that needs dry cleaning isn't all that practical."

You'd have thought I'd told her she would have an ugly child.

"Why can't you just be supportive!" she cried.

Truth to tell, I wondered the same thing. What did I care that the bedding belonged on a pampered woman's bed when she was, say, sixty-five, postsex (unless she was my mother) or anything else that might mess up the linens?

"I'm sorry, Savannah. It's beautiful, really."

Janice was in the kitchen when I went downstairs. She sat at the table looking glum.

"What's wrong?"

"Morgan doesn't like the dress."

Fresh off the debacle with my sister, I managed to swallow back a less than kind *No one liked the dress.* Unless you counted Ruth.

"I know what you're thinking," she said.

"You do?"

"Yes, that it's beautiful, but not right for Morgan and I shouldn't be making her wear something that you and I both know would be stunning at an event like this."

"Ah, something like that."

"Even after four kids, I still need a manual."

Noise erupted upstairs. After a moment of listening, Janice leaped up and raced to the foyer. Assuming this meant it was an emergency, I followed and found Lupe muttering some very unflattering Spanish. Ernesto kept saying "Ah, Dios."

"What's going on?" Janice wanted to know.

"Is Mother all right?" I asked.

"You mother ees no here."

I realized it was Wednesday at noon, reminding me that since I had been home my mother was never home on Wednesdays at noon.

"Where is Savannah?" I probed.

"*Hijole.* Mees Savannah ees upstairs and no ees happy."

Janice and I bolted up the stairs, Lupe following at a more se-date pace. At the top we found Cinco in the hallway looking like his usual food-stained self, though uncharacteristically stressed. The little princess, Priscilla, just tsked and said in a singsong voice, "Someone's in trouble."

Savannah stood in the doorway to the nursery fit to be tied. "It's ruined," she cried.

"Oh, great," Janice muttered like a mother who knows one of her children has done something wrong.

I saw the grape juice stains all over Cinco and shuddered to think of grape juice and all that white silk in the nursery.

With no help for it, I followed Janice into the room, expecting a new purple and white design. But purple wasn't the problem.

Two-year-old Robbie had crawled into the baby bed and was sound asleep. There was no grape juice stain, no ruined anything as far as I could see. I turned to look at my sister, and just before I started to say something, the smell finally registered in my brain.

"PeeU!" the little princess squealed with a laugh. "Robbie made a stinky!"

On closer inspection, underneath the little angel, the white silk was decidedly yellow. Even a little brown had seeped from young Robbie's nether regions.

I admit it, I sort of gagged.

"It's ruined," Savannah cried again.

Janice's reaction was the strangest thing I had ever seen. She was militant, no question, but underneath her brusque "Calm down, Savannah," I swear her face was red.

Our sister-in-law marched to the crib, leaned down, hauled out her toddler (who never woke up), and departed, her troops following in the rear. "I'll pay for the mess," she said from the bedroom down the hall where I could hear her changing Robbie.

Savannah stared at the brown stain. "It's all ruined," she whispered.

"Nothing is ruined," I said, "except some ridiculous baby bedding. You'll get new sheets."

"But he ruined it."

"Savannah, he's a child. I'm no expert,

but it seems to me that's what kids do. Are you sure you want kids?"

She wheeled around to face me. "Of course I do."

"Fine. Then go to Wal-Mart or Target or regular old Baby World and get some washable baby bedding. Again, I'm no expert, but I think you've just had your first lesson in what it's like to be a mom."

The doorbell rang but my sister and I didn't budge, our eyes locked. Yes, me, Miss Has No Children of Her Own but Acts Like an Expert.

The bell rang again.

"That will be the girls with their escorts," I said. "I better go."

Downstairs, I found Janice, with Robbie still in her arms sucking his thumb, staring at our guests in the receiving room. The sight of said guests made me wish I had been born to a poor mother on the wrong side of the tracks who had never heard of a debutante ball. If we had second-rate girls, they had managed to produce fourth-rate boys.

My mother walked in, shuddered at the look of them, boots scuffed and dirty, hats still on in the house. Not one of them stood when the ladies walked into the room.

"We're doomed," she muttered.

I couldn't believe it. How was it possible that this confident girl, raised in this modern world of equality, could fall back into insecurity when meeting a boy? Did hormones get in the way and make her forget who she was? Or was it that we all wrap ourselves up in the trappings of a life we have created, relying on what we build to provide our confidence? When India met someone new, someone not from her world, did she feel vulnerable?

I wondered suddenly what would happen if you stripped my mother of her wealth and her beauty. When she was taken down to her soul, who would she be?

Was I afraid to add the trappings of beauty, wealth, and men to my life for fear that the dormant gene I had felt when I was younger with Jack would resurface and I would lose myself?

It was all way too Self-help for me. I shook the confusion away and concentrated on the girls.

The other intros went much the same. Morgan looked on with suspicion at her escort, as did her mother. But I had worked hard to find a boy who would be intriguing enough for my niece and acceptable to my sister-in-law. Derek Clash was better looking than Gary, though without an ounce of pretty boy in him. Plus he was editor of the academy's student newspaper.

I'm no dummy.

The only other girl who had taken a good deal of consideration was Betty. Not only was it important to make the right match, but I wanted her to have one. When I introduced her to Thurmond "Bud" Thomas they both blushed, but couldn't take their eyes off each other.

"Thank you for coming. I hope each of you received the instruction sheet that I faxed over to Colonel Winters."

"Yes, ma'am," they stated.

Not a "yo" or "dude" in the bunch.

"Then you know that you will be wearing your dress uniform when you escort the girls."

"Yes, ma'am."

"Today we are going to practice the presentation and the waltz. Let's start with the waltz."

Janice and I lined the couples up, facing each other in a straight line down the room, the carpets rolled back.

I explained the formal, three-step movement, then grabbed Janice and said, "Let's show them how this is done."

"Me?"

My sister-in-law looked horrified and I realized she must not know how to waltz since I couldn't imagine that she was shy.

"Janice," I hissed, though my smile was so wide my mother would have been proud.

With a jerk of her arms, she brought them up.

"Here, let us show you."

Which was a gigantic mistake since the two of us did little besides step on each other's toes until we had the whole group laughing.

"What is this?" India scoffed. "Some demented dance school for debutantes?"

Funny. Or not.

"Good," I improvised, "we wanted to put everyone at ease. Now it's your turn."

The laughter cut off sharply.

Despite the return of terror, they did as instructed, but truth to tell, they were no better than their instructors. The only two who managed not to maim each other were Betty and Bud. Who would have thought?

"This isn't going well," Janice said; unnecessarily, I might add.

Then I remembered something.

"I'll be right back!"

I dashed out of the front room, up the stairs, then up another set of stairs to the attic. The mix of cedar closets, stale air, and heat hit me in the face. But I persevered since I knew that my mother never threw anything away.

I rummaged around until I found what I was looking for. As I raced back downstairs, dust floated in my wake, enough so that when Lupe returned and came out of the kitchen just as I made it downstairs, she went on and on about what a mess I was making.

I stopped on a dime, kissed her cheek, and said, "I'm teaching them to dance!"

The kiss did it. She grumbled, said some of her infamously uncomplimentary Spanish, but this time she was smiling as she shooed me toward my mission.

"Violà!" I announced, flipping out a thin rubber sheet that looked not so unlike a Twister mat, only significantly smaller, rectangular instead of square, and with two sets of footprints on it instead of round multicolored circles. Okay, so not like a Twister mat. Anyway . . .

I let it float to the ground, and everyone came closer.

"It shows the steps," Morgan said.

"Awesome," Tiki added.

"Exactly. For both the girl and the boy. Who wants to go first?"

India normally would have wanted to show off, but today she hung back.

"Morgan?" I asked.

"Sure. Why not."

She grabbed her escort's hand (clearly she wasn't shy) and stood on the girl's side. Derek stood opposite her.

"Now," I said. "Give it a try."

They did. And didn't do badly; that is, if you don't mind watching two people dance like automatons, their heads bent (not in prayer, though maybe, but in an intense need to make sure their feet were following the pattern).

"Step, step, together," I encouraged, clapping my hands in a three-step beat.

Once they got that down, I added, "Now, look up."

They did, then practically killed each other when their legs tangled and they fell to the floor. Janice gasped. Fortunately our cadet was nimble and he caught himself, on top of Morgan, but not crushing her. And let me just say that when their eyes met it was a shock felt around the world. Okay, around the room. But still. Her mother was there!

Morgan blushed, as did Derek, and they hastily rolled apart.

"Next!" I called out.

One by one we went through all the couples, until each of them could dance

275

without hurting the other.

"You'll need to practice on your own."

Morgan looked at Derek.

"How about tonight?" he said.

"Sure," was the breathy response.

"Great!" Janice enthused in a way that I knew wasn't enthusiastic at all. "Tonight, here. Let's say seven. Does that work for everyone?"

Morgan shot her mother a genuinely unenthusiastic scowl, and probably would have said, "Mother," with that teenage disdain, had there not been an audience.

No one else could make it.

"Then it will just be the three of us," Janice added.

"Great," Morgan said with a groan.

Janice put her arm around the boy in his starched khaki uniform, and led him off, but not before we heard the grilling.

"Tell me, Derek, what are your thoughts on dentists?"

"Dentists?" he asked.

"And pets. Have you ever felt any compunction to hit, maim, or kill small animals?"

He looked as if he thought she might hit, maim, or kill him.

"And your parents? Have either of them ever done time in prison?" she added just as she pushed open the kitchen door. "Lupe? Is there any lemonade for this boy?"

Morgan and I exchanged a glance of the "Is She Insane?" variety. But Morgan wasn't my daughter, ergo, none of my business. If she wasn't allowed to date yet (hello, Janice, she's eighteen) who was I to make judgments. Plus, who was I to say anything about starting to date late. Besides, there was the whole thing re: Morgan getting kicked out of all those schools. Perhaps her mother had good reason to keep a tight leash on her daughter.

"God," India said, coming up beside Morgan and me. "I would die if I had a parent who acted like that." India looked at my niece with grave sympathy. "You must be so embarrassed."

Morgan didn't look like she knew what to think.

"Thank God, my dad would never embarrass me like that," India added, as she headed for the door. "Girls," she called out to the Entourage. "Time to go."

CHAPTER SEVENTEEN

The next day I woke up in my childhood white eyelet canopy bed with a bad case of regression \re-gres-sion\ n (c1600) 1: reverting to previous behavior patterns 2: a return to a less complex or less perfect state of being 3: waking up out of breath after dreaming I had missed my calculus test because I was too busy standing in the main school hallway. Naked. And let me just say, my family does a lot of things, but we don't do naked.

I repeated over and over again that I was no longer sixteen and had never ever been caught in any hallway, at least naked. But that didn't assuage the fear that I was slowly spiraling back into Little Carlisle Cushing of Willow Creek, Texas, daughter of the outrageously fabulous Ridgely Wainwright.

During the previous few days, I had spent hours working on my mother's case, answering e-mail from the office back in Boston, and working with Phillip on the phone providing detailed instructions as to how he could help Morton further with his own divorce. Becky Mumps had proven the perfect choice, providing all the dirt Morton needed to prove his wife was cheating on him. If I closed my eyes, I could almost pretend I was back in Boston with Phillip holding my hand, laughing together as we made dinner and discussed our latest cases.

Still groggy with sleep, I rolled over and picked up the phone, dialing Phillip's number at the office, needing to hear his voice.

It was early, but he was already at his desk.

"Hey," I said when he picked up.

"Hey?"

"Sorry, it's a Texas thing. Good morning. How are you?"

I heard the familiar sound of his chair creaking as he leaned back. "I'm good now that you've called."

Smiling, I curled down into all that white eyelet. "Do you ever wonder if you're on the right track in your life?"

He hesitated. "Where did that come from?"

"I don't know. Just wondering if I'm doing the right things. Making the right decisions."

"Carlisle, are you all right?"

I could hear the concern in his voice and suddenly I felt myself ease completely, remembering why I wanted to marry him. I drew a deep breath then exhaled slowly. "I am now," I answered truthfully.

"You're sure?"

"Yes. I just had a bad dream."

"If you were here, I could have held you until you felt better."

"That would have been nice," I murmured, imagining the feel of his arms wrapped around me, holding me through the night whenever I needed to feel that I wasn't alone. He might wake up in the morning with a sore arm, but he never once pulled away.

"If you're sure, then I'm glad," he said. "Tell me, are there any new developments with your mother's divorce?"

I would have loved to talk to him about my mother's case, but he still didn't know she had any money. Which made it a little on the difficult side to discuss.

"No, nothing new." Other than that Jack was trying to take my mother to the cleaners.

"What's all that noise?" Phillip asked.

I became aware of banging coming from

outside, obviously being amplified over the phone.

"I'm not sure. And as much as I hate to go, I better. I have tons to do today."

"Okay. We'll talk later, then?"

"Absolutely. And Phillip?"

"Yes?"

"Thanks."

There was a slight pause, a comfortable pause. "We make a good team, Carlisle."

"Yeah, I know."

I hung up then rolled out of bed, the dreams of the night before dissipated. It didn't take me long to get ready then make my way downstairs.

"Coffee?" I said, just as Lupe extended a perfectly made cup in my direction. "Bless you."

"You welcome."

Lupe went about her work in the kitchen.

"Who's making all the noise?" I asked.

"Cinco."

I glanced toward the window. "What's he doing?"

"He making bike-cleaning business. He finding Weendex, rags, bucket to take around neighborhood and clean bikes." She looked impressed. "He make people pay feety cents for clean bike."

"Who's going to pay a ten-year-old to

281

clean their bike?"

Lupe scowled at me. "Bah. You have no faith. People good. People pay to be nice to boy."

For the record, it hadn't gone unnoticed by me that Lupe had developed a soft spot in her cagey and callous heart for my young nephew.

"I hope you're right," I added, pouring myself some more coffee, then went back upstairs and got back to work.

On the debutante ball front, I had hired the caterer, planned the menu, found an event planner who would decorate Symphony Hall for cost and a mention in the ball brochure. I could check off teaching the waltz (though practice the waltz was still there). I ran a line through "Find Escorts."

My ball to-do list was getting chiseled away.

Next priority was getting Morgan a new dress. Janice had suggested the three of us go together to Michel's House of Brides on Pine Avenue, a quaint white clapboard shop that had once been a home. The front yard was perfectly kept, and the house had royal-blue window boxes filled with red geraniums that matched the royal-blue window awnings and the front door. The shop catered to brides, bridesmaids, debutantes, mothers of the bride, and any other sort of woman who needed a formal gown.

Morgan didn't look happy when we pulled up, and Janice's smile was forced as we entered and went through rack upon rack of long white dresses. A saleswoman tried to help, but had been around enough brides- and debutantes-to-be and quickly left us alone.

For every form-fitting gown Morgan loved, Janice found a current-millennium-challenged monstrosity. I braved a suggestion or two, but decided I preferred my status as cool aunt and tolerable sister-in-law to what I quickly realized was devolving into my becoming a pariah to both parties. I'd let them slug it out between themselves.

I had just planted myself in a chair and had picked up a copy of *Insights* magazine (it was that or *Modern Bride,* which I really wasn't in the mood for) when the velvet curtains leading to the back room parted and a tall stack of gift boxes appeared, being carried by someone I couldn't see.

The boxes teetered, and I leaped forward to help.

"Thanks for the save."

It was Ruth.

"Miss Cushing!" The girl dropped the

load on the floor. "What are you doing here?"

Ruth stood stock-still, her practical clothes dusty and wrinkled. Her mouth opened and closed but she didn't utter another word.

"Is something wrong?" I asked.

"With me?" She made a big exaggerated snort. "No way. I'm great. I was . . . just leaving. See ya!"

Sure enough she bolted, leaving the boxes in a tumble at my feet. But she didn't depart through the front door. She disappeared into the back.

Curious, I followed and found her pacing in the storage room where it looked as if she had been cleaning.

"Ruth, do you work here?"

The sensible girl whom Janice admired stopped pacing, and I could see the gears churning in her brain. After a second she nodded authoritatively.

"Yes, as a matter of fact, I do work here. I found myself with some free time and knew that a job would be just the thing to punch up my college applications."

One, at this late date I suspected she had already gotten into college. And two, even if for some reason she hadn't, I doubted a cleaning girl at a dress shop would do much punching.

"Ruth, if you need someone to talk to —"

"Miss Cushing, I'm fine. Now, I've got to get back to work."

In quick order she returned to the showroom and cleared up the boxes, then put away the broom and cleaning supplies. But when she was done, she took her punch card and checked out. "I'm starved," she exclaimed and rushed from the store.

I was given no time to digest what had just happened before the bell over the entrance rang again and in walked Betty with her mother.

"Carlisle," Merrily exclaimed, wearing some sort of blue tent dress, her swollen feet shoved into blue patent leather shoes. "How are you, darlin'? You look good, you do. I'm here with Betty. She made me come, though I told her I was making the perfect dress."

I wasn't sure what to say, not that Merrily gave me a chance.

"But I gave in and here we are," she added. "If she can find something here that will make her happy" — she shrugged — "well then, what am I going to do?"

I ended up following them back to the fitting room where the saleslady brought several gowns for Betty to try on.

Both Betty and Morgan tried on gown

after gown, Morgan ruling each one out for herself, Merrily ruling them out for Betty.

Clearly excited, Betty emerged from the fitting room in yet another gown, but Merrily's brow creased. "Good Lord, child, what are you thinking? I will not have a daughter of mine dressed like a . . . floozy."

Just so you know, the dress Betty wore was a puff of taffeta and lace that would be hard-pressed to make anyone look like a floozy, or even desirable.

Betty looked dejected. "But Mama —"

"No buts, missy. I will not let you fall into the trap of being like all these girls without an ounce of decorum. Paris what's-her-name and that Jessica Simpson. It's a disgrace, I tell you. A disgrace that those little girls are allowed to parade around like nobody's business. And the Simpson girl a daughter of a preacher."

"Mama —"

"Don't you dare talk back to me, young lady. If I've told you once, I've told you a thousand times, pretty is as pretty does. You are a daughter of a decent, God-fearing family and you will conduct yourself as a child with high moral values. Now get out of that dress, it's time to go home. I'll wait for you in the car."

Janice, seeming confused by the interaction, watched the other mother depart, then she turned away and sorted through the racks with renewed purpose. Betty kept looking wistfully at herself in the mirror, the long lace sleeves and high lace bodice giving way to a taffeta skirt so full I suspected she had hoops and crinolines underneath.

"Here," Janice said to her daughter with determination. "Try this one on."

Morgan looked on the verge of mutiny but did as she was told.

The bell at the front of the store rang again, followed by a second of silence.

"Hello. Am I supposed to wait on myself?" India.

She strolled into the back area wearing a neon ruffled blouse, tight designer jeans, high-heeled platform shoes, and a Gucci bag. Morgan came out of the fitting room, her face set in grim lines, though I wasn't sure if it was about the dress or the arrival of India. Betty looked ecstatic about the new arrival.

"Hi, India!" she said, beaming.

"What is this, a party?" India asked, ignoring Betty and giving Morgan the once-over. "Tell me you're not planning to wear that dress."

"India," I stated.

"Well, excuse me," Morgan said, holding her arms out, displaying the gown. "She's right. This dress is hideous."

India smirked, then walked over and started looking through the gowns.

"I thought you already had a dress," I said to her.

"Of course. My dad took me to New York to get my dress. At Saks Fifth Avenue. I will totally rock. I'm here because I'm meeting my mom to find her a dress."

"Really?" we all asked.

"Yes," she snapped, then turned to the racks. She flipped through the gowns, her hot-pink nails glittering in the overhead lights as she pulled out a silk and lace cap-sleeved dress that was nice though certainly not a stunner. "Here, Morgan," she said, "this will look great on you."

But Morgan had found a dress on her own. "Oh, my gosh!" She whipped out a gown. "This is the one!"

She raced into the fitting room and returned seconds later. "It's perfect! I love it!"

"Gosh, Morgan," Betty said. "It's amazing."

Morgan stood on the small dais in front of a full-length mirror in a truly stunning gown. I'm not that big into fashion, but I'd say it was a cross between Oscar de la Renta and a bit of Vera Wang, and was surprisingly demure. The sleeves were long, the neck high, with a fitted bodice in white silk satin that flowed into a long sweeping satin skirt. Somehow the gown managed to make Morgan look both young and sophisticated, sexy even, without showing much skin.

Morgan swept from side to side, gazing at her reflection. I had a sense that my niece was startled by what she saw, not sure how to absorb this new Morgan.

Janice pressed her hand to her mouth. "Oh, baby," she breathed. "It is perfect."

The mother and daughter who before had hardly been on speaking terms actually smiled at each other. Though barely. A step in the right direction.

India's cell phone rang, playing a song that sounded suspiciously sentimental. When she glanced at the readout, her eyes went wide.

"Mom?" the girl sort of squeaked. "Where are you?"

Her face glowed. She was breathless and excited as she listened to whatever her mother said.

We all watched, like watching a play, until India's smile started to fade and I would swear her eyes glistened with tears. "But you promised," she said, turning her back to us. "We were going to find you a dress today."

Janice's brow creased. I felt a strange lump in my throat. Morgan looked on with concern.

"All right. I understand. But you promised you'll be at the ball, right?"

Still more listening, before India nodded. "Okay, that's good."

As soon as she flipped her phone shut, we whirled around, pretending to be engrossed in gown selection. But the strange lump I felt wouldn't go away, even when India narrowed her gaze on Morgan and snapped, "Your dress is way too big."

We focused on my niece.

"That dress," India clarified, pointing at Morgan. "It's like a whole size too big. It'll look hideous on stage."

"It is?" we asked.

Though when I looked closer, I saw that the bodice did look loose, the shoulders extending beyond Morgan's.

We looked at the saleswoman for guidance.

"Yes," she conceded, nervous about not getting her sale. "It should fit better. Let me see if I can find the smaller size."

The saleswoman disappeared through a curtained doorway and we could hear her pick up the phone and dial.

Morgan looked crushed, and while I could see the dress actually was too big, I had to wonder if India's concern was genuine.

"Maybe it could be altered," I suggested.

"You don't want to alter a dress a whole size," India said. "It'll look even more hideous. And I know that dress has been here for a while, so I doubt you'll find it anywhere else."

"I found it!" the saleswoman added, rushing back. "There's only one in her size and it's in Dallas, but I found it!"

For a second, I thought India looked furious. But when I looked closer, she just smiled. "It's going to be perfect, Morgan!"

Janice paid for the gown and left her phone number so the saleswoman could call when it came in. As we were walking out, Janice slipped her arm around Morgan's shoulder. It was awkward, no question, but I saw the emotion that flared in India's eyes at the sight.

I felt like the knot in the middle of a tug-of-war rope, one second being pulled toward being suspicious of India, the next being pulled toward feeling sorry for her.

"I've got to go," she said abruptly.

Truth to tell, I was glad to see her disappear as my rope was getting frazzled. Not that this was about me, but really, one of the reasons I was cut out for the law was that I didn't allow myself to get all emotional over other people's problems. Which reminded me that I seemed to have done nothing but get involved in other people's problems since I crossed the state line.

By the time Janice, Morgan, and I pulled up to the house we were feeling pretty good. But inside, a concerned Lupe offered a dejected-looking Cinco a tall glass of chocolate milk.

"What happened?" I asked.

"Meester Cinco, he no find jobs."

Janice strode forward and ruffled his hair. "I told you no one would pay to have their bikes cleaned, sweetie."

Savannah pushed in wearing a gossamer robe fluttering with boa trim. "What's going on here?"

"Cinco went door to door trying to make money by cleaning bikes," Janice explained.

"That's ridiculous," Savannah announced.

Great. Salt to the wound.

Lupe glared at her, though, as always, it was wasted energy.

Cinco took a dejected sip of chocolate milk. "It's okay. I don't care."

Savannah marched forward. "It's ridiculous because no one around here owns a bike." She snorted. "Everyone around here is old."

Cinco looked up, confused.

"You should have come to me. There are three bikes out in the storage bin that need to be cleaned." She looked at him. "But really, does anyone think that I have time to clean a bike? No, no, no. So a bike cleaner is just what I need."

"Really?" Cinco's eyes went wide.

"Of course, really. Come on."

They headed out, Cinco in cargo shorts, T-shirt, and baseball cap, Savannah in pink gossamer and feathers. Had I not been there to witness the scene, I never would have believed it.

"Mees Savannah. Being nice." Lupe shook her head and snorted. "Always surprises around here."

Janice stood staring at the door in surprise. And if surprise was the emotion of the hour, then sheer unadulterated shock followed on its heels when Savannah returned to the kitchen, cobwebs in her hair.

"He's set up outside with the bikes," she explained.

She stopped when she noticed that everyone was staring at her. "What?"

But she didn't wait for an answer. She marched out of the kitchen, trailing dust and cobwebs in her wake.

Amazingly, when all was said and done, Savannah doled out a dollar fifty per bike. The only person in Wainwright House who wasn't surprised by this was Cinco, as if it never occurred to him that his massively spoiled prima-donna aunt wouldn't be nice.

But if anyone thought that Savannah's bout of niceness would translate across the board, they were sadly mistaken.

"Where are my sunglasses?" she demanded the next day, marching into the kitchen. "One of those rugrats has taken them. I know it."

"Mees Savannah ees back," Lupe announced.

CHAPTER EIGHTEEN

Whenever I wanted time to pass quickly in my life, the minutes seemed to slog by like molasses in the freezing cold, the days creeping forward with the hesitancy of a deer peeking out of the woods. Whenever I needed more time for something, the minutes swept by like the hands on a funhouse clock and the days bolted forward like a deer flushed out of the dense greenery in hunting season. As the debutante ball approached, the days passed with dizzying speed. Before I knew it, the girls' individual deb parties were upon us like the rains of Kuala Lampur, moving in to wreak havoc with the topsoil of people's lives and emotions, and pretty much make everyone go crazy.

No one had been surprised when India insisted on being first to have her party.

Her extravagant invitation of ecru linen with gold engraving and satin tassel arrived the requisite two weeks prior to the event. I was more relieved than impressed that she was starting off on the right foot. Fingers crossed that there would be no replay of my very first foray into Blair entertaining.

True to her announcement that first day she arrived in my mother's kitchen with her trailing Entourage, she was taking all of the debutantes, their parents, and a few other assorted VIPs to dinner in Manhattan — and not Manhattan, Kansas.

"I am most certainly not going to New York City," my mother stated from her bed, a breakfast tray with fine bone china off to the side. "The notion is absurd."

In the Reasons Not to Go category, I could think of several excuses \ex-cus-es\ n pl (19c) 1: Who had the time 2: April in New York could still be cold 3: Flying up and back in a day sounded like more trouble than it was worth. But my mother's "The notion is absurd" seemed more a generic answer along the lines of "Because I said so," or a cover for "No way no how am I going anywhere with India Blair and her family."

"If you don't go," I cajoled, taking a bite of her croissant slathered with imported rouge jam, "then it appears you don't approve."

"I don't approve, certainly not of a flashy affair put on by a tacky girl who doesn't know the first thing about being a lady."

I dropped the bread back to the plate. "That isn't the point. It isn't about what you do or don't feel for the girls; it's about showing support for the hundredth annual ball founded by your family. Appearances, Mother. Something you taught me at your breast."

She waved the word away. "Don't use such language."

"What? Breast?"

She shook her head and turned away. My mother — the woman who had been married more times that I'd had dates — the prude.

"Fine. You taught me about appearances from the time I was born. Better?"

She glared. "All right, I'll go. But only for our family name."

The Blairs loaded up the eight girls and their parents, all eight escorts, a military academy chaperon, assorted guests, my mother, and me onto two planes. A Gulfstream IV and a 737 with BLAIR AIR painted across the side. Three and a half hours later, dressed in our finery, we landed at a small airport in New Jersey called Teterboro, then were transported into Manhattan on a plush bus that wound its way into the city through the Lincoln Tunnel.

As promised, we arrived in Midtown at seven o'clock and were whisked up to the top floor of Blair Tower where we walked into an extravagant display of champagne fountains, ice sculpture, coffee-table-book-worthy food, and the spectacle of city lights spread out before us like diamonds on black velvet.

"Hmph," my mother said.

"Is that a good 'hmph' or a bad 'hmph'?" I asked.

"It's impressive," she admitted. "Though it seems a terrible extravagance for a teen-age girl who doesn't appreciate anything that is handed to her."

My mother, philosophical?

The first guest hadn't taken her first sip of champagne before my mother sniffed. "Looks like the guest of honor is throwing a conniption."

As in: throwing a fit, and my mother wasn't lying.

"Where is the cake?" India demanded.

With a little detective work, I learned that the Sylvia Weinstock cake, which India had made such a to-do about, had not arrived. The frazzled party planner was on her cell phone.

"The cake's ready, but the delivery service I hired never arrived to pick it up. They have called another service but it will take time," the planner explained frantically as India's face grew redder by the syllable.

"I'll go get it," I said, surprising everyone, including me.

Not one to give a gift horse a chance to rethink, the planner wrote down the address and stuffed it into my hand.

"I'll go with you."

We turned and found Jack standing there.

A shiver ran through me. He looked great. I know, I know, he always looked great.

"Uncle Jacky! You came!" India said, and raced into his arms.

He turned her face up to him and made her smile. That was the thing about Jack, the minute you thought you knew who he was he shifted and changed.

In short order, Jack took my elbow and guided me to the elevator where once inside I couldn't help but think of all those movies with elevator scenes in them. The doors sliding shut, a beat passes, then two strangers fall together. However, we were neither strangers nor in a movie.

Since kissing was out, I opted for polite conversation. "I didn't see you at the airport."

A hint of a smile surfaced and he glanced over at me. "Were you looking for me, Cushing?"

"Agh. No." Don't laugh. "But I had assumed as India's uncle you'd be here."

"I came in last night."

It wasn't until we were down the elevator and he held the cab door for me that I asked, as casually as I could, "Where's your fiancée? Racine, right?" just as I stepped past him into the car.

No sooner were the words out of my mouth than we heard, "Jack, love, I'm coming."

The woman I recognized immediately as Racine strode out through the revolving door in stilettos, as smooth as smooth can be. "I heard about the emergency, and of course I am going to help."

She stepped past Jack who still held the car door, her shimmering evening attire fluttering in the April breeze, and slid into the cab, forcing me to scoot over. "You're Carlisle, right?"

Jack got in and shut the door, raking his hair back with his hand, giving the driver the address.

"I don't need to go," I said, though not before the car surged away from the curb, making it clear the only way I wasn't going

300

was if I opened the door and jumped. Which probably wasn't a bad idea.

"It's nice to meet you finally," Racine said, as the cab went from flooring it to inching down Fifth Avenue in Saturday-night traffic. "You don't mind me calling you Carlisle, do you?"

Up close she was as pretty as she was at a distance. And having spent a lifetime preparing to be a lawyer, I knew right away she was a perfect match for Jack. Tall with sleek, long brown hair, perfect skin, and a body to die for. Not that I was intimidated. Okay, maybe a little, but in my defense, she was gorgeous.

She spoke with a cultured Texas accent, her dark green eyes looking at me in quiet assessment. "I've heard so many stories about the Great Carlisle Cushing."

This was a surprise.

"You're a living saint around Willow Creek."

"Racine," Jack said succinctly.

She turned to face him. "What, love? Even if she isn't your favorite person, that doesn't mean everyone else doesn't like her." Then she turned back and patted my leg. "My apologies, I didn't mean to say that about Jack not liking you. I'm sure it's simply the lawsuit. If it weren't for that, no doubt he'd be singing your praises like everyone else."

Obviously she wasn't a member of the Junior League of Willow Creek and hadn't been to tea at Brightlee where my praises definitely weren't being sung.

Racine turned to Jack and just looked at him. I couldn't see her expression, only Jack's, but when she placed her hand on his forearm, the hard contours of his face seemed to ease. Then he smiled at her, and it was as if they were alone in that tiny space.

Uncomfortable, I glanced away.

When Racine finally turned back to me, her dark eyes smoldered like embers. "Have you seen the ring he gave me?"

She extended her hand. "It's beautiful, isn't it?"

Beautiful? Sure. If you went for diamonds the size of golf balls.

"I never would have guessed Jack could be so romantic, taking me to the Mansion on Turtle Creek in Dallas to propose."

"Racine, I'm sure Carlisle doesn't want to hear the details."

She just smiled at me — coolly, to be exact. "Women love that sort of thing. Don't we, Carlisle? Unless of course the woman is jealous."

Excuse me?

"Though I know for a fact Carlisle isn't

jealous. Isn't that right?" Another pat to my leg, and I had never wished for traffic to move faster in my whole life.

Through the starts and stops as we crept downtown, Racine told me about their wedding plans ("the kind of wedding every little girl dreams of"), described the house they were building just west of Willow Creek ("twenty acres with the most amazing views all around"), and ended with the honeymoon plans, when her smile went sly. "Of course I'll keep those details to myself."

When we pulled up to the cake maker's building, I had never been so glad to be out of a cab in my whole life. And when someone had to sit up front on the way back to accommodate the cake in the back, I leaped in next to the cab driver without giving Jack a chance to do the gentlemanly thing.

The party was in full swing by the time we returned. No sooner had the party planner placed the multitiered extravaganza of white icing and marzipan roses in its spot on a designated table, than a reporter and photographer arrived.

"Look who's here, everyone!" India cooed, her arm hooked through the reporter's. "*Texas Monthly!*"

The photographer snapped a photo, catching the assortment of unhappy, jealous, and disgruntled debutante faces.

India preened. She wore a minidress made of pleated metallic silver satin with tiny, fluttery sleeves that looked like wings, topped off with a flirty silver satin bow at the scooped neckline.

"Can you believe how much my daddy loves me!" she boasted. "I swear, he'd do anything for me."

I glanced over at her father in his midnight-blue suit, his wiry hair tamed back against his scalp, as he stood huddled in a corner with a group of businessmen in deep conversation, completely unaware of his daughter's declaration. India noticed as well. For half a second her lips pursed, but then she smiled and launched into a monologue on all the wonderful things she did in Willow Creek.

"You've probably heard about all the work I've done with little children."

"Like what?" the reporter asked, his pencil poised.

"Like what?"

Clearly a question she hadn't anticipated.

"Well, like . . . I help everyone."

It must not have occurred to her that the forty-plus people she had brought with her from Texas could dispel the image she was conjuring with little more than an *Are you on drugs?*

"You know . . ." I heard her say, touching the reporter's arm with her fingertips in a conspiratorial hush, guiding him away from the curious guests. "They are saying the Texas press is going to name me Debutante of the Year." She pulled back from boasting in a surprisingly good imitation of being demure. "Of course, I would be honored. Simply honored. But I am just thrilled to add my name to a cause that will help bring in money for the betterment of my Texas hometown. You know, my father has purchased four tables for the ball."

You'd think a reporter would see through her marginal acting ability and obvious agenda regarding her bid to be named Debutante of the Year. Though maybe they did see through it, because when Morgan walked into the room, the shutterbugs straightened in surprise then turned their shutters on my niece.

Morgan wore a sleeveless bright yellow silk sheath dress with a square neckline and a wide yellow silk sash at her waist. With her brown hair down and loosely curled, she looked like an A-list teenage movie star. Just the sort of girl photographers are drawn to.

Despite the color of her dress, she was no longer Cyndi Lauper, but she wasn't her mother either. And I saw Morgan's surprise at the attention, so unlike India, but she was learning to manage the fine line between belligerence and self-consciousness. I had the fleeting thought that it would be interesting to see who she would end up being when she finally grew into herself.

India looked even more unhappy than usual over the attention Morgan was getting, before she stormed off, not bothering to respond to Sasha when Miss Perfect made some snide remark about lying through her teeth to reporters.

But India didn't get very far because her father caught her arm. I'm not sure what he said, but he didn't look happy. I cringed to think he might be saying some of the very same things Sasha had said.

Whatever the case, the father and daughter shared a few words, none of which appeared very friendly, after which India scowled and changed direction. Just before she reached a small stage, her grandmother caught her hand. Unlike Hunter, Gertrude pulled her granddaughter close and hugged her. India stiffened in her arms, but at the very last second I could see her ease. I recognized that feeling, the same one I experienced when I had heard the concern in Phillip's voice. Kindness. Caring. The notion that everything was going to be okay.

"Hello!" India called out seconds later on the stage microphone.

It took a minute, but soon the crushing noise quieted.

"Thank you, everyone, for coming," India stated confidently. "I know it's a great party, how could it not be, here in New York! And thank you for all the great things you're saying about me being so beautiful and talented and all."

Hunter scowled. If he had told her to thank her guests, her form of gratitude didn't appear to mesh with his.

"But it's all because of my great father who totally did all this for me because he says I'm worth it!" she added with a little rah-rah fist in the air like a cheerleader.

If she had been going for sincerity she missed the mark, and judgmental whispers swept through the room. Her father scowled some more. India's brows knitted and I swear she stamped her foot in frustration.

Only her grandmother looked on with love gleaming in her eyes.

India sighed. "Thank you, Gramma," she said softly, the sound amplified through the room. "Thank you for believing in me."

Then she looked out across the crowd. "Thank you to everyone for coming all this way to celebrate with me. I feel honored that you would do that."

I wouldn't bet anything on it, but I swear this time she sounded sincere.

She dropped her hand, and after a startled moment, the crowd burst out in applause. Hunter raised his chin and seemed to study his daughter, then smiled at her across the room in a way that made me feel he believed that there was hope for her yet. They stared at each other, before finally India smiled, photographers' cameras going off in a blinding flash.

India waved to the cameras, posing like a pre-jail Paris Hilton on the runway, this way, then that way. She'd been at it for a good five minutes when I saw her father starting to leave. She must have good eyes to see through all the flashing, because she gasped then leaped off the small stage in her silver dress, and raced through the crowd. When she caught up to him, they weren't more than a few feet away from me.

"Daddy, where are you going?"

He was impatient to be gone. "I have business in Kuwait. The 737 will take everyone back home."

"But Daddy —"

"What, India? You got your party. Now I have work to do."

He left her standing in the doorway. I couldn't see her face, but the tension in her shoulders said everything I didn't want to know.

By the end of the evening, as the Blair Air 737 made its way south (Jack and his fiancée departing early for "our St. Regis penthouse suite," as Racine said with a cryptic — gloating — smile at me), most of the other girls were awash with varying degrees of envy and dismay. How to compete with that kind of party? However, Betty, ever faithful, ventured back to where India sat glumly. One row ahead of her, I was trying to sleep rather than think about the fact that the girl must be on a roller coaster of emotion. No sooner does she eke out a reluctant smile from her father than he stays in New York and sends her home without him.

No one had spoken to India the whole first hour of the three-and-a-half-hour trip, not even her entourage, who were busy planning who knows what at the front of the plane, which probably explained why she didn't send Betty away in the first place.

"Hi, India," Betty said.

"What do you want?"

"Ah, the party was great. I mean really great."

She shrugged. "Yeah, it was, wasn't it? Though everyone's jealous."

"Of course they are. How could they not be? You took everyone to New York City. I mean, that is amazing!"

I could barely make out India shifting in the seat, making a bit of room. Betty promptly sat down next to her. "I wish I could be as cool as you."

"Don't get your hopes up," India said.

My jaw went tight.

"Okay, not as cool as you, but at least in the same universe."

India didn't say anything for a second. "Where did you say you buy your clothes?"

"Ah, I didn't. My mom makes them."

"Why am I not surprised? You need to tell her that Little Commune on the Prairie dresses don't work at Willow Creek High. You can't be cool looking like a twit."

Even over the plane noise I could hear Betty's painful intake of breath.

"I didn't mean that mean or anything," India continued with an exasperated sigh. "I'm just being helpful. How do you expect to be cool if you dress like that?"

I could almost feel Betty's blush.

"And, hello, your hair. Go look in the mirror. You might even be halfway okay looking if you did something with all that bushy hair. Now, go on. Look."

Betty pushed up and went back to the bathroom. I stood and glared at India.

"What?" she said, put out. "It's the truth. At least I'm trying to help her."

I shook my head and followed Betty. When she came out of the tiny bathroom, her eyes were red.

"Don't let her see you like this," I said. "She knows that you care; that's the only reason she does that stuff. Because she knows she can hurt you."

"It's all right, Miss Cushing. I'm fine. But I'm really tired. I'm going up to see if I can get some sleep."

Betty hurried back to her seat. I started forward and stopped cold when I saw Morgan, my little niece, entwined like a pretzel with her escort.

"Morgan," I said.

But I didn't get any further. Janice came up behind me, saw what was going on, and well, freaked. No definition necessary.

"What are you doing, young lady?" Janice demanded, and with it every ounce of progress the mother and daughter had made over the dress flew out the pressurized window somewhere south of New York City.

Morgan and young cadet Derek leaped apart, or actually, young cadet Derek leaped away. Morgan hardly moved, just sat there with a defiant scowl on her face.

"Ma'am, I'm sorry," the guy began, but was cut off.

"If you know what is good for you, young man," Janice bit out, "I suggest you get back to your own seat."

Derek scrambled out of the row, no doubt remembering Janice's interrogation regarding prisons and dental practices.

Morgan still just sat there, arms crossed. "What are you going to do, Mom?" she hissed.

"You're grounded, for starters," Janice shot back.

"Oh, great, treat me like a kid. Hello, when are you going to accept that I'm eighteen? An adult!"

"So kissing on a plane in front of half of Willow Creek is mature?"

"Since when did you start caring what anyone thinks?!"

I swallowed back a no doubt uncalled-for "touché."

"I care that my daughter is making herself look cheap!"

Morgan leaped up, her face going red.

"Maybe I am cheap! Cheap and not totally brilliant like you, okay! I'm just me! Regular old Morgan who hasn't won any stupid Pulitzers. And FYI, I don't want to. I don't want to be like you, okay. I just want to be me. So get over not having Little Miss Intellectual High School Newspaper Editor for a daughter!"

To say Janice stood there stunned would be an understatement. Quite frankly, I was stunned, too, as was everyone else within earshot.

We flew the rest of the way in silence, landing at Willow Creek Airport and pulling up to the Blairs' private hangar at six in the morning, neither Morgan nor Janice having moved since Janice staggered back to her own seat.

When the engines powered down and the door was opened, we all saw the news crew and photographers waiting on the tarmac. India marshaled a smile, then hurried to the front.

"Top that, girls," she said, then exited to the welcome party I suspected she had planned.

CHAPTER NINETEEN

You've never seen seven girls (and their mothers) scramble so hard to compete. Tiki Beeker and Abby Bateman defied convention and had their party together. They bussed five hundred guests, including reporters, photographers, politicians, Dallas Cowboys football players (forget the cheerleaders, who needed the competition), and Texas movie stud Matthew McConaughey to South Fork Ranch for an extravaganza worthy of J. R. Ewing himself.

Tuxedoed waiters served marinated quail eggs, javelina sausage in gold gilt casing, and melt-in-your-mouth venison pâté on wafer-thin cheddar biscuits, washed down with the finest North Texas Llano Estacado sparkling wine.

They served a dinner of mesquite grilled rib eye steak, potatoes en croûte, and pencil-thin asparagus. Dinner was followed by country western dancing under the stars and decadently sweet Texas mud pie. And liquor. Plenty of wine, beer, bourbon, and fifty-year-old single malt scotch.

India was the only person there who wasn't having fun since even she was smart enough to know that New York Big was one thing. But in the mind of Texans, especially Texas media (i.e., the people who would vote for Debutante of the Year), nothing could compare to Big done Texas style. Texans were all about Big. Big hair, big smiles, big parties held inside big tents under a big Texas sky filled with infinite stars glittering in the night.

It had been a misstep on India's part, and her sulking pout all night made it clear she knew it. But her pout turned to a tantrum when Tiki and Abby were photographed by a slew of Texas newspapers as they raffled off a prize Texas longhorn steer at the end of the night, proceeds benefiting the oldest musical institution in Texas, the Willow Creek Symphony.

My mother stood next to me reluctantly pleased with the outcome if not impressed with the display. Old Texas money was about making it clear that there was plenty of it without ever shoving it down people's throats. Better to constantly and subtly rub their noses in it with quiet power — a power

315

that my mother was desperately trying to hold on to.

Janice stood there with her mouth hanging open in shock. I couldn't tell if she was offended by the display, or worried that her party would never measure up.

She and Morgan were solidly back to not speaking. Not that Janice hadn't tried. I had witnessed the mother's attempts to "talk" to her child, getting little more than monosyllabic grunts in response. One step forward, two steps back, I suppose.

"Close your mouth, dear," my mother said. "It's not a good look for you. Moreover, after what I have seen tonight we have some planning to do. I am not about to let my granddaughter have an inferior party."

"Ridgely, we are not having an inferior party. A luncheon to support community service is far superior to jetting people off to New York or serving gold-gilt sausage."

"Yes," my mother said with cool sarcasm, "I'm sure that's how everyone will perceive it."

Sure enough, we returned to Willow Creek and first thing the next morning my mother woke Janice and had her huddling in the kitchen, like a general and reluctant soldier planning a war. I was thankful my mother

316

was spending more time out of bed than in it, but I was in a state of disbelief that a lifelong socialite and a card-carrying NOW member would ever come up with a party on which both could agree.

Whatever the case, I left them to the party replanning and sat down to work. Discovery was going better than great with the divorce and I had more than enough proof that Vincent did little more than loaf around Lucky Stars and made no contribution to the bottom line. Mentally, I started calculating the damage I anticipated causing to Jack's case.

I was feeling pleased and couldn't wait to call Phillip. He picked up on the first ring.

"Is this the most amazing man on the planet?" I asked grandly.

I could almost feel Phillip's smile come across the phone. "You sound much better today. I take it your case is going well."

True, nothing like work going well to make everything seem right in the world.

"I'm hoping to have this wrapped up sooner rather than later," I said. "How is the deal going with Morton's divorce?"

"All is good," he said, sounding pleased. "He comes to my office every afternoon to catch up — as if we're best of friends now that I saved his ass by getting the dirt on his wife." I heard him lean back. "Thanks for that."

"Anything for you."

"Does 'anything' include setting a date for the wedding?"

My phone beeped. I glanced at the readout. "It's the office on the other line."

"You better take it. But I'm serious. Set a date."

"I will. I promise. In fact, I've been thinking of a fall wedding." Then I clicked over.

My assistant had heard from Mel Townsend again, this time practically threatening her if she didn't give him my cell number since I hadn't called him. On the surface, I expressed my exasperation. Secretly, I was pleased at his persistence, though not for pride issues. Rather, I liked the proof that when I returned to Boston I wouldn't have lost my momentum.

Someone knocked on the door just as I disconnected from my assistant.

"Miss Wainwright?"

Betty entered my makeshift war room, the sun streaming through the windows, reflecting off her thick eyeglasses. She wore a blue-jean jumper over a white button-down shirt, and black and white oxford shoes, making her look like an oversized first-grader, her wild bush hair springing all over her head.

"Hi, Betty. How are you?"

"Good. Fine. Not bad." She twisted her lips. "Okay, not so good. Worse than bad."

"Are you training for the thesaurus Olympics?" I smiled kindly.

"What?"

"Nothing. Tell me what's wrong."

"Did you hear the news?"

"What news?"

"India isn't speaking to Tiki and Abby anymore. They're in this huge fight. India says Tiki and Abby stabbed her in the back."

"How?"

"By having their deb party together, without her. I was thinking maybe I should invite her over, or something. What do you think?"

"Why do you want to be friends with India?"

"Because she's nice. She wants to help me."

I shook my head and sighed. "Betty, I don't think she's really trying to help you. India has problems of her own."

"No way India has problems."

"Of course she does. We just don't know what they are." Actually, I could guess. I had lived my whole life trying to ferret out true meaning from a word or gesture under the notion that if I knew what someone was really thinking I could better navigate around potential disasters. Not that it really worked, and certainly this way of functioning caused a person (namely me) to spend more time worrying than the average person should. But habits are hard to break and I figured that India's mask of words and smiles concealed a little lost girl. Specifically, I could guess that she wanted more of her father's attention and bragged all the time thinking this would make everyone believe she was adored by a man who spent very little time at home.

"Why else would she be so mean to everyone?" I asked.

"But she isn't mean. You heard how she was trying to help me on the plane. I was just being too sensitive."

"Betty, you weren't too sensitive. Your inner radar was saying, Alert, run, don't let her attack you with mean insults wrapped in syrupy smiles and the promise that she's only doing it for your own good. That's crap, Betty."

She didn't look convinced.

"All I ask is that you think about it."

She looked so dejected I wanted to cheer her up.

"How's your party planning going?"

"It still isn't planned."

"Well, your party date isn't until the end of the month. If you hurry, you can make it. Pearl's Paperie on Willow Creek Square can get invitations done in twenty-four hours."

"But Mama and I can't agree on anything. She wants to do a hoedown in the backyard. A hoedown! I told her that India really isn't into hoedowns. When I said it, Mama got really, really mad and said that she didn't care what India thought."

Hard to blame her.

"Whatever about that," she added. "I don't want a hoedown. Only geeks and nerds hoe dance."

"Don't get upset. I'm sure you and your mother can come up with something else."

"But what!"

"Let's see. If you could have any party you wanted, what would it be?"

I expected her to say some huge glittery event like India had, or an extravaganza like Tiki and Abby's. Weren't my mother and Janice regrouping that very instant?

Betty clasped her hands like Dorothy in Oz and said, "I wish I could have an elegant tea, something they would do in England. Proper and lovely. Grand." She dropped her hands. "But my mother doesn't know the first thing about grand. Or even proper and lovely."

I searched my brain for something helpful to say. But dealing well with a parent had never been my specialty, especially a mother who had a strong personality.

"Listen, tell your mother what you want. Tell her how you feel." The answer felt right and I might have preened a little, feeling smart and very in tune with the needs of young girls everywhere. "I'm sure she'll help you make it happen if she knows what it is you want. You could hold it at the Brightlee tearoom. Or the country club."

"Do you think?"

"Of course." Moreover, a tea would be perfect for serving up just the sort of grace, wit, and style this deb season needed. "Run home and talk to your mom. If you need some help convincing her, just let me know."

The next two weeks went by in a blur of invitations, parties, and final preparation. For all the stress of juggling, I woke up one morning and realized I was enjoying myself. I was too busy to worry about succeeding or not succeeding. I simply was having fun.

Sasha Winthorpe had her party next. A luncheon at Brightlee for the girls and their mothers.

Ruth Smith hosted a brunch at the Willow Creek Public Library, though we were surprised when all the guests arrived and the hostess was nowhere to be seen.

Ten minutes after the party began, Ruth careened into the library, her sensible party dress looking as if she had thrown it on in the car.

"Hello! Sorry I'm late. Thank you all for coming."

Once the guests were settled in with their tea, I took her aside. "Are you sure you're okay?"

"Of course!" she said with great cheer. And I had never seen Ruth Smith do "cheer" since I met her.

"Ruth?"

Her face gave way like a house of cards. "I might be a little frazzled. And maybe money's a little tight. But everything is going to be fine. I'm working two jobs to pay for my dress."

"Ruth, if money is a problem, why did your parents agree to your becoming a debutante?"

Her nose wrinkled, she glanced around, then leaned closer. "My dad is doing it for business reasons, said he would make a lot of contacts through this. Plus my mom is crazy wanting to be social, and it's not like I've ever been much good to her on the social side of things."

My heart did a little jig at her words. How well I knew that feeling.

"So we said yes, but then everything has turned out to be way more expensive than we realized. So I'm doing what I can to help out. This party?" She gestured to the library. "It's practically free. And my mom and I were up all hours making the food." She smiled. "Pretty good, huh?"

"It's great, Ruth. Listen, why don't you let me at least help you with the dress."

"No way! I can do this. And please, please don't tell anyone. My parents would kill me."

What was I going to do?

"Please, Miss Cushing. Let me handle this."

The next week Nellie Morgan surprised us by partnering with Saks Fifth Avenue for a What Every Girl Needs in Her Closet fashion show in San Antonio.

When it was Morgan's turn, I didn't think that my mother, Janice, and Morgan would ever agree on anything. But in the end they put on a costume party (concession to Morgan), where every guest had to bring cans of food to give to the needy (concession to Janice), held at the Willow Creek Country Club (concession to my mother). The party was a surprising success, both with the guests and with the media. As we were leaving the club my mother leaned close and said, "I think Morgan has a shot at Deb of the Year."

"What was that?" Janice asked, scowling.

My mother and I exchanged a glance.

"I think Morgan has a big pot of no fear," my mother equivocated.

Janice muttered, then veered off to join Henry.

"I think Morgan has a big pot of no fear?" I repeated incredulously.

"You didn't provide anything better."

She had me there.

The final party was held on the last Saturday of the month. Betty's invitation arrived, and indeed she was hosting a tea. But instead of holding the festivity at Brightlee or the country club as I had suggested, the chosen venue was the Bennett home.

With a grimace, I glanced down the long expanse of our lawn, through the arching live oak trees dripping Spanish moss, and could just make out the family of brightly painted gnomes and geegaws (as my mother called it) decorating the Bennetts' yard across the street.

My mother glanced over my shoulder at the invitation. "A formal tea with the gnomes?"

"Mother," I said with a warning tone.

"Aren't you the protective one of little Betty Bennett."

I did feel protective, maybe because if I hadn't protected myself with school and studying, I would have been Betty Bennett. Teased and needy. A walking target for mean girls and gossips. But was the price I had paid for cutting myself off from other kids any better than what she was paying now?

On the day of the party, I woke up to a beautifully blue, warm Texas sky. A perfect day for a tea.

I dressed with care as if the party were mine, feeling nervous for Betty. When I came downstairs Janice and my mother waited for me in the kitchen.

My mother took one look at me in my borrowed beige and nodded her approval. She gave Janice's muslin shift a resigned sigh.

"At least it's beige," Mother conceded. "Now come along, girls. If I have to go to another of these travesties, I might as well get it over with."

A glum Morgan was at our side; we were the first to arrive at the Bennetts'.

The yard "decoration" was still present,

but I thought my mother would have a heart attack when Morgan said, "Look how cute. They dressed the gnomes."

In tuxedos.

We walked along the path, then up the three wooden steps to the wraparound porch. A man pulled open the front door, also dressed in a tuxedo. "Welcome," he intoned. He was tall, regal, and I couldn't imagine where they had found a butler.

"Oh, man," Morgan whispered excitedly. "He's the guy from the Willow Creek Dairy ads!"

"May I take your wraps?" he asked, starting for my mother's sweater.

She slapped at his hands. "Absolutely not!" She hurried out of reach and we followed.

Merrily Bennett and Betty greeted us formally in the foyer of the big house. Just like the last time I was there, everything was just as casual, but now (as with the gnomes) furniture, clocks, paintings, and family photographs were spruced up with something fancy. Silver bells, silver crepe paper streamers wrapped around the banister, silver candlesticks with burning candles despite the midday sun. Glass vases filled with elegant white flowers standing next to homespun bric a brac. Topping it off, both

Merrily and Betty were dressed in the elegant attire of Victorian ladies.

"How do you do?" Merrily said, as if she'd been watching too much *Masterpiece Theater.*

Betty looked half terrified, half hopeful that this display could in any way impress. I couldn't imagine the conversation that had led up to this, but I guessed that Betty had said something along the lines of *Mama, please can you just be grand and elegant for once,* bringing us to this odd display that was supposed to pass for good breeding.

"What do you think?" Betty asked hopefully.

What did I think? The deeper we went the more my heart started to pound with what I believed might be an anxiety attack.

"It's . . . amazing."

I mean, really, what was I going to say? Your party has disaster written all over it?

"Oh, good." Betty sighed her relief. Then she straightened and smoothed her skirt. "Welcome to my home," she said properly. "You'll find refreshments in the parlor."

My mother looked at me with a raised brow. "Amazing?"

I ignored her and hoped the refreshments were spiked.

In the parlor, I found Betty's grandmother. The tiny woman didn't notice me as she picked up petit four after petit four (homemade, I assumed, given their larger than normal size and less than perfect appearance) and poking the bottoms like a child trying to determine the flavor of a chocolate-covered candy before committing to it.

"Hello, Mrs. Bennett."

The woman dropped a pink-iced cake with a lime-green icing rose onto the platter and whirled to face me. She had crumbs on her lips. Furtively, she tried brushing them away. When my mother entered behind me, Mrs. Bennett's eyes went wide and she bolted from the room.

"I take it you two aren't on friendly terms," I said.

"I've never spoken to the woman in my life."

"Mother. How is it possible that you've lived across the street from her forever and you've never spoken?"

"She's as mad as a hatter. Always has been. What is there to say?"

The rest of the girls and their mothers arrived, India with her grandmother. Our teen diva entered with a look of disdain, wearing a pink organza wraparound blouse, the neckline bordered by an elegant ruffle, the elegance ruined by an orange push-up bra, ripped jeans, and purple stilettos. She strode in and glared when she saw Tiki and Abby, then went over to Nellie.

"Can you believe this place?" She snorted. "Did you see those psycho trolls in the yard? Hello, no wonder Betty is such a loser. She's from a family of freaks."

"India," I interjected, "can't you just be nice?"

"Oh, great." She looked at Nellie and rolled her eyes. "Miss Superior is going to lecture me again. Whatever."

She turned and walked away.

"Sorry, Miss Cushing," Nellie said.

"Popular, are you?" my mother quipped, coming up behind me.

Over the course of the next hour, the party took on a surreal quality, tensions running high among India, Tiki, and Abby. It was all subtle, barely a word spoken, the adults unaware of the building pressure that ran through the room like a fault at the bottom of the ocean. I held my breath for the impending tsunami.

The girls were on opposite sides of the room, Ruth and Nellie standing with India, Sasha standing with Tiki and Abby. Betty fluttered from group to group, constantly having to take petit fours out of her grandmother's hands and returning them to the silver tray. Morgan was the only girl who sat back and observed.

I approached my niece. "So tell me," I began with a nonchalance I didn't feel. "I've heard rumors."

Morgan glanced over at me. "About what?"

"That, well, India has . . . gone all the way."

Morgan rolled her eyes. "*Gone all the way? What are you, from the Middle Ages?*"

"Okay. I've heard she's had sex."

This time Morgan scoffed. "One, she's like eighteen, so whatever if she has."

As if this meant of course she's had sex.

"But two, I heard she started the rumor herself, and that she really hasn't even been felt up. She talks about psycho trolls. Hello. She's a psycho bitch."

"What's going on?" Janice asked.

Morgan and I exchanged a glance. "Nothing," we said in unison.

Janice's eyes narrowed.

"India, Tiki, and Abby have had a parting of the ways," Morgan answered with bored impatience. "India said all of us have to take sides. All three of them are like campaigning."

"Who did you side with?" Janice wanted

to know.

She made a disdainful sound in her throat. "Hello. No one. I'm not stupid."

You'd think Morgan had handcuffed herself to the front gates surrounding the White House demonstrating against world hunger for as happy as Janice was. Though when she tried to give her daughter a hug, Morgan scoffed, and scooted away.

Merrily entered, making a to-do over the flowers, cut from her own gardens, pretending that the house hadn't filled up with smoke just before a maid delivered a china plate of cucumbers with a touch of mayonnaise served on burnt toast. Betty desperately tried to placate the growing tension between the girls. But the party came to a screeching halt when India bit into a not-so-petite petit four and suddenly gagged.

"Oh, my God!" she mumbled dramatically over the mouthful of cake, choking. She tilted over, her long chunky blond hair swinging forward, cake and icing falling into her hand. "Agh!" she cried in staggering shock, holding up an undeniable partial set of icing-and-cake-covered dentures.

The group gasped.

Grandma Bennett ran forward, mumbling something that no one could make out. Then she grabbed the teeth and shoved them into her pocket. "Thank you, dear," she gummed to a traumatized India.

"Oh, my God!" India's grandmother cried.

"Heaven have mercy," my mother added.

"Lordy," Merrily Bennett said, though I swear she swallowed back a laugh.

I was just glad the parties were over.

CHAPTER
TWENTY

Over the following week, I was surprised when both Phillip and the office started calling less frequently. Even Mel Townsend had finally gotten the message and stopped calling.

I told myself that the churning sensation I experienced in my gut had nothing to do with concern that I was losing hold on my life in Boston. I reminded myself of Phillip telling me we made a good team. And since I don't do the weak emotion thing, and ruling out the possibility of Phillip's potential desertion, I decided I needed to come up with a plan to introduce my fiancé into my family *and* let him know that I wasn't exactly who he thought I was.

Fortunately, by juggling the girls' parties, whipping the girls and their escorts into shape for the big night, and working the case, my days were consumed. Who needs time to think, really?

Thankfully, on those occasions I had to deal with opposing counsel, I managed to do so without throwing myself at him. However, I didn't like admitting that it was harder than it should have been, and I'm convinced the only thing that saved me from the pressing need to have my way with him on his conference room table was his constant digging, his repeated demands of more money for his client. A real turnoff. Thank God. Plus, he was engaged. I was engaged. And while I hadn't been completely forthcoming to my coworkers in Boston about my past, I was not someone who had her way with men who were not her fiancé.

Also in the plus column, Jack's constant digging into my mother's net worth helped me refine my own case as to why there was no way in hell my mother was going to give up one red cent more than was prescribed in the prenup. I would conform to the letter of the law, no question, but that didn't preclude doling out the info in tiny pieces as it suited me.

I had been in Texas nearly three months, the days growing warmer, and with those strange exceptions of Wednesdays at noon, my mother still spent an inordinate amount of time in bed. I would have questioned her about the Wednesday thing if I hadn't been so relieved by the better mood it brought about.

Savannah grew bigger by the day, probably more so because of her determination to eat for two. My always tiny, looks-obsessed sister suddenly didn't care about anything but the child she was going to have. Ben, ever vigilant, watched over her as if he could ensure nothing bad happened to his precious wife. It was as touching as it was cloyingly sweet.

Janice and Morgan existed in a suspended standoff that I prayed would hold until after the ball was over. Then they could do whatever they wanted. Run away from home. Send daughters off to boarding schools. Whatever. Just don't screw up my ball.

With the parties over (and the gnomes not making the news) I felt a growing sense of excitement \ex-cite-ment\ n (1600 — give or take a few years) brought on by 1: finding proof that the prenup should stand 2: knowing I could show that Vincent hadn't contributed to any bottom line that had anything to do with Lucky Stars Farm 3: making headway with turning the girls into ladies. Soon I would accomplish it all, and then be able to return to my other life with a clean conscience.

I was sitting on my mother's veranda to get away from the growing afternoon heat inside, my case notes in my lap, and all seemed surprisingly right with the world when Jack pulled up into the front drive.

"We need to talk," he said, stepping out of his black Suburban.

"About what?"

"The case."

"Then talk."

"Not here. Somewhere private."

"How very Deep Throat of you. If you want, we can find a parking garage somewhere, though that might entail driving to San Antonio."

"Do you want to hear what I have to say, or not?" he added, striding up onto the veranda.

The phone beside me rang. We both glanced at the caller ID. Massachusetts. I knew right away whose cell phone number it was. Uh-oh.

"Phillip, I take it," Jack noted.

I made a face. "No."

Sue me.

I ignored the call. I didn't want a replay of the last time I spoke to Phillip with Jack looking on.

"Let's go in the kitchen to talk. Lupe has gone to the grocery store. My mother is upstairs in bed. Henry is at work. Savannah is at Willow Creek Collegiate demanding a spot for her future child. I can't swear where Janice is, but the kids are upstairs doing who knows what. Basically, that's about as much peace, quiet, and/or privacy as we are going to get around here."

I stood and headed inside, not waiting for an answer.

In the kitchen, I poured two glasses of sweet tea to ward off the heat. The back door was ajar, the windows open. Despite my mother's wealth, she flatly refused to turn on the air conditioner before the first of May regardless of the temperature. It was a rule, sort of like no white shoes before Easter.

"What's up?" I asked, motioning him toward the table.

"I thought we might talk settlement."

Interesting. It seemed both too late and too soon to be talking settlement. "You can talk, I'm happy to listen."

He walked over to the table. He wore a white button-down shirt with enough starch in it to make it stand on its own, tucked into pressed Wrangler jeans, roper boots, and a sport coat. Typical Texas menswear.

Sitting down across from me, he pulled a piece of notepaper from his jacket pocket.

No briefcase, no folder, nothing. Just a folded piece of paper in his pocket. Unfolding the sheet, he spread it out in front of him.

"As I see it," he began, "I can clearly show that Lucky Stars has dramatically improved since Vincent has been spending time there —"

"Gambling."

"That's not the point."

"What is the point?"

"Improvement. Lucky Stars was a mess. Now it's making money."

"No thanks to Vincent."

"Vincent was there during the turnaround."

"Again, gambling."

"I say he was there working."

"There is absolutely no evidence of that."

"There is circumstantial evidence."

"As in?"

"He was there, and during that time they made more money. A lot more money, based on what I can see. Speaking of which, I'm getting tired of your piecemeal method of disclosure."

"Me? Piecemeal?" I gave him an innocent smile.

"Not funny."

"I wasn't trying to be."

Noise erupted, no surprise there, from the upper regions of the house. A crash, followed by yelling, screaming, and fighting.

"God, what now?" I said with a groan.

Cinco banged into the kitchen. "It's a lunatic asylum up there," he announced, then studied Jack. "Who are you?"

"I'm Jack." He extended his hand.

Cinco shook, then let go. Jack smiled wryly, then reached for a napkin to wipe away chocolate.

"Hey, you want to play poker with me?" Cinco asked.

Without waiting for an answer, he dashed out, his footsteps banging through the house, before he returned with cards and a container of poker chips.

"Cinco, Mr. Blair is here on business."

Jack shrugged. "I could play a round or two."

Within seconds, they were deep into the game. Cinco provided chocolate cigars for both of them, which Jack surprised me by accepting. When I realized I was not needed, or wanted, and the heat of the kitchen was growing by the second, I left. And amazingly, the game continued and was going strong when I returned an hour later. With one difference. Each player had several empty cellophane wrappers in front of them, and chocolate covered just about everything else in the room.

I cringed at the trouble I knew was coming from Lupe over the mess, from Janice over the inevitable sugar buzz, and my mother over the fingerprints on her tablecloth.

Jack looked up. "Hey," he said.

"Hey, yourself."

I walked over to the table. "If I were you two, I'd get this place cleaned up before anyone else finds you."

"In just a second," Jack said, tossing in some more pennies.

"Yeah, in a second," Cinco echoed, tossing in his own pennies.

The players sat back and eyed each other.

"Am I bluffing?" Jack teased.

Cinco looked on with the seriousness of a general. He twirled the melting cigar slowly, chocolate coating his fingers. Then he shoved every last penny he had in front of him into the center. "I call."

The boy set his cards down like a chocolate-covered fan. Jack debated, then said, "You got me."

Cinco's eyes went wide, then he leaped up. "I win! I win!"

Jack folded his cards without showing them, but Cinco was too high on sugar, apparently, to notice.

Cinco swept up the pile of pennies, and raced out of the kitchen.

I glanced at Jack, then picked up his cards before he could stop me. "A straight flush. Hmmm, I guess this is a new version of the game where that doesn't beat a pair of aces."

And right there I felt something different for Jack. Different from the need to take him on conference tables or even strangle him. Different from the need to run every time I was afraid he was the one man who could turn me into my mother.

I felt something warm and soft inside which I suspected would be called emotion \e-mo-tion\ n (1660) 1: sensory stimulation 2: subjective reaction experienced in response to a state of mental agitation 3: those things I didn't do.

I folded the cards and set them down. "Who would have guessed Jack Blair, former bad boy and current ruthless killer lawyer, could be nice to a kid?"

He pushed back in his chair and stood. He came so close to me that my heart banged against my ribs. It was hard enough to stand near him when I wanted nothing more from him than something physical. But now, with those unfortunate feelings coursing through me like hormones in a thirteen-year-old girl, I felt like, well, a thirteen-year-old girl.

Jack stared at me. I couldn't tell what he was thinking, but I can safely say that darkly brooding Jack had returned.

I felt rattled.

Concentrate, Carlisle, I told myself.

Forcefully, I managed to turn away and retrieve 409 and paper towels. I told myself to clean. Chocolate was everywhere. Lupe and my mother would hit the ceiling if they walked in and found the mess.

"Why does it keep coming back to you and me?" Jack asked, as if he were trying to understand and wasn't particularly thrilled with the answer that came to mind.

I hated that I wondered the same thing. Year after year, encounter after encounter, no matter how I pushed Jack Blair out of my mind, he always came back again.

"I'm happy. I have a great life. I love the idea of spending the rest of my days with Racine." He sighed in frustration. "I'm not going to screw this up."

There had been so many near misses with him. Each time my breath held for fear I would dive headlong into Jack Blair. It was no different three years earlier when I did finally dive in, like leaping from a bridge, praying a bungee cord was attached. Unfortunately it wasn't.

I was in the WCU law library where I had gone to cram before I took the bar exam. I had graduated top of my class, but that didn't stop me from being obsessively nervous about the bar.

Concentrating in the echoing silence in the law library, I wasn't aware Jack had walked up to me until he sat down at my table, the scrape of the hardwood chair legs against hardwood flooring echoing in the quiet space.

I looked up, startled.

"Hey," he said, crossing his arms on the heavy wooden table, the arching green shaded lamp casting light on my stack of books and papers.

"Hey," I managed.

"How've you been?"

"Great. Fine. Better than fine."

My mother had wondered (not without cause) how someone as sexually unsophisticated as I came from her loins. And I swear she uses the word "loins."

"And you?" I asked.

Other than seeing him a few times when I was a first-year law student, he a third year, I had managed to keep a safe distance from him.

He tugged the study guidebook away from

me. Turning it around, he read a question from the page I had been working on, answered it, smiled with the arrogant pride that on him only seemed endearing, then said, "You look like you could use a burger at Moe's."

He closed the workbook and started to stand. I lurched across the table and grabbed it.

"I can't. I have to study."

We stood on opposite sides of the table, the library's echoing silence surrounding us, the oversized paperback book caught in our hands.

"Come on," he cajoled.

I stood my ground.

"I tell you what," he said. "We'll go to Moe's, sit in a back booth, and I'll quiz you."

"I'm serious, Jack. No." I tugged hard on the book and he let it go. "I can't go to Moe's."

Then, almost frantically because I wanted very much to damn all I knew about men and women and especially this kind of man and how things would end up, I gathered my stack of books, papers falling around me, my pencil dropping with a clatter on the floor. Without stopping to pick it up, I said goodbye and dashed out of the library.

It was the hardest thing I had ever done. I wanted him. Had since that first day I laid eyes on him. And based on the look in his eyes, he wanted me too. Still.

But fleeing, I told myself I couldn't.

Really.

It would never work between us.

I couldn't deal with the kind of need for a man that had ruled my mother's life — the kind of need that made it impossible to breathe when self-worth was wrapped up in "I love yous."

I banged outside through the heavy wooden doors of the law library, hurrying down the wide stone steps, my books held in my arms. My senses were heightened, the smell of budding honeysuckle hitting me in the face, the sound of the door opening behind me.

"Carlisle!"

I didn't stop.

"Carlisle, come on."

Despite all the screaming my brain was doing to keep going, my feet stopped of their own volition. Squeezing my eyes shut for half a second, I told myself no. But I turned around. It was a shame how little control I had around this guy.

Jack strode toward me with a crooked smile on his face. When he stopped in front of me I held my breath.

"You forgot this," he said, holding up the pencil.

I stared at it for half a second, then dropped my stack of books and took the steps that separated us.

I swear.

After years of avoiding just that, standing outside the WCU law library, I was in his arms. That day my cell phone rang, my mother's number appearing as if she had an unerring ability to find me just when I was about to dive into Jack Blair. But unlike the other times, I ignored her, ignored her call, refused to listen to any messages. I turned off the phone, and let him take my hand and drive me to his apartment on his Harley, my arms wrapped around his black leather jacket.

For one amazing month I dove in. We came together on the dining table, the kitchen floor, the back booth at Pete's Bar and Grill. I raced through Willow Creek on the back of his motorcycle, oblivious to the stares, the talk. I lost myself to everything I felt for Jack Blair.

I ignored my mother and her latest marriage to a handsome poet half her age who made her laugh and cry in equal measure. I pretended that I was born of a woman who had at least a fleeting awareness of sane and stable marriage. I acted as though I knew all about normal relationships. At least I did until I woke up in Jack's bed one morning, tangled in his sheets, only to realize belatedly it was the day of the exam.

In a panic, I leaped out of bed. When Jack woke and tried to pull me back, I slapped at his hand.

"I have to go! I'm late! I'm going to miss the bar."

He just smiled that crooked smile and reached for me. "Take it later."

As if it were that easy. They only gave the exam two times a year. I'd have to wait six months in order to take it again.

"That isn't acceptable. I'm not like you, Jack, irresponsible, only doing whatever suits you," I said as I threw on my clothes, hopping around on one foot as I crammed on my high heels without the panty hose I couldn't find, then careened to the university where the bar exam was being given. But I was twenty minutes late, the doors already locked. I stood outside that exam room hyperventilating, begging the moderator through gasping breaths to let me in. To no avail.

That day, standing outside the closed oak doors of the testing room, I couldn't believe what I had done. My plans, the timeline of my life, shot. And when my mother called to tell me she was divorcing the poet, demanding through her tears that I tangle myself in yet another mess of extracting her from the disaster she had made, I felt the moment I cracked. I started to cry, me, sensible Carlisle Cushing, right there in front of the guard manning the door.

To the world my mother was amazing — vibrant, alive — beautiful like fine porcelain. But what no one else seemed to understand, not even my sister, was that while our mother was indeed like porcelain she had been broken, more than once, then repaired each time so expertly that only I could see the cracks. I had learned that my mother's happiness and self-worth came from being loved by a man. When they'd inevitably had enough and left, she broke a little more.

Standing there next to the door monitor who stood between me and my goal, I felt the fissure snake through me, not from my self-worth being wrapped up in a man, but from the pressure of a life I finally admitted I didn't know how to manage.

I was drowning in Jack and my mother, ir- responsibility and unwanted obligation like cement boots pulling me under. So I did the only thing a sensible girl could do. I opened the big atlas in the Wainwright House study to the map of North America, closed my eyes, and took a stab at the page. My finger landed in the Atlantic Ocean, but it was reasonably close to Nova Scotia, Maine, and Boston. You know the rest.

I left Willow Creek without a word to anyone, including Jack and my mother.

In retrospect, it sounds ridiculous. I'm not proud of not being brave enough to think things through before departing to what seemed like saner climes. And maybe, just maybe, I had come back to Texas to undo that mistake — not to stay, mind you, but to stay longer than those quick trips I had made home in the past. Maybe this time I could make amends to my mother for leaving her in the lurch, putting her in a position that allowed her last divorce to become a line item on the Wainwright family ledgers, and to Jack for leaving without explanation. Perhaps this way I could move on and finally set a date to marry Phillip.

"Fuck," Jack said, though this time it was a proverbial fuck and in the present day.

We stared at each other in my mother's kitchen, neither wanting to feel all we felt for the other, though neither of us knowing how to break the hold.

"Aunt Carlisle!"

Tiny footsteps raced down the corridor toward the kitchen, jarring us, before little hands hit the swinging door with a boom, throwing it open.

"Aunt Carlisle!" Priscilla yelled despite the fact that I wasn't more than three feet away. "You got company!"

Jack and I glanced at the door, just as it swung open again.

"Carlisle?"

"Phillip!" I managed, and dropped the 409 on the floor.

Chapter
Twenty-One

"Carlisle?" Phillip repeated, peering over my shoulder at Jack.

My mind started spinning, and not just because of the exceedingly awkward situation. "Phillip! What are you doing here?"

"I came to see my fiancée," he stated, never glancing away from Jack.

Jack raised a brow. "Fiancée?"

To say that Jack looked unhappy would be an understatement. "A dangerous fury" might be more accurate but would also be completely melodramatic, so I'll leave it at "unhappy."

The thought jarred me out of paralysis. For half a second I tried to figure out how to extricate myself from the mess. But I knew my moment of reckoning had finally come. And even I knew that if you can't beat the charge you better go with it and make the best of a bad situation.

I pulled up mental fortification, then

walked over and took Phillip's arm. "Jack Blair, I would like you to meet my fiancé, Phillip Granger."

The two men who were such complete opposites stood eyeing each other like two gunslingers at a Wild West showdown; that is, until the menacing shock on Jack's face shifted and changed, settling into what I can only call an amused grin. Maybe even relief.

"Nice to meet you," Jack said, extending his hand.

After a second, Phillip shook, then grimaced when he pulled away covered in chocolate.

"Sorry, man," Jack said, not that he looked it.

"Jack was just leaving."

"Right," he said, but didn't budge.

I pushed him toward the door, but just before we got there he spun back (I lurched forward) and added, "First, I really should clean up. Don't want to get chocolate all over the Suburban." He strode over to the sink. "So tell me, Phil."

"It's Phillip."

"Sure. How did you come to be engaged to Carlisle?" The man I was beginning to think of as the King of the Underworld actually chuckled. "We've heard about you,

353

of course. Sort of. But we're a little short on details."

I glared at him. "*We* don't need to know any of this. Especially since *you* really need to go."

Phillip looked confused.

Jack held up his dirty hands and gave me a menacing look. "I'm going. Just give me a second."

I walked across the kitchen to the counter, shooting daggers at Jack the whole way, grabbed up a linen towel, and forced a smile when I turned back and handed it to my fiancé. "The chocolate," I explained.

Phillip glanced down at his hand, only then remembering. "Oh, yes."

With no help for it, I knew that I couldn't delay cleaning up the chocolate, regardless of the potential disaster brewing before me. Lupe and/or my mother could walk in at any second. I didn't need a disastrous kitchen hanging over my head as I finally came clean to my mother about my fiancé. Beyond which, I wasn't fool enough to think that any amount of pressure, coercion, or insistence was going to get Jack Blair out of there one second before he was ready to leave.

I found an apron and tied it on, picked up the 409 from the floor, wet some paper towels, and got to work.

Phillip stared as if seeing me for the first time. "Carlisle?" he said. "I can't believe that with all the work you're doing here, they're making you clean as well. What kind of employer does your mother work for?"

Jack stopped drying his hands, his head cocking. "What is this? Employer?"

"Jack, really," I said with tight determination, "I know you have lots to do."

"On the contrary." He tossed the towel aside, crossed his arms on his chest, and leaned back against the counter. "I have nothing better to do than stay here and get to know your fiancé." He glanced between me and the chocolate-covered kitchen. "Though you better get a-crackin' on this mess before your *employer* arrives." He turned back. "Hey, Phil, looks like you got a spot on your tie."

Phillip's head dropped (I grimaced), and sure enough, chocolate did streak what I knew was his favorite Hermès tie.

With a jerk, Phillip's head popped up. "Who are you?" he asked Jack in continued confusion.

"Just think of me as . . . a friend. An old friend. So sit." He walked over, slapped Phillip on the back, then guided my fiancé to a chair and pushed him into it.

Satan turned up the charm and it didn't take my "old friend" long before he had Phillip revealing the highlights of our life together in Boston. I swallowed back a groan when Phillip started in on just how proud everyone should be of me given how I had pulled myself up by my bootstraps and succeeded.

"Bootstraps?" Jack said to me, repeating the word in an exaggerated use of syllables. "Aren't you clever to go off all poor and make good. Your mother must be so proud."

"Really, Jack, you need to go."

"Right. Probably should get back to it."

He stood, but before he got far the back door opened and in walked Lupe, dressed in street clothes (hand-me-downs of my mother's in the form of a perfectly preserved, decade-old Ralph Lauren shirt dress, low-heeled Cole Haan shoes, and matching purse), groceries held in her arms, keys to the Volvo dangling in her fingers.

She stopped dead in her tracks at the sight, not of me, Jack, or even the stranger, but the chocolate-covered kitchen.

"What ees theese!" she cried. "What is theese mess you make?"

Phillip leaped up, his eyes wide. "I'm sorry. It's my fault it isn't cleaned up."

"Yes," Jack interjected happily. "As Car-

lisle's *employer*, Mrs. Hernandez runs a tight ship here at Wainwright House."

Lupe looked at him as if he had lost his mind. Then to make matters worse, my mother walked in.

"Carlisle? Who is here?"

Mother wore a simple housedress and low-heeled slippers, as if she had just been dragged from bed. When she saw Jack, she scowled, though her scowl turned to curiosity when she saw Phillip.

I debated whether or not I could hide.

"Mrs. Ogden," Jack said grandly. "I'm sure you've met your daughter's fiancé. Phil."

My mother couldn't seem to move.

Phillip extended his hand. "It is a pleasure to meet Carlisle's mother."

"Fiancé?" she said.

"I'm the one," he said with solemn pride. "I managed to get your daughter to agree to be my wife."

She glanced at me, then back. "Fiancé," she repeated. "Of course you are," she carefully.

Jack got that wicked-smile thing going. "know you're just going to love hearing the impressive *achievements* of your ter."

"Jack, stop."

357

"Now, now, Carlisle, don't be modest."

He then proceeded to regale my mother with all the unfortunate details of my "fake" life.

Mother glanced from person to person, pressing her beautifully manicured hand to her chest. "Me? A humble servant?"

I groaned. After a lifetime living with my mother, I knew, as I knew my own name, what was coming next when she turned those violet-blue eyes on me.

But I was wrong.

"Carlisle, you sly puss. Aren't you full of surprises. Such a life you *haven't* boasted about." Then her mouth turned up in a mischievous smile. "Though I'd best get back to my chores before I get fired for shoddy work."

The stabbing pain behind my eyes resurfaced.

Lupe started to say something, but my mother cut her off. "Now, now, Mrs. Hernandez, I am here to serve, sugar. All I ask is to be given a small stipend and a bit of bread and water for my labors."

Now this was thick. Which made me feel better since if my mother had really been upset she would have stormed to her room, jammed the door, and pulled her secret bottle of Johnnie Walker Blue out of her

dressing table. Instead, she launched into her role as servant with the enthusiasm of a method actor.

I stood in shock as my mother tied an apron around her waist, then smoothed it with those perfect hands.

My mother smiled her schoolgirl's smile. "Would you like some tea, Mr. ah . . ."

"Granger," he offered.

"Mr. Granger. It has a nice ring to it."

She set out to serve tea in the kitchen (no servant could entertain their own guest in the receiving room, she informed us) with a flourish.

"As much as I'd like to stick around for the rest of the show," Jack said, "I've really got to go." He extended his hand. "Phil, nice to meet you."

"Yes, you too."

Though Phillip looked more stricken than anything.

"Now, let's sit," my mother said, then leaned forward and added in a whisper, "Though truly I only have a second before Old Battle-ax Hernandez cracks the whip."

Lupe started a heated diatribe, fortunately in Spanish so that Phillip hadn't a clue what was said.

The pain increased and I was sure my head would explode.

"Mother," I warned.

"Now, Miss Lupe, you don't mind me having a spot of tea so I have a chance to get to know my future son-in-law. Lord have mercy, fiancé!" She looked at Phillip. "Mrs. Hernandez and I are practically family, you know."

"Enough!" I said.

"Now, sugar, is that any way to talk to your mother?"

"Yes, Carlisle, you really shouldn't be rude to your mother."

Mother smirked, then coughed as she served. And not particularly well when ice-cold sweet tea sloshed over the side of the silver pitcher and into Phillip's lap.

He leaped back, coming out of his chair. Lupe muttered in Spanish, retrieved a dish towel, and started wiping at our guest's private parts. Phillip was too stunned to do anything at first, then finally regained his wits and took hold of her wrist. "I'm fine, Mrs. Hernandez, really."

The kitchen went still, Mother barely holding back laughter, Lupe's face beet red in a way I never would have dreamed possible.

"Mother, stop this game right now."

"What game, dear?" she asked, straightening with the silver tea server still held in her hand. "I'm just being kind to this lovely man who has come all the way from Boston to surprise you. And you can imagine how proud I am of my daughter for having risen from her *poor, humble* roots to become a top lawyer in her field." She smiled wickedly at me. "You can imagine how that would make any mother feel."

Given Phillip's expertise as a man of the law, he seemed surprisingly oblivious to my mother's charade. He took her smiles at face value, her sweet words as the truth, the apron as something she wore every day.

"Phillip, there is something I need to tell you."

This time Lupe groaned. "Et was just geeting good."

My mother scoffed.

I glared at them both, then reluctantly turned back to Phillip.

"My mother is not a maid."

She sighed, disappointed that the game was over. "But I think I did a magnificent job of pretending to be one. Don't you think, Lupe?"

Lupe rolled her eyes and muttered.

"Like you did much better as the lady of the house? Good Lord, you felt the man up."

"Wha?"

"You heard what I said!"

"Stop, you two," I demanded, then turned back to my fiancé who watched in stupefied shock as my mother and her maid went at it. "Phillip, I am not poor." Just like that.

His brow furrowed.

"My mother isn't really the maid."

"I don't understand."

"Good God," my mother interjected, "what's there not to understand? She is not poor. I am not poor, and Lupe here is really the maid. I am the lady of the house, and Carlisle is my daughter."

Phillip's head swung back and forth between us.

"Is this true? You aren't poor?"

I cringed. "Yes."

"You're rich?"

"Well, rich is relative."

"You are a Wainwright of the Wainwright family?"

"Yes. But in my defense, I never said I was poor."

He sputtered over words that made no sense.

"I just never clarified the misconception," I hurried on.

My mother sniffed. "As if that makes it better. I can't believe you were up there with all those Yankees pretending to be poor.

What were you thinking, Carlisle?"

"Yes, Carlisle, what were you thinking?" Phillip's tone was ominous.

I cringed. "Would you buy: I wasn't thinking?"

No one liked my answer.

Phillip stared at me, his mouth opening and closing, no words coming out.

Finally he said, "I'm sorry, but I really have to go."

He looked at me one last time, shook his head, and disappeared through the swinging door.

CHAPTER
TWENTY-TWO

Great. Just great.

I couldn't get Phillip to answer his cell phone the rest of the day, and that night I found myself in Ernesto's truck driving from every better to moderately priced hotel in Willow Creek. But he wasn't registered at any of them.

By the time I pulled up the drive to Wainwright House, my unmanicured nails curled around the steering wheel, I was in shock. And not just because of Phillip's surprise appearance, then disappearance. I couldn't believe that I had spent hours doing exactly what my mother had spent most of my life doing. Driving around at night looking for a man. The realization careened through my head like billiard balls cracking together in a smoke-filled pool hall.

Though as horrified as I was about that, I was equally worried that it was over between Phillip and me. What if he couldn't forgive me for having money — which in itself felt like a bizarre thought on a bizarre night in a bizarre situation that I couldn't believe I was in the middle of.

But then I thought of Phillip, my Phillip, the man I knew from my life in Boston, and while I couldn't have explained why (a voice in my head might have been laughing and repeating the word "denial"), I knew he wasn't like all the men who had paraded through my mother's life.

The next day, Thursday morning, May 1, I walked into the kitchen to a stack of newspapers from around Texas. No one had to tell me that the Spring Debutante Season had started and my mother was keeping track.

In Dallas:

BIG D SPRINGS INTO THE SEASON WITH RARE ROSES FOR GIRLS

In Austin:

DEBUTANTES IN FINE FORM RAISING MONEY FOR GOOD CAUSES

In Fort Worth:

FINEST FAMILY WITH THEIR FLOWERING FEMALES

365

There were more, and I'm sure if Janice took a look she would groan over the ridiculous headlines. But I'm sure all my mother saw was that the events had been glowing successes. Ours was still iffy.

I pushed the newspapers away and tried Phillip's cell phone again. But still no word from my fiancé, and my mother and I were due in court at nine.

Fortunately I calculated that I could get back to finding him sooner rather than later since it couldn't take more than an hour or two in front of the judge to prove that Vincent hadn't contributed to Lucky Stars's bottom line (unless it was in the category of net loss) and that he hadn't signed the prenuptial agreement under duress. My mother kept everything, and she had a detailed timeline of when Vincent had been presented with the document, the extensive meetings they had had in regard to the matter, and the top-of-the-line attorney he'd had to represent him. No judge in the land was going to invalidate the document in this case.

"Order," the bailiff called. "The Superior Court of Willow Creek County is now in session, the Honorable Edward Melton presiding."

We stood as the judge entered, Jack not so

much as looking at me.

"All right," the judge began without preamble. "Where do we stand, counselors? Since we are here, clearly the parties didn't get this mess straightened out."

"Correct, Your Honor," Jack and I said in tandem.

"Mistake," I was almost certain the judge muttered.

"Fine, let's get on with it, then. Mr. Blair, which issues still remain unresolved?"

Jack looked grave, his brown eyes dark, ruthless. I could guarantee that whatever traces of humor he had felt up until that point were gone.

"Your Honor, nothing is resolved," he said. "We have no stipulations at this point."

"Miss Cushing?"

"Your Honor, as I have provided in copious detail in my prehearing filings, there is no evidence whatsoever to support counsel's claim that his client was pressured into signing the prenuptial agreement. Furthermore, I have provided extensive evidence both to the court and to counsel that supports the claim of Mr. Ogden's *lack* of economic contribution to Lucky Stars Farm, LLC. I see no reason to continue wasting the court's time."

Jack nodded at me with the seriousness of

a priest, as if truly considering my words, then said, "Unfortunately, Your Honor, neither pressure nor economics matter any longer in this case. I move that the prenuptial agreement between Mrs. Ridgely Ogden and Mr. Vincent Ogden, dated February of last year, be nullified immediately."

I looked at him as if he had lost his mind. A murmur swept through the gallery like a wave.

The judge didn't even bother to bang the gavel. "If not based on undue pressure or economic contribution, then on what grounds?" he demanded.

Jack didn't look at me. "Adultery, Your Honor."

The courtroom erupted. Judge Melton hammered his gavel. "Good God almighty, Mr. Blair," the judge barked. "What did you say?"

"Adultery, Your Honor," he repeated, as cold as a winter day in my beloved Boston.

"Adultery?" I practically bleated. "That's ridiculous." Or was it?

"Miss Cushing," the judge ordered. "Sit down."

I sat very still, my fingers curling around my pencil. I had the sudden realization that Jack wanted to win this — bad — for reasons that had nothing to do with helping his client. Was it possible he would go after my mother to get back at me?

"Your Honor," he continued, "this new information only just came to my attention yesterday."

"Explain, counselor."

"Yesterday at noon, I was called to visit a *friend* of Miss Cushing's who was staying at the Lazy 6 Motel. It was while I was there that I learned of the adultery."

Things were going from bad to worse. I knew "yesterday" was Wednesday and I also knew my mother had a suspicious habit of disappearing every Wednesday at noon.

I leaped to my feet again, objecting. But in the back of my mind I also realized that my "friend" could only be Phillip and he must have been staying at the beyond modest and completely unPhillip-like Lazy 6 Motel and had called Jack, not me, to talk.

Angrily, the judge ordered Jack and me into chambers where we were read the riot act (hello, I didn't do anything) then told to present evidence on both sides by the end of next week. Quite frankly, I thought adultery deserved more than a week. But the man, apparently, had had it with extensions, delays, and continuances. Perhaps we would have been better off with one of the judges who had dated my mother.

I sank back into the leather seat of the car as Ernesto drove us home. With my eyes closed, I asked, "Mother, are you going to explain what is going on here?"

Ridgely reapplied her lipstick in a small compact mirror, admired the shade, before snapping the case shut. "Vincent is no gentleman."

"Mother, get serious. You are on the verge of losing a great deal of your worth if the prenup is voided. I'd think you'd be interested in telling me why in the world Jack would accuse you of adultery?"

"He's desperate."

"Mother, Jack Blair is many things, but we both know he isn't desperate."

"Don't be naïve, Carlisle. All men are desperate."

"Mother, we are going for serious here."

"I am serious. But even if I did have an affair, which I didn't, that doesn't mean Vincent should get one blade of grass from the farm."

"If you had bothered to read your prenup you would know that the only thing that could make it null and void is if you have an affair."

"What?"

"You heard me. That was the single stipulation we agreed to when we drew up the agreement."

"Oh, my Lord! Then you have to fix this."

Yet again.

We pulled up the drive, headed around back, and stopped. Lupe came out the back door at a dead run, and from the look on her face she had already heard the news. I was wrong.

"Miss Ridgely, Miss Ridgely, Meester Ben take Savannah to hospital."

I forgot all about Vincent, adultery, Jack, and even my need to track Phillip down at the Lazy 6 Motel. We entered Memorial Hospital not more than five minutes later. Savannah's doctor met us in the white-walled and linoleum-tiled hallway outside her room.

"What's happened?" my mother demanded of a young resident.

"You should ask the patient," the man said.

"You must not know who I am."

"Ma'am, unless you are the woman's next of kin, it doesn't matter who you are. I have doctor-patient confidentiality. And the form here lists Ben Carter."

"Doctor" — I glanced at his name tag — "Pressman. I am Carlisle Cushing, Savannah's sister. This is our mother."

But the doctor was off the hook when Ben

came out of the room, his tie loosened, his eyes bloodshot. He looked beaten and much older than his forty years. "She miscarried," he said without preamble. "Again."

Then he walked down the hall and out of the hospital.

My sister had miscarried three times before but she had never given up on her belief that she would have a child. That was the thing about denial. It's hard to know the difference between lying to yourself and giving up on a dream that just needs perseverance.

We walked into Savannah's hospital room and were met by the usual prima donna grandeur, but now the confidence that normally brightened her eyes was gone.

"It's about time you showed up," she snapped.

My mother went to her side and took her hand. "I told you nothing good could come of this." She tsked. "Ben told you the same thing."

Savannah's blue eyes flashed a dark shade, then she turned to me. "I'm surprised you came at all."

I had to remind myself that she was lashing out, meanness thrown around to cover the pain. "Of course I would come."

After talking at length to the doctor and

learning that Savannah would be fine, I stayed awhile longer before my mother shooed me off to deal with her divorce. Unlike our mother, Savannah had never reached out to me when she was in trouble.

Ernesto drove me to the house and dropped me off. I walked in the back door, set down my briefcase, and pulled open the refrigerator. Popping a soda, I knew I should start making sense of my mother's predicament. Though I was all too happy for the diversion when the doorbell rang.

When I opened the front door, Phillip stood on the veranda looking half contrite, half defiant.

"Phillip!"

He just stood there and stared at me, his blond hair barely combed, his always perfect clothes rumpled, his eyes red-rimmed from lack of sleep.

"Oh, Phillip. I'm so sorry. I meant to tell you, wanted to tell you, but one thing led to another —"

"I forgive you," he stated.

Just like that. I mean, really, just like that, and I wasn't too happy.

"We can survive this," he continued in a voice I had heard him use countless times in court — controlled, dispassionate. "We'll go back to Boston, get married, and continue on as we always have. No one has to know about this."

Phillip had always cared what people thought more than I thought he should, but didn't we all have flaws, and I had ignored it. I was having a hard time ignoring it right then.

"Phillip," I said carefully, "why do you want to marry me?"

The question seemed to come out of nowhere, at least to me since it never occurred to me to question why. He appeared surprised.

"Because you are . . . nice-looking, smart, levelheaded, and you're going places in the firm. You're just like me." Then he grimaced. "I guess not quite like me given your money. But we've invested too much in each other to throw it away. As I said, I can forgive you the lie. Eventually, I'll forget and we'll have the perfect life we've always planned."

I realized then, standing in my mother's entry hall, that I didn't love Phillip. I even took a step back at the thought. At least I hadn't been *in* love with him, and it had taken him saying something so businesslike and devoid of emotion to jar me out of the cocoon I had been all too happy to exist in. And that was what it was. A cocoon. A safe, warm place where I was comfortable.

I remembered then that I had compared the ease I felt with Phillip to the ease I saw pass between India and her grandmother. Probably not the best recommendation for marriage.

My anger faded as quickly as it had surfaced when I realized that I was guilty, though not because I hadn't made it clear I had money. That was the least of my crimes. Phillip had allowed me to exist in the safe place of no intense feelings. My real crime was thinking that existing in that place could possibly make for a fulfilling life — for me or for Phillip.

Messy is good. Jack's words.

Not that I suddenly believed it, but I did concede that living an anesthetized life was bad. A very different proposition from messy being good, I consoled myself.

"Oh, Phillip," I said. "Admit it. We're not in love."

His eyes crinkled with confusion. He didn't appear upset, not angry, just confused, as if love had nothing to do with anything. "But we make a good team."

"That's where you're wrong. We don't make a good team. Two people have to love and respect each other to make a good team, at least in marriage. They have to be committed down to their cores in order to survive the ups and downs of life."

"What are you saying?"

"That we have no business getting married."

"Carlisle," he said sternly. "You're a lawyer. A good one. And both of us know that there is no room in success for waxing poetic or letting emotion rule the day. That is why we're perfect for each other."

"I'm not a child to be reprimanded or a case to be won. More than that, I believe there is a woman out there who is perfect for you because you won't have to forgive her for who she is, or who you think she is."

He looked abashed. "Okay, I'm sorry. I came on too strong." He started to panic, tripping over the entry hall rug when he stepped toward me. "I'm sorry. Really, I'm sorry. I'm sorry for getting upset," he pleaded. "I just sort of . . . flipped."

"Phillip —"

"Let me finish." He took my hands in both of his, studying them. "I was jealous, so I found your friend Jack because I wanted to understand. Maybe I even wanted to see what was up with him."

My eyes narrowed.

"He didn't tell me much, but I could tell there's nothing going between you two." He sort of snorted. "No love lost there, I'd say."

Not that I didn't know this, and not that I cared, but you'd think Jack might have harbored a tiny soft spot for me, enough to smile at Phillip and congratulate him on his good fortune for winning my hand.

"Carlisle, I love —"

"Phillip." I held up my hand. "Thank you for coming to Texas to find me. That means more than you know. But it's over."

Emotion circled through his face, like a game-show spinning wheel of assorted prizes — anger, frustration, confusion, disbelief, ending on what I can only call resigned acceptance. We talked for a while longer, but nothing changed other than I felt a growing sense of relief when he finally left.

As soon as I heard the tires crunch on the gravel drive, like a moth drawn to a flame, I knew what I was going to do about my mother's case. She kept everything in the attic. With the exception of my one foray to retrieve the dancing template, I had avoided the upper regions of the house at all costs. But with little help for it, I ascended the two flights of stairs.

Under the sloped eaves of the hundred-year-old house there were several lifetimes of possessions. Books, trunks I knew were filled with clothes, old toys, memories. Everywhere I turned I was faced with my family's history and memories. The very thing I had left behind.

Rather than get sucked in, I pulled open a file drawer that contained records of my mother's debts, assets, and all previous litigation including prenups and divorces. I wasn't sure what I was looking for that could possibly help me, but I stopped when I came to a file on Lucky Stars Farm.

Sitting down in the old rocker by the window, I read through the file, then found pictures of my parents on beaches I didn't recognize, in a boat on a lake with my mother's hair down and flying in the wind, the two of them opening a new barn at the farm, newspaper photographs of my mother cutting the red ribbon, my father looking on, looking stunningly handsome as he stared down at his very young wife. I had never seen my mother look so happy. No cracks visible.

I was young when my father died and I hardly rememberd him. When pressed I could pull him up, but only in the context of my mother and how happy she was before he died. Everything else I knew about him, I had learned from the larger-than-life tales of a man who had lived well and loved my mother with the grand passion of a novel. I had always half discounted the stories. But looking at the photographs, I wondered if maybe they were true.

It was as I was putting the albums away that I saw my sister's diaries.

Stay Away!

Keep Out!

Don't You Dare Open!

My sister's handwriting scrawled the words all over the box.

I can't begin to explain why sensible Carlisle popped the lock on the first diary.

Dear Diary,

I had the most amazing day! I love junior high! I wore my favorite pink sweater, got tons of compliments (as usual), and Betsey Tanner was soooooooo jealous because everyone loves me better than her. At least everyone loves me but Mrs. Finkel. She HATES me. I mean, really, I do all my work. I might not get the best grades but I am totally the prettiest girl in the whole class. I should be her favorite!!!!!!!

Mother is in one of her @&%$ moods again, so I'm doing my best to ignore the drama of her latest boyfriend. Geez! What kind of mother has boyfriends!!!! It really is the most embarrassing thing EVER! Of course I pretend that it is so

379

awesome that my mother is so beautiful and that every man for miles around chases after her. But what I would give to have a NORMAL family.

Henry is as big of a freak as Mother. But I think Carlisle might actually be normal. Not that it matters. She's way too busy being smart and together to even notice that she has an older sister, one she should be looking to for advice! What I would give to have a sister who I could talk to. Someone I could curl up in bed with at night and share secrets. If we did, I would tell her about this completely amazing new guy, Nicky, who is madly in love with me.

Oh, well.

Gotta go. I think I'm going to wear the navy blue mini tomorrow. Better make sure it's in my closet!

xoxoxoxo,
Savannah

My throat felt oddly tight when I turned to another.

Dear Diary,
I was at Cindy Henley's house and her mother just had the cutest baby. I know I'm way too young to be thinking about

babies, but I know when I get older I will be the best mother in the history of mothers. Unlike certain mothers we know in this very house!!!!!

Anyway, it was weird to watch someone who actually took care of a baby. I mean, really, she held her!!! No maid anywhere to be found. That's the kind of mother I am going to be. I swear.

On top of that, I wore the polka-dot bikini to the country club yesterday and of course turned every boy's head. I'm like a goddess or something. The girls were snippy, as usual. But I just ignore them.

I met this new guy. Frank Winters. He is soooooo cute and I swear he's totally in love with me, but not all drooly like the other boys. He has some dignity. Plus he's on the football team! I've decided I'm going to be a cheerleader. Head cheerleader. I started to tell Carlisle about my plan because of course Mother was nowhere to be found. But C was building some moronic science project and totally was not listening. Whatever.

More later . . .

xoxoxoxo
Savannah

Most of the entries were the same. How great she was, the latest boy who was in love with her, the outfits that were much loved and the cause of great jealousy, and her wish that we were closer as sisters.

I couldn't have been more surprised if she had written diary entries in blood and spewed on about Satan. I also couldn't have been more surprised that my sister had been as lonely and frustrated about our mother as I had been.

An hour later, I returned to the hospital. The door to my sister's room was partially open. Inside she was alone, looking out the window, unexpected tears in her eyes. The prima donna was gone and for the first time I saw the daughter, not so different from me, overwhelmed by a parent whom we didn't know how to absorb. A parent who needed comforting, who never comforted. Probably didn't know how. I had always seen my sister as a girl, then a woman, who was used to getting her way simply because she was beautiful, her fine cheekbones and high brow lined with entitlement. I realized then that her beauty moved around her face with pain, not entitlement, like partners in a reluctant dance.

I walked into the sterile white room, the metal blinds down, the slats angled open.

"Hey," I said.

She dashed her hand across her eyes, and when she looked at me I saw the mask return, the pain pushed back to the edge of the dance floor, the arrogance pulled forward like a life preserver.

"I thought you went home?"

"Yep." I shrugged. "But now I'm back."

"You look terrible."

I laughed. "Thank you."

"Why are you smiling?"

"Because I feel like it."

She scoffed. But the sound cut off when I walked to the side of her bed, then carefully climbed up next to her.

"Good Lord, Carlisle! What in God's name are you doing?"

I was careful of the IV in her arm as I stretched out on my side, propping my head on my hand. "Just wanted to be with my sister."

Truth to tell, she looked sort of panicked, like a crazy person had just gotten in bed with her. I swear she eyed the nurse call button. And maybe I was crazy. Maybe it was too late to be her sister, at least as she had wanted when we were young.

"I thought we could braid each other's hair, talk about boys, the usual girl stuff." I shrugged. "Then maybe you can tell me how to avoid screwing up my life."

Suspicion mixed with confusion on her perfect face.

"I seem to be in need of some wisdom these days. And who better to give me advice," I added softly, "than my sister."

Which made her eyes fill with tears, though I could tell she fought them.

I rolled over on my back and stared at the ceiling since I didn't really want her to cry any more than she wanted to cry. "Then after that, I thought we could share our secrets," I added, though it was my voice that actually cracked. "Like real sisters do."

With a strangled moan, she broke down. "Oh, Carlisle. My baby."

She cried as I have never seen any woman in my family cry during daytime hours, hard, her body heaving.

There was nothing to say, so I snaked my arm under her neck, pulled her close, and held her as she cried.

"What am I going to do?" she said through her tears.

"There's plenty you can do."

She sucked in a gasping breath. "I don't have a law degree like you, or even any degree for that matter. All I am is pretty."

The last words were whispered like a confession at the Catholic church in the south part of town. I didn't have a clue how to respond.

"If I can't have children, then what good am I?"

My mother and sister spent their lives slashing their way through life with the sharp edge of blond hair, blue eyes, and physical beauty. I had always felt they took the easy way. Now I wondered. Looks eventually, always, fail.

"Oh, Savannah." I wrinkled my nose as I searched my brain for something to say. "You are plenty good, and you can be anything you want. Besides, I believe you'll have a baby one day."

She stiffened in my arms. "Don't say that."

Foolish, I know. But something in me rose to the surface and wouldn't be pushed back. "You've always believed in yourself and have never been afraid to persevere." I had to believe that in this case persevering wasn't denial. "That's what you've got to do now."

She leaned back and looked at me.

"Just don't give up on yourself. And don't force Ben out of your life. Remember, you said he was a keeper. The two of you will figure this out."

She gave me a pathetic look of hope, making me feel exceedingly uncomfortable.

The wide hospital door pushed open and

Janice walked in. "What are you two doing?"

I glanced at Savannah. "Being sisters."

Janice's brow furrowed and she looked ill at ease, out of place, and sort of gritchy at the same time. But I had spent enough time around my sister-in-law for the first time in our lives that I actually had an idea of what she was feeling. I groaned, and then extended my arm.

Janice's militant eyes went wide, then the next thing I knew she dashed across the room and climbed up on the other side of Savannah. I'm not making this up.

"I'm sorry about the baby," Janice whispered, tears welling in her eyes. "I feel responsible."

Savannah scooted over more to make room. "Of course you're not responsible, Janice. Just inventive."

The three of us laughed until the door pushed open again. This time Morgan walked in.

Unlike her mother, she didn't look wistful. "God, could you guys be any weirder?"

Just in case I was wrong, I extended my arm to her. Savannah and Janice followed suit. Morgan backed up a pace. "No way. Though it does suck about the baby, Aunt Savannah."

Savannah's eyes got teary again and Morgan looked concerned. "Sorry. I'll go. I just wanted to tell Mom that I went to pick up my gown and the saleslady said it was gone."

"What?" we demanded.

Without warning, tears sprang into Morgan's eyes, which she dashed at angrily. "Can you believe it? My dress. It's gone."

"But they just called and said it was here."

"I know. And I went to the shop to pick it up like we said, but when I got there they couldn't find it."

The door opened again and my mother walked in.

"What in the world is going on here?" she demanded.

Ridgely and her granddaughter exchanged a pained glance.

"Don't look at me," Morgan told my mother. "They're more your responsibility than mine."

Savannah, Janice, and I burst out laughing again.

"Laugh all you like," Mother snapped. "Though when you can spare a moment, Carlisle, you might want to have a look at this. Your Willow Creek debutantes have gotten their first newspaper headline."

With a grimace, I rolled to a sitting position on the hospital bed and took the afternoon newspaper my mother extended. There on the front page of the *Willow Creek Times* Lifestyles Section:

NEW DEBS ARE A SIGHT WE'RE NOT SURE YOU WANT TO SEE

The article that ran with it was less than complimentary to the girls, my mother, and myself.

Savannah and Janice read over my shoulder.

"You've got to be kidding," Janice snapped.

"Oh, dear," Savannah said.

"Oh, dear, indeed," Mother added. "I told you this would hurt the symphony, our family, and the debutantes. What do you plan to do about it? What brainchild are you going to come up with next?"

I hadn't a clue.

"I'll figure something out, Mother."

"Fine. And in the meantime, do whatever it is you need to do to settle this case with Vincent. I have no intention of returning to that courtroom."

CHAPTER
TWENTY-THREE

Unraveling \un-rav-el-ing\ pp (1603) 1:
coming apart at the seams 2: inability to
hold together 3: what I was doing at a dizzying pace.

Not to put too fine a point on it, but suddenly:

- I was no longer engaged,
- my sister had miscarried,
- my debutantes were on the verge of
  devolving into the laughingstocks of
  Willow Creek,
- and my grandmother's cherished symphony association debutante ball (not
  to mention its financial stability) was
  threatening to collapse.

If that wasn't enough, in the bonus round
there was:

- Jack going for the jugular,

- me not sure I could win against him,
- leading us all to my mother's reputation (not to mention *her* financial stability) on the verge of swirling down the drain with the remnants of last night's bottle of good sherry.

Oh, and one other thing. I had started questioning who exactly I was. Yes, me.

Though really, what would you expect. My perfectly ordered life was exploding in my face, and I knew that if I allowed the girls to become fodder for the gossip mill as I had been, I would never forgive myself.

I sat at my childhood white French Provincial student's desk, with gold gilt trim. My grandmother's letter lay on the desk in front of me. For about the millionth time, I reread the note, holding her heirloom pearls like rosary beads, still unable to put them on. To say she had overestimated my abilities to save the day would be an understatement. No sooner had I felt confident about the way things were coming together than boom, everything fell apart.

None of this felt good, which reminded me just why I didn't do emotion. Quite frankly, it never helped, which was why I had always scoffed at the notion that "messy is good." Hardly.

If I had been the type to indulge in said beliefs, I would have gone to the dollar movie house downtown and watched B movies all afternoon and stuffed myself with day-old popcorn. Given that I could be counted on to be just like me, I decided there was no time like the present to deal with a settlement, thereby allowing me to ignore said emotions of vulnerability.

Taking the Volvo, I headed for Jack's house. I didn't know if he still lived there until I pulled up and saw the Suburban and Harley. As I sat in the front drive, my fingers curled around the steering wheel, my heart did double time as I told myself that I would under no circumstances touch him in any way. He was engaged, even if I wasn't any longer.

Which reminded me of his fiancée. Was it possible, even in Willow Creek, Texas, that they lived together?

I knew Jack drove the Suburban, and I doubted Miss Long, Tall, and Svelte rode the Harley, so she either didn't live there or wasn't home. I got out of the car and knocked on the door.

His home was one of the small cottage houses that had been built in the 1920s. It was a perfectly kept stone house with bronze metal roof, and a cobbled circular drive. I knew he could afford more, but for whatever reason he stayed in the place he had bought for himself once he had started paying his own way. Neither his brother's wealth nor his more recent success as an attorney in the hottest boutique law firm in Central Texas had changed him. Still wild. Still daring. Still didn't seem to care what anyone thought of him.

Knocking again, I turned and looked back at the tiny yard and street. The house was on a rise, the rolling hills undulating out into the horizon. I had forgotten the power of that view, the big Texas sky overhead a nearly painful blue, blocked only by the long, twisting stretch of live oak branches.

I didn't hear the door open, but I wasn't startled when he stood behind me and said, "Carlisle?"

I turned back and yet again felt that surge in my chest. I mean, really, you should have seen him. He wore Wrangler jeans, work boots, a sweat-stained T-shirt as if he had been engaged in some sort of manual labor.

"Why are you here?" he said, his expression dark and not just a little forbidding.

I would have appreciated a hello. Even a grunt of welcome would have done in a pinch. His accusatory question made me blush. Quickly, I cleared my throat. "I would like to discuss settling after all."

He studied me forever, and for a second I would have sworn he wasn't going to let me in. But finally he nodded. "Fine. But it'll have to wait a minute. I'm in the middle of something."

My mind ran amuck with all sorts of things he could be in the middle of.

"Is Racine here?"

Jack rolled his eyes. "Get your mind out of the gutter."

"I'm just asking," I said, and followed.

The house was the same inside as it was the last time I had been there (on the floor, on the dining table, on the kitchen counter) three years earlier, with no sign of a female inhabitant. If Racine lived there, she had the same masculine taste in furniture and clothes as Jack. Which meant we were really alone. I swallowed back heat and another blush and reminded myself of my goal. Settlement. No sex. I do not have sex with other women's fiancés.

The space was done in warm earth tones, a rustic motif that thankfully didn't look as if he were trying to create a country cabin in the middle of town. There were over-stuffed leather sofas with heavy wool pillows thrown on them, and heavy overstuffed wool chairs on either end of a pine coffee table. The walls were painted an earthy terra-cotta, the ceiling simple cream with rough-hewn beams.

When I focused, Jack was nowhere to be found. After a second, I heard him, and given that I was reasonably smart, I deduced his project had something to do with power tools given the noise that suddenly erupted through the house.

Following the din, I went down a short hallway to the kitchen of warm granite and rustic wood, then on through a screened-in porch where he had more of the simple, casual furniture and a ceiling fan. I could see Jack in the backyard working with a chain saw.

A pile of branches lay on the ground, another more orderly pile of cut branches forming a second pile. A massive grill made of bricks, mortar, steel grates, and some sort of pulley contraption lay beyond the growing pile.

As soon as the power tool stopped, he looked up and saw me.

"Mesquite wood," he explained.

"I gathered as much."

"For grilling."

Call me what you will, but no one will ever say I don't know how to appreciate a good meal. And anyone in Texas will tell you that real mesquite-grilled anything is beyond wonderful, and not something you get in Boston. I felt my mouth water at the thought.

"You look like a lion with a zebra in its sights." He actually smiled for a change, before it was gone. "I have some lobster tails and T-bones in the refrigerator. Do you want to stay for dinner?"

"Me? You're inviting me? The woman who you made it clear to my former fiancé that there was no love lost between us?"

"Former, huh?"

"Yep."

"Just as well, I suppose. He didn't look like your type."

Clearly, he wouldn't qualify for a Mr. Sensitive award anytime soon. "What is that supposed to mean?"

"Just what I said."

"And I suppose Racine is your perfect type?"

There went that smile again. "Jealous, Cushing?"

I snorted.

"Are you staying for dinner or not?"

Well, really, who was I to be rude and turn down such a kind invitation? Besides, he had smiled. "I don't want to put you out," I said with grave politeness.

"Sure you don't."

"Will . . . Racine be joining us?"

"No, she's in Dallas." Then he pulled the cord on the saw, the air filling with the deafening roar.

Not knowing what else to do, and wanting to avoid flying wood chips, I returned inside. Without thinking, I went to the refrigerator and found everything needed for a perfect dinner.

Rolling up my sleeves, I got to work. I made a salad of romaine lettuce, dried cranberries, tomatoes, walnuts, with an olive-and-feta vinaigrette on the side to toss in later.

Next, I found everything I needed for my mother's famous scalloped potatoes that made the regular kind look tame in comparison. The recipe called for too much butter, too much cheese, too much cream, and even corn flakes to provide the crunchy top. It might sound strange, but take one bite and I dare you not to fall in love.

I found the steaks from Slim's House of Meats cut to perfection. Seasoning both sides, I set them on a plate and returned them to the refrigerator. Then I found the lobster. Four tails — the perfect part for grilling.

Given that the potatoes would take forty-five minutes to bake, I made a batch of quick biscuits and found a jar of homemade jam I was certain his mother had made.

Between all I had whipped up, combined with the steak and lobster, I'd have to starve myself for a week afterward. That and run, which I hadn't done in years. Preferably in the heat of the day. A cross between exercise and punishment.

But I wouldn't think about that just then. There was an amazing meal with my name on it, and I wasn't about to let a few potential (guaranteed) pounds deter me.

Just when I finished mixing up the biscuit dough, Jack came in through the back door, sans T-shirt. He wiped the sweat on his chest with a towel.

He glanced around. "Looks like you've been busy."

What could I say to that? "Seemed the least I could do."

"I'm going to take a shower while the grill heats up." He tossed the towel into the laundry room, opened a bottle of red wine, and poured two glasses. He extended one and looked at me with the sort of intensity that made me wish for an invitation to the shower. I swear he nearly asked, but he cursed instead, then disappeared.

You'd think he could get over my leaving

him without a word, and my not bothering to tell him I was engaged. Hello. Then I slapped myself upside the head.

No sex, I repeated, adding, *engaged, off-limits,* and *don't even think about it.*

When he returned, his glass empty and his hair still wet, he wore a clean black T-shirt tucked into 501 jeans. And we know what I think of 501 jeans. At least on Jack Blair.

He poured us each a second glass, and while my brain started to do the red alert thing again, I accepted the wine then let him guide me outside.

We stood on the back porch, the sun sinking on the horizon, splashing the sky in varying shades of purple. When I looked over at him, I remembered all those ridiculous feelings from the past, a larger-than-life love and, well, hot need. When I looked at his hands, all I could remember was the way they felt on my body.

"So, the case," I interjected into my wayward thoughts, dragging up my very best professional mien.

"Dinner first."

The smell of mesquite filled the air and, really, it would have been rude not to truly appreciate the lobster tail.

In short order, we had everything on the

table. He sat down across from me, and for a second, just looked at me. I swear it was as if three years hadn't passed.

"Jack —"

The front door banged open, cutting me off.

"Sweetie?"

Jack didn't move a muscle.

"Jack, sweetie, where are you?"

"Racine?" I asked.

"Racine," he confirmed.

"I can hide if you want," I said, my smile as wicked as any Savannah could have doled out, which was a knee-jerk reaction to the fact that I was massively disappointed.

"You are not going to hide." He stood. "We're in here, Racine."

His fiancée swept into the kitchen, an oversized handbag on her shoulder, then stopped. "Well, well, look who's here," she said. Then she turned to Jack. "You bad boy. Are you trying to charm Carlisle, hoping to win your case with a meal of steak and lobster?"

She walked over and gave Jack a long, deep kiss.

"I got back early, dropped my things off, then decided to surprise you. Little did I know you were here with Carlisle."

She laughed, and seemed completely unfazed by my being in Jack's house eating dinner, as if it had never occurred to her that I might be a threat.

I was almost insulted. I do have womanly pride, after all.

Racine talked about her trip to Dallas, retrieving a place setting and a glass of wine, then sitting down at the table.

"This looks fabulous. Carlisle, did you make all this?"

She didn't wait for an answer before going on about something else. We spoke of inconsequential things until Racine leaned back and gave me the once-over. "Tell me, do you really like Boston?"

"Sure."

Jack studied me, turning his wine glass slowly on the tablecloth.

"Hard to imagine," Racine said, blotting her mouth. "Though Jack told me about your fiancé. Phillip, right? I think he sounds just right for you, so maybe I'm wrong about you and Boston. That's where he lives, right?"

Jack just continued to consider me, and I felt uncomfortable.

"Actually, Phillip and I are no longer engaged."

Suddenly Racine didn't look quite as confident as she had a moment before.

"Not engaged?" she said. "What happened?"

"Hard to say. I guess we just weren't right for each other."

"Oh." A deep line appeared between her eyes. "I'm sorry to hear that."

"So listen, I don't want to intrude any longer. Jack, we really need to talk about the case."

He studied me, then nodded. "Racine, can you give us a few minutes?"

She glanced between us. "Of course. I'll just go freshen up." But before she left, she looked Jack in the eye and I was embarrassed by the intense emotion I saw pass between them. Then she kissed him softly on the lips. "I missed you," she said, then she left without so much as a glance over her shoulder at me.

"Shoot," he said, as soon as she was gone.

"As I mentioned, we'd like to settle."

He took a sip of his wine, considering me over the rim of the glass. "When I wanted to settle, you said no."

"We've changed our minds."

I spelled out the details, but this time his answer came back as no. Forgetting how he made my heart flutter, I pushed my wine aside. I reasoned, I made generous offers, I even resorted to batting my eyelashes.

He smiled at me and shook his head. "Come on, Cushing, you can do better than that."

Obviously not.

"Fine. I'd better go." I pushed up from the table, but he stopped me, taking my arm, his smile gone.

From his expression I couldn't tell what he wanted from me. Everything? Nothing? Which was probably more like it since Racine wasn't more than a room or two away.

His voice was deep, rough, when he spoke, catching me off guard. "Why didn't you say goodbye before you left?"

"Left?"

Impatience flared. "Left Texas."

Everything inside me froze, organs ceasing, heart stopping. I had no idea how to answer or even if I wanted to. But I suspected I owed him, at least that.

I raised my chin and looked him in the eye. "You want the truth?"

"Of course."

"I was afraid if I did you'd ask me to stay and I wouldn't be able to leave."

He started to smile, an utterly not-nice smile.

But then the whole truth came blurting out of me before I could stop myself. "Or maybe I was afraid you wouldn't ask me to stay."

I was all too aware of those strong fingers of his circling my arm. Very aware that Racine could walk in at any minute. Very aware that he wasn't more than inches away and I badly wanted him to kiss me. Just like at the Foley Building. Or us at the country club. His fiancée within earshot. Sanity forgotten. I know, me!

But after what seemed like forever, he simply nodded and let me go, turning away.

He got as far as the door when I stopped him. "My turn."

His expression grew wary.

"Why didn't you try to find me?"

His brown eyes flickered like a movie screen in the dark, the contours of his face hardening.

"Jack, love! Are you done yet?" Racine called out in the distance. "I have a surprise for you."

The dark edge faded and I could see ease come into his body like a deep breath. Ease, rightness. That same emotion I had seen pass between the two of them before she left the room. I understood then why Jack was with Racine. She gave him a sense of peace that neither of us had been able to give each other. I also understood then that he would marry her, just as I had been dead set on marrying Phillip. Only Jack hadn't started out living a lie with this woman. They had nothing to get over.

He smiled, that crooked smile that made hearts melt. "Like you said yourself, you're not like me, irresponsible, only doing things when it suits me. Let's just say it didn't suit me to find you, and leave it at that."

He left me standing there and headed for Racine. I'm not sure if I was more surprised that he remembered what I had said to him three years ago or that his smiling dismissal of the whole thing felt suspiciously like a javelin thrown straight through my heart.

CHAPTER
TWENTY-FOUR

As if my psyche needed more of a kick than it had already gotten at My Dinner with Jack . . . and Racine, the next day Janice dragged me over to Michel's House of Brides to reason, make generous offers, and bat eyelashes in hopes of obtaining the return of the missing dress.

At the eyelash maneuver, Michel himself gave me a strange look and asked if I needed to sit down. And it didn't go better from there.

No matter what I did, the outcome was the same. The dress was gone, but there was no receipt of sale except for Janice's — and Janice didn't have the dress.

"I do not know where eet is," the man said. "We cannot find eet anywhere."

"But it has to be here," Janice pleaded.

The older woman who had waited on us entered the store, her handbag swinging on her wrist. "Oh, hello! You've come for the dress."

"You have it?"

"Of course. Let me just put my things aside." She put her purse in a bottom drawer then pulled open a side closet. She flipped through the gowns, then flipped through again. "Well, I'll be." She turned around. "I must have put it in the back."

"Don't bother, Meez Montoya," Michel said. "I've looked everywhere. Zee dress is gone."

"But that's not possible. Who would have taken it?"

"India!" Janice blurted.

The woman appeared startled, and quite frankly, so did I.

"India Blair?" the saleslady asked.

Again, my sentiments exactly. Why would India take the dress?

Michel scowled. "Do you know theese India, Meez Montoya?"

"Well, yes. She's such a sweet girl."

There were many adjectives I would use to describe India, but "sweet" wasn't one of them. Though "thief" wouldn't have been on the list either.

"She has been coming in to visit young Ruth. Quite the odd pair, really," she mused. "Ruth is such a hard worker. Though just the other day, India helped me unpack

406

boxes. I'd say that is quite extraordinary for a girl in this day and age." The woman's brow furrowed. "Though come to think of it, she hasn't been back since." Her hand came to her chest. "Do you really think she could have taken the dress?"

Since we had no definitive answer, Janice asked about the dress that had been too big. Unfortunately, it had been sold to a WCU student who was getting married that summer.

After Michel made a big production of saying he would do anything he could to make things right (sans producing the dress, and sans calling up one of the richest men in Willow Creek and asking if by chance there was a missing gown lying around his house), we left. What were we going to do? We had no proof.

Outside on the front pavement, Janice and I stood in the growing heat.

"Why do you think India took it?" I asked.

"I know her type. She has to have the best everything, including the best dress. And it was one amazing dress. So she went to the store and got it before we could."

"I know girls can be competitive, but —"

"Carlisle, you're a divorce lawyer. Don't be naïve." She headed for the car. "Come on, we're going to speak to her father."

"We?" I asked.

Indeed, we headed for the Willows and were in luck that Hunter Blair happened to be home and let us through the gates. The man waited for us in his study.

"What can I do for you, ladies?"

"Mr. Blair," Janice began. "I believe that India has *mistakenly* taken my daughter's ball gown." Not even Janice wanted to accuse Hunter Blair's daughter of outright stealing.

Hunter, who hadn't stood when we entered his huge study filled with massive furniture and thick velvet draperies, studied us. After a second, he barked, "India!"

The teen entered, though not before a servant scurried off to find her. "What, Daddy?"

"The ladies here say you went and took a dress that was supposed to be for another of the girls."

"Mistakenly took," Janice reiterated.

Hunter ignored her. "Is this true?"

India scoffed. "I don't know what they're talking about, Daddy."

"We're talking about the dress you mistakenly took from Michel's last week," Janice clarified.

India gave one of those scrunched teenage faces. "Hello, I already have my dress. The one my dad bought me in New York."

Hunter rocked back in his chair and considered.

"Sir," Janice said, "I'm sure she's mistaken."

"There's a lot of 'mistaken' flying around."

"Perhaps we could have a quick peek in her closet," Janice suggested.

"Daddy! That is so unfair!"

Hunter stood. "Let's have a look."

"They are lying about me!"

She made a big production about not being trusted, her eyes narrowed with anger. But that didn't deter her father. The four of us went up to India's room where she carried on and wept though I wasn't sure why.

"I know you hate me!" she screamed at him.

"Stop acting like your mother."

Which pretty much made us all freeze.

India's face went hard, her tears drying. "If I acted like my mother, I would have run away and not come back, just like her."

They stared at each other, locked in a war that I realized had been waging for years.

He stormed through her closet. Just so you know, there are whole houses in South Willow Creek smaller than India's closet. There were rows of shoes, glass drawers filled with jewelry, and racks lined with more clothes than I had probably owned in my entire life. If things could make a person happy, India Blair should have been dizzy with joy.

"There's nothing here," he announced bitterly, then turned and left the room.

"India," I began.

"Just shut up." She raced away, her bathroom door slamming shut.

Janice and I looked at each other. "Come on," she said. "Let's get out of here."

Outside, we were heading for the Volvo when I noticed India's Jeep.

"Let's look in her car."

We were peering into her Jeep in seconds.

"No dress," Janice lamented.

"Wait. Look." I pulled out a big Michel's shopping bag, though there was no sign of a gown.

India slammed out the front door. "What are you doing?" she screeched.

I held out the shopping bag.

"So?"

"What's the big Michel's shopping bag doing in there?" I asked.

Red burned through the girl's face.

"How should I know," she stated. "Tiki or Abby probably left it in there."

"Really," I countered. "I thought the three of you weren't speaking."

"What is this, an inquisition? I don't have the stupid dress, so leave me alone!"

"I can't believe this!" Janice bit out as we left the Willows. "India has the dress, I'm sure of it, but who knows where. Morgan is going to be crushed." She sighed. "Though I guess every girl has to learn the reality of life sometime, and the reality is that people can do hateful things. And isn't it my job to prepare my daughter for the world she's about to step into, the world that we are supposedly launching these girls into?"

Was she really asking? Or was this one of those trick rhetorical questions where the person didn't expect an answer, and quite frankly didn't want one.

I rolled the dice. "Actually, it seems to me that your job as a mother is to help your daughter believe in herself."

Janice went very, very stiff. "What are you implying?"

"Nothing. It was just a rhetorical statement." If there was such a thing.

We drove back to Wainwright House. When we walked in we found Savannah home from the hospital, ensconced on a chaise in the garden room, surrounded by plump pillows and a cotton rather than cashmere throw in concession to the grow-

411

ing heat. She was riding the roller coaster of hormones, a rockier ride than even my sister was used to. I reminded myself of the Savannah in the diaries and braced myself to take whatever she doled out.

My mother entered from the kitchen. "There you all are." She huffed, then turned to Savannah. "What are you doing out here? You should be in bed. Resting. Recovering." Then she focused on Janice. "And why are you just standing there? Your children are upstairs acting like . . . your children."

She left without waiting for a response. My mother's mood was getting worse and I was concerned that the cracks might start to show.

Janice stood there half furious, half frustrated. "That woman is the most unsupportive mother I have ever met," she stated. "All she wants is for her daughters, and even me, to do things her way and only her way!"

Savannah and I exchanged a glance and smiled. Janice's brow furrowed, before her eyes went wide. "I am not like your mother!"

"You don't have to wear cashmere and pearls to expect your daughter to be just like you."

You'd think we had shot her, as wounded as she looked, though I am certain she was remembering the tiny little uncomfortable discussion she'd had with Morgan on Blair Air.

Savannah pulled the throw closer. "Did you find the dress?"

"No," I said. "We think India took it."

Savannah rolled her eyes. "Of course she took it. Who else would have? Did you go to her house?"

"Yes," I said, "but it wasn't in her room or in her car."

"Then it's in her locker," my sister predicted.

Janice blinked. "Her locker? If she wants the dress why would she stuff it in a high school locker?"

"Get real, Janice. India doesn't want the dress. She just doesn't want Morgan to wear it." She folded her arms over the blanket. "Look. Debutantes are pretty much the same. You have the girls who just want to survive, the girls who want to have fun. There are the ones who are doing it because their parents make them. Then there are the girls who want to win and will do whatever it takes to do it. India wants to win."

"Win?"

"Deb of the Year."

"Errr," Janice growled. "I am so tired of hearing about Deb of the Year!"

Savannah shrugged unapologetically.

"So what am I going to do?" the mother of the gownless teenager asked.

"Go to the high school, of course," Savannah stated.

Janice thought for a second. "Okay," she said with a nod. "I will not be an unsupportive mother." She actually glared at me. "I'll go and talk to the principal, get him to open up the locker."

"You're going to request a little unlawful search and seizure?" I asked. "Our family is in enough hot water as it is."

Janice arched her back and roared her frustration. "You're right. But what am I supposed to do?"

Unfortunately, I was fresh out of solutions.

CHAPTER
TWENTY-FIVE

Despite my mother's wishes that she not set foot back in the courtroom (and regardless of the strange difficulty I suddenly had in regard to the simple act of breathing), the courtroom was exactly where we found ourselves the following Thursday.

During the intervening time, I pored over Jack's evidence and interviewed witnesses. He had copious photographs of my mother at the Lazy 6 with an unidentified man, along with photos of her car in the parking lot, not to mention her disappearing into one of the rooms. At the end, all I could say was, "Mother, you're sunk if you don't give me something, anything, to prove you didn't have an affair."

She remained stubborn and closemouthed for the duration, my frustration level building even as the whole breathing thing became more pronounced.

"Mother, you have no way to prove that

you didn't have an affair."

"I have my word."

"Unfortunately" — there might have been a trace of sarcasm in my voice — "in a court of law that doesn't amount to much. Are you willing to leave your fate up to what the judge believes? We've both seen the pictures Jack has of you at the Lazy 6."

She eyed me in a way that could curdle a lesser woman's blood. "You're supposed to be such a great lawyer, dear. Here's your chance to prove it. It's your job to find a way to make the judge believe me," she added. "Surely if you're as good as they say, at least you can do that."

"All rise," the bailiff called.

We launched into our day in court, the gallery filled with Willow Creek society types. I wore a black Calvin Klein suit and a white sateen high-collared blouse I found in San Antonio. With my hair pulled back in a sleek chignon, I added my black-framed glasses to finish off my power look.

The preliminaries were quickly dispensed with, including my mother's flirting smile to Judge Melton, before Jack stood.

"Your Honor, I call Oscar Hemmel."

A tall lanky man with sandy blond hair, nondescript eyes, and ill-fitting shirt and tie took the stand, swore he would tell the truth, then folded himself into the spindle-back chair.

"Mr. Hemmel," Jack began, "please tell the court where you are employed."

"I work at the Lazy 6 Motel," Hemmel stated proudly. "I'm the front desk manager," he added with a nod of importance.

"In your capacity as front desk manager, have you ever seen this woman?" Jack asked, pointing to my mother.

Ridgely sat up even straighter, tilted her head up a bit, no doubt to tighten any hint of a double chin, and smiled.

Hemmel sort of waved at her. "Why, yes sir, I have seen her before. Every Wednesday at noon."

Jack retrieved photographs from his table and extended one to the witness. "What do you see here in exhibit one, Mr. Hemmel?"

The man peered close. "That's her," he said, pointing to my mother, "going into room 5 like she always does to have her affair."

"Objection!" I stated. "Your Honor, this is pure speculation."

The courtroom buzzed.

"Based on this photo," I continued, "there is no evidence of an affair whatsoever."

Mr. Hemmel made a condescending noise in his throat. "As much as I see going on around that place, I know an affair when I see it. I'd say I'm something of an expert. Isn't that right, Mr. Blair?"

"Your Honor," I bit out, glaring at Jack, all too easily imagining opposing counsel implying without saying to Hemmel that he was an expert. "I would like the witness's statement stricken from the record. While the position of motel desk clerk is a perfectly respectable job, we all know there is no such thing as an *expert* on affairs."

"Agreed. Strike that," the judge told the court reporter.

But the fact was, by getting the word "expert" out there, it couldn't be taken back.

The judge turned to Jack. "Objection sustained. Mr. Blair, please inform your client that he is only to answer when he is asked a question."

"Yes, Your Honor."

Though I could see the hint of his satisfied smile.

"Continue."

Jack extended another photo, this time of my mother at the door with the unidentified man.

"Mother," I hissed, "why won't you tell me who he is? If we could find him, then he could testify to your assertion that you weren't having an affair."

After the day Jack saw my mother with the man, he had disappeared. No one, not even Jack, could find him.

"If he's not at that motel," my mother bit out, "then as I've said, I have no idea where to find him."

I still didn't know if I should believe her.

"Carlisle, there is no need to find him. He's no one."

"Mr. Hemmel," Jack said, "in your knowledgeable *opinion* as the desk manager of the Lazy 6 Motel" — aka the Expert — "that rents out rooms by the hour, would you say that based on this photo it is easy to ascertain that Mrs. Ogden is engaging in an affair?"

My mouth dropped open. "Objection." I couldn't imagine how Jack thought he could possibly get away with that kind of question.

"On what grounds, Miss Cushing?"

I blinked in disbelief at the judge. "Leading," I said as if speaking to a mentally challenged first-grader.

"Objection sustained. Mr. Blair, rephrase your question."

"Of course, Your Honor. Mr. Hemmel, what do you think is going on in this photograph?"

"They're having an affair."

"Your Honor, I object," I stated firmly. "Again, speculation."

The judge considered. "It is his opinion. But proceed carefully, Mr. Blair."

My jaw cemented and yet again I saw that hint of a satisfied smile on Jack's face. My game was off, way off. What was worse was that I couldn't put my finger on exactly why.

"Mr. Hemmel," he continued, "what other evidence led you to conclude Mrs. Ogden was engaged in an affair?"

He shrugged. "Well, there's the seeing them like that," he said, pointing to the photos, this time of my mother kissing the man on the cheek, "then every time she left, the sheets were a mighty big mess, let me tell you."

The gallery twittered.

"No further questions," Jack said.

"Miss Cushing?"

I stood and approached the witness, my mind spinning as effectively as tires on ice. Me. The woman who had been written up in several law journals, all under the auspices of who to watch in law.

"Mr. Hemmel," I began, trying to calm down, "how do you know the sheets were messed up after Mrs. Ogden left the motel?"

"The maid, Hortensia, told me."

Jack grimaced.

Finally. I didn't let the smile I felt show. "So you never actually saw the sheets messed up."

"Well, no, ma'am. But Horty has no reason to lie."

"I am not accusing anyone of lying, Mr. Hemmel. Just pointing out to the court that you didn't actually see the alleged mess. The testimony is simply hearsay," I said pointedly to the judge. "No further questions."

Not one to be outdone, Jack stood and called Hortensia Murtado to the stand.

Miss Hortensia Murtado went on about the handsome man and the beautiful woman, and their big love. The court, gallery included, was witness to more photographs of my mother with the same unidentified and suspiciously not-to-be-found man, kissing as she entered the motel room, then others of her car, parked outside the door, her license plate, and still more of her leaving the room fixing her hair. I wasn't sure when Jack had had a second to talk to Phillip for the sheer amount of time he must have spent in his car snapping photos with the camera he no doubt kept in his glovebox for just such an occasion.

Regardless, I objected for every reason I

could think applied, and for several reasons that I knew didn't, but I wanted to break the mesmerizing spell Jack was casting with his case. None of said objections got me anything more than increasing scowls from the bench.

"Miss Cushing, do you have any questions for Miss Murtado?" the judge asked.

"Yes, sir."

I gripped the edge of counsel's table for a second before I stood and approached the stand.

"Miss Murtado?" I began with a kind smile. She glanced from me to Jack a little dreamy eyed. "Over here," I said, waving my fingers.

She turned back with a frown.

"Miss Murtado. Isn't it possible that the sheets were already messed up before Mrs. Ogden arrived at the motel?"

The maid drew herself up. "I make bed each morning. I do my job. I good at my job. You no say otherwise. That woman," she said, pointing to my mother, "come to motel and mess up sheets. I have to change every time after they make their bad love!"

I swallowed back a groan. Now I even had the maid implying my mother was having an affair.

My heart thumped against my ribs and I

felt hot perspiration beading on my forehead.

Forcing a smile, I focused on the witness.
"Ms. Murtado, did you actually see Mrs.
Ogden and the man having . . . intimate
relations?"

"What?"

"Having sex."

More twittering.

"Well, no, I no actually see, but I know
what I know," she sniffed.

"Yes, fine, but you did not see them, correct? You only assumed because of the
rumpled sheets?"

She didn't look happy.

"Ms. Murtado, your answer, please?"

"No, I no see."

"Thank you. I am through with the witness, Your Honor."

"You may step down."

Jack stood, but didn't follow up with the
maid. "Your Honor, I call Bertram Wicker."

The motel handyman found his way to
the stand, ambling up to the front in his
plaid flannel shirt despite the eighty-degree
heat.

"Mr. Wicker," Jack said, "you have stated
that you believe Mrs. Ogden was having an
affair with the man who rented room 5 at
the Lazy 6 motel."

"Yes, sir."

"Did you actually see Mrs. Ogden and the man engaging in sexual relations?"

"No, sir, I did not."

The gallery tensed and I cocked my head.

"Then how, Mr. Wicker, did you come to the conclusion that Mrs. Ogden and the man were engaged in sexual relations?"

"Well, sir, I heard them with my own two ears."

As calmly as I could, I flipped through my notes. There was no mention of anyone hearing anything.

"How did you happen to hear?" Jack asked.

"You see, we got ourselves a bat problem at the Lazy 6, and I was using one of those listening-recording devices against the wall of room 4 to find where their colony was." He chuckled. "I didn't hear any bats, but I did hear what was going on in room 5."

Then Jack surprised us all by pressing play on a handheld recorder. Instantly a female voice echoed in the high-ceilinged court-room, moaning.

I leaped up so hard and fast that I knocked the wooden table forward a good three inches. "Objection!"

"Mr. Blair, turn that blasted thing off."

"Your Honor," I said, when the voice

ceased abruptly. "I have no prior knowledge of this tape. Mr. Blair has clearly violated the rules of ethics. I request a mistrial."

Judge Melton wasn't happy. But before he could rule, Jack launched into an Academy Award–worthy speech.

"Your Honor, I apologize to the respondent and the court for my unique method."

Unique method? I might have snorted, must have snorted since everyone turned to look at me.

Jack continued. "But Mrs. Ogden and her lawyer still remain less than forthcoming in regard to information my client is entitled to. I find myself operating under extenuating circumstances, and am forced to act in my client's best interest."

The judge shot a glare in my direction, then said, "I want to hear the rest of the tape."

I couldn't believe it. I was back on my feet. "Your —"

"Don't bother, Miss Cushing."

"Sir —"

But Jack was no dummy. He didn't wait. He pressed play and the moan restarted. *"Oh, yes"* a woman said, *"more. I want more."*

"Your Honor," I bleated. "There is no way to determine who is on this tape."

"Patience, Ridgely."

425

I groaned, then wanted to disappear altogether when an orgasmic *"Oh, my stars, you are wonderful"* washed through the courtroom like a wave.

My mother sat stoically in her chair, ramrod straight, proud despite her precarious position. I made copious notes as to why I deserved a mistrial. I couldn't imagine how things could get worse. But of course they did. A man entered and slipped Jack a note.

Opposing counsel read, then glanced at me before turning to the judge. "Your Honor, I have just learned that we have located the unnamed man in the photographs. I would like time to question one Martin Pender who has just arrived at court."

The back doors banged open and everyone turned to find a man who faintly resembled the blurry image in the photos.

"Martin?" my mother said as she sucked in her breath.

I had no idea what was going on, and I would have objected, though who knows on what grounds, if my mother hadn't outdone herself. As the man headed up the aisle, she whispered, "Oh, my," and fainted dead away.

CHAPTER
TWENTY-SIX

I have never been more grateful for my mother's dramatics in my whole life.

The bailiff raced over to her, even Vincent started to go to her, though Jack held him back.

"Your Honor . . ." I started, but didn't need to.

"This court will reconvene first thing tomorrow morning." Judge Melton crooked his finger at me to come forward.

When I stood before his bench, Jack scrambling to come up next to me, the judge said, "I will not tolerate a trial filled with your mother's shenanigans."

Then he stood and was gone just as Jack arrived at my side.

"What was that about?"

"Oh, nothing," I managed.

Who better than I to know that my mother's "shenanigans" couldn't be controlled. At least by me. "You know how men are regarding my mother. He was concerned about her health, is all."

Jack cursed, his brow lined with worry. And why shouldn't he worry? Jack knew as well as I did that he had been given more rope that day than he should have been given. And this judge was known to be fickle. Whatever Jack's reasons were for going after my mother, if he wasn't careful, he very easily could have reeled off enough rope to hang himself.

I smiled to myself, then went to my mother's side as she was helped out of the courtroom.

Once in the car, my mother smoothed her skirt. "I was good, wasn't I?"

"Not so much since the judge is on to you. If you pull a stunt like that again he's going to throw you in jail on contempt."

"He can't do that!"

"He can, and he will."

We pulled into the driveway and my mother shooed me out of the car, and told Ernesto to hand over the keys.

"I have someone I need to see."

"Mother, don't you dare go talk to anyone about this case!"

"Someone's got to do something."

Short of lying down in front of the Mercedes, I didn't know how to stop her. And quite frankly, I wasn't sure my blocking the way would have done more than leave me with tire tracks across my back.

She returned an hour later looking quite pleased with herself. She even had Lupe pour her a glass of sherry.

"Mother, we need to discuss Martin Pender. Without the alcohol."

She waved me away. "There is nothing to discuss."

"What do you mean?"

"Martin Pender will not be back in court tomorrow."

I gasped. "Mother, what did you do?"

She smiled her particular brand of satisfied smile and took another sip.

"You killed him!"

She sighed in exasperation. "Good Lord, Carlisle. Don't be ridiculous." The smile returned. "I just convinced him it was worth his while to leave town."

I slapped my hands over my ears. "I don't want to hear it." And quite frankly, what were my choices? Turn my mother over for tampering with a witness? Or pretend I hadn't heard her? I opted for the latter, and why not. It wasn't like I was the only person in this hearing who had lost sight of how to be a lawyer.

I left the room, wondering how I had ever gotten tangled up in this mess with a lunatic mother, crazy judge, and an opposing counsel who played fast and loose with the rules.

I had to shift my regular dance school for debutantes to the evenings given my court schedule. During the deb sessions I stopped messing around. The girls were going to become proper young ladies who could carry themselves with grace if it killed me.

I drilled them like a marine sergeant, running them through their paces like they were in a debutante boot camp. We walked, talked, practiced pleasantries. And we did more Dips than royal courtiers in front of a queen. Unfortunately, the girls weren't getting any better. Tiki and Abby didn't even try to do much more than bob their heads. Sasha spent most of her time talking on her cell phone to her boyfriend. And I was really nervous that Ruth still had money worries.

The Smiths had only taken one table instead of the unwritten rule of at least two, and they were paying for it on the installment plan — which I suspected was a first for Willow Creek debutantes. When I had asked Ruth about her dress, she had been evasive, simply exclaiming it was going to be great. It was her cheer again that gave me pause.

In court, if possible, the gallery grew even more crowded. Savannah had warned me it was coming, mentioning at breakfast that everyone who was anyone in town was talking about my disastrous debs and the titillating divorce proceeding. Wainwrights had become the best source of entertainment in town.

At the news, my mother had gone all out by dressing in a stunning royal-blue suit that highlighted her eyes, her blond hair, and supple skin luminous even under the harsh court lighting. She wore pearls at her ears and neck, and greeted people as we arrived as if we were entering a gala in her honor, not a hearing that could take her down.

"Don't ever let them see you sweat," she whispered to me under the flash of newspaper photographers.

"Your Honor, I call Martin Pender," Jack announced.

My mother smiled confidently.

But Jack looked at me with a raised eyebrow as if he knew what my mother had done. Then he nodded toward the inner door, which opened spitting out one Martin Pender led by two court officers.

My mother's confident smile faltered, and

I could tell she was on the verge of fainting, this time for real. "Don't you dare," I hissed.

Martin Pender was a tall, handsome man, with deep brown eyes, his light milk-and-coffee skin speaking to a Spanish heritage.

My brow knitted. Something was off.

Pender stood in front of the bailiff, his hand placed reluctantly on the Bible.

"Do you swear to tell the truth, the whole truth, and nothing but the truth, so help you God?"

He shrugged. "What is truth, anyway?"

Judge Melton glared and started to say something, no doubt something unkind and of the punishable-by-another-night-in-jail variety.

"Fine, I'll tell the truth. And the truth is I am here against my will," he stated more to my mother than anyone else.

"Your Honor," Jack said, "I would like the court to recognize that Mr. Pender is a hostile witness."

"So noted."

Jack cleared his throat. "Mr. Pender, for the record, please state your name."

His name came out reluctantly, hesitantly. But the sordid details of his and my mother's "alleged" affair did not.

"I met her at a café on the Riverwalk in San Antonio."

I knew my mother loved the Riverwalk, and went often.

"She flirted with me."

No surprise there. She flirted with every man.

"Then I saw her again the next week, at the same café. We started to talk."

Jack hammered away, asking questions, ruthlessly grilling the witness, going from their encounters of harmless flirting to furtive dating, to their first physical encounter, all in San Antonio until they made a regular date at the Lazy 6 Motel.

As Pender warmed to his subject, he regaled the audience with a tale of inventive sex that had everyone on the edge of their seats even if their faces were flushed with embarrassment. He threw around words like "naked" and "hot," "sweaty skin" and "sliding together" as easily as if we were in an X-rated porn shop.

Only Jack stood through it all with the implacability of a warrior used to seeing blood. And by the time he finished his line of questioning, the courtroom felt much too hot and not a little dirty, though based on the detailed description given, there was no doubt in anyone's mind that my mother had indeed had an affair with Martin Pender. Even I couldn't see how he could make up the sordid tale.

"This court will reconvene tomorrow at ten," the judge announced, pushing up so abruptly that his high leather chair banged back against the wall, and the bailiff had to scramble to do his job.

In the car on the way home my mother and I were silent. I didn't have a clue where to begin. I also didn't know how to look her in the eye given all I had heard in the courtroom.

As if reading my mind, she huffed and looked out the window. Willow Creek passed by as I studied her profile. "Why would Jack Blair have it in for you?"

She jerked her head back to look at me. "What are you talking about?"

"Truthfully? I don't know. At first I thought it was about me. But now I'm not so sure. If I were a betting woman, I'd say he was going after you." I flinched involuntarily. "God, Mother! Did you have sex with him too?"

"Carlisle! Heavens no."

Right or wrong, I believed her. "Then why?" I persisted.

She sighed. "Who knows. Though whether it's those Bennetts or those Blairs, they've never been particularly friendly."

Actually, she had never been particularly

friendly to them.

"Whatever the case," she continued, "he's being as rude as I have ever seen a man be."

"Mother, lawyers aren't supposed to be minding their manners."

"Carlisle, everyone should mind their manners no matter where they are."

My mother — Emily Post.

We were silent, tension riding between us like another unwelcome passenger in the car.

"This isn't going well," she finally said.

"First clue?"

"Stop acting like a child."

"I am not a child."

I might have stamped my foot.

Note to self: you are a successful adult and an accomplished attorney.

"I don't get it," I said. "You've done nothing but criticize everything about me since I got home. Why did you want me to deal with your divorce when you don't have any confidence in my abilities, and you won't do anything to help!"

"Good Lord, Carlisle. What is wrong with you?"

I sat up straight with a start. "What is wrong with me? Why don't you take a look in the mirror for a change, and not simply to notice how beautiful you are."

She went very still, a bad sign, but I was too caught up in the moment to take notice. "You have spent my whole life getting into trouble and expecting me to fix it somehow, which is bad enough," I said. "But you're never, ever satisfied with how I get it done. Why don't you stop getting in trouble? Why don't you stop demanding everyone's attention? Why can't you be like every other normal mother out there?"

I expected at least a bit of contrition. I was mistaken.

"Because sweet, shy doormats don't get anywhere in life," she said with a cold voice. She looked me up and down. "Besides, what's so wrong with wanting to be noticed?"

"Nothing, I suppose, if you're an actor, or an opera singer, or a politician, or a . . . whatever. But not a mother at the Willow Creek Elementary PTA meetings, or at my birthday parties, or when I was in the final round of the Central Texas Debate Competition. You weren't the one who was supposed to be noticed. You were an adult, a mother, not one of the kids. But no, you could never be a regular mom. No apron, no cookies, no simple questions like 'How was school today, dear?' "

My heels jammed against the floor board

in surprise at all I had spilled.

Ernesto shot us a nervous glance in the rearview mirror, and why not given the unwritten Wainwright rule of avoiding confrontation at all costs.

My mother and I both drew a breath and cut ourselves off. We drove in silence the rest of the way. When we pulled up the long brick drive, I was frustrated and confused. I started to get out but she caught my arm and told Ernesto to go on without us.

While I was frustrated, my mother had a strange, almost melancholy expression on her face. She sat for an eternity, not letting me go, but not speaking either. Finally she said, "Do you want to know a secret?"

I wasn't sure. This could easily go in any number of directions, most of which I had no interest in going.

"I've never thought I was beautiful."

I narrowed my eyes. My mother, the great boaster of her beauty, never thought she was beautiful?

"I wasn't when I was young, you know," she continued, smoothing the perfect lines of her skirt. "As I got older, I guess I grew into myself, and it was quite a surprise when people started calling me beautiful. And you know how one thing leads to the next; soon I started working to be more beautiful. I can't tell you how differently people treated me once they saw me as the perfect beauty. It was unnerving, especially since I never thought I was perfect. In fact, more than anything I was sure that I wasn't. But I learned that if I showed the perfect front, didn't let anyone know that I had any weaknesses, then that front was what people believed."

Was this what had caused the cracks?

"Is it so wrong that I need to feel beautiful?" she asked.

How to answer that? Or, realistically, *was* there an answer? And was the trouble she constantly found herself in a trade-off she was willing to make in order to feel noticed?

"Do you remember when you were a little girl," she continued, and I could hear the fond smile in her voice, "how you used to pull the red beach towel out of the linen closet, tie it around your neck like a cape? You would sit for hours seriously tackling whatever you were doing. It was cute, but I always thought it a shame that you didn't run up and down the yard in that cape, have fun. You know, let loose. But you only put it on to work. Even at four."

I felt heat in my cheeks, and didn't dare tell her that while the red towel was long gone, I still thought of the cape, almost as an anchor against the storm.

"Just one more time, pull out your cape and find a way to fix this, Carlisle." High dramatics even for my mother. "Then I promise not to bother you with another deb ball or divorce ever again."

CHAPTER
TWENTY-SEVEN

I sat in the car long after my mother went inside. I hadn't a clue what I felt. Being out of practice in the emotion department, I didn't know how to make sense of it all.

The first person I saw when I entered the house was Janice, and I understood then what I was going to do.

"Come on," I said, grabbing her sleeve and tugging her from the room.

"Where are we going?"

"To the high school."

My sister-in-law gave me a worried look. "What for?"

"We're going in for the dress."

"You're joking."

"Surprisingly, I'm not. But if India really took the gown, she can't get away with it."

"This is insane. We can't go to the high school."

I gave her a look. "You want the dress, don't you?"

"Yes. But I'm calling around. Surely someone in the whole state of Texas has that dress."

"And how is that going?"

She growled. "No one can find another one."

"So, *Mom,* what are you going to do about it?"

"Oh, man," she groaned, but allowed herself to be pulled upstairs where I enlisted Savannah's help.

"Make us look like teenagers."

"Good Lord, I'm talented but not a miracle worker," Savannah said, giving Janice's thirty-seven-year-old gauze-and-muslin-clad form a once-over.

Despite that, she did a remarkable job, I thought, using a combination of makeup, clothes inappropriately borrowed from Morgan's closet, and some old Halloween costume paraphernalia.

Once decked out as "teenagers," Janice and I procured the Volvo and wheeled through the streets, radio blaring.

"To get us in the mood," I supplied, as I turned up the local Top 40 station, feeling young and reckless. Which probably wasn't the best way to go into a breaking-and-entering stint in a high school in Central Texas.

"How exactly are we going to get the dress?" Janice asked nervously when we pulled in to the Willow Creek High School parking lot, smacking the gum I insisted we chew to complete the look.

I whipped a fingernail file out of an over-sized WCHS canvas bag I had found.

"What?" She sounded panicked. "We're going to break into India's locker? We can't do that!"

"And you call yourself an investigative re-porter."

"You were the one who went on about unlawful search and seizure."

"That was before I pulled out my red cape."

"What are you talking about?"

"Forget it. We need to hurry." I rolled out of the car, smacking the gum, dragging the bag with me, and tripped on the pair of chunky heels Savannah insisted I wear. "We need to get inside while the kids are chang-ing classes so we can see where India's locker is."

Janice couldn't seem to move from the car. I raced around and opened her door. "Weren't you the one saying that you wanted to be a supportive mom?"

"Yeah, supportive mom, not serving-eight-to-ten mom."

I laughed. "Come on, Janice."

She drew a deep breath and got out of the car. "You know this is insane, right?"

"Sure," I said, and dragged her along beside me.

Thankfully, it didn't take more than a yard or two before Janice got into her role. "We'll blend in," she stated, though I wasn't sure who she was trying to convince.

Taking the cement steps to a west side door, we slipped inside, hurrying down one corridor, then another, making our way through the maze of hallways of WCHS.

The deeper we went, the more Janice got into her role. By the time the bell rang and students flooded the halls between classes, my cohort in crime "jived" with the masses. "Hey, dude. What's up? Awesome."

"Dude," some boy said. "What's with the grammas in school?"

So much for blending in.

"Keep your head down," I instructed.

Just before the bell for fifth period rang, we saw India at her locker. Sure enough, she barely opened it, tossing a book in, slipping another out, before she banged it shut then walked away.

As soon as the bell rang, we raced forward. I was struck by the sudden, nearly deafening silence once the kids were back in class.

"This is the one," I said, dropping the bag and taking out the file.

I glanced up and down the wide deserted hall, lockers lining each side, and a large round clock extending out. One thirty-two.

I took the file to the lock and got to work. But no matter how I pried, the latch wouldn't give.

"Hurry," she said.

"I'm working as fast as I can."

"Here, let me try."

She grabbed the file, but made no progress.

"Someone's coming," I gasped as I suddenly heard the faraway sound of sensible heels echoing in the corridor.

I grabbed the file, and stuck it between the outer metal trim and the door, jimmying hard (no doubt adrenaline kicking in) until the door popped open. We leaped back in surprise as the dress fell out. I barely caught it before it hit the floor.

"We got it!" Janice squealed.

The footsteps grew louder.

"Oh, my gosh, we've got to hurry!" she cried in a whisper.

Like crazy people, we stuffed the billowing satin, tulle, and organza into the bag, nearly zipping our fingers in our haste. Then we flew in the opposite direction of the footsteps, careening through the hallways. Both of us having graduated from WCHS, we knew our way by heart despite the years that had passed between graduation and the present.

Right then left, our chunky heels sliding on the shiny linoleum like kids from *The Breakfast Club.*

"Just one more hallway and we're home free," Janice bleated.

We rounded a corner that took us back to the side door. And came smack-dab in front of Mr. Sisk, assistant principal of WCHS for as long as anyone could remember.

"What the devil are you two girls doing out of class?"

CHAPTER
TWENTY-EIGHT

Escape \es-cape\ vb (1425) 1: to evade 2: to avoid confinement 3: to elude a completely and totally embarrassing situation of being caught in a high school that you didn't particularly enjoy when you were supposed to be there and certainly would not enjoy in a second go-around under less than auspicious circumstances.

But maybe that's just me.

All I can say is, thank God Mr. Sisk was a hundred if he was a day, and unlike his real students, he couldn't tell that "the girls" he had come upon were considerably older than the girls under his charge. I guess age really is relative.

"Mr. Sisk!" I stammered.

"What is going on here, young ladies?"

"Ah . . ."

"Ah . . ."

A Pulitzer Prize winner and a top lawyer, and we couldn't do better than two "ahs."

"Come with me," he barked.

I knew this couldn't be good. One, I wasn't interested in getting detention this late in my life, and two, it would probably be detention at the Willow Creek County Jail for trespassing on school property, breaking and entering private property, and, well, theft.

Yep, I was in the process of saving my sacred family legacy and reputation, all right. Yeah, my cape was back. Truth was, I was going to make the episode with Conductor Rinaldi look like a real treat in comparison.

There was only one thing to do.

I glanced over at Janice as we walked behind the man.

Run, I mouthed.

What?

RUN!

Which is how we solved our precarious position. We bolted.

"Hey!" he bellowed after us. "Come back here."

Yeah, right, as our young debutantes would say.

While I am a full supporter of full-time security checks in schools, I thanked our lucky stars that WCHS hadn't yet had to resort to such tactics. We careened out through the side door and into the parking lot, leaped into the car, and headed away before poor Mr. Sisk hit the sidewalk, his heart no doubt forced to work harder than it had in years.

"I feel bad," I told Janice once we were well away, my heart beating so fast I was afraid I'd pass out.

"Yeah, me too."

"You don't sound like you feel bad."

She glanced over at me, then smiled. "We got the dress, we got the dress!"

However, we were not feeling so cocky when we got home and pulled out the gown.

Janice's jubilant expression contorted. "What's wrong with it?"

Oh, dear.

After a second, she cried, "Crap! It's ruined!"

She wasn't exaggerating. The white ball gown, was crumpled and filthy as if India had taken it out to the Willow Creek High School parking lot and stomped on it.

Lupe bustled in, took one look at the gown, and tutted. "Me fix." She swiped it from Janice's arms and disappeared.

Janice started pacing. "After all that, the dress is ruined!"

"You underestimate the Power of Lupe."

I left Janice to pace, went to my makeshift

study, and got to work. Time flew by and before I knew it I heard Morgan arrive home from school with the rest of the kids, while Robbie woke up from a nap to let everyone know he was around too.

When I came downstairs, I arrived just in time to see Lupe come out of the utility room, white ball gown hanging beautifully on a padded hanger.

"For you, Mees Morgan."

Morgan gasped. "Oh, my gosh! Where'd you get it, Lupe?"

"You mama get it for you."

Morgan turned to her mother. "Are you kidding? How?"

"Well . . ."

Clearly this wasn't a question Janice had anticipated answering.

"I found it?" she offered.

I raised a brow.

"Okay, I . . . found it in India's locker at school," she confessed.

Morgan's eyes went from wide to popping out. "No way! You were the gramma who was cruising around school!!! Oh, man!"

Janice looked more panicked than happy. But then Morgan raced across the kitchen and threw her arms around her mother. "You rock, Mom," she said.

Later that evening all smiles and feeling

good were gone, however, when none other than Hunter Blair arrived at our doorstep unannounced. For the first time in my life I saw the wisdom of living in a gated community.

"What the hell is going on?" he wanted to know.

He wasn't happy, though oddly, I wasn't sure why. You'd think he was being protective of his daughter. More than anything, though, he just seemed put out.

"I don't know what you're talking about," my mother said. "And don't raise your voice to me, sir."

Amazingly, the roughneck oil fighter had the good grace to look uncomfortable.

"When I got home from work," he continued with more control, "India was caterwauling about someone stealing the debutante dress."

India stood behind him, the usually pushy teen shifting her weight uncertainly. "Daddy, really, I said it was no big deal. Forget it."

"Really?" Mother said. "What dress?"

"Her ball gown."

"You mean the one she told us about that you had bought her in New York? The one that is heaven and astoundingly expensive that she's dying to wear?"

"That's the one," he said.

"Daddy, really, forget it. Let them have the dress."

"Money doesn't grow on trees, young lady, despite what you think. I bought you the dress and I'm not about to sit by and let someone else steal it." He turned to my mother. "I am here for the dress that was stolen out of my daughter's school locker."

My mother eyed us all. "I'm not sure what this is all about. What I do know is that we have one ball gown, a dress that we have a receipt for, and no other. Morgan, go get your gown."

India's eyes went wide with panic, and I figured she must have complained to her father before she realized just what she was complaining about, and once the train left the station, well, there was no turning back.

Morgan returned with the dress.

"Is this the gown you paid for, Mr. Blair?" my mother asked.

While the man probably couldn't tell the difference between one gown and the next, I knew that India's gown was covered with hand beading. There wasn't a bead to be found on Morgan's dress.

"That isn't the dress I bought you." His craggy face turned redder.

"My guess is," my mother continued,

"that if you go home and look in your daughter's closet, her gown will be there."

Hunter turned to India, his eyes narrowed. "Is *this* the dress the ladies came looking for the other day?" he probed.

"Daddy, I can explain."

"You bet you will."

Taking his daughter firmly by the arm, Hunter Blair bid us good night and led India away. Whatever she deserved for her misdeeds, I didn't envy what she would face with a father like Hunter Blair.

My mother closed the door. Janice, Morgan, and I stood like three kids ready for our own lecture. Savannah stood by with an amused smile.

"What?" my mother asked. "Do you possibly think that I don't know every little thing that goes on under my roof?" Then, she smoothed her hair. "I believe it's time for dinner."

She headed for the dining room. At the last minute, I dashed out the front door and just as India was getting into her father's car, I stopped her.

Hunter didn't look happy. "What the hell do you want now, Miss Cushing?"

"Just a second with your daughter," I said.

India shot daggers at me, but didn't resist when I pulled her to the side. "Look, I know it's none of my business, but, well . . ." My brain froze. What in the world did I think I was doing? But somehow I felt sure the pieces that were India were falling into place.

"Listen, you keep doing these weird things, but I don't think you really want to be mean."

From the look on her face I'd have to say that I had finally lost my mind. But on the other hand, she didn't stop me.

"I think you do it because you don't believe you deserve good things. But you do, India. You deserve to be loved by your mother and your father. And maybe if you start letting people in, start letting them love you, they will."

Finally, I was diving in and getting messy in a real way, instead of doing everything possible to stay on the surface. I wasn't standing on the sidelines watching people hurt while doing everything I could to stay out of it. I felt light-headed with insight and goodness.

The girl stood stiffly in front of me, her perfect complexion red, her eyes going glassy. I swear she was on the verge of crying. Then she shook herself.

"Get real, Miss Cushing. I'm a bitch because I want to be a bitch. There's no afternoon special crap here, got it?"

She got in the car and slammed the door, and left me standing in the Wainwright front drive with my mouth hanging open.

CHAPTER
TWENTY-NINE

The next morning, I bypassed the new batch of Texas newspapers my mother had spread out on the kitchen counter, with their Society Section headlines about the continued slew of other balls in cities across the state. Though even I couldn't miss words like "Fabulous" and "Dazzling" she had circled with a red Sharpie. As if I needed her to remind me that our ball was just around the corner and all of Texas would be watching us as well.

I drove to court myself because I wanted to get there early. If my family had been the best entertainment in town before Martin Pender's sordid testimony, I realized we were fast becoming recognized on the world stage when I arrived to a Court TV news crew setting up in the parking lot.

But not even that could dampen my foolish pride in retrieving Morgan's dress, even if we had resorted to idiotic tactics. Now I needed to find my footing in this Texas courtroom.

Inside, I took in the dark wood paneling, the marble floors, telling myself I could do this. By the time the gallery started to squeeze in so tight I didn't know how they could breathe, I had done everything from visualizing to affirming that I would find a way to make the judge believe my mother hadn't committed adultery.

Nerves threatened to get the better of me, however, since the fact was I had written out copious notes the night before, detailed questions, an entire course of action to take in the courtroom that day. But at the end of the night I had known my plan would get me nowhere. There was something I was missing, something needed in order to make magic. And I hadn't a clue what it was.

Jack walked in, and I would be lying to say I wasn't surprised when I saw Racine on his arm. He directed her to the front row where she kissed him.

"Carlisle," he greeted me crisply, no dark brooding looks, not even a teasing smile.

"Jack," I responded coolly.

Our clients pushed their way to the front of the crowd, Vincent helping my mother.

"Thank you, Vin," she said, meeting his eyes.

Jack and I both stared. We couldn't imagine how after yesterday's testimony Vincent could be speaking to her.

"Glad to help, Ridgely," he said solicitously, "since not everyone around here knows how to be a gentleman."

She briefly smiled her gratitude, touched his forearm, and came to sit beside me.

"Miss Cushing," Judge Melton intoned after formalities were dealt with.

My turn.

I took a deep breath, then stood.

"Thank you, Your Honor. I call Martin Pender back to the stand."

"You are aware that you are still under oath?" the bailiff asked the man.

"Yes," he stated curtly.

I walked to the stand. "Mr. Pender," I began, and even I could hear the hesitancy in my voice.

"Yes?" Pender said.

I felt frozen. Hello, wake up. No time like the present to get your act together.

But reprimanding myself didn't work.

"Miss Cushing?" the judge said. "We're waiting."

"Of course." I nodded. "Mr. Pender, please state your name."

Jack stood, raising his arms to his sides,

457

palms up. "Your Honor, we've been over this."

My heart raced fast enough to send off warning bells in an ICU. "But he didn't say his full name," I explained. Like this mattered. Though somehow I was certain it did.

"Fine. Continue, Miss Cushing."

"Sir, your name?"

"Martin Pender."

"Don't you have a middle name?"

"Oh, ah. Yes. Of course. Wilbur. Yes, Martin Wilbur Pender."

The gallery looked on, their brows creased with a mixture of impatience and disdain, ready for more titillating testimony. My palms started to sweat, but my mother hadn't had an affair with this man, I was sure. There had to be a way to make the judge believe it. But nothing came to me.

"Thank you, Mr. Pender."

I hesitated.

"Is that it?" the witness asked.

When I didn't say anything, he started to stand.

"Where were you born?" I blurted.

He stopped halfway out of the chair.

"Sit down, Mr. Pender," the judge instructed.

The man resumed his seat angrily. But sweat had broken out on his upper lip. "I said everything I had to say yesterday. I had an affair with Ridgely Ogden. That's the only reason I'm here."

Judge Melton leaned toward him. "Mr. Pender. Answer the question."

"Fine," Pender said. "I was born in the United States."

"Where in the U.S.?" I persisted.

His eyes narrowed. "San Antonio."

"What hospital?"

"Objection," Jack said, tired and bored. "Relevancy?"

"Miss Cushing, I have to agree with Mr. Blair. I can't imagine what this has to do with anything."

"Sorry, Your Honor," I said, my hands visibly shaking.

"Counselor," the judge asked, eyeing me, "are you all right?"

I smiled wryly. "I'm fine, sir. I was up all night working on this and you've probably heard I'm also in charge of this year's debutante ball. I've got bags under my eyes to prove it."

The gallery chuckled. Even Pender smiled, clearly relieved to see how ineffectual I was. At the sight, my brain went still. Something was wrong, but my mind couldn't bring the answer to the surface. Then it hit me.

I didn't have time to think things through.

But hadn't this judge established a certain leniency he couldn't deny?

Not knowing if there would be water in the pool, I dove in headfirst. "Your Honor, did you hear the joke about the Aggie who went to the doctor's office cut up and bruised?"

The judge blinked, as did everyone else.

"You know," I hurried on, "the one where the doctor asks the Aggie what happened to him, and the Aggie says, 'Well, I was in this horse race and I fell off my horse. And then the horse started jumping up and down on top of me.'"

The judge smiled, just as I had gambled he would. He was a University of Texas Longhorn. Undergrad, graduate, and UT Law School. The sort of man who couldn't resist a Texas A & M Aggie joke regardless of where he was.

Jack leaped up. "Your Honor?"

Melton held his hand up. "Mr. Blair, a little humor never hurt anyone."

Jack was incensed.

But just as Jack had the day before, I rushed on in case the judge changed his mind. "So the doctor looks him over and says, 'That must have been terrible!' and the Aggie replies, 'I know. I could have been killed if the Wal-Mart man hadn't unplugged the machine.' "

A child's joke, but one that broke up the courtroom, at least everyone who wasn't an Aggie. And Martin Pender wasn't an Aggie. He chuckled with the rest of them.

"Okay, enough, Miss Cushing," the judge said, amused.

"I'm sorry, Your Honor," I rushed on, trying to sound contrite. But my heart raced, this time with stunned amazement.

I hadn't looked closely enough to see the truth, hadn't seen what was right before my very eyes. I had fooled myself into believing that being smart alone made me strong when in truth there was a whole lot more to it than that. In Boston I could construct a life that made me feel strong. But to be truly powerful, I had to be able to succeed no matter where I was — no matter what the obstacles.

"Mr. Pender, what hospital were you born in?"

"Your Honor, not again," Jack complained.

"I have a point, Your Honor."

"You better get there," the judge warned, but he still had the ghost of a smile on his face.

"The hospital, Mr. Pender?"

"I don't remember."

"Really? With as much time as you've spent in San Antonio, seems like you would know the name of the hospital where you were born. But okay, so you don't."

He settled back, but he looked wary.

"Do you do business in Mexico?"

"No! I do not!"

"*Doctor* Pender?"

"What?" he snapped.

I sucked in my breath, and the judge's eyes narrowed. I had hit pay dirt, I had the answer. I knew he was a doctor.

But no sooner did elation rush through me, than it evaporated with the realization of what I was about to do to my mother if I continued to show the court what kind of doctor this man really was.

The court buzzed with speculation. I stared at the man with his pink-tinged, newly glossy skin, the hint of pinpricks around his eyes, the plumped-out laugh lines around his mouth, and the frozen face that didn't move even when he laughed. This was my mother's secret for looking so significantly younger than her years. Not her good genes, not great moisturizers as she claimed. Not even a dedicated cleaning regime that she boasted about with not a little holier-than-thou superiority. Rather it was because of this man and what I was sure were his treatments: illegal human growth hormones, antiaging therapies, placenta gels, and the alphabet soups of hormone supplements. I figured she dabbled in them all since even I knew no one went for Botox once a week.

Turning around, I met my mother's eye. Now that I was here, on the verge of disproving the affair, I couldn't say the words and give my mother away. I knew her entire identity was based on her beauty, the beauty she didn't entirely believe. It was something she wrapped around herself so tightly that she would take the risk of people thinking she'd had an affair and potentially losing a good deal of her net worth rather than admit her famed beauty was manufactured.

She sat in the courtroom, her society peers sitting behind her, terror in her eyes.

It is no exaggeration to say that I couldn't breathe. My head swam, and I had to steady myself on the table.

"Miss Cushing," the judge asked, "are you all right?"

"Your Honor," I managed, "I need a recess."

I must have looked as bad as I felt because the man's brow furrowed with what I knew was genuine concern. "Thirty minutes," he declared, then banged the gavel.

"Carlisle," my mother snapped.

But I didn't respond. I didn't bother with files or my purse, or anything else. I walked with as much calm as I could down the center aisle, then started running as soon as I burst out the doors. I had no idea where I was going, couldn't get my brain to work cohesively enough to think beyond the reality that my mother was manipulating me once again. *"Just one more time. Pull out that red cape and find a way to fix this."* Prove she wasn't having an affair *and* don't let anyone know that her perfect beauty was as fake as the plastic trees she disdained that people put up for Christmas.

I didn't realize I wasn't alone until someone stopped me. Whirling around, I expected to find my mother. But it was Jack.

"What's wrong?" he asked.

It wasn't the question of the impatient, ruthless opposing counsel who didn't like me. It was concern from the Jack I had known years ago. And for reasons I couldn't get my head around, I felt tears burn in my eyes until I gasped.

At some edge of consciousness, I knew that people were beginning to notice. Jack must have noticed as well, because he did his infamous cursing thing, glanced around, cursed again, then dragged me through the first door we came to. I didn't know where he was taking me until I saw the men's urinal with an unfortunate and completely startled man standing in front of it.

"Out," Jack commanded.

It didn't take more than that before said man zipped up and dashed out. I was so thankful he was gone that I swallowed back the knee-jerk reaction to tell him to wash his hands.

As soon as we were alone, Jack slid the bolt home on the door.

"What's wrong, Carlisle?" he asked.

Yet again, it was the way he went all gentle and concerned that undid me entirely. Tears turned into out-and-out crying.

At first he paced, cursing again, muttering something about real pains in the ass, then he stopped and forced me to look at him. "What is it?"

"She'll never change," I managed.

"Who?"

"Deep down I think I always hoped things would be different between us. That we could have a real relationship."

"Who, Carlisle?"

I couldn't tell him what I knew about my mother given his position as opposing counsel. I wasn't that far gone. But emotion rode me hard, like an angry bull finally let out of the gate.

"I'm tired," I choked out, surprising both of us. But standing in the men's room with Jack, the truth hit me in the gut. "I'm tired of trying to figure out who my mother really is. Tired of trying to get her to accept me for who I am. Tired of always disappointing her by not caring about being fabulous, or putting myself together, about dances or even boyfriends."

I knew it sounded like I was feeling sorry for myself, but excuse me, I was. "I'm tired . . ."

The words trailed off because I couldn't say more, not to him, not to anyone, because I could never say out loud that my mother was selfish and shallow and needy in a way that no matter how hard anyone tried, nothing would be enough for her.

The realization hit me like light flooding a dark room, making me squint against the pain. And right then, I didn't care if my mother won or lost. I just wanted out.

"I'm tired of being safe," I whispered.

He stared at me without a word, until finally he whispered, "Fuck," then pulled me to him.

CHAPTER THIRTY

No matter how we look at it, there are always things we could have done differently in life. There are two possible ways to deal with this. If we're smart, we live with no regrets. If we're not, well, we wallow in what could have been, living in a world of If Onlys.

I didn't like either possibility, and being the resourceful sort, I came up with a third. Righting wrongs. Which, given the circumstances, seemed the only sensible thing to do. So when Jack pulled me to him with what I can only call hungry need, I went.

We came together, crashing against the bathroom stall, hands tugging at clothes, searching out skin, completely forgetting things like where we were and who was sitting in the front row of the courtroom. We kissed with TV movie desperation until we both pulled apart. He looked at me and I felt as if I had never been seen before. I became aware of the drip of water from the sink faucet echoing faintly against the tile floor and walls, panic mixing with a prickling excitement.

My breath shuddered in when he ran his thumb across my lips.

"Kiss me," he said.

Well, really, what was I going to do?

I reached up on tiptoes, my body trembling, and pressed my mouth to his. Then whatever patience there had been disappeared and he pulled me back. We pressed together, like trying to get beyond the barrier of flesh and skin. In the tiny stall, he pulled my blouse free, kissing my bare skin, stopping at my shoulder.

"What's this?" he asked.

I tried to pull the material back. "Just a scar," I said, hating the reminder of running out of the building where the bar exam was being held, crying, half crazed, and tripping on a crack in the sidewalk. I had flown, my arms tangled in my books, unable to get free fast enough to break the fall. My shoulder took the brunt of the hit, my loose blouse from the previous night Jack and I had spent out late, flimsy and shredding along with my skin. No one had seen the mottled skin since, not even Phillip back in Boston.

"Stop," Jack said, pushing my hand away, kissing the scar in a way that made me shiver with something more than desire.

After that, I forgot all about scars and pavement and him seeing a whole lot of my naked skin. He ripped my stockings free in a very Neanderthal (but totally hot) motion, then lifted me up, my back pressed against the metal divider. His kiss was intense, his hands pulling my knees up around his hips, cupping what I have to admit was a whole lot of bareness. I shivered and, yes, moaned, and wanted what I knew was coming in the worst sort of way.

"This is such a bad idea," he groaned into my neck. And when he lifted me up just a bit and slid my body down on his, well, we both cried out.

It was one of those moments in life that you hear about, where time stands still, reality suspended as if nothing in the world existed beyond the tiny metal stall. We moved together, touching, kissing, whispering, the world locked out. And when we both finished, everything seeming to stop, I could feel the muscles in Jack's back shudder then relax before he seemed to cave in on me.

We stood that way, locked together, braced against metal, his heart pounding in his chest. I could feel his breath against my neck as it slowly steadied. Then in a hoarse whisper he said, "Your mother is proud of you. You shouldn't give up on her."

"What?"

Not quite the postcoital talk one would imagine — especially when it was coming from the lawyer who in minutes would be reseated on the opposite side of the aisle.

I tried to push him away just far enough so I could see his face. After a second, he said, "The other night you asked me why I didn't come and find you after you left."

"Yes," I said carefully. "And you said something to the effect that it didn't suit you to find me."

"Well, that part is true. But I left something out. I did try to find you."

I felt the cold metal against my spine.

"When you didn't come back and I couldn't find you at your house, I went to your mother and asked her where you had gone. She wouldn't tell me."

"What? She wouldn't tell you?" I couldn't believe it, and I made a great production of gasping and gaping.

"Calm down," he said.

"I'm calm!" Or not. The truth was, as soon as I got to Boston I realized I had overreacted. I called my mother, talked to her, and for once in my life I had asked her for advice, told her what I was feeling. And for weeks I'd had this crazy certainty that Jack would come after me. But he never did.

"I can't believe she didn't tell you."

"Actually, it was more along the lines of her saying you were the first Wainwright woman who was going to do something more than rely on her beauty and wealth, that you were born to do 'fabulous' things. And I was distracting you."

"She said that? About me?" Frankly, I was amazed. Then shook it away. "Still, it was my decision to make, not hers."

"All I'm trying to tell you is that she's proud of you. Don't self-destruct in the courtroom because she isn't who you want her to be."

Whoa, bring in the couch, a box of Kleenex, and the man with horn-rimmed spectacles and a close-cropped beard.

"I don't get it," I said. "First you go for the jugular, now you're trying to help me win?"

He straightened his shirt and adjusted his tie, bringing him back to himself. "Don't fool yourself, Carlisle. I have every intention of winning. I just don't want it to be because you threw in the towel."

Someone pounded on the door. Hard.

Then hard again.

"Open up!"

Either someone needed to pee really bad or security was wise to us. Either way, their timing was unfortunate.

"Damn," Jack muttered. "It's Bart."

Bart, as in the former covert operations CIA man who currently ran courthouse security.

Just perfect.

We banged out of the stall straightening our clothes. I caught a glimpse of myself in the mirror, and swallowed back a gasp. One look at me and everyone would know just exactly what we had been doing in the men's room.

"Let me talk to him," Jack said, once we were as together as we were going to be.

Amazingly, he used his cell phone. Then I heard a ring on the other side.

"Bart, my man." Pause. "Yeah, I know you're busy, but wanted to let you know I'm the one in the bathroom."

I could hear the profanity coming through the phone at a slight delay from what I heard coming through the locked door.

"I know, I know. But remember, you owe me."

More profanity ensued.

"Bart, I know. But you help me out on

this and we'll call it even."

Still more profanity, but issued with a fraction of the intensity.

Finally Jack flipped his phone shut just as I heard what was obviously Bart clearing the hallway.

"Well, um," I said, buttoning my blouse, smoothing my skirt. "Shouldn't we talk about what just happened? You know, the sex part? Your fiancée in the gallery part?" Me feeling stupid and totally guilty part?

He studied me, his expression grim. "I'd say we've talked enough for one day."

Bart gave two sharp pounds on the door.

"Time to go," Jack said.

He undid the lock and opened the door. Once he determined the coast was clear, he thanked the court officer, then tugged me out of the men's room. As soon as we were out with no one besides Bart the wiser, he stopped.

"You go in first."

"Bart, give us a minute. Jack, we can't just leave it this way."

"Carlisle, we're already late."

Well, there was that. But it just seemed like we should have said something, even if it was a tossed-off "I'll give you a call." Clearly Jack had done all the talking he was going to do.

■ ■ ■ ■

Inside the courtroom, Racine looked decidedly unhappy, and I doubted it was because
she envied my new postbathroom-romp
hairstyle. But I had enough problems just
then without adding Jack's fiancée to the
mix.

My mother still sat there, looking even
more worried now that she'd had time to
wonder what direction this was going to
take. For the record, I wondered the same
thing.

I looked at her, trying to fathom why she
really hadn't told Jack where I had gone.
Had it been concern about me? Or had it
been about Jack and his family? My mother
barely tolerated India — and only out of
desperation. Whatever the case, I knew I
had to fix this.

With that goal in mind, I considered my
options. As I saw it I had two:

1. throw my mother under the bus by
   proving her beauty was manufactured, namely by Mr. Pender, who
   had been treating her with illegal
   hormone therapies, not making il-
   licit love to her every Wednesday at

noon, or,

2. throw my mother under the bus by letting Mr. Pender off the hook and allowing the judge to believe my mother had had an affair, thereby nullifying the prenuptial agreement, and in the process vaporizing half of her net worth.

Not a great menu of options.

I glanced over at Jack, and was thrown off balance when I saw that he was looking at my shoulder, as if remembering. What? The scar? How much he hated me? Us together? Me naked?

My head whipped back when it hit me.

Sitting there in court with Jack looking at me, I realized something. It was all I could do to stay in my seat and not jump up and sing at the top of my lungs, "There's a third option!"

Hurriedly, I scribbled a note and handed it to Bart, who had followed us into the courtroom.

He read, then scoffed.

"Please, Bart. Do it for me." I batted my eyelashes, and this time it got me somewhere. That, or as I had gambled, underneath the gruff exterior Bart was kind. He'd saved me from complete humiliation in the courtroom hallway, hadn't he?

Sure enough, he muttered some things that don't need repeating here, but suffice it to say he barreled down the center aisle and out the door.

By then Jack had stopped looking at me. He stared at the closing door, then turned back to me with a question in his eyes.

I gave him a quick shrug across the aisle, then thanked my lucky stars when the bailiff brought the court to order.

"Miss Cushing?" the judge inquired.

My heart whipped around in my chest like a car on a Tilt-A-Whirl. "Thank you, Your Honor," I said. "I would like to call" — I drew a deep breath — "ah . . . Ms. Murtado."

Jack was on his feet. "Objection," he stated. "Your Honor, we've been over Ms. Murtado's testimony in copious detail."

Like that mattered? Hello? Forget that I had nothing else to ask the woman. I needed to buy some time while Bart was out rounding up my quarry.

As I knew would be the case, I got my chance with the motel housekeeper. Though then I had to move on to the desk clerk and even the handyman when Bart still hadn't reappeared. When I had asked every question I could possibly think of with still no

Bart, I was getting desperate and was just about to tell my mother to faint or have a spell or make some sort of scene when the head of security entered with three men behind him.

At the sight, my mother gasped. Vincent scowled. I smiled and gave a quick wave as Bart directed them to take their seats in the gallery.

Turning back to the bench, I said, "Your Honor, I would like to recall Martin Pender to the stand."

The bailiff led the witness back. Once everyone was settled, I started in. "Mr. Pender, do you or don't you go by the title of 'doctor'?"

"This is ridiculous. My name is Martin Pender. *Mister* Martin Pender."

"So you're telling me you do not go by the title 'doctor'? And just so we're all clear, I would like to remind you that you are still under oath and lying can get you thrown in jail."

The man's face flared red with anger, his lips pursed.

"Mr. Pender?" the judge prompted.

Martin exploded, leaping up from his chair. "This is ridiculous. I've already told you, I am having an affair with Ridgely Ogden," he yelled, panicking. And why wouldn't he? Trafficking in illegal human growth hormones for use in athletic-performance enhancement or antiaging therapies was a federal offense.

"Mr. Pender," the judge barked. "Calm down."

He settled warily back in the chair, his muscles twitching.

"So the sex," I fired off, unrelenting.

An uneasy (if titillated) murmur ran through the courtroom.

Pender looked like a caged animal. "What about it?"

"You said you engaged in wild sex with my mother." Not my client. Not Mrs. Ogden. But my mother. I was making this personal.

"Yes!"

"Really?"

"Yes." Though this time he didn't appear as convinced.

"You're sure we're talking totally hot, wild sex on Wednesdays at the Lazy 6 Motel?"

The gallery twittered. My mother was on the verge of fainting again, for real. Vincent looked on the verge of murdering someone, namely me. Jack looked more worried by the tick of the courtroom clock. Good.

Pender pursed his lips.

"Mr. Pender," I prompted. "You were telling me what you said about the sex."

"Ah, I don't remember exactly what I said."

"Really? Or is it that you lied?"

"I did not lie! All I'm saying is that I don't remember the exact words!"

"Then let me help." I addressed the court reporter. "Could you please read back the witness's testimony?"

Jack groaned. "Your Honor, objection. Where can this possibly be going? I don't think the court needs to endure any more discussion of the sex."

"Your Honor," I interjected, my voice cajoling. Sue me, but I was starting to have fun. "A little talk about sex never hurt anyone." I turned to Jack. "In fact, I believe that a bit of discussion afterward is more than warranted. It helps everyone understand *what* happened, *why* it happened, and more importantly, *where* we go from here."

Jack's expression went hard. The judge looked confused. My mother looked impatient. Racine looked like she might leap over the balustrade and wrestle me to the ground.

"Miss Cushing," the judge said. "Just hurry this along."

"Yes, of course, Your Honor." I nodded at the court reporter, who found the section of the testimony.

In her dry, monotone voice she read, " 'Every Wednesday we had wicked wild sex, Ridgely Ogden naked and sweaty and asking for more.' "

The gallery oooohd.

"Thank you," I said, unfazed. "Mr. Pender, is that true? Or, perhaps, did you get it wrong?"

"I did not get it wrong!"

"Fine. That's all. Now I would like to call Wendell Jameson to the stand, Your Honor."

Jack was back on his feet. "Your Honor, there is no Wendell Jameson on the witness list."

"That is correct, Your Honor. However, I have every right to call into question the testimony of Mr. Pender. And I plan to do that with three of my mother's former husbands."

The gallery went crazy and Martin Pender leaped up from the witness stand where he hovered. "You can't discredit me! I don't care what anyone says. I spent every Wednesday with your mother making mad, passionate love!"

Judge Melton hammered his gavel, not that anyone paid attention.

My mother and I stared at each other as she realized I had come up with another way to deal with her dilemma.

Option three: prove Ridgely Wainwright-Cushing-Jameson-Lackley-Harper-Ogden doesn't do wild, or for that matter, naked. And I was going to put Wendell Jameson, Alton Lackley, and Lionel Harper on the stand to prove it. We Wainwright women go to a lot of trouble to *not* do naked.

I swear a smile of surprised pride flitted across her lips, before she rolled her eyes and stood, the scrape of her chair gaining everyone's attention.

"Give it up, Umberto," my mother snapped. "It's over." She turned to the judge. "He is Dr. Umberto Velasquez. Also known as the 'Fountain of Youth Doctor' from Mexico." She turned to face the astonished, snickering crowd. "Yes, I work hard to look like this. But at least I do something about it instead of letting myself go," she said pointedly to several women with their sun-beaten skin, who immediately snapped their mouths shut, pursing their wrinkled lips.

Umberto appeared to be on the verge of a full-fledged panic.

"You're Umberto Velasquez?" the judge demanded. "The Mexican doctor wanted for practicing medicine with a fraudulent medical license?"

The court clerk typed something into his computer. "It's him, Your Honor. He's wanted by the IRS, the FBI, even the INS."

The newly revealed Umberto wasn't interested in answering questions, or waiting around to see what happened next. He made a run for it, leaping off the stand and heading for the masses.

"Stop him!" the judge called.

Fortunately, Bailiff Medina was a former running back for WCU and he caught the fleeing pseudo medical man before he could get through the swinging gates. Medina re-cuffed him and dragged him away, leaving a stunned and mostly snickering gallery behind.

My mother turned to Vincent, her perfect face lined with hauteur. "So now you know. You were right all along. I'm not as pretty as I pretend to be, and certainly not as young." Everyone had stopped talking, her expression softening, and I swear her eyes had tears in them. "But I hated for you to think I was less than the woman you thought you fell in love with."

I could hardly believe it: my mother showing vulnerability, especially in front of most every well-heeled and well-connected person in town. And I was almost certain she was sincere.

Vincent stood from his seat and approached my mother. "Ridgely. I'm so sorry I've put you through this."

"Vincent," Jack said, "we're not done here."

"Yes we are," his client replied. "I withdraw my petition for divorce. That is, if you'll have me back, Ridgely."

"Oh, Vin, you know I wasn't the one who wanted the divorce."

The minute my mother stepped into Vincent's arms the crowd went wild — half disappointed, half enthralled.

Formalities were dispensed with quickly and the courtroom emptied, my mother and Vincent filing out with the crowd until only Jack and I remained.

"So," I said, and offered him a crooked smile. "I guess this Yankee convert won after all."

He didn't smile back, just nodded gravely. Racine was waiting at the back of the courtroom for him. "Congratulations, Carlisle," he said. Nothing more.

"Oh, well, thank you."

Then something occurred to me. It had nothing to do with winning or losing or anything regarding the case. My mind went back to what he had told me in the men's room.

My eyes narrowed against the image of Jack arriving at Wainwright House to talk to my mother, her reluctantly letting him in wearing his standard jeans and leather jacket. I doubted she would have offered him a seat, much less a glass of sweet tea, her stiff formality and Wainwright lineage worn like a crown in front of the bad boy from the wrong side of the tracks — regardless of what his brother had managed to achieve.

And with that thought came another. Jack had walked into my mother's house with trouble written all over him and she hadn't simply told him he was distracting me.

He snapped his briefcase shut and stood to go.

"I get it now," I said. "She told you that you weren't good enough for me. That's why you went after her."

"What?"

"My mother, and the things she really said to keep you away from me. By taking the case, that was your way of making her pay."

He hesitated, then his mouth crooked. "Give me a little credit. It was a case. A good one. It was nothing more than that. Besides, we both know that all your mother did was say out loud what everyone else said behind my back. You and I never did belong together. I never cared much for rules, still didn't even though I was a lawyer by then. But you, Carlisle, you are about nothing but rules."

He retrieved his briefcase then strode from the courtroom with Racine, the massive oak doors banging open, my mouth gaping much like the doors.

CHAPTER
THIRTY-ONE

It was hard to imagine that my mother's hearing was over, the prenuptial standing. Not that it mattered since the Ogdens had kissed and made up. And if rumor had it, Jack and Racine were still together. Either she had forgiven him, or she hadn't asked questions, turning a blind eye to what she didn't want to know.

More important to me, really, I was happy for my mother, proud of (and equally amazed at) her for standing up and telling the truth. I wanted to talk to her, but hadn't a clue what to say. Besides, the pressure was still on.

I might have retrieved Morgan's dress and proved my mother hadn't engaged in adultery, but I still had the debutante ball to deal with, which, quite frankly, mattered more to the inhabitants of Willow Creek than the truth behind my mother's beauty, though barely. If the grand event proved to be a disastrous night there would be no convincing a single other girl and her family to debut at the Willow Creek Symphony Association Debutante Ball — i.e., funding would evaporate. But more important, I didn't want my eight girls written up in newspapers across Texas as disasters.

Wainwright House had already been crowded, but with Vincent back in residence, and he and my mother acting like hormonal teenagers, it felt as though the place would burst at the seams. The Hundredth Annual Symphony Association of Willow Creek Debutante Ball was less than a week away and for the next 6.5 days I focused on the debutantes. I fielded calls from frantic mothers, ironed out last-minute wrinkles in the preparations, helped the girls practice walking down stairs in ball gowns and doing the Dip at all hours of the day and night. But the day before the grand event I was completely unprepared when India called saying she quit.

"What are you talking about?"

"I'm not going because it's stupid and dumb and I don't want to be a debutante."

Then I heard her sniff.

"India," I said kindly over rising panic, "what's wrong? What happened?"

"Nothing." Though her voice cracked.

"Sit tight, I'll be right there."

"What?"

I hung up and raced to the Willows, threatened the guard with his life if he didn't let me in pronto, and was at India's front door in minutes. The teen opened the door and her eyes were red.

"What's wrong?" I asked.

"I'm not doing it!"

"Hey," I said softly, "it's okay."

It might have been the soft, gentle voice, or maybe simply that someone seemed to care, who knows, but India started to cry.

"My mother isn't coming to the ball. She called and said she's too busy." She scoffed through her tears. "She'd rather grocery-shop than be with me."

For a second she resisted when I took her in my arms, then she relented. When she calmed down I put her at arm's length. "Do you want to go to her house and talk to her? I'll go with you."

The girl looked conflicted. "What would I say?"

"That you'd really like her to be there."

"But what if she still says no?"

"All you can do is try."

India had the address for a house on the south side of town, but had never been there. Whenever they got together, they met on neutral territory in town. When we drove up the street, the shock of her mother's new life was palpable.

Perhaps because we were in South Willow Creek, India had assumed her mother's life was broken down. Instead we found a whitewashed cottage with black trim, matching shutters framing the windows, and a cheerful cherry-red front door. The tiny lawn was immaculately kept, flower beds exploding with spring color. No question a great deal of love and care went into the home.

The front door opened and a woman came out who even from this distance I could tell looked like India. She was straight out of central casting and could easily have gotten a part in *Ozzie and Harriet.* Granted, *Ozzie and Harriet* hadn't been on the air in decades, which might explain why India's mother had given up on acting.

She came down the steps, pulled on a straw hat against the sun, and got to work in the garden. The mailman stopped and handed her the mail. They chatted for a second, then she waved goodbye to him.

"She's happy," India whispered.

Translation: she's happy without me.

"She has this great new life and she

doesn't want me in it," she said, her voice choked.

"You don't know that, India."

"Forget it. Just take me home."

"India. You don't strike me as the type to give up so easily."

She scowled at me in exasperation. "Okay, let's go."

She got out of the car before I had it in park. I had to hurry to catch up.

The woman turned at the sound of our doors. It took a second, then she said, "India! What a surprise."

Renata Blair, now Renata Frazier, looked older up close, fine lines showing around her green eyes. But even then, you could feel her happiness.

"Hi, Mom."

It was like the happiness wore off on her daughter, and the teenager's hard expression eased. This India was the one I had seen a flicker of in New York when she thanked her grandmother.

I introduced myself. "I'm Carlisle Cushing. I'm in charge of the debutante ball."

"Oh, yes, India told me what a great job you are doing."

I raised a brow at the teen.

"Whatever," she said, then turned back to her mother. "I really wish you would come to the ball. I know you're totally busy, but it will be fun, and I don't know, something special we could do together."

The woman peeled off her gardening gloves and set them aside, then cupped her daughter's cheek. "India, I can't come."

Happiness fled like blue sky chased out by a cold front. "Fine."

"India, listen. You don't want me there. I don't fit into that world anymore."

"You don't have to fit in! It's just one night! Just one night to be with me."

Renata sighed. "I don't even have a dress."

"I said I would buy you one." Her voice rose with each syllable, and quite frankly, I wished I had headed out with the mailman.

"India, I'm the adult," her mother explained. "A child shouldn't be buying me a dress."

"I'm not just some random kid. I'm your daughter!"

The woman looked surprised, as if she had forgotten that fact. India saw it, too, and her jaw went tight.

"Yes, my daughter," the woman rephrased. "But a mother doesn't let her daughter buy her clothes either."

"Forget it," India said. "Though why you care what a mother should or shouldn't do is beyond me. Last I heard mothers aren't supposed to leave their daughters."

India walked away, leaving a stricken Renata standing on her perfect lawn. I stuttered for a second, then got my tongue to work. "She's hurting. She doesn't see that maybe you might be embarrassed or might have a difficult time dealing with her father or who knows what your reasons are for not going. But she's eighteen, trying to find her way into being an adult, and whether you realize it or not she needs her mother. Every girl needs that."

I turned to go.

"Miss Cushing, you have to understand. I just can't."

"You can't or you won't?"

"Truly, I'm no longer a part of that world —"

"I'm not the person you need to make understand."

I left her standing on the sidewalk. India was in the car when I got there, and her mother didn't try to stop us from leaving.

We drove home in silence, the teenager slumped against the passenger door. I didn't know how to fix this. I had a hard enough time understanding my own mother.

As soon as I pulled up to the Blairs' house India got out without a word. I wanted to say something, anything, to help and maybe to get her to remain a debutante.

Good news, bad news . . . my conscience got the better of me and I let her go without a word about the ball.

The morning of the event arrived with perfect weather. It would get hot during the day, but by nightfall the rolling hills would cool, the stars coming out like ice in the black velvet sky. The night promised to be dazzling . . . that is if you discounted eight, or now seven, decidedly undebutantish debutantes at what was once the premier event of the Willow Creek social calendar.

I was decidedly nervous as I pulled on a pair of khaki shorts, a button-down shirt rolled up at the sleeves, and a pair of boat shoes. When I walked into the kitchen, Lupe, Janice, and my mother were already there. Each raised a brow as they looked me over.

"Last I heard," my mother began, "there wasn't a yacht club in Willow Creek."

"Funny," I said.

"Why the long face?" Janice asked.

"Well . . ." I hesitated. "I just want the ball to work."

"It's going to," Janice stated emphatically. And how could she afford to believe otherwise given her daughter was one of the debs?

Janice handed me a cup of coffee.

"Thanks."

"It's going to be great," she said.

"This from the nonbeliever?"

"I'm still a nonbeliever when it comes to these things. But I'm resigned to making the best of it."

"How is Morgan doing?"

"Great. Her dress is perfect. We're going to get her hair done this afternoon. I just wish she wasn't spending so much time with that escort of hers."

"Every time I see them they're studying. Not such a bad thing," I ventured.

Janice sort of laughed. "Yeah, my daughter starts getting good grades after she gets a boyfriend, not the other way around."

To prove her point, Morgan walked into the kitchen, dressed in a simple cotton top and jeans, her long dark brown hair pulled into a ponytail. She looked cute and sophisticated at the same time, far far different from the Cyndi Lauper look-alike she had been only a few months before.

"Gotta run," she said, picking up a piece of toast. "I've got to go to a government study group before we go get my hair done. Finals start on Monday and I'm going to kick . . . do really good."

Savannah entered the kitchen. She still

494

hadn't recovered, not really. She was actually more beautiful in this new quietness, but I could tell that her blue eyes were icy with loss of hope rather than calm.

"Here you tea," Lupe said, putting an heirloom china cup in front of her with a pot of cream and a bowl of sugar.

Savannah nudged them away and took up her cup, drinking it straight. Yet again, someone was hurting and I hadn't a clue what to do about it.

Ben walked in behind her. He looked as stressed as his wife. When he saw all of us he hesitated.

"What?" we asked.

He hesitated. "Herb Pennings has gotten word that a baby has become available."

Savannah stiffened.

My mother looked confused. "Herb Pennings, the Dallas lawyer? What is he doing with babies?"

"He's been helping us find a child to adopt."

Tears welled in my sister's eyes.

"Savannah," Ben said. "Last year you agreed that adoption was the best way to go."

"Only because I didn't think it would come to this. I assumed I would have our own baby."

Ben ran his hand over his face. "Just drive up to Dallas with me. Listen to what he has to say. If nothing else, it would be good for you to get out of town for a few days."

In a fit of the old Savannah, she jerked up from her seat. "No! I am not going to talk to a lawyer about adopting."

Ben muttered something unflattering, grabbed his briefcase, and headed for the garage.

"Ah, *Dios,*" Lupe said.

"You can say that again," my mother added. "Tonight is the ball. How could Ben think about going to Dallas and missing it?"

I shook my head and left the room.

"What?" she demanded. "What did I say?"

Savannah returned upstairs. Mother went in search of her husband. Janice and I were left to the whirlwind of last-minute preparations. The phone rang incessantly with last-minute questions, about dresses, makeup, decorations, caterers.

The ball started at seven-thirty with a cocktail reception for the parents and guests.

At eight, the gala would begin with the girls making their debuts, then dancing with their fathers. The escorts would bring mothers onto the floor to dance, then after a few minutes they would switch so that fathers danced with mothers, and escorts danced with debutantes. As soon as that was accomplished, dinner was served, followed by a big Texas night of drinking and dancing. I knew I wouldn't breathe easy until every last guest had left the premises.

At six-thirty, I dressed with care in a ball gown I had purchased in San Antonio. An ivory organza blouse with high full collar that plunged to a low (for me) neckline that gave way to a billowing blue-black taffeta skirt that swept the floor. I splurged on black satin strappy sandals with a four-inch heel that I knew I would regret thirty minutes into the night. I took more time with my makeup than I ever had in my life, pulling my hair up in a loose twist at the back of my head.

Sitting at the little desk in my bedroom, I hesitated. After a second, I pulled out my grandmother's pearls. I held them, rubbing each pearl between my fingers, then just before I was about to put them back in the box I put them on instead.

"This is it, Grand-mère," I whispered. "Do or die."

I swear I felt a rush of warmth surround me.

The doorbell rang just as I was heading for the back door. Janice and Morgan were still upstairs and Lupe was helping them.

When the bell rang again, then again, I picked up my skirts and retraced my steps.

"Ruth," I said when I opened the door.

She stood on the front veranda, as white as a ghost, her eyes wide with terror. "I don't have a dress."

"But . . . but I thought you . . ."

"Oh, Miss Cushing, I thought I could get enough money but those dresses are so expensive and then I thought I could find one somewhere for less so I went from store to store and even drove to San Antonio but I couldn't find anything in white that would work and —"

"Ruth, calm down. We'll fix this."

Though how I couldn't say.

Janice came down the stairs dressed in her own finery, looking as beautiful as I've ever seen her. "What's wrong?" she asked.

"Ruth doesn't have a dress."

"What happened to it?"

"It's a long story. But suffice it to say that we need to come up with something for her to wear. Any ideas?"

Janice's face brightened. "Yes!"

She raced back up the stairs in her ball gown, banged around, then came rushing back. "Here, wear this."

"Oh, my, I couldn't," Ruth breathed.

I had to smile. The suffragette gown was

going to be worn after all.

"I didn't have the heart to take it back because I loved it," Janice explained. "Plus, I figured, better be prepared in case of an emergency. And look. An emergency."

Amazingly, when we got Ruth into the old-fashioned-looking gown, it suited her.

"I love it!" the girl stated. "Thank you! But I promise, I'll pay for it."

Janice fussed with the seams. "Don't you give it a thought, honey. Think of it as a present to me. Someone needed to wear this dress and I'm glad it's you."

I'm sure the saleswoman at the suffragette store would be glad, too, on the outside chance Janice had gotten it into her head to finally make the return. I really couldn't think of a single other soul in Willow Creek who could have pulled that dress off except Ruth Smith.

With the emergency averted, I took the Volvo to Symphony Hall by myself with Janice, Henry, and Morgan following in one car, and Ruth in her own. Thank God I had taken the time to put myself together because the first person I saw when I strode into the magnificently decorated grand room with its gold-domed ceiling was none other than Jack.

Dressed in a midnight tuxedo, his dark

hair swept back, he looked as if he had stepped out of the pages of *GQ*. What I hadn't expected, no doubt foolishly, was that he'd be with Racine. I guess deep down I had assumed that he would tell her what had happened eventually, and she wouldn't be able to forgive him. Jack was many things, but he wasn't one to lie about something like extracurricular sex.

Since he was standing next to my family's table, I had no choice but to approach. "Jack," I said. "Hello."

"Carlisle. How are you?" he asked.

"Good. You?"

"Good."

"Hello, Carlisle," Racine said coolly, taking firm hold of Jack's arm.

So she knew what had transpired, but had forgiven Jack, if not me.

"Hello, Racine."

Savannah arrived looking ethereal in a stunning cream strapless gown with a white satin sash. Ben was at her side. Janice and Henry came up behind them. Henry looked his usual handsome self. Janice wore an earth mother ball gown that really was lovely.

"Carlisle," my mother called out when she approached in a long golden taffeta skirt with a puff of cream organza blouse. She stopped as soon as she saw me, and I could tell she'd noticed my grandmother's pearls. She stared at them for a moment, then nodded her head without a word, her fingers coming automatically to her own strand.

When she noticed Jack, she dropped her hand and turned away without a word of greeting.

"Look who's joining us tonight," she enthused.

My maiden great-aunt Penelope flitted up to us. She was a hundred if she was a day, though she dressed and acted like a teenage princess in a play. She wore a voluminous ball gown made from tulle and taffeta, with hints of stiff white crinoline and stays showing from underneath. Bright spots of pink rouge marked her powdered white cheeks.

We all loved Aunt Penny, but no one ever brought her out in public. I couldn't imagine why she was there that night.

"I'm your date!" she cooed proudly to me. "Your mother called this morning and said you were going to be alone, alone, alone, and would I mind sitting in so you didn't appear to be without a friend in the world."

My cheeks felt hot underneath Jack's and Racine's stares. I swear Racine smirked.

I stood stock-still and surveyed the people in front of me. More specifically, the couples in front of me.

Mother with Vincent.

Janice with Henry, smiling even if she still hadn't completely gotten her head around the fact that her daughter was making an old-fashioned debut.

Jack with Racine.

And me . . . with my maiden aunt.

I told myself I wasn't embarrassed, that I was stronger than the typical woman who defined herself by a man. I told myself I would stand there proudly, make intelligent conversation. Though no sooner did I have the thought than I did what any other self-respecting chicken would do.

"If you'll excuse me."

I walked away as quickly as I could without looking like I was fleeing. I swear I could feel Jack's eyes boring into me.

As soon as I went backstage, I was swept up in the prepresentation panic of the girls.

"My hair!"

"My makeup!"

"My shoes!"

The girls and their near-hysterical problems were just what I needed. I worked on makeup, dresses that were suddenly too tight, or too loose, even elaborate hair that threatened to unravel.

The girls were nearly ready to go on, their

fathers nearly as nervous as their daughters. The president of the Symphony Association Society committee, Yolanda Shoemaker, went to the podium and called for attention. Peeking out through the curtains from stage right, I could see the glittering ballroom filled with beautifully dressed people. Senators were there, the governor had arrived. But all I saw was the gaping hole that was India's empty family table. Only Jack and Racine sat there as if they hadn't received the memo not to attend.

Janice came up behind me, peering out as well. "She's really not coming?"

"It doesn't look like it. Though I tried. I called her father and her grandmother. But it looks like she was serious."

"What are we going to do?"

I had no idea, though I suspected I'd have to resort to pulling people off the street to fill the empty seats so it wouldn't be so obvious.

Morgan hurried in, breathtaking in the elegant white satin gown and a white heirloom cape trimmed with white fox. I was almost certain someone must have told Janice it was faux fur, otherwise she would have been compelled to douse her daughter in red paint.

"I'm still on record as not approving," Janice said, "but doesn't Morgan look beautiful!"

I smiled at her. But any smile I had froze when Betty arrived.

The teenager wore what could only be termed an ill-fitting white dress. I had no doubt it was the dress Merrily said she was making. To top off the "look," Betty's hair was done up in two tight braids coiled on top of her head.

Anger surged up in me. How was it possible that her mother could be so clueless?

I wasn't the only person who gasped, though even my gasp cut short when none other than India walked in. Unlike Betty, India was dressed fashionably in a gown of silk faille, lace, and satin, the strapless bodice skintight, decorated with crystal beading and lined with handmade white satin roses. The skirt was as full as any antebellum ball gown Scarlett O'Hara would have worn, made of voluminous white satin. Her hair was pulled up in a chignon, set off with crystal headbands.

"God, Betty, who are you trying to be?" she demanded. "Little Swiss Miss?"

No question India was out of line, but she wasn't wrong.

"India!" Janice and I said, both of us relieved. "You're here!"

She made a face. "What was I going to do? Throw away like a bazillion dollars and waste the chance to wear this dress?"

I stepped close to her. "Are you okay?"

"Of course. In fact I'm totally glad my mom isn't coming. I mean, really, what was I thinking. She's not worth the energy."

Given the last three months, I knew no matter what the girl said she didn't mean it, though I wasn't sure what it would take to break through the hard shell she kept around herself to keep hurt out, and as a result, keep everyone else out in the process.

India turned to Betty. "So really, what's up with the hair?"

The other girls snickered at Betty, whose face immediately collapsed. "I don't look okay?" she asked. "My mom said she couldn't get my hair to behave so we did the braids."

The girls laughed out loud. Except Morgan. She stared at Betty, her face angry.

"You look ridiculous," India said.

Betty's eyes flowed over with tears.

"Stop crying."

"Shut up, India," Morgan snapped.

India gaped, but I didn't hang around to see what happened next. I took Betty's hand. "You are going to be great. But maybe we could fix your hair a bit."

"Yeah," Janice said, leaping forward. "You just need your hair fixed."

"And maybe a little makeup," Morgan added, hurrying after us.

Janice, Morgan, and I turned into a quick-change makeover team using makeup, hot rollers, and hairspray I had brought along for emergencies. When we finished we handed Betty a mirror.

"Oh, my gosh," she breathed.

With the help of hot rollers, we tamed her hair, then pulled it back into an updo of loose curls and tendrils. Morgan had worked wonders with the makeup, mascara, eyeliner, and blush.

"You totally look like Drew Barrymore," Morgan announced.

Actually, she did.

"You're going to be great," Janice said, squeezing her shoulders.

Betty's excitement died when she took in her gown. "But my dress. It's awful compared to everyone else's."

"No it isn't," I assured her.

"You're an original," Janice offered, unhelpfully I might add, since I knew Betty's goal was to look normal.

But there was nothing we could do about the dress at that late date.

"It's going to be fine," I assured her.

Or maybe not.

Her mother bustled backstage and at first didn't recognize her daughter. A tremor raced through her when she finally did. "Betty Bennett, what have you done?"

"Merrily —"

She cut me off, marching over to her daughter. "How many times do I have to tell you, you are an eighteen-year-old girl. Not some . . . some —"

This time Betty cut her mother off. "Some what, Mama . . . er, Mom?" She fisted her hands at her sides. "Someone who looks halfway normal for a change?"

You would have thought Betty had told her mother she was pregnant. Merrily gasped and shuddered. "Betty!"

The teen's anger instantly caved, but she surprised me when she didn't back down. "I'm sorry. I know you like your gnomes and crazy teas, and you even like being the woman who does as she pleases regardless of what anyone says. That's great, Mom. I love you no matter what. I just wish you would do the same for me."

Merrily stared at her daughter, didn't move.

Betty sighed. "Is looking like the rest of the girls really so bad? Just this once? Can you possibly understand that unlike you I don't get a charge out of not fitting in?"

Merrily's lip sort of quivered. "Did it ever occur to you that I wasn't given a choice?"

I could tell from the look on Betty's face that she didn't understand what her mother was saying. As far as the girl could tell, the end all of fitting in had to do with fixing your hair and having the right clothes. She hadn't yet come to understand more deeply that the surface was only the beginning. But I remembered my mother spurning Merrily, going on about the crazy family. Merrily was a woman who had come to town and married a man everyone would have sworn was gay. Then the father-in-law taking her under his wing in a way that raised more than one eyebrow. I knew that a simple makeover never would have helped Merrily Bennett fit into Willow Creek.

"Oh, Mom," Betty said. "I'm so sorry if I've hurt your feelings. I love you and I love Mama Bennett and even the gnomes. But just tonight, let me . . . be like everyone else."

Merrily grumbled, but I thought maybe she was actually embarrassed rather than disgruntled. "Well, as long as you like the gnomes."

They hurried away together to find Mr. Bennett just as I heard Yolanda's voice come over the speaker system asking everyone to take their seats.

Once the crowd had settled, she said a few words, then turned the microphone over to the president of the board of directors for the Willow Creek Symphony, Bernard Hall.

"Ladies and gentlemen, it is my great honor to introduce to you this year's debutantes."

The symphony flared, Purcell's Trumpet Tune in D Major filling the ballroom as the curtains drew back to reveal the traditional sweep of stairs that led down to the stage. Young cadet Milton Harvey strode to the bottom of the steps, at military ready, then Abby Bateman and Grady Bateman appeared at the top like a young bride and her father. Grady beamed though I could tell Abby was terrified as she looked out into the bright lights and audience.

"Miss Abigail Bateman," Bernard Hall announced. "The daughter of Mr. and Mrs. Graham Donald Bateman of Willow Creek. Escorted by her father and Master Sergeant Milton Harvey of Willow Creek Academy."

The crowd clapped as the father and daughter took the first few steps. Abby wore a perfectly respectable silk satin gown with long sleeves, plenty of beading, and a full skirt, though she had chosen Jimmy Choo satin stilettos. I held my breath when she wobbled. Her father quickly pressed his free hand over her fingers and they made it to the bottom without mishap. But they weren't out of the woods yet. As I well knew.

At the bottom of the staircase, Milton and Grady flanked the young deb. Abby let go of her father's arm and for one time-stop moment, the three of them stood there, her father in his black tuxedo, Abby in her gown, her escort in dress uniform, all of them wearing white gloves.

Then she extended her hands and started the Texas Dip.

Given that we were in Willow Creek, Texas, no one in the audience gave it much thought. They simply expected the Dip, though I could see the lines of tension around my mother's eyes. I thought Abby's mother was about to faint dead away from the stress. And with good reason because as Abby started to sink to the floor she wobbled again and I was certain she was going down. Not one to let his daughter fail, her father caught her arm and she popped back up, half embarrassed, half relieved.

When the crowd realized that was all they were getting, they applauded, if without much heart, as the debutante, her escort, and father strode to the left where they had been instructed to stand.

Not perfect, I thought, but not a disaster either. One down, seven more to go.

The music swelled as the spotlight followed the next escort to the bottom of the stairs. I stepped back and took in the rest of the girls and their fathers huddled nervously backstage waiting for their turn to ascend to the platform at the top of the staircase. It barely registered that Morgan had disappeared.

"Miss Tilda Kay Beeker," the president announced.

From my place in the wings, I could see Tiki and her father appear at the top of the stairs. Tiki looked terrified, her brown eyes wide, her demurely painted mouth hanging open. I could almost hear my mother tsking.

"Tilda Kay is the daughter of Mr. and Mrs. Armand Beeker of Willow Creek. She is escorted by her father and Master Sergeant Kenneth Kenan of Willow Creek Academy."

Tiki's dress was almost identical to Abby's, silk satin and plenty of beading, though her heels were half the height. She and her father headed down the stairs for the Dip. Nearly to the bottom, Tiki's heel caught in her hem and she pitched forward. The crowd gasped, but thankfully, Master Sergeant Kenan had quick reactions, and after one startled moment, he reached out and caught her before she tumbled to the floor.

Mortified, Tiki curtsied awkwardly, then raced to her spot next to Abby with her father and escort trailing behind.

The crowd began to murmur its displeasure.

"Oh. My. God!" India cursed backstage. "Could this be any more embarrassing? We're going to be laughingstocks, what with Gunny Sak Betty, and the rest of these messed-up girls."

The music flared and it was Betty's turn. But Betty had gone missing.

"Where's Betty?" I asked frantically.

Yolanda careened around the corner. "Where's the next girl!"

"I'm here! I'm here!" our missing deb shouted.

"Betty?" My mouth fell open in shock at the sight of her. She wore a different gown.

"Betty!" the girls gasped, with the exception of India.

With her new hairstyle, makeup, and now new gown Betty was beautiful, like Drew Barrymore playing Cinderella.

"Hurry," I said, my brain spinning. "They've already announced your name!"

She took her father's arm and they hurried to the stairs, then stepped through the curtains.

I didn't have a clue how Betty had transformed herself. All I knew was that when I turned around I found my niece standing backstage in nothing more than her slip.

Janice raced in from the audience. "Betty's wearing Morgan's dress!"

She stopped dead in her tracks at the sight of her daughter.

"Oh, my God, Morgan, what have you done now!"

CHAPTER THIRTY-TWO

Janice stared at her daughter, her eyes blazing. "Morgan," she barely managed. "What have you done?"

Morgan raised her chin. "I couldn't let Betty go out there and make a fool of herself. And the dress fit, so I told her to wear it." She grimaced. "Though I didn't think much beyond that. I'm sorry. I wasn't trying to be stupid."

Her mother sucked in her breath, then stepped forward, taking her daughter's hands in hers. "I've never been so proud of you in my life."

It took a second, but eventually Morgan's stiff shoulders eased. When they stepped apart, the girl dashed at her eyes. "I guess you're getting your wish after all."

"What wish?"

"That I'm not a debutante. I sure can't go out there like this."

Janice took her by the shoulders and

looked her in the eye. "Do you want to be a debutante, sweetheart?"

She shrugged, almost shyly. "Yeah, I do."

"Then you're going to be a debutante. In fact, dress or no dress, you are going to be the best damn debutante this freaking town has ever seen."

Morgan looked terrified. "Mom! I can't go out there in my slip!"

Janice muttered, "No, I guess not."

Mother and daughter turned to me. "What do we do?"

This, it occurred to me, I could fix.

"I have an idea, but we have to work fast." I scribbled a note. "Slip this to Yolanda so that India changes places so Morgan can go last. We need time."

"What?" India demanded. "Morgan is going last? She can't go last! I'm going last!"

"India," I said, "we have no choice."

She looked over at Morgan who was nearly naked. "That isn't my problem! I'm supposed to go last."

"I'm sorry, India, but this is an emergency."

She stood very still and her lip started to tremble. "It isn't fair. Morgan has everything."

Her whole body shuddered and I watched, stunned, as the shell around India finally broke away.

"She has a mother," the girl choked out. "She has a father. And sisters and brothers and aunts and uncles. All living together in one house." Tears streamed through her makeup. "She can't have this too."

"India —"

"India," Morgan said, cutting me off.

My niece walked over to her, then glanced at the other girls. "You guys better get in line or you're going to miss your cue to go on."

The remaining debs leaped and raced to the stage.

Morgan's nose wrinkled as if she were trying to figure out what to say. "You have a totally cool life, India. God, you have like the most amazing house and car and clothes."

By now India was crying into her hands, her gloves smudged with blush and lipstick. "But my dad hates me."

I felt my heart twist.

"Oh, man," Morgan said, "he doesn't hate you."

"He's never there. Nothing I ever do is good enough. It's like he wants some perfect daughter, someone like you."

"Me?" Morgan glanced uncertainly at her mother, then leaned close. "Look, I am so not perfect, believe me. And it's not like my life is so perfect. Hello, my dad is hardly ever around either. But don't get stupid about it like I did."

"What do you mean?" she sniffed.

Morgan hesitated, then I watched as right before my eyes my niece grew into herself. "India, listen to me. I got kicked out of just about every school in San Francisco trying to get my father's attention. And all it did was mess me up." She struggled to find words. "It was a waste of time and my dad didn't even notice. But I figure one of these days he'll see how great I am." She smiled wryly. "The point is, we deal with what we got." Her mouth tilted at one corner. "Plus, if it helps, when I was in the wings getting Betty into my dress, I saw a woman come in with your grandmother and your dad and some other man. I'm guessing they're your mom and stepdad."

"What?" She jerked her head back and forth between me and Morgan. "My mom's here?"

I didn't say anything about how I'd called her father and suggested (strongly) that for his daughter's sake it might be nice if the woman were made to feel welcome by the man she left. I peeked through the curtains.

"Yep, she's here," I said, feeling tremendous relief. "I think your dad called her and asked her to come." I squeezed her hand. "Your dad loves you, sweetie. Let him in."

"Oh, my God! I've got to see her."

India bolted, getting three steps away in her ball gown before she stopped, raced back and gave me, Morgan, and even Janice a hug. Then she dashed out into the audience despite the fact that she wasn't supposed to be seen until the moment of her debut. Though truth to tell, India had always been a rules-optional sort of girl.

"The clock is ticking," Yolanda barked at me.

Crap.

I followed India out into the audience on a separate mission. My footsteps came up short when I saw India's mother stand awkwardly in a gown I suspected she had purchased at a thrift store, but India didn't even notice. She threw her arms around her mother and started introducing her to everyone who was within earshot.

I knew things weren't perfect, but it was a start.

Unfortunately I didn't have time to linger. As discreetly as I could, I grabbed my aunt and pulled her backstage.

"Oh, my," she said when I told her I needed her billowing undergarment.

Just as I yanked the dress over my aunt's head Savannah appeared. "What is going on?"

Janice filled her in while I continued to work. Aunt Penny covered herself with Morgan's white satin cape while I hurriedly got my niece into the slip that was made of white organza and taffeta that in the current millennium looked something like a dress. The bodice was thick, smooth, and tight with thin spaghetti straps, and the skirt was full and flowing all the way to the floor, the crinoline underneath giving it a beautiful bell shape.

Savannah took one look and said, "It doesn't look finished." She glanced around, focusing on our aunt. With one yank, Aunt Penny was capeless.

"I can't wear that!" Morgan said.

"Not this," Savannah offered, retrieving a pair of scissors from my emergency sewing kit, and fiddling with the fur trim.

"You're going to cut Mother's cape?" I gawked.

"I only need the fur."

With an expert's touch, she made a single snip, tossed the scissors aside, then pulled the white fur trim away from the satin in one easy tug.

Aunt Penny, despite her barely clad state,

understood what needed to happen next. She stepped up with a needle and thread. "I'll tack it on in a jiff."

Working like a race crew at a NASCAR pit stop, Janice and I whipped the slip off Morgan, Savannah snipped away the spaghetti straps, then Penny tacked the fur along the new strapless bodice, before we shoved the stunned teenager back into the new, improved "gown." After one last inspection, Savannah whipped off her own white sash and tied it around Morgan's waist with a big bow. A little Linda Evans *Dynasty* action, but amazingly, Savannah made it work.

"There," she announced, "you're ready."

My mother bustled backstage. "Where is everyone?" she demanded.

When she saw her eighty-year-old aunt standing close to naked, she nearly fainted. "What's happened?"

Morgan stepped forward and extended her arms. "How do I look?"

My mother's hand came to her chest. I couldn't tell if she was going to have a heart attack or smile with joy.

"Morgan. You look like a Russian princess."

With Janice's dark hair and the Wainwrights' violet-blue eyes and alabaster skin, she truly was stunning.

"Here," I said, reaching for the clasp on my pearls. "Wear these."

My mother stopped me. "Keep those on. It's taken long enough for you to finally wear them." She reached back and unhooked her own pearls. "Here," she said, coming up behind her granddaughter. "Wear mine."

When she was done, we stood back to admire our handiwork. "See, Mom," I said to Janice, "being a debutante didn't ruin your daughter."

My sister-in-law's eyes shone. "She's a good kid."

"Yeah, she is."

Janice hugged her daughter. "I'm so proud of you."

This time Morgan held tight. "Maybe I have some of that Pulitzer Prize stuff in me after all."

My mother scoffed. "Of course you do. You're a Wainwright." But this time my mother wasn't scowling.

"You're up next!" Yolanda called.

Holding her long skirt, Morgan raced to the stairs where Henry waited, the puff of white fur around the top of her bodice gently fluttering.

When I got back to the wings, I arrived in

time to watch India. Standing at the top of the stairs with Hunter, she looked like a princess.

"Ladies and gentlemen, may I present Miss India Elizabeth Blair. She is the daughter of Mr. Hunter Blair of Willow Creek. She is escorted by her father and Master Sergeant Derek Clash of Willow Creek Academy."

They came down the stairs with elegance, stopping at the bottom where India struck a superior pose. Then she began her formal bow. The entire room held its breath as she sank toward the ground. For a second I thought she would stop as the violins held a long expectant note, but then she kept going until her forehead nearly touched her skirts. She had done better than anyone so far.

Unlike any other deb crowd I had ever witnessed, this one gave India a loud cheer of applause. Her father looked stoic while her grandmother openly wept in the audience. Her mother had tears in her eyes in what I could see was both pride and regret.

I expected India to accept the admiration as nothing more than her due. Instead she waved at her mother, then threw her arms around her father. "Thank you, Daddy."

Hunter Blair stood very still, awkward,

uncomfortable. The crowd felt the tension, the cheers dying down. India felt it too and she let go, her angry arrogance starting to resurface.

But Hunter stopped her, tilting her chin to look at him. "You did a great job." Then the man who had gone from abject poverty to staggering wealth by means of fire and the danger inherent in manipulated crude oil flaunted convention and picked his young daughter up and twirled her around.

The crowd cheered as Hunter led India to the side to join the line of debs. Then the music swelled one last time. This time Morgan appeared at the top of the stairs.

Where India had been a princess, my niece looked like a young queen as she stood with my brother. Her white gown of organza, taffeta, and satin trimmed in white fur was simple in its elegance, her dark hair swept back to tumble down her shoulders in soft curls. She smiled confidently, her gloved palm placed formally on the back of my brother's extended hand, Wainwright family pearls resting against her collarbone.

"Ladies and gentlemen, may I present Miss Morgan Wainwright Cushing. She is the daughter of Mr. and Mrs. Henry Herbert Cushing the Fourth, descendant of Duke Ridgely Wainwright, founder of the

Willow Creek Symphony."

I could see that my mother had tears in her eyes at the sight as they came down the steps. At the bottom of the staircase Morgan smiled at her escort and her father, then began her slow descent. She had been the first to tumble on the Wainwright black and white marble entry hall floor, so no one was more surprised than me when she hit that midway point where most girls ceased, and kept going. She sank lower and lower, my breath held until, I kid you not, she bowed her head so low that she touched her forehead to the voluminous folds of her makeshift debutante skirts, her arms extended on either side of her like wings.

The audience erupted, this less than proper crowd cheering for a less than proper group of girls who had proven they were perfect just as they were. And standing there, I realized this wasn't about money, my family's history, my past, or even my grandmother. It was about eight girls, and what was just one of many ways of making them feel capable of taking on the world.

The orchestra flared, the crowd roared its approval, and I fell back against the wall in relief when the girls and their fathers began the traditional waltz. It was done. The girls had shone and right then I didn't care about symphony finances or family legacies. All I cared about was my girls. It might not have been the most traditional of debuts, but I was proud of what they had accomplished in three short months.

The escorts exchanged mothers for daughters, and I decided it was time to head back to my family's table. But when I walked out from backstage I saw Jack with Racine wrapped around him like a cheap spandex sweater.

I veered off in the opposite direction, but Janice was there, catching my arm. "What's up with you two?"

I considered my sister-in-law, then grimaced. "You know that thing you said about having sex in the men's room?"

Her eyes went wide as saucers. "You and Jack?" she squeaked.

"Yep. Me and Jack in the courthouse men's room, with Racine sitting in the gallery, no less."

She burst out laughing. "You bad, bad girl. And to think we gave Savannah trouble about the country club men's room!" She hooked her arm through mine like we were best friends. "Come on. You can't let a little slut action scare you off."

We wove through the tables, people stopping us every step of the way.

"It was a beautiful presentation!"

"The girls were lovely."

"Congratulations!"

But more than the praise, I noticed that my mother was sitting at our table all by herself. Aunt Penelope wasn't there. Vincent was gone.

Ridgely sat stiffly in her seat, surrounded by empty chairs, her smile plastered on her face. She wore the perfect expression, pretending to adore sitting there alone while everyone else danced and the women of Willow Creek, old and new to the society ranks, whispered behind her back.

We might not have had a disastrous ball, and I might have proved that she wasn't an adulterer, but she would not soon be forgiven for lying about her looks.

I felt that age-old need surge up to save her and I beelined it to the table. But before I made it, Jack stood and walked over to her.

Oh, no! Don't confront her here, I wanted to holler.

But before I could get there, before I started to call out to them, I saw him extend his hand and ask my mother to dance.

She looked from his hand to his face, then said something I couldn't hear. But when I practically slid to a stop at the table, I heard his laugh.

"Mrs. Odgen, when it comes to you, hate isn't what comes to mind. Beautiful. Larger than life. Willing to go after what she wants. That's what I think when I think of you."

"Why, Mr. Blair," she cooed.

"Now, are you going to sit there all alone or are you going to dance with me?"

She took his hand, and when they walked past me, she smiled and whispered, "I can't imagine why you ever let him go."

I gaped. But all gaping was cut off when the music did the same.

Confused, I saw India, Morgan, and the rest of the debs talking to the conductor. After a furtive shake of his head, then more whispering from the girls, I saw the man relent.

"Ladies and gentlemen," he called out. "We have a special request."

He whirled back, said something to the orchestra, who hurriedly whispered among themselves, and launched into a new piece.

"What?" I whispered.

I watched with the rest of the audience as my group of eight debutantes linked their arms at the front of the room and started singing along . . . to the orchestra, no less, playing the Dixie Chicks' "Not Ready to Make Nice."

CHAPTER
THIRTY-THREE

WAINWRIGHT ROYALTY STILL RULES

In a day and age when the world is filled with war, hunger, and poverty, debutante balls seem frivolous and outdated. But this year Carlisle Wainwright Cushing, daughter of former Debutante of the Year Ridgely Wainwright managed to pull together a Hundredth Annual Ball that raised record amounts of money for the Willow Creek Symphony. To accomplish the feat, she brought together both old and new Willow Creek families, and presented us with eight young women of elegance and charm, who showed us they won't be bound by outmoded ways.

This isn't the Peace Corps, but it isn't your grandmother's or even your mother's debutante ball anymore.

Overnight I had become something of a celebrity. Following in my mother's footsteps, Morgan had been voted Debutante of the Year by the Texas press corps. Even India experienced a reprieve from haut bitchdom when she promised to spend more time getting to know her mother and new family just as soon as she returned from a trip with her father to the Middle East, where he spent so much of his time working. Not anyplace I'd take a child, mind you, but who am I to judge. As the man said, it was time his daughter saw more of the world than her own backyard.

And maybe that was the case. Maybe you had to get out, see the world beyond your own backyard, in order to understand what you have, or to be bigger than ideas that never have a chance to grow beyond the strictures of a single place.

Janice got a job writing for the *Willow Creek Times* editorial page, not society page, as they had initially offered. Janice and Morgan immediately started planning a mother-daughter trip to Barcelona. My brother couldn't believe the change in his life.

"What about me?" he asked, regarding the trip.

"We certainly don't want to take you away from work," they said, then laughed like schoolgirls.

After the article ran, my mother quickly found redemption among the women of Willow Creek. She told me she was thrilled with the outcome of the ball, telling me she had never doubted my abilities, and she swore again that she would stay out of trouble. I half believed her on both counts.

Then there was my sister. The morning after the ball, we found Savannah in the foyer, packed and ready to go with Ben to Dallas. They returned two weeks later after adopting not one baby, but two. Twin girls. And if our mother has anything to say about it, I have no doubt they will be future twin debutantes.

As for me, after all that had happened I couldn't imagine that I would ever marry. But who knew. The sight of my sister with those babies made me believe in miracles.

One thing that I told myself wasn't possible, however, even with my new status as minor celebrity, was staying in Willow Creek. But that was the rub. Where would I go?

Sure, I could go back to Boston, and it made perfect sense. I might even convince Mel Townsend it wasn't too late to take on his case. But how to explain to everyone why I hadn't let them know I had money?

And how would I work with Phillip every day? Not that I couldn't get beyond those things, but quite frankly, I didn't want to. I wanted the chance to start over in a new place where I'd have the freedom to reinvent, the mistakes of the past not known.

With everything done, there was no reason for me to stay any longer. I went to the office on the second floor of Wainwright House. I found the old atlas I had used when determining my last destination. There was comfort of ritual, I suppose, when I pulled the old leather-bound book from its place in the floor-to-ceiling shelves.

Laying it out on the desktop, I opened it to the map of the United States, but then turned a few more pages until I found a double-page spread. Why limit myself? It seemed only appropriate to open myself to the world this time.

Closing my eyes, I tried to empty my mind. But oddly, all I could think about was the attic.

When I couldn't get it out of my head, I resolved to return to the atlas later and trudged up the flight of stairs. The late afternoon sun streamed through the windows, motes of dust caught in the yellow-orange light.

I rummaged through boxes and cabinets

until I came to a box marked "Carlisle." I sat on the floor and opened the top. Inside there were debate trophies, report cards, certificates of achievement. I could see my orderly workings on everything I had done. A tiny handprint dried in clay, mounted on a piece of painted plywood with young but still neat block letters providing my name, age, height, and weight. A fifth-grade report I had written then bound with cardboard and neat stitching along the spine.

At the sound of footsteps I turned.

"I thought you might be up here."

My mother came up the stairs wearing her signature tasteful attire and heirloom pearls, her low-heeled bone shoes ladylike as she crossed the wooden plank floor. When she came up behind me she glanced over my shoulder, then smiled. "Ah, the report you did in fifth grade. 'Six Reasons Why Eleanor Roosevelt Should Have Been President Instead of Her Husband.' " She tsked. "Since you lived in a house with me and your sister, I never understood where you got all that seriousness. No interest in dances or boys or, later, sororities. You were always different, and needed something different than what I could give you here."

"Is that what you told Jack. When I left?"

She cocked her head. "So, he told you."

"Yep. He told me everything."

"I wondered what you were doing when you were gone for so long from the courtroom, and Jack gone too." She nodded. "Good. I'm glad it's out there."

"You should be. When I figured out the real reason you wouldn't help me with the case I was ready to let you fry."

She rolled her eyes. "Don't be dramatic."

Which made me laugh. "I learned it from you."

"At least I can claim credit for something."

Which made us both laugh.

We were silent then, both lost to our own thoughts.

"He also told me you were proud of me," I added.

"Really?"

"Yes."

She hesitated, then said, "I ran into Jack today."

I glanced at her. "Based on your expression, either you ran him over or you have decided to direct your charms his way."

"Carlisle! Really." Then she smiled. "Though he is a nice-looking man. Young, of course. And I am blissfully happy with Vincent." She straightened. "But that isn't the point. He's moving."

"What?"

"I was shocked too."

"What about that house I heard he was building? And what about Racine? Is she going with him?"

"As I understand it, he broke up with her. Not that he said that. I heard it at the Velvet Door beauty salon. Apparently Racine was in there yesterday making quite a scene, saying that he had broken up with her, broken her heart."

Jack moving? On the heels of which came, Jack not with Racine?

Mother walked over to the window and ran her finger along the sill. "I wasn't wrong to tell Jack he wasn't good enough for you," she said. "He wasn't. Though it had nothing to do with his family or anything else you might be thinking. He wasn't good enough because he was wild and disreputable, and you always had a soft spot for him. That kind of love can ruin a girl. And let me tell you, Carlisle Cushing, he would have ruined you."

"Mother —"

"I should know. Your father was like that."

"What?"

My mother's perfect features went dreamy in the early afternoon sun that streamed in through the window. "Your father was amazing, dashing, filled with life, and if he hadn't run that little sports car of his into a tree he would have made me miserable."

That I hadn't expected. The tree part and the miserable part.

"When I married him he was older than me but still a boy with good looks, easy charm, and a wild streak as wide as the Missouri River. My daddy told me not to marry him. He'd only make me unhappy, he swore. But he was wrong, at least at first. I was delirious with happiness when we first married. We opened Lucky Stars and traveled and made love —"

"Mother."

"Well, we did. But a grown man can't live life as a boy, at least not when he has a wife and children who depend on him." She looked at me. "I loved your daddy, Carlisle. But our life together was already spiraling out of control before he died. And Jack Blair was just like your daddy. Can you understand that I didn't want the same life for you?"

I had heard more about my father in the last five minutes than I'd ever heard. And had seen more of my real mother than I knew existed.

"You always had so much promise," she continued. "You could be anything you wanted. And I knew that by leaving, you'd be able to realize all that potential. It was the least I could do to let you go."

"And make Jack let me go too."

"Exactly," she said without an ounce of apology.

She walked over to a tall file cabinet and pulled open the top drawer. She dug around then pulled out a small box. "Here."

I took it warily then started with surprise when I opened it and found the plastic ring Jack had given me in high school. "Where did you get this?"

"From that little house you lived in by campus. After you left — without so much as a word, mind you — Lupe and I went over there to pack everything up. I found it hanging on a chain in your bedroom." She walked back and kneeled down in front of me. "You have loved Jack since you were thirteen years old, Carlisle. And whether you want to admit it or not, you're not just attracted to him —"

"Mother —"

"You still love him."

I dropped my gaze, my throat idiotically going tight. "For all the good it's done me."

"It's certainly doing no good with you sitting here on the floor rummaging through a hundred years of clutter."

"But you didn't want me to be with him."

"I didn't. Not back then. But things change. And it turns out, Jack isn't completely like your father."

"What do you mean?"

"He let you go." She touched my chin and raised it. "It was the right thing to do, and he did it. That's the kind of man who's worth a lifetime. I might not have been much of a mother to you, but I did the best I could. And the best I can do for you now is to tell you to get up and go after your man."

As only my mother could put it.

I thought of Janice and Morgan, Merrily and Betty, even me and my mother. It occurred to me, sitting on that floor with a hundred years of family history around me, that my mother was right and if we're smart, mothers are strong enough to let their daughters find out who they really are, and daughters are strong enough to realize that mistakes or no, every mother has done the best she can . . . and if she's lucky, her own daughter will one day give her the same gift of understanding.

That's what my mother had done. For all my complaining about her and her larger-than-life drama, I realized that she had seen to it that I could be who I wanted to be. She hadn't forced me to wear ruffled dresses as I knew she wanted. She hadn't made me take the dance lessons Savannah had been so great at. And when I fled to Boston, she hadn't forced me to come back. She had let me find my own way. That had been her gift without my even realizing it.

"But you're forgetting one thing. Jack has made it clear he doesn't love me." He might want me in some sexual way — or maybe it hadn't even been that, and had just been the whole men's room thing that got him going, as Janice had predicted about men.

Mother shrugged her delicate shoulders. "Well, that might be."

Ouch.

"But you'll never know for sure if you don't go over there and find out. Wouldn't you rather know one way or the other?"

Not necessarily, at least not when I suspected there was a fair chance the truth wouldn't go in my favor.

She gave me a look. "Carlisle."

"You're right. You're right. Better to know."

I pushed up and headed to the stairs as if walking toward a guillotine.

"Good heavens, Carlisle, where's that red cape?"

Which made me laugh out loud, a bud of

excitement pushing at the fear of rejection. "Tell me this, how did you know the ring was from Jack?"

She scoffed and waved me away. "How many times do I have to tell everyone around here that I know everything that goes on underneath my roof."

Then just as India had done, I ran back, gave my mother a hug, before I hurried down the stairs and out the back door to the Volvo. I shot through town and pulled up to Jack's house with my heart beating hard. When he pulled open the door and just looked at me, my mouth went dry. Though said mouth turned to sawdust when I saw how far along he was with the packing.

He leaned up against the doorjamb. "Hey."

Just like that.

"Hey."

You can imagine how I felt, what with him dressed in those 501s and a T-shirt just tight enough to make me dream of his broad shoulders. But that didn't help me figure out how to proceed from there.

"You know, leaving town is overrated," I ventured. "I should know. Though if anyone understands the draw of going someplace new, it's me. Finding another town where you're not that Wainwright girl who face-planted into the floor . . . or that Blair kid who had to follow in his big brother's foot-steps."

But still nothing.

"Though, really, how can you leave lobster and mesquite-grilled anything? Or what about all this wide-open sky and everyone knowing your business? You can't buy that in a new town."

I was trying to make him laugh, for all the good it did me. So I took a deep breath and dove in deep. I swallowed my fear of letting myself love, knowing what I had to do regardless of the outcome. "I'd really hate it if you left."

He didn't answer right away, just continued to study me. "Why?" he said finally.

There was no hint of a smile, just the seriousness that spoke of all that deeper stuff in him.

"Do you remember this?" I asked, and pulled out the plastic ring.

He was totally confused.

"It's from high school, when you brought the gum machine egg to thank me for giving you the answer to the question?" I prompted.

Those dark eyes sparked. "You kept it?"

"I kept it for years, then my mother found

it and kept it for me."

He looked back. "What does it mean?"

A smile crooked on my mouth this time. "It means that I have loved you since you sat down next to me in Mr. Hawkins's math class, and after fifteen years it's time to get things right between us."

Call me melodramatic, but that's what it was. Who knows if my mother was right about how things would have been between us if I had stayed? Who knows what would have happened if I had done things differently? That wasn't the issue.

I shrugged my shoulders, feeling like a thirteen-year-old again. Which maybe wasn't so bad.

"I love you, Jack Blair, and I thought maybe we could start over. Forget the past."

He still didn't move. "You want to do that?"

I bit my lip. "I'd like to try."

He hesitated. "We could," he said, but didn't look convinced. "Or we could keep everything just like it is," he added, then took my hand, that sweet molasses smile surfacing, "and keep going. I'm not sure I want to erase the memory of you in the courthouse men's room."

Okay, so Janice really was right about men and their fondness for sex in strange places.

Blood rushed to my cheeks and I laughed. Looking at him, I felt all those ridiculous feelings from the past and a huge all-encompassing love. I had never felt it before him, or since, which was why I had always done my very best to steer clear.

But then things had changed, circumstances I hadn't created bringing me back to this place. I had returned to Texas and saved the symphony from bankruptcy. I had saved my family's connection to the debutante ball, and my mother's assets. But standing there, I realized that maybe I had saved myself in the process. Not from Boston. Not from Phillip. But from the continual denial that what I had been doing my whole life was running.

I still didn't know what the future held. I didn't have a map or even a plan. But I had learned that's what life was — risky, messy, no way to tie it up in neat little packages despite my desire for it to be otherwise. So when he tugged me inside the house, I went. When he picked me up and carried me to his bedroom, I held on tight. Because I knew that I was one of the lucky ones. I had reached beyond denial and found that rare sliver of grace where the dream of what life should be meets the reality of what it really is. And in doing so,

I had found my way back to my roots. To my family. I had found my way home.

ABOUT THE AUTHOR

Bestselling author of nineteen novels **Linda Francis Lee** is a former Texas debutante who has high hopes that all photos of the experience are long gone. She currently lives with her husband in New York City, where she is at work on her next novel. Visit her at www.lindafrancislee.com.